HOLLYWOOD PRINCESS

DANA AYNN LEVIN

Park-Hill Press

Hollywood Princess

No part of this book may be reproduced, transmitted, down loaded, distributed, stored in or introduced into any information storage and retrieval system, in any form or by any means, whether electronic or mechanical, now known or hereinafter invented, without express permission of the author, except by a reviewer who may quote brief passages for review purposes.

Hollywood Princess is a work of fiction. Names, characters, places and incidents either are the product of the author's imagination or are used fictitiously. Any resemblance to any person, living or dead, or any events or occurrences, is purely coincidental.

Cover design by Sarah Jordan Levin

ISBN: 0990737004
ISBN-13: 978-0-9907370-0-1

DEDICATION

To Paul, for not only never laughing at me,
But for supporting my dream,
Supplying me with yellow pads and Disney pens,
And allowing me to retreat to my cave.

.

CONTENTS

ACKNOWLEDGEMENTS

Writing a novel was never my aspiration, but then Elizabeth and Daniel's story came to me, and it wouldn't stop. Everywhere I went, I composed new material. At home I spent countless hours writing, inputting, and editing.

Thank you to my husband and children for allowing me to sometimes pay more attention to Elizabeth and Daniel than to you, but I never missed the important stuff. I appreciate your support and that you never laughed at me, except maybe Sarah did.

Adam, in your own quiet way you were always there for me. Your nightly living room piano concerts helped keep me focused.

Caiti, my chief cheerleader, you still have to wait a few more years until I'll let you read this book. My apologies for not writing a YA book for you. Thank you for choosing my cover font.

Sarah, who often made fun of me, and still does. I love the cover! Thank you for designing it, and for designing my website and other social media sites. We have the best bartering system: shoes, designer bags...

Paul, for all your encouragement. You always believed in me and my project, sending me to classes and conferences. You even supported what might have seemed ridiculous, but worked. Yes, I'm referring to a certain one night trip to Las Vegas solely to attend an All-American Rejects' concert. I knew it would boost my creativity, and it did. I probably should thank Tyson Ritter and Nick Wheeler, because every time I saw them live, I had similar results. I have no idea why this happens.

Thank you to Avery, Esther, Harriett and Yada for reading various drafts of Hollywood Princess. Esther, it was your comments that led me to find a home in the New Adult genre.

Finally, thank you readers, for taking a chance on a debut author.

CHAPTER 1-ELIZABETH

Could today get any better? From across the room of my intermediate-level French class, an adorable-looking guy with smooth, dark curls flashed me a shy smile that set my heart aflutter.

If a flirty smile counted, then this was the second good thing to happen this morning. The first had been…no, maybe this was the third. Definitely, the second. Though "Gives You Hell," the perfect mood-boosting song to start the day woke me, it didn't count.

A longtime favorite, this song was ideal for imbuing me with the confidence needed to face the first day of freshman classes at exclusive Donnelly College in New York State. I wanted to give them hell, unless my usual insecurities and shyness surfaced. Often a possibility.

Rising slowly, I had opened the window shade a crack. The sixth-floor view, all treetops, but after yesterday's rain, at least the sun shone through. Certainly, that was a good omen.

A passing glance at the clock confirmed the early hour; enough time to leisurely check my e-mails and choose my clothing for the day.

Quickly scrolling my iPhone confirmed my hunch. Today was already a good day! A late-night love note from Mom made my eyes tear. Far away from my Santa Monica home, I missed Mom and Dad more than I imagined, though it had only been a few days since move-in.

Silently, I tiptoed into the bathroom, enjoying the privacy that came with being the only one awake. I shared a suite with two other girls on the seventh floor of a ten-story tower, Donnelly's tallest building. The tower appeared to be sitting on the broad shoulders of ivy-covered Berkeley Hall, an otherwise four-story, C-shaped brick building.

Loud, rapid knocking interrupted my reverie while I brushed my teeth. "You almost done?"

With the water running, I couldn't tell which impatient roommate it was. I spit into the small sink to answer.

"One more minute," I called. Jeez! It was bad enough having to share the facilities, but really, I hadn't been in the bathroom for that long.

Rachel was leaning against the doorjamb to her bedroom, shower caddy in hand, staring. I smiled to diffuse the tension and returned to my room. Learning to live with other people was more difficult than I had imagined.

Born into A-list Hollywood society, I led a rarefied existence where you never wanted for anything, nor waited for anything. The downside, everyone assumed they knew you because of the latest gossip blog entries.

At Donnelly, for the first time in my eighteen years, I'll have the opportunity to be me. I'm three thousand miles from home, just another anonymous freshman. It's time for me to discover who I am.

It was time to get dressed, too. I had been mulling this over since I'd arrived. Before going to sleep, I rifled through my wardrobe once again, never having selected first-day clothes before. The schools I attended in Los Angeles had required uniforms.

What was a simple decision for most tied me up in knots. I wanted to dress like a typical Donnelly student. But who exemplified typical for me to emulate? In my few days on campus, I observed fashion that ran the gamut from prep, goth, punk, hippy, jock, and Walmart to fashionistas like my roommate Chloe.

Chloe boasted designer labels without fear. At worst, she would be teased and called a Jewish American Princess. For doing the same, I'd face sneers and derision while being called a stuck-up Hollywood bitch.

That my flippy khaki skirt and lavender cropped polo, both courtesy of J.Crew, were appropriate soon became apparent. As I approached the classroom door when French ended, cutie, dressed just as preppy, stopped me. Only then did I take in his pale blue eyes, a distinct contrast to his smooth mocha complexion.

"Bonjour, mademoiselle," he said, smiling warmly. "Je m'appelle Cameron Reynolds."

"Elizabeth Jacobs," I answered.

"I'm meeting my roommates for lunch. Want to join us?" Cameron asked in English, his voice smooth and lacking any discernable regional accent.

At midday, the quad, the most public of public places on the Donnelly campus intimidated me. Companionship would insulate me from the gawking students I detected almost as soon as my toes touched the concrete path. Focused on me, Cameron, of course, was oblivious, for he had not been born into my life.

"That's her, isn't it?" a student walking behind us whispered to a buddy.

"I thought Miranda Jordan's daughter would wear better clothes," her friend said.

"I know, right? Ms. Jordan can easily afford Ralph Lauren. Why the J.Crew knockoff?"

Crap! Didn't they realize I was trying to blend in by dressing like everyone else?

I pretended that I hadn't heard them. If Cameron noticed, he graciously did not say anything.

As we stood on the century-old dining hall's front steps waiting for our roommates, I took in the grandeur of the Donnelly campus. Initially wait-listed and headed for Swarthmore, I had never visited Donnelly, my first-choice college. The website didn't do it justice.

"How were your classes?" I greeted Rachel and Chloe when they finally arrived. The wait seemed longer than it probably was, but I was fidgety, praying not to be noticed again.

Rachel bubbled with excitement. "You'll never believe who is in my class."

Her morning class, "Survey of Motion Pictures," left me curious. Nobody I knew from home was enrolled at Donnelly. It must be someone New York-based.

Noticing Cameron lingering a step behind me, she answered, "I'll tell you later."

Once inside the lobby, Cameron's phone buzzed, an incoming text. He read the message and frowned.

"Looks like Shane won't be joining us," he said.

"What about your other roommate?" I asked. Three girls at a table with only one guy was awkward, especially when we barely knew each other.

Cameron smiled. "He'll be here," he said with certainty. "My roommate's always late."

After purchasing our food, we found an empty table. Preparing to place my lunch down, a confident male voice came up behind me.

"Cam, you've been busy this morning," it teased.

Instinctively, I turned my head toward the speaker. Our eyes locked, green on blue. The power of his dark sapphire stare overwhelmed me.

"Eli?"

Only one person ever called me Eli. I was dumbstruck that not only was he here, he was apparently Cameron's roommate. My heart catapulted into overdrive. I lost my grip on the plate, and it slammed onto the table with a jarring bang.

"Danny!" I breathlessly responded, and he pulled me into a bear hug, his now taller six-foot frame towering over me.

Danny Newman's strength and muscularity surprised me. He had been hitting the weight room since we last hugged.

My head was spinning, my pulse racing. I thought I might faint, though whether from the shock of seeing him or from Danny's innate sensuality, I couldn't discern.

Why hadn't anyone told me that Danny was attending Donnelly? My parents must have known. Our families had been closer than close for over twenty years. As youngsters, we were inseparable. Nearly a year and a half older than I, Danny was like an older brother. Then once puberty began to kick in, my sisterly love morphed into a full-fledged infatuation. But after Danny left for prep school in New Hampshire, our relationship changed. So why did my insides quake? I was eighteen years old, a mature college student now.

Yet my eyes clung to Danny. Incredibly handsome, his mesmerizing eyes with long, dark lashes caught your attention and held it. Danny's face had thinned. His cheekbones were more prominent. Emphasis fell on his full lips, posed in a wry smile aimed in my direction, and his straight, sun-streaked hair was shorter, though still shaggy. I couldn't stop staring.

Danny Newman had morphed from teen heartthrob into full-fledged hunk.

"Mom told me you were attending Donnelly," Danny said. "I planned on calling you after classes. Now I don't have to."

"My parents didn't tell me," I answered, dumbfounded by his revelation.

"Strange." Danny shrugged, then pulled me back for another emotional hug. "You look great," he whispered. "You're older now."

"Of course I'm older." What did Danny expect? Five years had passed since we'd last seen each other.

Rachel stared. Danny must be the student from her morning class. As a film major, she would have found Steven Newman's son being in her class exciting.

Danny released me and took the seat next to me.

"Eli's like my kid sister." Danny answered the unasked question in everyone's eyes.

"Eli? Kid sister?" Rachel asked, stunned by this revelation.

"I couldn't pronounce 'Elizabeth.'" Danny quirked a brow. "Can I still call you, 'Eli'?"

"If you must," I sighed. This battle was unwinnable, so why fight it.

Danny grinned, victorious. "Eli's my dearest friend in the world. I've known her since before her birth."

"Dad and Steve roomed together in college," I added as an explanation.

"Steve?"

I regretted uttering his name. The wheels in Rachel's head spun.

"So your father is Steven Newman? The director?" she confirmed.

"Guilty as charged. Good old dad." Danny winked at me.

Rachel eyed me suspiciously. Now she knew. The Newmans and Jacobs were frequently linked. Would she keep my identity quiet?

"What other classes are you in?" I asked Danny, quickly changing the subject.

CHAPTER 2 - ELIZABETH

Danny and I discovered we were in the same political science class. As everyone dispersed after lunch, we headed off to the squat brick social sciences building, a short walk across the residential quad.

Entering the cavernous lecture hall, I led the way into the third row. Two vacant seats in the center called to us. I sat down in the first one. Then Danny stepped by me to reach the other. From this vantage point, I would spend the semester gazing into Danny's potent sapphire eyes.

Though the professor took to the lectern, commanding every student's attention, I sensed eyes on me. I turned my head to the side. Two girls sitting toward the end of the next row were staring, and I turned away.

This was not what I wanted. Please let it be first-day curiosity. I wanted to engage in class discussion, but the professor was lecturing, affording no opportunities for participation. I needed my classmates to see that I was just another Donnelly student. News flash folks: celebrities' children have brains.

I turned back again hoping their attention would be on the professor, as it should be. But no! The girls continued staring. And they weren't even embarrassed at being caught. I followed the trajectory of their pupils. Oh! I blushed. Danny. Of course; I should have expected as much.

After class, Danny led me to a nearby bench bathed in late-summer sun. What a beautiful afternoon for the outdoors, and at a time of the season when such opportunities were fleeting. Fall would be upon Donnelly soon enough.

I curled my legs under my skirt to face Danny. It was wonderful being with him. The comfortable familiarity we'd always shared had returned in an instant. I enjoyed having my "big brother" around.

"Amazing," Danny said. "I move three thousand miles for college and find my dearest friend in the world."

"It's great," I agreed, then changed the subject. "Danny, I want to keep a low profile. People shouldn't guess who I am."

Danny picked up the end of my long, thick braid and twirled it.

"So that's why this?"

I swatted his hand away. Danny was right. I only braided my hair for sports or the beach. Loose auburn waves were my trademark in a town where everyone did whatever they could to have straight, glossy hair.

"I haven't even told my roommates. Chloe and Rachel think Dad's an attorney."

Danny laughed. "Well, Mike did go to law school." I frowned. "Eli, I've always loved your folks. Are you ashamed of them?"

"Of course not. I just don't want people saying, 'There goes Miranda Jordan's kid.' It's already happened."

I glanced around, my eyes darting in all directions. Sure enough, a student passing by stopped to tie his shoelace and did a double take. In the distance, two girls chatting with each other turned onto the path that would take them past our bench. I frowned.

"And you think being my friend will make people notice you?"

"You do draw attention."

"So do you." I scrunched my face, disappointed. Danny continued: "Have you looked in the mirror lately? You look so much like Randi, it's freaky."

"No, I don't. Mom is stunning. I'm not," I protested. "Our coloring is different too, and I'm not built like her."

Danny eyed me and smirked. I blushed a deep crimson. "Okay, so your eye color is different, but you're both always in sunglasses. You have to get very close to notice," Danny said, and he playfully inched toward me.

Our noses touched, and I gasped. Widening, my eyes jumped to his. Yeah, he'd felt it too, an unmistakable electric current.

Danny abruptly backed up. "Even a blind person could figure out who your mother is. Except I think your figure is more appealing and you're prettier than Randi."

Wide-eyed, I stared at Danny. He couldn't possibly mean it. "I'm prettier than Mom? Nobody thinks that." Mom was an actress and a former model.

"I do." Danny smiled. "You can't hide from it, Eli."

I sighed and dropped the subject, not wanting to ruin our reunion. I love Mom, but I envisaged college as the way to escape the giant shadow she cast.

"What was prep school like?" I asked, thinking this would be a safe topic.

Danny paused and stared down at his fingers, fidgeting, unusual for him.

"Difficult. Academics were great, but at times I felt socially inept."

"You, socially inept?" This admission surprised me. "You're, you're you," I stammered. "You're Danny Newman. How could you feel inadequate?"

"My fan club!" he laughed. "That's what I missed at Bromley."

"I am not your fan club. I don't even know if I still like you. It's been years."

"Of course you still like me, and yes, you are my fan club."

"You're so arrogant."

"Not really. I've humbled," he smirked

6

"Humbled?" I laughed. "Danny and humble do not belong in the same sentence."

"Elizabeth, at Bromley, L.A. didn't count, Wall Street ruled. The guys were quick to remind me that Dad had attended the wrong university in New York."

"If Steve hadn't gone to NYU, he wouldn't have become Steve. And he wouldn't have met Ellen or my dad. They would have married other people. We wouldn't exist." I paused for a breath. "I'm beginning to sound like *Back to the Future*, aren't I?"

Danny laughed. "That whole time-continuum thing."

"Scary. I'm glad Steve went to NYU. I enjoy existing, don't you?"

"Yes." Danny continued laughing. "I forgot how funny you are, Eli."

I turned serious again. "They were probably jealous. When have any of them ever attended an awards show or gotten backstage passes to their favorite band? I'll bet they can't get into the hottest clubs just by showing up, like you can. How did you put up with that crap?"

"The preps ran everything, and they weren't shy about letting me know they thought being Daniel Newman was less than impressive."

"That's absurd. Danny Newman has always been impressive. In Brentwood, you're royalty."

"Brentwood doesn't exist to those guys. But they did like that I usually won matches for the golf team and was a tough bastard in the rugby scrum and at lacrosse."

Danny paused and smiled at a memory. "I was popular for one week. Gibby sent me passes for a performance in Boston. He invited us to hang out with his band. It boosted my standing for the week.."

"I'm sorry. I wish I'd been there."

"I considered calling you, but I don't know. Remember, the last time we'd seen each other, you were a little kid who worshipped me."

"You knew that?" I asked.

"Everybody knew that," Danny laughed. "That's why I couldn't call. I needed to believe your feelings hadn't changed. If I had called, I risked learning that perhaps even you had turned against me."

"Oh, Danny." I almost cried over the pain he had bravely endured while I had been safely oblivious in Santa Monica.

We continued filling in the gaps of the last five years. Being back in each other's life, a void had closed. Danny had always been the one person I could completely trust, and he felt the same toward me. Danny and I could discuss anything.

"The boys at home are envious," I smirked. "They say you bed a new girl every time you go out. Is that the truth, Daniel?" I cringed picturing anonymous girls hanging on his every word.

Danny glanced down at his hands, then back to me.

"Eli, I enjoy a good time," he said quietly. "I'm not ready for a relationship. What about you, Elizabeth? I'm sure you left plenty of broken hearts along the way."

"Not at all," I laughed.

"Oh, c'mon, Eli. A hot girl like you?"

"Oh, shut up!" I exclaimed, both surprised and flattered.

"They must have been blind."

"Maybe they wanted a blonde," I deadpanned and Danny laughed. "It was me. I didn't want the entanglement of leaving someone behind."

Danny raised an eyebrow. He always read through me, sometimes too well. Distance and time had not changed that.

"I've had dates, just not boyfriends."

"You're still a virgin. Aren't you noble," Danny replied sarcastically.

I rolled my eyes. "I am not noble. My personal life should not be all over the Web. It's not like I'm the famous one in my family."

"So if you're ever in *People* magazine with a guy, he's the one you lost it to." Danny laughed. "That's why you're at Donnelly—to hide from reality."

"That did enter into the equation," I said bitterly.

CHAPTER 3 - ELIZABETH

"Show me your room," Danny demanded as we returned from dinner.

"I'm sure it's the same as yours."

"Eli...."

Irresistible like a yapping puppy, Danny was hyper and gleeful all at once as he followed Rachel, Chloe and me into the elevator.

"This is great! I've never been to the tower."

Rachel rolled her eyes, a favorite habit.

Then Rachel unlocked the door to our suite and she and Chloe retreated to their rooms. Danny wandered over to our new sofa, a bed covered with a brightly colored spread and fingered the throw pillows. Then he proceeded to examine every inch of the room.

"A private bathroom! No shit!" he exclaimed. "I have to go down the hall. So not fair."

Hah! I laughed. Rachel peeked out from behind her door and shook her head disapprovingly.

"Show me the rest, Eli."

When I knocked on Chloe's door, Danny glanced in approvingly. Only an orange beanbag chair punctuated her muted décor.

Smiling sweetly, Chloe peeked out from browsing through her closet. "Hi, Danny."

"Nice room, Chloe. Great chair," Danny answered, giving Chloe's highlighted blonde good looks a quick once over.

Rachel's door was open. A phone was poised in her hand to make a call.

Danny's eyes were drawn to the movie paraphernalia decorating her wall, including a poster from a film directed by Steve.

"Dad." Danny said quietly. The five year-old movie had been nominated for an Academy Award but didn't win.

Danny remained glued in place, as though he were afraid to come nearer. Danny appeared wounded; disturbed, and his posture sagged.

"Take that off the wall!" Danny insisted.

"I love this film," Rachel protested. "It was Vanessa Rogers' big break and one of Steven Newman's best. This film should have won that year," she said knowledgeably.

Danny shuddered. "I'll replace it with a poster from any other film Dad has ever made and he'll even sign it. Please, get rid of that. I don't want to see it again!"

"Then don't come in my room!"

"That film makes me sad." Danny said quietly, and he backed out of her doorway.

"It was a comedy," Rachel muttered.

"I can't look at that poster, Eli."

"What's wrong?" I calmly asked, once Rachel couldn't hear our voices. I'd never seen anyone react that way to a poster. It was just paper, wasn't it?

"Bad memories."

"Didn't that wrap right before my bat mitzvah?"

"I guess," Danny replied flatly.

"Steve and Ellen were so tense at the reception. Even when I danced with Steve, he wasn't with me. It was weird."

Something was missing from my memory. A crucial piece of the puzzle had eluded me in the excitement of that day.

"Eli, you didn't know?" Danny asked. "Mom and Dad weren't living together."

What! How had I not known? I was family.

Was there a link to that movie? What had happened to lead Steve and Ellen so far apart that they weren't living together.

"Hey, let me see your room," Danny said, changing the subject. Anticipation was back in his voice. "I bet it's fluffy and pink like at home."

"My room is not fluffy!" Color rose in my cheeks.

A moment later I regretted denying its "fluffiness." Danny stood in the doorway and at once noticed the white shag area rug. He couldn't restrain his laughter.

"Okay. There is some fluff," I sneered. Then I glared at him.

"Kate Spade linens. Why am I not surprised," Danny flashed a mischievous grin.

Then Danny glanced at the mound of decorative pillows arrayed on the bed. He launched himself backwards into the pile like a diver, only Danny was laughing too hard.

"This is what I'm missing. I only have two," he teased.

How cavalierly Danny had messed my carefully made bed.

"Get your shoes off my bed!" I scolded and then I swatted Danny's large feet. I thought he would sit up, but instead Danny kicked off his Topsiders, piled up the pillows, and propped himself up against them, while stretching out his long legs.

"Make yourself at home, Daniel," I stated sarcastically.

"Elizabeth, no man will ever want to sleep in this bed."

"The décor is for me. Worry about your own sex life."

"There's nothing for me to worry about," Danny responded with a devilish grin. I flushed crimson, wanting to smack him. Instead I rolled my eyes and growled.

Danny leaned into the pillows. "This is so nice." Then Danny pressed his hand against the mattress. Surprised to find a pillowtop, he pressed two more times.

"A real mattress? Eli, how'd you get a real mattress?"

"And box springs," I gloated. "I bought them at Sears."

"No shit! I've never been to Sears. Tomorrow you're taking me. You're such a spoiled little princess."

I laughed. This was either the ultimate compliment or insult coming as it was from the most spoiled person I had ever met.

Danny took out his phone and dialed. "Hand me your Mac," he commanded, spying the laptop on my desk. Curious, I obediently brought it.

"Hey, Mom," said Danny into the phone. Then he paused to listen. "No, everything's great. Let's Skype." Danny ended the call and grabbed the computer.

"Eli, over here," he ordered motioning me next to him on the bed. The physical closeness made my pulse race. I hoped he didn't feel it.

Danny turned the laptop toward himself and logged-on. "Hi Mom! Guess where I am?"

"In a girl's bedroom, Danny?" Ellen answered.

"And she's the most amazing girl too." I glared and Danny grinned.

"You haven't been at Donnelly for a week and already you've found a girl? You sound happy, though."

"I am. It's as though we've known each other forever."

Then Danny burst into laughter. I lunged across his chest for the computer, but he pulled it out of my reach.

"What's going on there?" The commotion was audible to Ellen, plus, the video was jerky.

"Lovers' quarrel," Danny answered, still laughing.

"We are not lovers! Ellen, it's me."

"Elizabeth!" Danny adjusted the computer. Now we were both visible. "Daniel, don't give Elizabeth a hard time."

"I can't help it, Mom," he could barely speak from laughing. "It's so much fun."

I smacked Danny's upper-arm.

"Ouch!" Then he crushed me close.

"Now we'll be in the frame together," Danny smirked.

The warmth of his arm around me had a calming effect. Danny's touch was cozy like a chenille blanket you wanted to run your fingertips over.

"We got home this morning," Ellen said. "Elizabeth, we'd hoped to see you, but Steve had meetings in London. Danny, I'm sorry we couldn't have been with you."

"It's okay, Mom."

Danny's downcast expression told me it was not at all okay. Danny might be a muscular six-footer, but today he was vulnerable, a little boy putting on a brave front.

Hidden from Ellen's view, I hugged Danny's waist. Now I understood. Danny needed me to be his family.

"No, it isn't okay," Ellen answered. "You needed me too."

"I'm fine, Mom," Danny said flatly to end the discussion.

"Did everything get delivered?"

"Yes, Mom. And my car arrives Monday."

"You shipped the Porsche?" I asked. At home his car was legend.

"No. Mom said I needed a four-seater. I bought a convertible M6. Red." Danny lit up. "Really sweet. We picked it up at the BMW factory and drove around Germany. I've been waiting for it to clear customs."

"I'll tell Dad it's coming."

"Thanks, Mom. Oh, and tell Dad I'm shopping for a bed tomorrow. Dorm beds suck. Eli bought her own bed and I want one too."

"Poor baby,' I said sarcastically. "Jealous?"

Danny gave me an impish grin. "Yes. I have mattress envy," he answered and turned back to Ellen. "Mom, if I don't get a real bed I might do something drastic."

"Drastic?" she asked, smirking.

Smiling mischievously, Danny answered, "I might be forced to sleep with Eli."

I flushed crimson, but Danny's arm around my shoulder kept me glued in place.

"That wouldn't be drastic," Ellen responded.

"Hey! What about me?" I protested. "I have my reputation to consider."

"Which would be enhanced." Danny sniggered. "Only for a couple of nights, please Eli? Until mine gets delivered."

"If my Mom heard this she'd castrate you."

"Ouch!" Danny laughed. "Mommy, don't let Randi come near me with a knife!"

Now Ellen was laughing, too.

"If I were Randi I'd agree, but I'm your mother, Danny. I'd love to see you with a girl like Elizabeth, but if I had a daughter, I'd never want her anywhere near you. Danny, be honest. You're not ready to be a boyfriend. You don't even know what it means to be one."

"I've had girlfriends," Danny answered, somewhat indignantly.

"No, you haven't. You've never made an emotional commitment to any girl."

"It's not going to happen, Mom. I'm not ready to settle down." Danny looked over at me and smiled. "That's why I'm glad I have Eli. I can be emotional with her and sleep with someone else. It's perfect. There are no entanglements to worry about."

CHAPTER 4 - ELIZABETH

Chloe was spending an inordinate amount of time primping for our first big social event, the Freshman Fete. I was summer tan. A little mascara and pale pink lip-gloss were all that I required. I doubted Rachel with her perpetually frizzy hair every primped for anything. She was on the phone.

So I sat on the edge of my bed dressed and waiting.

"Let's go!" Chloe called out as though we had been keeping her.

"Wait! I almost forgot."

I smiled provocatively while I scampered back to my room and removed a folder from the top drawer of my desk.

"Don't tell anyone where you got these," I warned. "Promise? I'll be in so much trouble. My parents don't know."

"Promise!" they both swore though without knowing what they were swearing to.

I opened the folder and removed two drivers' licenses, one from New York and one from Connecticut. The girls scrutinized them.

"These say we're twenty-one!" Chloe gasped.

"How did you...?" Rachel was stunned.

"A prop master friend; she can get anything," I replied smugly.

Shortly before ten we arrived at the second floor of century-old Daughtry Hall dormitory. Decked out with balloons and posters, a table manned by two upperclassmen blocked the entrance to the party. IDs would be checked and purses searched for alcohol. From their stares, it was clear the students used their jobs to check out the freshman girls.

Before Rachel, Chloe and I got that far, Danny accosted us. He guided us to where Cam and their other roommate, Shane, were lurking, in an alcove down the hall. Shane Mills' angular pale face, with straight blonde hair and deep brown eyes, was a sharp contrast to Cameron's softer features.

"Here." Danny grabbed a glass bottle from Shane and pressed it to my lips. "Drink."

I had no choice but to take a gulp. Otherwise the liquid would have spilled down the front of my dress.

"What was that?" An unfamiliar rasp came from my throat as Danny passed the bottle to Rachel who took a quick swig before passing it to Chloe.

"Vodka," he smirked. "I thought you might need something to take the edge off."

Admittedly shy, I did not like large parties, but Cam had promised me a dance. I wouldn't be stuck alone on the sidelines. And if nothing else, Danny was good for at least one dance out of obligation.

The bottle had quickly made its round and Danny took a long pull before passing it back to me. I took another sip, a small one this time, before handing it off. With my low alcohol tolerance, I already felt the buzz.

Danny took my elbow and escorted me into the party, already in full swing, wall-to-wall with freshmen.

"Do you mind?" I groused, "I'm not your date," and I pulled my arm free.

"Aha! So you do want to meet someone," he teased.

"I don't know. Maybe. It could be nice. I know I don't want you."

Thankfully Cam appeared. "Is my roommate bothering you?"

"Yes," I answered, and I flashed Danny a victorious smile.

"Then let's have that dance you promised me." I stuck my tongue out at Danny as Cam led me to the dance floor. So mature.

Cam was an excellent dancer, and we enjoyed dancing to several songs before breaking for a cold drink. While I waited for Cam's return, I observed Danny through the corner of my eye. He danced with several different girls, none of whom kept his interest. I sighed. Danny was an excellent dancer, effortless in his movements.

After Cam and I finished our drinks we danced a few more dances. Then a slow song played. Out of nowhere Danny approached.

"May I cut in?" He asked, all polite good manners.

Cam had no choice. He handed me to Danny as though I was chattel.

Danny reached for my hand and held me close. Our feet went gliding across the floor as he masterfully led. The hand Danny had positioned on the small of my back sent unwanted shivers up my spine. I hoped he didn't notice.

When the music ended I smugly curtseyed. Before I could take my leave, a skinny blonde preppy approached us. There was something about him. I couldn't put a finger on it, but my reaction was visceral. The little hairs on my neck prickled. We'd never met, but intuitively I knew this guy was bad news.

He must have had a similar affect on Danny, for he instinctively wrapped his arm across my shoulders. Did Danny want him to think I was his date?

"Hey, Newman," he said, lasciviously eyeing every inch of me. I cringed. "Who's your babe?" His voice was soft, a muted southern drawl. Usually I found this somewhat sexy, but not this time.

"Duncan, meet Elizabeth," Danny responded stiffly.

Danny calling me Elizabeth confirmed that for me, Duncan was to be avoided.

"Elizabeth. Lovely," he said with sarcastic bite. "I'm Duncan Lebeau."

"Charmed, I'm sure," I replied tersely, but with a sweet forced smile.

A barely visible tattoo on Duncan's collarbone appeared to be a dark-hued snake. A goth preppy. That was interesting. Or was it a warning?

"The after party's at my suite. Be there." Duncan said.

"I wouldn't miss it," Danny answered.

"And bring your babe." Duncan aimed his devious smile at me. "Pretty girls are always welcomed."

"Elizabeth won't be coming," Danny responded definitively.

Duncan shrugged indifferently and left us. I deliberately removed Danny's arm from my shoulder and indignantly turned to face him.

"Why won't I be going?"

"You wouldn't have a good time," he answered flatly.

"I make my own decisions. I'm not a kid, Daniel." How dare he!

Danny put his hands square on my shoulders and met my gaze with an intensity I had previously not experienced.

"You will not be going to Duncan's. I will not permit it."

"Permit!" Who was Danny to give me orders?

"Danny, why are you all over my date?" Cam's laughter interrupted us.

Danny quickly dropped his hands. His usual laid-back demeanor replaced the intensity of a moment earlier.

"Your date? Eli your Cam's date?" Danny was surprised.

"I guess I am now," I answered. "Cam, let's dance." I sarcastically blew Danny a kiss as I walked away with Cam. Let Danny stew.

Midnight found me cozy in pajamas, attempting to read for political science. Distracted, I kept replaying the exchange between Danny and Duncan. There was something off-putting about Duncan. Recalling his tattoo made me shiver. I clutched my pillow.

Chloe staggered in with Rachel in tow. I wasn't sleeping anyway.

"How was the party?" I asked.

"Be glad you didn't go," a sober Rachel answered. Chloe was grasping the walls to stay upright. "I got her out just in time."

Chloe stumbled toward my bed. One whiff and I understood. She reeked.

"I thought Chloe didn't smoke," I said to Rachel. Chloe giggled. Rachel glared.

"Everyone was wasted," Rachel explained. "I would have left as soon as I arrived but Chloe wanted to stay and I thought I might be needed."

"Looks like you were."

"Danny's so hot. And he's such a good guitarist," Chloe sighed. "And his voice... Lizzie, can he play for us?" Chloe giggled.

"Sure. I'll call his agent tomorrow and book him," I said sarcastically.

"Would you?" She sighed again. "Then he can kiss me again."

I sat bolt upright. "What! Rachel, what went on there!?"

"Let's get Chloe to bed and we'll talk."

We dragged Chloe to her bed, removed her shoes, and covered her with a blanket. She fell right to sleep. Now Rachel could fill me in.

"Everyone at Duncan's was getting wasted, including Chloe. Then she jumped on Danny and started kissing him." Rachel rolled her eyes in disgust.

How awkward! Danny didn't like Chloe that way. And I didn't want to feel self-conscious if Danny showed me attention like at the dance. Had Chloe noticed? Is that why she had gloated about kissing Danny? What a mess! Why couldn't she like Shane?

CHAPTER 5 - ELIZABETH

The next evening I met Danny, and we headed to the library. What an incredible week it had been. The trepidations I'd felt before arriving at Donnelly were laid to rest. I was enjoying my classes, dorm life was fun, and I had made several good friends.

Then there was Danny. What an amazing reunion. We had picked up right where we had left off five years earlier including the comfort we felt with each other.

When Danny and I arrived, we found the library was relatively empty. It was early in the term and we were able to snag a soundproofed study room that by next month would require a reservation.

Danny and I settled in to review political science. We both had extensive outlines. While I impressed Danny with my mastery of the material, he overwhelmed me with his.

"How do you know all this?" I asked. "You spent half the weekend wasted."

"It's the other half that matters," Danny shot back arrogantly. "Where were you at ten o'clock this morning? This is what I was doing." Danny held up his book.

To say that I was shocked was an understatement.

"How were you up at ten? I know what went on at Duncan's."

Danny smirked. "Well, after Chloe was forcibly removed from me... It could have been sweet except she's your roommate."

"I'm so glad there's a code," I replied sarcastically which he ignored.

"I stayed a while longer and was snug in my bed asleep by two. I got my eight hours and hit the books. No way was I showing up tonight with less than my A game."

"You're so competitive."

"Same as you. Admit it, Eli. You want to show me up just as much as I want to show you up." I flushed, deep red. Danny laughed. "I'm right, aren't I?"

I launched the rubber band I'd been wearing on my wrist at Danny's head. As it bounced off his shoulder, Danny laughed. I sneered and returned to my book.

After a time I caught Danny stifling a yawn, and I raised an eyebrow. Aha!

Caught, he glared at me. "Let's see how the coffee is."

Danny guided me out of the room. After several wrong turns we found the lounge where vending machines sold coffee, cold drinks and snacks. Danny grabbed a cup of coffee and bought me a bottle of water.

Pressed against the side of one tall machine, I tilted my chin toward Danny, maintaining eye-contract while we chatted. Towering over me, his height apparent, Danny leaned, supporting his hand against the metal machine.

An average looking blonde girl passed by, glancing at Danny, offering a plastic smile. She failed to get his attention that was riveted on me. How could Danny not notice her? The girl was boring into me with a deathly stare.

After she paused on her return, I whispered to Danny, "What's with the blonde giving me the death stare?"

Danny brushed it off. "She's nobody."

"Let's get back to our books. 'Nobody' is giving me the creeps."

In our study room, I gave Danny my own version of death stare.

"Who is that blonde, Daniel?" I asked sternly.

"I don't know," he answered uncomfortably.

"You don't? Why would someone I don't know, if you don't know them either, be giving me death stare?"

"I met her at Duncan's," he replied sheepishly. "I didn't catch her name."

"Great." I rolled my eyes.

"She's an upperclassman. They have singles."

"Do I really care?"

"You asked," he shrugged shamelessly.

"A simple she's a girl I met at Duncan's would have sufficed. No need to get graphic," I said indignantly.

"I didn't get graphic. I could if you really want me to, but you wouldn't understand." I rolled my eyes again. Danny was infuriating.

"The girl is stalking us! It must have been quite memorable evening."

"I guess so. For her," Danny laughed.

"What a cad!"

"No, I'm just having fun, Eli. A girl that wasted understands things can happen that do not mean anything. She has to deal with it."

"That's why you wouldn't let me attend that party."

"I wanted to protect you from a room of wasted people behaving badly."

"Yourself included?"

"Yes. Especially myself. Despite where you grew up you're still naïve. I want to keep you that way. It looks right on you. It's charming. I don't want you to change."

CHAPTER 6 - ELIZABETH

After a busy morning, my ire softened. It was difficult to reconcile Danny's reckless behavior with the deference and kindness he bestowed upon me. Then again, they often said that about gangsters and their treatment of female relatives. The Godfather's Don Vito Corleone was a wonderful husband, once you got past the fact that he murdered for a living.

Like it or not, I was more or less Danny's female relative, and I didn't like it.

Cam waited for me after French class. *"Le dejeuner, mademoiselle?"* he asked.

"Oui, monsieur," I replied. So this was to be the new routine; lunch with the guys after French class. Works for me!

Danny approached as I was deciding what to eat and he planted a yogurt cup on my plate. He flashed that boyish grin, the one that most women, okay I, found irresistible. The accompanying twinkly sapphire eyes were what really killed.

"What's up buttercup?" he smiled at me.

"Is this a peace offering?"

"Are you still angry?"

"No," I answered truthfully. "I can never stay angry for long."

Danny followed me to the salad/sandwich bar line. "I'm glad. I would hate if you stayed angry."

Danny lingered, watching me assemble turkey with lettuce and tomato, a dollop of mayo on whole wheat. I gave him a questioning look that surprisingly puzzled him. Sandwich making was really not that interesting. Why was he so intent on watching me?

Later, Danny and I strode triumphantly out of Political Science. Proud of having tackled several complicated questions posed by the professor, we were giddy with success.

"Let's hang out. We've earned it," Danny suggested. "I'll buy you ice cream."

When Danny and I arrived at the Café in the Student Center, we found an unoccupied round table on the patio. Despite being designed for five, Danny sat as close to me as possible, while we enjoyed our snacks and spent the afternoon talking.

Later, Danny opened his iPad to Notes, a serious expression on his face. What the?

"I'm making a list. Eli. You need a boyfriend and if you tell me what qualities are important I can find him."

"Are you serious?" I asked angrily. "I don't need your assistance. I'll find my own boyfriend when I want one!" Should I be embarrassed, humiliated or just plain furious? How dare he!

Danny looked at me with concern. "I doubt it. You haven't had any success to date, Eli."

I felt as though I'd been slapped in the face.

"What do you suggest I do? Place an ad? Eligible bachelors please respond to P.O. Box Danny Newman," I blasted him. "Why do you even care?"

"I'm your friend. I want you happy."

"I am happy. I have friends. And I'd rather hang out with them than date anyone you'd fix me up with. Do you know how bizarre this is?"

"He's got to be from a prominent family so you can trust him," Danny continued while ignoring me. "That's the big one, trust. Intelligence – no problem if he's a Donnelly student. What else? Looks? Does he need rock star glam, or do you like to be the one who shines? Help me here, Eli."

"You really are nuts."

"Blonde or brunet?"

"You've lost it, Daniel." I scolded while trying to keep my voice from carrying.

"You're eighteen years old, Eli."

"That's what this is about. You're hung up on me being a virgin. My sex life is none of your concern, Daniel."

"It is my concern. I'm your big brother."

"You are not my brother," I snapped.

"I've got a better idea. Remember our agreement? If you haven't found someone by winter break I'll take you out to Malibu. Nobody's ever at the house."

My blood was boiling. White heat. I couldn't believe Danny remembered, nonetheless intended to hold me to a deal made when I was thirteen.

"Go die in a hole, Newman!" I jumped up from the table, picked up my books, and turned to leave. Danny grabbed my wrist.

"Don't go, Eli. Stay." He looked at me with sad, sapphire eyes. "I'm sorry. I won't ever bring it up again."

Those damned eyes were impossible to resist, and he knew it.

Exasperated with myself for giving in, I sat down. Danny grinned triumphantly. Some things never changed.

CHAPTER 7 - ELIZABETH

Danny's interest in my love life became apparent the following evening at dinner. Danny was absent. This bothered me more than I wanted to admit. I was distracted. An uncomfortable emptiness filled me.

As I toyed with my salad, every new male voice garnered my hopeful attention. My eyes darted around the dining hall seeking Danny's. Where was he?

"Hey, guys!" Danny breezed in and greeted us, startling me as I was glancing in the other direction. "This is Juliette."

My eyes popped open. My stomach sank. The loud metal clank of my fork hitting the floor as it slipped through my fingers brought unwanted attention from my tablemates. I forced composure. They shouldn't see my queasiness.

Beside Danny stood a tall, waif-like girl with waist-long, stick-straight hair the color of ice and her face had the palest complexion. Coal black eyes were all that kept her from looking albino. I couldn't decide if she was attractive. Maybe I didn't want to.

There was something ethereal about her. Juliette wore a long gauzy dress of pale yellow and flat tan sandals. A lack of makeup and nail polish only accentuated her blandness. She seemed frail while she had the overall appearance of a sixties' hippy. I was certain if I bumped into her she would fall over.

Who was this Juliette? Why was Danny bringing her to dinner? There could be only one reason and that conclusion made me ill.

"If Rachel moves down there's room for you by Elizabeth," Cam volunteered.

"Thank you, Cameron," Juliette answered. She had a soft, almost musical southern accent. Ethereal.

She had met Cam! Danny had previously introduced her to his roommates while I was blind-sided? Why?

Rachel complied and moved. Juliette took the now vacant seat beside me. Great! Just what I wanted; this strange girl sitting next to me.

I did not want this girl joining our table. I was perfectly happy with my friends as they were. Thank you very much.

"Juliette," Danny said, bubbling with enthusiasm, "This is Eli, my oldest and dearest friend."

Oh, joy! So I'm the 'oldest and dearest friend' tonight.

My heart sank. It was too obvious to ignore. Somehow, Danny had acquired a girlfriend. When had this happened? He always spent his time with me!

Danny could do so much better than Juliette the washed-out waif. He could have a tanned, auburn-haired girl. I silently brooded. I needed a Tony Award quality performance to make it through this meal, my pride intact.

I pasted on my brightest smile and vowed to be as charming as possible.

What claim did she think she had on Danny? Juliette had to be supremely confident not to be bothered by seeing that his 'oldest and dearest friend' was me.

"Eli," she purred, "So pleased to meet you."

"My name is Elizabeth," I answered with emphasis.

"My mistake. I thought Dan called you…" her voice tailed off. Dan?

"Eli. He did. Only Daniel calls me Eli," I answered in a voice as icy as Juliette's coloring.

Danny squeezed Juliette's bony shoulders. "Once you and Eli get better acquainted, you're going to be great friends," he said with confidence.

Chloe shot me a sideward's glance of support. I felt Rachel's eyes rolling. No way on earth was I ever going to be "great friends" with Juliette.

"Dan, don't eat that," Juliette gently admonished Danny as he stuck his knife into Chicken Parmesan.

"Juliette's vegan," Danny boasted. Of course she was.

Juliette stared at him with wide, pleading eyes. Danny received her message and forced a smile. It was not the carefree smile he reserved for me.

"Who wants my chicken?" he relented.

Cam and Shane looked at each other. "We'll split it," Shane said.

Danny lifted the piece of chicken and placed it on Shane's plate. Shane cut it in half and gave one section to Cam. Danny dug into his spaghetti marinara.

Amazing! Burgers and steaks had always been Danny's go to staples.

I wanted to laugh, but at the same time I wanted to cry. What was this girl doing to him? I wanted the real Danny back! I wanted my Danny back.

"How did you meet Juliette?" I asked Danny.

"After I left the library Sunday, I went to The Cellar. Juliette works there on Sundays." Danny grinned, pleased with himself.

"Sunday? Like two days ago?" The rapidity! I pushed the disappointment from my voice.

Danny shrugged. "Sometimes things happen fast," he answered, reading my mind.

I wanted to wipe the grin off his face. Danny had to realize how hurt I was.

"I live in the Exchange. We do our own cooking," Juliette volunteered. "I'm only here tonight because Dan wanted me to meet his friends. I could never live on this stuff, and I don't want you to either, Dan," she purred. Purred?

Should I smack her or kill myself? I deferred making a decision, hoping my carnivorous boy would soon come to his senses.

Trying to be pleasant, I asked, "Where are you from, Juliette?"

"Atlanta," she answered. "If you're Dan's oldest friend, does that mean you're from Los Angeles?"

"Yes. I live around the corner from Danny." He let my exaggeration slide.

"How nice," Juliette responded.

I looked directly into Danny's amused eyes and targeted him with my brightest smile. "Yes," I said, "It is nice. It's very nice."

I caught Rachel's smirk. She knew exactly what I was doing. I was rather transparent.

"What do your parents do?" There! I sounded both polite and interested. See, I'm not a jealous bitch.

"He's an executive at Coca-Cola and my mother teaches autistic children," Juliette bragged.

"That's terrific," I said sincerely. "I have a lot of respect for her."

I hated admitting that, but anyone who would devote themselves to a career of helping the disabled was a hero. I couldn't compete against that. My mother's career was far from saintly.

"Thank you," Juliette answered, taken aback by my sincerity.

"Does your father send you freebies?" Shane asked. This levity cut through the tension, if only for a moment.

Juliette smiled. "I can get you coupons." Juliette turned back to me. "What do your parents do, Elizabeth?"

I smiled at Danny with a look of defiance. Well, she'd asked.

"Dad's a movie producer and Mom's an actress," I answered nonchalantly.

Shocked, Danny gave me a hard stare. Accustomed to my usual evasive answers, telling Juliette the truth was in sharp contrast.

My friends wondered where this would go. They were sworn not to disclose my parents' identities, but, hey, they were my parents. I could do whatever.

"Who are your parents?" Juliette asked playing into my hand.

"Michael Jacobs and Miranda Jordan," I answered, filled with pride.

Well, she had asked a direct question. I couldn't help it if my parents were recognized world-wide, and hers weren't.

These thoughts were distasteful even to me. I was angry with Danny and envious of Juliette. And for once I didn't care. This girl had come out of nowhere and stolen my man! So what if Danny wasn't really mine for her to steal. If Juliette hadn't appeared, perhaps Romeo would have become mine.

"I'm sorry, I don't know who they are."

How did she not know who my parents were! Had she never heard of IMDb?

"I only go to foreign films," Juliette explained.

I was dumbfounded. "Shame," I answered, filled with contempt. "Danny spent last year working on his dad's latest film. They were all over Europe and even spent a month in Africa," I bragged. "I'm sorry you won't see it. Steven only directs blockbusters. I'll gladly report back to you when I return from the premiere."

Danny's fork crashed against his ceramic plate. All eyes turned his way. His glare directed at me made me spasm. Shit! He was pissed.

Much to everyone's relief, dinner finally ended. I left with Chloe, relieved to leave Danny and Juliette behind.

"What was he thinking having that girl dine with us?" Chloe asked as soon as we were far enough down the path that no one could hear us. "She was awful. 'I only go to foreign films.' Like she thinks she's superior to us. You put her in her place."

"Not really. She didn't know who I was bragging about."

"She had to. Your mother's won two Oscars. Juliette wasn't born in an art house."

"Thanks, Chloe. I'm not proud of myself. I've never done that before and I didn't like it. Danny didn't either."

"I'm sorry, Elizabeth. It had to hurt having this girl shoved in your face. What was Danny's point?"

Tears pricked my eyes. "It's Danny's way of telling me that to him I'm his kid sister and always will be." My voice quivered. The tears I'd kept bottled inside through dinner released in a torrent down my cheeks.

"You want more." Chloe embraced me. "Oh, Elizabeth. I truly am sorry."

CHAPTER 8 - ELIZABETH

It's difficult finding time to spend together when you're not a couple, and even more difficult when one of you is part of a couple. Now I treasured any time I spent with Danny even more than before.

Danny was spending an increasing amount of time with Juliette, and a diminished amount with me. It took great effort to put on a believable happy face. Yet within moments of glimpsing those sapphire eyes, I could put Juliette out of my mind and enjoy the relationship I had with Danny, one she would never experience.

One afternoon, a few weeks later, I was enjoying a cup of hot chocolate on the Café patio while Danny drank his usual black coffee.

"Eli," he began tentatively, playing with my fingers, "I'd really like if you and Juliette ate lunch together sometime."

"Why would I want to do that?" I asked curtly.

The question had caught me off-guard. Other than to assuage his guilt, I couldn't imagine why Danny thought I should socialize with Juliette. It was like asking your wife to lunch with your mistress. And I was the wife.

"You'd like Juliette if you got to know her."

"I have no desire to do lunch or anything else with that condescending albino."

"Albino?" Danny laughed.

"She's completely colorless."

"Eli, Juliette's my girlfriend and you're like my sister. I want you to be friends."

"Daniel, I am NOT your anything." I angrily turned away. My eyes stung. "There is not a single drop of Newman blood coursing through my veins," I stammered.

"You're jealous!"

Of course I was. Juliette had the one thing I'd always wanted. I fought the tears that were forming and fiercely looked Danny down.

"Of Juliette? Never," I said emphatically.

I turned away. On the verge of crying, I needed my control back.

"You're jealous of me!" Danny gasped. Then he brought his cup to his lips to sip.

"What? I don't want to date Juliette. I'm not gay, Daniel!"

Coffee sputtered out of Danny's mouth as he choked on laughter. "Of course you're not. I mean you're jealous that I'm getting laid and you're not." He wiped his face with a napkin.

How obtuse could Danny be?

"I am not jealous of you," I said deliberately.

What did Danny not understand? Or was he afraid to?

By mid-October, there was only one flaw in my otherwise perfect relationship with Danny– I wasn't in one. Danny remained with Juliette whom he wisely didn't discuss. He enjoyed the best of both worlds: a strikingly beautiful woman he was sleeping with but had nothing in common with, and a strikingly beautiful woman he was not sleeping with but had nearly everything in common with.

I worked this to my advantage, spending as much time with Danny as possible, but controlling my frustration so as not to piss him off.

As weeks passed, Juliette was having an increasingly difficult time with my role in Danny's life. Sorry Juliette.

I thoroughly enjoyed the day Juliette caught up to us in the Café. Danny and I were next on line to order lunch when she appeared, ruining his gastronomic plans.

I smirked at Danny's frustration as he ordered, "Veggie burger with tomato and sprouts. No fries, please. I'll have carrot sticks."

Juliette preened like a proud peacock. Holding back giggles, I smiled prettily and ordered, "Bacon burger, please, medium-rare, and extra crispy fries."

Poor Danny! The longing in his eyes was painful. He had to exercise every ounce of control not to leap across the table and steal my food.

"Want a bite?" I asked, a mischievous glint in my eyes.

The glare I received said it all and I smirked. The enticing aroma had to be killing Danny. The Café made the best burgers!

I was poised to take my first juicy bite when Juliette interrupted my musings. "Elizabeth, you really shouldn't. Beef is bad for your body."

Bad for my body? I'd show her. I jumped up, thrust my chest toward Danny, and slowly pirouetted so he would not miss a single curve on my perfect size zero figure.

"Daniel, anything wrong with this body?" I asked while sending a flirty smile in his direction.

"No, Eli," he stammered. But Danny's eyes couldn't hide their pleasure.

The following Sunday, Danny suggested we go to The Cellar after our study date.

"Doesn't Juliette work there on Sundays?" I asked. That would certainly ruin my night.

"Not tonight. Juliette lives in that co-op. Tonight's her turn to scrub the kitchen."

"I'm glad I don't live there. When I get my own kitchen, it comes with a maid."

"Agreed. There is no glamour in housework."

Sunday was a slow night at The Cellar and we had no problem finding a table. Danny ordered a pitcher of beer. After the waiter served it, I poured us each a foam-free glass. We raised our glasses and tapped them together. "Cheers," we toasted.

The cold amber felt smooth going down. The tensions of the day vanished. Danny and I sat easily talking and laughing. We always had such good times together.

"Eli, let's dance," Danny suggested after he consumed a couple of beers.

Danny took my hand and led me to the dance floor. Fast rock tunes were playing and we danced non-stop through three songs. I laughed when Danny purposely bumped my hip and he laughed when I pivoted and tripped over my own foot. Two friends having fun!

A slow song played next.

"I love this song," I told Danny, expecting him to lead us back to our table.

Instead, Danny placed one hand on my waist and held my other hand up at his shoulder. I placed my hand around him and Danny held me close, our bodies touching. I gasped at the electricity. Danny grinned; he felt it too.

A second slow song began. Dreamy happiness consumed me as I tilted my head upwards looking into his sapphire eyes. They smiled back with gentle pleasure. He was as content as I.

Danny pressed me against his body. Powerful current made us inseparable and I gasped at feeling him harden.

I glanced at Danny who was smiling. He moved our joined hands to where his knuckles lightly skimmed my cheek. Shivers ran through me. The intensity was so powerful our hearts were racing.

Unexpectedly, Danny leaned toward me and tenderly kissed my lips. My head began to spin. I felt unfamiliar urges. The raw pleasure was all consuming.

Abruptly Danny pulled back. "I shouldn't have done that, Eli."

I followed his panicked glance. Juliette was approaching, steam spouting. She was not happy finding another woman enjoying her boyfriend's arms. Damn you, Juliette!

Danny immediately dropped his hands. Should I help Danny or make him suffer Juliette's wrath? I had a split second to decide. The high road would serve me better.

"Juliette! How nice to see you," I said enthusiastically. "We thought you were working here tonight."

CHAPTER 9 - ELIZABETH

Until arriving at Donnelly I believed I was a good dancer. At home I worked my way through the Royal Ballet curriculum culminating with principal roles in recitals. So when the professor demoted me a class level early in the semester, I was humiliated.

Insecurities overwhelmed me. Had my academy not properly prepared me? Should I have attended a more competitive program? Worse, had another student been more deserving but their parents weren't famous?

The professor assured me that "fine-tuning" student placement happened every year. The bar at Donnelly was set higher. So here I stood, hard work personified. I had never tried so hard in my life. My blisters spawned blisters. Some days I cried in the shower after class.

Today we were learning a new combination. I didn't need to master it. I simply needed to get it. Following the professor as she demonstrated, I seemed to get it, at least I thought I did. Instead, every time the pianist played the music, I became distracted by visions of Danny in a clinch kissing Juliette while in The Cellar last night.

Concentrate, Elizabeth. Concentrate.

The pressure was intense. I found myself concentrating more on the need to concentrate than on the combination. Sweat trickling from my brow and I wiped it.

After a water break I was more determined than ever. Failure was not an option.

Then came my turn to solo. The pianist began to play. This time I didn't get confused. The steps came fluently. Three grand jetes and it would be over. Then two.

"My ankle!" I cried out as I landed the second grand jete on a twist.

CHAPTER 10 - DANIEL

Professor Nash was lecturing on guns versus butter. A society with finite resources had to decide on the optimal utilization of its resources. Should it produce more guns or more butter? If country A more efficiently produced butter, then it should produce fewer guns and trade with country B which produced guns more efficiently and needed butter.

As with so many macro-economic theories, a plotted line graph was at the heart of the discussion. Line A represented guns; Line B represented butter. Where they intersected was the optimal mix.

While the class was discussing the factors that determined where the lines intersected, my phone vibrated. I glanced down. Eli! Why was she texting? She knew I had a class.

I grabbed the phone and pressed the link to our thread.

"911. Infirmary," it read. "May have broken ankle."

Broken ankle! "On my way," I texted back.

As I pressed the send button I felt Professor Nash glaring.

"Daniel," she admonished as I closed my laptop, "There's no texting here."

"I'm sorry, Dr. Nash. It's an emergency. My girlfriend just broke her ankle. I have to go."

I collected my computer and textbook. Without waiting for approval, I rushed out the classroom door.

CHAPTER 11 - ELIZABETH

"A bad sprain, Elizabeth."

The doctor delivered the grim diagnoses. Then he wrapped my ankle in a neoprene-covered brace.

"Stay off your foot and come back in two weeks."

The nurse handed me printed instructions on how and when to ice it, a bottle of pain relievers, and my first ever pair of crutches. I studied them, confused by how to use them.

With the nurse's help, I mounted the crutches. Uncomfortable from the pressure under my armpits, I wondered, was I doing it wrong? I winced in agony. The ankle pain left me grinding my teeth. How would I survive the next two weeks?

Urging me onward, the nurse opened the door leading to the waiting area. Danny was right by my side and I collapsed against him, quietly weeping, needing his strength, both physical and moral.

"Baby, you're hurting," Danny said softly while stroking my back.

"Are you Elizabeth's boyfriend?" the nurse asked.

"Yes," Danny answered without hesitation.

Had I heard right, or was it pain-induced hallucinating?

The nurse handed Danny the instruction sheet.

"See that Elizabeth elevates her ankle. She's going to need these today," the nurse instructed while handing Danny the bottle of pills. "Follow the dosage. They're powerful. And keep them secure."

Danny steadied me. Then he picked up my tote bag, and I hobbled out the door to his car, parked illegally in the handicapped spot.

Danny studied my face, wracked in pain. "Eli, I am so sorry. Let me take those."

I handed Danny the crutches and he leaned them against the rail. Without warning, Danny scooped me up in his strong arms, so cozy on my body. And I was wearing nothing but a leotard and cut-off tights! Then Danny carefully placed me in the passenger seat of the BMW and went back for the crutches to put in the back seat.

No more than five minutes later, but feeling like an eternity, we arrived at Berkeley Hall.

"Don't move," Danny ordered as he completed parking the car.

My hands clenched. Hurting too much to even nod, and rendered incapable of making decisions, I was content to follow whatever Danny instructed.

Danny was removing the crutches from the car when I heard him call, "Hey Shane! Some help here."

As Danny opened the passenger door, Shane caught up.

"What's going on?" Then Shane noticed the crutches and my obvious pain. "What happened to Elizabeth?"

"Eli sprained her ankle." Danny handed the crutches to Shane. Then he leaned toward me, took my hand and wrapped his other hand around my back.

"Put your left foot on the ground," Danny said in a soothing voice. I obeyed and received the approval of his warm smile. "Now Sweetheart, press on that foot and lean on me, all your weight, and try to stand."

Standing was difficult. I feared accidentally leaning on my right foot. With caution, pressing as hard as I could on Danny, I righted myself.

"Good girl," Danny said.

I hopped away from the car and retrieved the crutches from Shane. After a few tentative steps I couldn't continue. The pain was increasing. Danny held me to his chest, and I cried.

"Eli, shh," he said in a soothing voice. "I'll get you upstairs and give you the meds." Shane took the crutches and Danny lifted me into his arms.

"Good thing you weigh nothing."

If I hadn't been in such extreme pain I would have enjoyed the close contact. I wrapped my arms around his neck and held on tightly as Danny placed one arm under my knees and the other around my back. Then he carried me to the elevator. Shane's starring made me blush.

"Drugs," I pleaded once we were in Danny's room.

Danny clasped my waist, gently placing me upright as though I were a fragile piece of china. I wondered if holding me felt as cozy to Danny as it did to me.

Shane placed the crutches against Danny's desk. He continued leering at me.

"Shane, why are you starring at me?" I scolded.

Shane exchanged sly smiles with Danny who hugged me. I winced from the pain.

"Sweetheart, you do realize that you're wearing practically nothing."

"Oh!" I gasped and pivoted to hide against Danny. Of course it made no difference. My tank leotard was low-cut in front, but it was high-cut at the thigh. The guys shared a good-natured laugh at my expense.

"Shane, get Eli an ice pack, please," Danny ordered while trying not to laugh.

He sat me down on the double bed as Shane left. Danny went to his closet and removed an oxford shirt.

"Here, put this on before Shane returns."

"I hurt so much," I cried.

"I'll get you a glass of water so you can take your meds."

As Danny left I pushed the leotard off my shoulders and down to my waist. I slipped the shirt over my head and fastened all but two buttons. Then, exercising the utmost caution, I pulled the leotard off and let it drop to the floor.

"Much better," Danny announced as he appraised my appearance upon returning. He came over and sat down beside me.

"Here." Danny handed me the glass of water and shook a pill from the bottle. I took it and swallowed, washing it down with the water. I leaned my head against Danny, surrendering to the pain,. He lifted his arm and brought it around my shoulder.

"It's going to be alright, Eli," Danny told me as he tenderly stroked my arm.

All I could do was nod.

"Let's get you more comfortable, Sweetheart."

Sweetheart? I knew it didn't mean anything, but maybe it did.

I smirked, imagining Juliette's reaction if she walked in and found me sitting on Danny's bed partially clad. How I wished that she would.

Shane returned with an ice pack as Danny propped plump, down pillows against the wall.

"Thanks, Shane. Show's over," Danny smiled.

Shane threw Danny the pack but otherwise ignored him.

"How's the ankle?" Shane asked.

"I don't know. Maybe a little better." My words came out unexpectedly slurred. I rose from the bed and I giggled. Shane raised an eyebrow.

"Catch you later, Danny. You have your hands full today, buddy."

"Bye, Shane," I flirted.

Danny glanced over as I blew a kiss. Then I lost my balance.

"Elizabeth!!"

Danny caught me around my waist just as my right foot was about to hit the floor.

"You scared me! Eli, are you trying to hurt yourself worse?"

Danny was angry. He never got angry with me. My heart felt hollow. I didn't like this sensation and I couldn't stop the tears from flowing.

"You hate me!" I wailed. Danny spun me around so we were face-to-face.

"Eli, those drugs are messing with you. I could never hate you."

I smiled, drunk, and then I wrapped my hands around Danny's neck. Completely uninhibited, I pressed my lips against his face. It was soft and warm.

"I'm a little loopy. Is this what being drunk is like?" My speech was slurred.

"For you, probably." Danny smiled an amused smile.

I might have to get drunk sometime. This was fun! I smiled at Danny and he smiled back, his sapphire eyes twinkling. Did he know how appealing he was?

"Let me ice your ankle," Danny suggested.

"Okay," I answered breathily, pressing myself against him.

I pulled Danny's face to mine and pressed my lips against his. Danny's lips were warm and soft. His hands firmly held my back. Our lips moved in concert. His tongue gently touched mine. This was heady. Danny Newman was kissing me!

Abruptly Danny broke apart from me.

"Eli, what are we doing?" He frowned.

I smiled. "I don't know," I shrugged, "But it sure feels good."

"Eli! You're worse than drunk. I'm not doing this."

"Danny, you're no fun!" I pouted.

"I'm lots of fun," he laughed, "But not when you're drugged."

"I want to have fun, Danny. Please." For emphasis I opened two buttons on my shirt, revealing my breasts. Danny gaped. His eyes lingered.

"Elizabeth," he nervously laughed, "Not when you're drugged."

"Daniel…" I protested, and I pulled him to the bed, on top of me.

"Elizabeth!" he said uncomfortably. I grabbed Danny's hand and placed it inside the shirt, pressing it against my bare breast. I flashed him a triumphant smile.

"This is so wrong, Elizabeth."

"Not to me it isn't. You feel so good."

"You do too, but I won't let this happen," Danny said firmly.

He removed his hand and buttoned the shirt.

"Daniel!" I pouted, disappointed.

"The nurse never said anything about those meds making you horny," he laughed.

I glared. How could Danny not want me? Tears welled in my eyes.

"Shit!" Then Danny tenderly wrapped his arm around me, "If we do this now, you'll regret it for the rest of your life. I won't do that, Eli. You're too important to me."

"Danny," I protested.

"Elizabeth, you want love and romance, not drug-induced horniness."

Danny lifted me up and placed me in a sitting position against the pillows.

"Let's ice that ankle and we'll forget this ever happened."

I still pouted. I wanted to win, but Danny was right.

With utmost care, Danny placed my foot on a small decorative Los Angeles Dodgers' pillow. He then removed my tights and the brace. Danny's smile faded to a grimace.

"Eli, your ankle's the size of an orange and it's all black and blue."

He reached for the ice pack from the desk. I sat straight up and tried to see, but Danny already applying the ice, obscured my view.

The cold sent a new wave of pain through me. I gritted my teeth and gripped the comforter, trying not to scream. "Ow, ow, ow!" I cried. "It hurts so much."

Danny lay propped on his elbow facing me. His left hand skimmed my cheek. "I'm sorry, Sweetheart. I hate when you hurt."

"It's passing now."

Danny smiled, relieved. "Is there anything I can get you? Do you want lunch?"

I hadn't thought about food, but now that Danny mentioned it, "Lunch would be good. And a change of clothes."

"Clothes," Danny laughed, "Good idea. It'll keep you out of trouble."

CHAPTER 12 - DANIEL

Remembering that we were missing political science, I called Professor Dennison, assuming I'd get his voice mail. Instead he answered. By the end of the conversation the professor was telling me to take good care of my girlfriend.

If Professor Dennison assumed Eli was my girlfriend, did others as well?

At the dining hall I was forced to endure Shane asking, "How's your new girlfriend?" followed by filing Rachel, Chloe and Cam in on every detail.

What was it with everyone today? Normally nobody bothered me about my friendship with Eli. Just because she was injured and needed help, didn't change anything. They knew I was with Juliette. I hurried back to the dorm with sandwiches.

Last stop, Elizabeth's crammed closet. Like a life-sized Barbie doll, she owned an outfit for every possible occasion. I pulled out an apricot colored short-sleeved polo shirt dress, perfect for Indian summer. I also grabbed light blue cotton yoga pants and a royal blue tank top for her to sleep in tonight.

Eli didn't know it, but with those drugs playing with her mind, she was sleeping with me. Otherwise I wouldn't sleep for worrying. My full-sized bed had room.

After taking a few more items including underwear, I returned to my suite. On the walk down, I reflected that for a girl who, as far as I knew, had never let anyone see her underwear, Elizabeth owned the prettiest, sexiest sets. Every piece came as a matched set in the softest, silkiest fabrics. There was a color to match every mood.

I didn't know the mood Elizabeth would be in. The white lace set would remind me of her virgin state and how I'd better keep her that way.

When Elizabeth flirted earlier, it was the painkillers. There was no excuse for the desire I had felt. I was completely sober.

Before entering my room I made the phone call I dreaded, but needed to make, telling Juliette that Elizabeth was convalescing in my room.

Eli didn't like Juliette. She felt we had nothing in common. Eli was almost right. Juliette and I had enough in common to keep seeing each other. But Juliette didn't know that she was not a keeper. Our relationship was casual enough that if it ended tomorrow, I wouldn't miss her.

Juliette answered on the second ring. I got right to the point.

"Dan," she finally said in a clipped voice, "I've had all I'm going to take of you and Elizabeth. Every time I see you, you're with her. Something is going on but you deny it by saying you're just old friends. But it's there Dan, and I've had enough."

"Juliette," I protested. Was she ending our relationship? That never happened to me.

"Dan, please," she answered more forcefully that I thought she was capable of doing. "Sunday, I arrived at The Cellar and you were holding her in your arms dancing. It was a love song, Dan!"

"It was?" I had been paying attention only to Eli. I hadn't noticed the music.

"Yes. And that was my regular shift. Everyone working at The Cellar knows I'm seeing you. It was humiliating."

"I'm sorry. I enjoy dancing, and you weren't there. It was innocent dancing." Had Juliette seen me kiss Elizabeth?

"It was far from innocent." Juliette's ire was rising. "Dan, it wasn't just that you were holding her in your arms, but the way you were looking at each other. Dan, she loves you."

"Elizabeth always has," I answered.

"Since childhood. So you've said," responded an exasperated Juliette. "Now you tell me she's sleeping in your bed. Even I've never slept in your bed! Do you expect me to believe that's innocent too?"

"I expect you to believe me. I'm being honest. I've never lied to you. Juliette, I can't date a woman who doesn't trust me and refuses to understand my complicated relationship with Eli."

"It looks as though you've made your choice. Elizabeth wins, Dan."

"Juliette…" I knew I had lost, but perhaps I had instead won.

"No woman is going to understand your 'complicated relationship' with Elizabeth. So admit to it already. You will never be happy with any girl until you do."

And so I, Daniel Newman, was single once more. Well, not really. I did have Eli. She was a more satisfying companion than ten girlfriends put together. What I was lacking was a sex partner.

I tip-toed into my room replaying the conversation. Juliette might be right. I had dropped everything when Eli called. I didn't hesitate for a moment. Eli needed me; of course I came running.

Elizabeth lay sleeping, the ice pack on her ankle. Ten perfect, pedicured toes greeted me when I gently removed it. Not a chip of magenta polish was missing.

Curled up on her side, Elizabeth's silken auburn hair falling across her face, I couldn't help but smile. I carefully smoothed her hair back. So beautiful. So peaceful.

I sat down on the bed next to Eli and propped myself against the wall. I opened the assigned film history book and glanced at her before beginning.

My eyes flitted between the book and Elizabeth. When I realized I was reading the same paragraph for the fifth time, I gave up. All I could do was stare at Eli and watch her breathe.

Could they be right? The nurse, the professors, Juliette, hell, everyone? Did they see something I was missing, or was perhaps avoiding?

I never had a girlfriend, only several longer-term flings. I would classify Juliette as one, but I doubted she realized it, or how I cringed whenever anyone referred to her as my girlfriend. The ownership implied by the word didn't sit right. It sat just fine when Dr. Nash and the nurse applied it to Elizabeth

I'd known many pretty girls, but I never trusted whether they wanted me or coveted entry into the world of Steven Newman. These future trophy wives assumed all I cared about was their looks when what mattered was intellect and soul. None had touched my heart.

I avoided the pressures of having a girlfriend. They were clingy, and they wanted to change you to fit their ideal. Juliette had tried, and that was after only one month. Now I was relieved that it was ended.

The roast beef sandwich I picked up at the dining hall, my first since meeting Juliette, felt wickedly rebellious. As soon as Eli was up to it, I'd have to take her to a local steak house I'd heard was good.

Eli. Why wouldn't I invite Shane or Cam to the steak house?

Should Elizabeth be my girlfriend? The thought unnerved me. We were already the closest of friends and Elizabeth was the most beautiful girl I'd ever seen. She had an amazing figure and soft skin I loved to touch.

Watching Elizabeth sleep was mesmerizing. How enjoyable seducing her would be. Now that she had removed her tights, she was wearing nothing underneath my shirt.

Anticipating her softness, I was getting hard. I wanted Elizabeth so badly I found myself reaching over to her. I deftly unbuttoned the first button on her shirt. She didn't stir, but I knew what would wake her. I went for the next button.

Crap! The phone. What a time for an interruption. I answered before the next ring. Elizabeth should only be woken when I wanted her to.

"Hello," I mumbled, barely audible.

"Danny?"

Randi! Shit! I'd forgotten I'd left her a message. The sound of her voice embarrassed me. Would Randi guess that I had just begun undressing her daughter? Randi and Mike trusted me to be Elizabeth's brother. These had not been brotherly thoughts.

"Is something wrong?" Randi fretted. I did not often call her.

I explained Elizabeth's injury. "The pain pills are working. Eli's sleeping."

"I'm glad she has you. I'd be frantic if she was alone."

"Don't worry Randi. I am Elizabeth's most humble servant."

"Danny, I'm sure you'd rather be out partying. It's Friday."

"No, not really," I answered automatically. Then I realized it was the truth. I wanted to be with Elizabeth. I could party next week when she recovered.

"Randi, Eli's sleeping in my room tonight. I'll take the floor. The meds made her pretty loopy. I'll worry too much if she's not with me."

"Thank you, Danny. I'll sleep better too if she's with you," Randi responded, oblivious to what she had interrupted by her call.

Guilt is a powerful emotion. Randi's impeccable timing had to be a sign, a sign that Elizabeth must remain hands-off.

Elizabeth woke a couple of hours later refreshed and in less pain. To my relief she didn't notice the open shirt button.

"I'm starving," she complained.

"We'll have an early dinner after we ice your ankle." I eased Elizabeth into a sitting position and applied a fresh ice pack.

Her warm smile melted my heart. "You take such good care of me, Danny."

I tingled inside, not a good thing. What was wrong with me? I thought Randi's call had chilled me.

"How's your pain?" I asked Eli when I removed the ice twenty minutes later.

"I think it's improving," Eli answered tentatively. "I want to move it, but…"

I took her small hands. "Eli, don't," I warned. "Give it time."

"I don't like being an invalid. I'm a burden."

"Not at all, Eli. I enjoy taking care of you. This is what friends do." I emphasized the word friends as much for myself as for her.

Then I dried her ankle and re-wrapped it. "There you go. Time to get dressed."

"Then get out," she playfully ordered me.

"Don't you need my help?" I teased.

Elizabeth laughed. "Danny! Are you trying for a free show?"

So busted. Was I that transparent?

"A boy can try," I laughed.

"Okay. You get two points for trying, but lose three points for being snarky."

"Snarky! Eli, you're killing me!" I loved our easy, playful banter.

"Can you please hand me my clothes?" Eli giggled.

I handed her the neatly folded bundle. Then I stood glued in place watching her, waiting. Eli looked at me, amused. "Daniel, please go," she finally demanded.

"Right. I'm out there." Flustered, I left the room. I never get flustered. Eli had this strange new power over me.

CHAPTER 13 - ELIZABETH

What was with Danny today? I examined the clothing he had handed me. His kindness and caring, touches that lingered, calling me 'Sweetheart.' I was baffled.

Did Danny want something more? Possibly? Maybe yes.

I blushed at the bra and panty set he had brought. Made of the finest white silk lace, I was goaded into the purchase by Steff and Emma.

Before parting for college, we were shopping in Beverly Hills. Steff spotted the set on a mannequin in the window of a boutique on Rodeo Drive. The ultra-feminine bra was a revealing push-up. Its matching panty was a revealing thong. The girls insisted I buy them.

Steff and Emma had each had boyfriends in high school. My friends were obsessed with my lack of experience and aimed to change it.

"The perfect ensemble for the big night," Emma had declared.

That was disappointing. The big night should be more spontaneous. I shouldn't know hours earlier to select the right underwear.

Steff had clinched the sale. "You will want these," she had insisted, because, "Someday you will meet a guy who makes you get over Danny."

I smirked at the memory less than two months earlier, and hugged Danny's shirt close to me. His scent on the cotton was intoxicating and left me grinning like a fool. I had yet to tell either Steff or Emma that Danny was at Donnelly.

In spite of my ankle, I was gleeful. Steff and Emma would die if they knew I was sitting on Danny's bed wearing nothing but his shirt ready to put on the white lace ensemble. The girls wouldn't believe I had him waiting on me hand and foot either.

What was he thinking? The set had been near the bottom of the drawer. Danny had obviously been looking for what pleased him. Did Danny want me to model? The thought sent a shiver through me as I struggled to pull on the thong. Perhaps Danny was hoping I'd ask for his assistance. I blushed.

After slipping the dress over my head, I hobbled to the bureau to use Danny's hairbrush. My ponytail, sweat dampened from dance class would have to do.

I opened the door. "Hi!" I called out.

Danny was speaking with Shane. His eyes opened wide, enjoying the body-skimming shape of the short dress. I smiled with satisfaction.

"Eli," he gasped, "You look great. Doesn't she look great, Shane?"

Shane smirked, enjoying Danny's reaction.

"Whatever. Except for an ankle the size of an orange, your girlfriend looks great."

"I'm not his girlfriend," I protested.

"Whatever. Live in whatever alternate reality you want," Shane muttered.

"Can we go to dinner? I'm starving."

"Of course you are," Shane teased.

"Elizabeth never ate lunch," Danny growled. Then he was at my side. "Let me help you, Sweetheart."

I let go of the doorframe and grasped Danny's shoulder for support. With his hand holding my waist, I felt safer.

"Can you please bring me my crutches?" I asked.

Danny lifted me up and sat me on the chair. Shane rolled his eyes. "You're such a couple," he taunted. Danny and I glared at him.

Then Danny entered his room and brought the crutches. "Thanks," I said, letting Danny help me to my feet.

"I'll drive if you want. The health center gave you a handicapped pass."

"It's nice to know that at least in room 313 chivalry is not dead," Shane said.

Danny and I chose to ignore his lame attempt at humor.

"Let's walk. I need to get used to these."

"This, I want to see. Can I come too?" Shane asked. "Unless I'd be intruding."

It was slow going to the dining hall. I stopped frequently. My frustration increased.

"I've got to master this," I complained when I stopped yet again.

"Don't be so hard on yourself. It's your first time. I'll help you, hon," Danny said with kindness filling his eyes. His words melted my heart.

Danny skimmed my jaw with his fingertips and smiled. My knees weakened.

Once we arrived at the dining hall, Danny led me to our table. He helped me to the chair at the end and placed my crutches on the floor. Then Danny gently lifted my right foot and set it down on a chair he had moved into place for that purpose.

Danny's eyes were twinkling like fine gems, his electric smile lighting up both his face and mine. I beamed while meeting his gaze.

"I'll get your dinner." As Danny straightened, he brushed his lips against mine. We exchanged smiles again and Danny squeezed my shoulder as he passed.

My eyes followed Danny as he walked away. Before he left my line of sight, Danny turned back and grinned. The warmth from his smile radiated throughout me and I knew my smile and glow were here to stay.

"What's going on?" Rachel interrupted my reverie. I turned to see her amused expression.

"Nothing," I abruptly answered. The color rose in my cheeks.

"Right," she said in disbelief. Rachel seated herself two chairs down.

Soon Danny returned and set our dinners down. From his vantage sitting beside me, Danny studied my every movement. Later, he caught me trying to hide a spasm of pain when a fleeting grimace crossed my face.

"Eli?" Danny raised an eyebrow, concerned.

"Just a little throbbing," I answered, though it was more than a little. I didn't want Danny to worry, or worse, insist that I take more painkillers.

Using caution, I lifted my foot an inch. I sucked in, holding my breath in anticipation of an increase in the pain that didn't come. This might actually help.

"Hey, Elizabeth," Cam joked from across the table, "Get your stinky foot out of my face. I'm trying to eat."

Then Cam tickled the bottom of my foot. Reflexively, my foot pointed sending a spasm of pain through me.

"My ankle!" I cried.

"Eli!" Danny exclaimed.

Everyone stopped and starred. I couldn't hold back. Pain tore through me. Tears spilled down my face. Danny cradled me to his chest for comfort. I cried into his shirt, his thumb stroked my shoulder.

"Cam, what the hell did you do that for?" Danny snapped, his anger showing through narrow, dark sapphires. "Eli's ankle is shot."

"I'm sorry. I didn't know it was so bad," Cam answered contritely.

"It's almost broken, dickhead," Danny shot back.

Aiming to lower the tension, I lifted my head and lied. "The pain's subsiding," I said slowly and Danny relaxed.

Later, everyone was going to The Cellar except for Danny and I. I felt miserable ruining his evening.

"You don't have to stay with me," I told Danny as we slowly walked back to Berkeley Hall after dinner.

"I want to, Eli," Danny insisted. "I won't enjoy myself if you're not there."

"I mean it, Danny. I'll feel guilty if you're stuck in with me."

"And I'll feel guilty if I'm not with you."

CHAPTER 14 - ELIZABETH

While I leaned against the pillows, Danny applied ice to my ankle. I received the most loving smile a girl could ever hope to receive from a man and I reflected that I had the most attentive boyfriend. Except that I didn't. Danny belonged to Juliette.

Now he snuggled with me while the ice sat on my ankle for twenty more minutes. His arm wrapped around my shoulders. Danny caressed my hands. His were warm and soft. The attention filled me with love.

Danny gave my shoulder an affectionate squeeze. Those damned sapphire eyes twinkled at me, the happiest smile on his full lips. It was infectious. Despite the throbbing pain, I smiled back. I had no choice.

Relaxed and content, Danny kissed my forehead. I snuggled closer, my head leaning against him as Danny held me close. We were a picture-perfect couple; except that we weren't.

"Time's up!" Danny's gentle voice jarred me.

"One more minute?" I pleaded.

"Cozy, Elizabeth?"

"Yes," I smiled, dreamy-eyed.

"Me, too," Danny agreed, and he kissed my head.

I was in serious danger of getting used to this.

Soon, Danny removed the ice pack and patted my ankle dry.

"How does it look?" I asked. I feared looking at my ankle.

Danny playfully examined my limb. "It's as beautiful as the leg it's attached to," he said giving me a wicked smile that sent a spasm of pleasure through me.

Surprising me, Danny kissed my ankle, and I giggled. If only Danny were my boyfriend. I sighed. Wishful thinking, for now.

Danny flashed another killer smile as he finished wrapping the brace around my ankle. "It looks the same as before."

Impatient, I wanted an instant recovery.

"Maybe by the morning?" I asked, disappointed by the lack of progress.

"Possibly," Danny answered. "Let's go watch a DVD."

It felt good to get out of Danny's small room. The spacious dorm lounge, all overstuffed couches and chairs, with a large flat-screen television affixed to the wall, was empty. It was our own private oasis.

Wearing pajamas, reminded me of when Danny and I were kids hanging out at home while our parents were out for the evening. Flora prepared the snacks then. Danny would set the television to Nickelodeon or some other parent-approved channel. Then he would pop in an R-rated DVD. Keeping an ear out for Flora and his finger on the remote, Danny would flip back to Nick whenever he heard her. Flora never caught on.

Tonight Danny did the honors. After placing cans of Diet Coke on the side table, he eased me on to the sofa and took the crutches, leaning them against a wall. Then he carefully placed my foot on a sofa pillow he'd placed on the coffee table.

Danny handed me the remote. "I'll go pop some corn," he said.

With a kiss to my forehead Danny disappeared into the adjacent kitchen. I could get used to this.

Danny soon returned with two large bags of butter-flavored microwave popcorn. He dimmed the room lights and settled in next to me. I continued flipping channels.

"There's your mother!" Danny exclaimed. We laughed, having stumbled across the latest Miranda Jordan film airing on HBO.

"Sorry, Mom," I shrugged and changed the channel to Showtime.

"Or we can watch this," Danny pulled out a DVD in a plain cardboard case distinguished by it's lack of artwork.

"What's that?" I never thought we were going to watch Mom.

"Dad sent it. I can keep it until Monday."

Right away I understood as I read the title printed in a plain black font.

"The new Ryan Gosling! I'm dying to see this. It doesn't open until next month," I exclaimed. "Pays to have the right Dad, Mr. N." I smiled at Danny.

"Pays to have the right girl to watch it with, Miss J," Danny returned my grin, and he rose to insert the DVD into the player.

Then Danny sat back down to start the movie. "Have some popcorn, Eli."

Danny lifted a few buttery pieces from his bag and placed them in my mouth. His fingertips lingered on my lips. My pulse quickened and our eyes locked. Danny waited, and I sucked the butter off his fingertips. Then the film began.

Once the popcorn bags lay empty on the table, I became aware of Danny's every motion, his every breath. The electricity radiating between us was undeniable. It was a fantasy high school first date I'd never experienced. The cool guys never asked out Elizabeth Jacobs.

Like an inexperienced fifteen year-old, Danny tentatively lifted his arm and carefully unfolded it across my shoulders. I inched even closer to him than I already was. In response he gave my shoulder an affectionate squeeze, and I smiled at him. In the dimness of the room, the pleasure registering on Danny's face lit the space.

Emboldened, his other arm wrapped around my collarbone, enveloping me, warming me, both inside and out. I leaned into Danny and my hand pressed his arm telegraphing the enjoyment his closeness brought me.

After the film, returning to Danny's room didn't take long. I was getting the hang of using crutches. My strides were more fluent and under control. Still it was tiring and the renewed pain was causing me stress.

"Let me take those, baby," Danny said as we entered the suite.

"You must be a mind-reader." I leaned against his strong body for support.

"Nope. I'm a face-reader. You look exhausted, Eli."

I hopped into his bedroom, both arms around Danny's waist for support. Inside, he leaned the crutches against the desk while I continued to hold him.

"Time to take your meds and go to sleep, young lady."

"You sound like Dad."

"I'm definitely not Mike."

"Good," I said, and I wrapped my hands around his neck.

Danny's arms were instantly around my back pulling me closer. His power gave me the strength to go up on my left toe, my weight supported by him. I brought Danny's face down to mine for our lips to meet in the kiss I had been waiting all night for.

Anticipation lit a fire inside me. My heart raced. I tingled all over from his magnetism. But just as Danny's lips touched mine, he jerked his head back, not far, but out of range.

"Not tonight, Eli," he whispered. Danny's expression turned downcast.

Throughout the movie Danny held me in his arms. Now that we were in the privacy of his room, it seemed the natural next step. Was it Juliette?

"We're alone now," I pointed out. "I thought you'd want to."

"I do, but not tonight," he said firmly.

Disappointed, I came down from my pointe and turned away.

"E," Danny said as he turned me to his chest, "This is not a rejection. Making love to you would be amazing. Just not tonight."

He wanted to! Danny thought making love to me would be amazing! My pulse quickened. I had been waiting all my life to hear Danny admit that!

I glanced up at sad, molten cobalt eyes. Nothing left to lose, I said, "I want you, Daniel."

He smiled. "I feel the same. But we have to wait."

I stared at Danny, bewildered. He felt the same! "You can't say that and not tell me what you mean," I stammered.

"You're right." Danny carried me over to the bed. In one fluid motion he was sitting beside me holding my hands.

"E, your ankle," he pointed out. "You're in pain."

"I'll take my meds."

Danny smirked. "I don't want you loopy your first time."

"I don't care," I protested.

"You won't give up, will you?"

"I'm a spoiled princess and I want my way," I teased.

Danny sighed. "Princess, we need to talk."

Shit! Nothing positive ever began with the phrase, "we need to talk."

"Is it Juliette?" I asked, afraid of the answer. The truth could ruin my evening.

Danny smiled warmly. "No, it's not Juliette. We broke up."

"You did! When?" Total glee. Then I tamped it down for show.

"A few hours ago. She didn't believe there was nothing going on between us." Danny laughed and so did I. How quickly things had changed, sort of.

"Eli, I need you to understand where my head is at." I nodded. "Elizabeth, what happens tomorrow if we make love tonight?"

"We wake up and do it again?" I shrugged with an impish grin.

"That might have been the wrong question." Then Danny sighed. "We have a very special relationship. I don't want to ruin it. You're the best friend I've ever had."

Danny glanced down at our joined hands, and them back up to my eyes.

"Mom was right when she said I'd never had a girlfriend. I've dated girls, including Juliette, but I've never had the emotional commitment. Then there's you. Eli, it's only since this morning that I began to realize we might be more than friends. When you hobbled out of the doctor's office, my heart broke. I felt your pain. It was unbearable. I'd have done anything to make it go away."

"And you did," I assured him. "You've been amazing."

Danny took a deep breath, crafting his next words with precision. His brow creased. He was troubled.

"Eli, I woke up happy and single this morning. If we make love, tomorrow I wake up in the most committed relationship I could ever imagine being in. I'll go overnight from having a casual girlfriend in Juliette to being practically married. It's overwhelming. I need to decide if I want that. I need time. Do I make any sense?"

Yes, yes, yes! I tried not to grin. If the end game was Danny and I together, he could have as much time as he wanted. Instead I kept my exterior calm and answered,

"I understand. I've thought about it before. You haven't."

Danny took my face in his hands. His devilish smile set my head to spinning.

"Time to take your meds, young lady." Then Danny chastely kissed my lips.

It was not a deep or passionate kiss, but it was a kiss nonetheless.

CHAPTER 15 - ELIZABETH

Pulsating ankle spasms woke me and I couldn't fall back to sleep. I should take something, but the powerful medication frightened me.

After I swallowed the pills last night, Danny tucked me in. I hadn't felt sleepy at first, but then wham! It was as though I'd been hit on the head.

Danny had held me against his chest and comforted me by stroking my back. My trust that he would not let anything bad happen was all that calmed me. Soon I stopped fighting the sedative effect of the drugs and I succumbed to sleep.

Rain was falling. In the distance a low rumble of thunder rudely announced the official end of summer. A cold front pushing in from Canada was arriving later today to visit the Donnelly campus until spring.

Danny's arms folded around me, holding me close. His unspoken love enveloped me. Danny may not be ready to be my boyfriend, but the way he held me contradicted his words.

The thunder was getting louder. Thunderstorms were rare at home. Years passed between storms. The loud claps startled me. I snuggled even closer.

Danny's room was cloaked in darkness. A flash of lightning startled me. My heart jumped. I clenched Danny's t-shirt. I marveled that he was sleeping through the storm, but Danny's ankle wasn't throbbing and he had experienced similar storms at Bromley Hall.

It was tortuous lying next to Danny. Powerful longings overwhelmed me. Yet I had to wait, acknowledging that when we became lovers, it was for the long-haul. That's what scared Danny. It scared me too, but my mind was made up. I wanted it.

I enjoyed sharing Danny's bed. His hand against my tank top covered stomach felt so right. What if his hand was against my skin instead? I smiled. It would be great.

Danny was deep in sleep, breathing rhythmically. Slowly, I slid the fabric up. I passed the soft cotton underneath his hand. Perfect! Danny's hand now rested on my skin. The warmth of his palm, and the softness of his fingers were intoxicating.

I quickly pulled my top down into place. If Danny woke now, he would believe that his hand had found its way by itself. But Danny's hand had a mind of its own. It inched upward. My pulse quickened as I determined its destination. Ah! This felt so good!

Cautiously I turned my head toward Danny. His eyes, as dangerous as

Medusa's but in a good way, were closed in sleep. A content smile formed on Danny's perfect lips. I turned away; my staring might wake him. Danny's hand slid up my torso. I gasped as it reached my breast and Danny began to caress me, squeezing me. I moaned. My senses heightened, the most insane pleasure I had ever experienced. Tortuous!

I could not remain quiet any longer. My gasps and moans would not be contained. As Danny continued caressing my breasts, I pressed my hands against his, my body wanting more.

No longer in control, my back arched against Danny's chest and my hand reached for his face to kiss him. My head twisted, my lips strained to share this moment of sweetness with his.

Danny began to stir, but he wasn't yet conscious. He moved his other hand down to my waistband and his fingertips reached my white lace thong. I gasped as his fingers thrust into me. I vibrated. My pulse raced out of control. This is what I wanted.

Abruptly, Danny's fingers withdrew. His other hand stopped caressing my breasts. My body on the verge, the verge of what I couldn't comprehend, felt extreme frustration. My thighs squeezed together trying to relieve it.

"Elizabeth, what's going on?" Danny asked. He was wide-awake.

"I don't know," I answered while fighting to regulate my breathing and pulse. "You were sleeping."

"And you were lying here innocent?" Danny raised an eyebrow.

"Yes?" I said shyly.

"No," he answered knowingly.

"Danny!" I protested.

"Elizabeth," Danny said, gazing into my eyes.

"Well, maybe I gave you a little encouragement." I was so busted.

Danny laughed. "You wanted me to seduce you." I turned my head away, humiliated.

"I'm not angry, Eli. I'm amused." Danny peered over my shoulder, smiling. "This has been the most enjoyable wake-up ever." Danny kissed my forehead. "But don't do it again. I almost did something we both would have regretted."

"I wouldn't have."

"You would have if I'm not ready to reciprocate your feelings."

Pouting, I turned away again. A long clap of thunder boomed directly overheard followed by a lightening flash. I tensed. Danny leaned over my side gently rubbing my bare arm.

"Hey," he murmured, "You're not scared, are you baby?"

"A little," I whimpered. Danny gathered me into his protective arms just as the thunder boomed again, followed by more lightening.

"It'll pass soon. You're safe," he murmured. "Elizabeth, what am I going to do with you?" he mused.

"I don't know," I answered.

"That was rhetorical. Until yesterday sex was never an issue with us. Now, it's the only issue. Can we please stop this? Please, Eli?"

"Okay," I relented. "I don't want to ruin our friendship."

"Thank you," Danny replied. "Eli, I know how you feel about us. Give it a rest, baby. I told you I need time to think and I've been sleeping ever since. No epiphanies struck while dreaming."

Another booming thunderclap sent me clinging to Danny all over again.

"It's okay," he said gently and rubbed my back. "Eli, let this be my idea."

CHAPTER 16 - ELIZABETH

Fortunately the rain stopped, and the sun was trying to break through when Danny came to get me for brunch.

Rachel and Chloe had returned from dining. Now Chloe was off to join friends and Rachel was editing the short screenplay she had written for Danny to direct.

Danny bounced into the suite full of energy.

"Good morning, ladies," he greeted them.

"Hi and good-bye," Chloe said breezily as she dashed out in Burberry rain gear.

"Where's my sweetheart?" Danny cheerfully asked Rachel.

"Elizabeth is in her room." Rachel snarled.

"How is she?"

"Fine, I guess. I haven't heard any screams or thuds."

"Thanks, Rach," Danny answered. His footsteps headed my way.

"Wait," she called. "What's wrong with this picture? It's nearly noon and you saunter in just out of bed. I've been toiling over our project. Since ten."

I imagined Danny employing his boyish grin. I smirked. Danny was not going to win this one. Rachel was immune to his charms.

"Rach, I can't write. I'm giving you space. When the script's finished, I'll read it."

"Some moral support would be nice," Rachel said bitterly.

"You have my support," Danny said, "But my lady and I need to eat."

Danny's lady? Was I now his lady?

Danny knocked on my ajar door, entering before I said, "Come in."

With a grin that lit his face, Danny approached the bureau where I stood supported by the crutches brushing my hair. His arms circled my waist.

"Hey, baby," Danny's eyes twinkled fiercely.

"Hey, yourself." I turned my head to his and Danny kissed the corner of my mouth. "You're happy today," I smiled.

"That's because I woke up next to you."

That was the most romantic thing anyone had ever said to me. "But we didn't do anything but sleep," I pointed out.

"That's what made it special," Danny answered, and he kissed me again. "Do you have any idea how nice it was to wake up with you in my arms?"

"I'm sure you've woken up with a girl in your arms before."

"Not really. Possibly once or twice, but I'm sure I wasn't sober."

What a contrast from last night! Had lightening struck while Danny showered?

"Is that a compliment?"

"Yes. Just like telling you how adorable you are in the morning is." Danny kissed me again. "You're not only beautiful, you're cuddly Eli. You're soft, feminine and cuddly. You smelled good too. It was like waking in a field of freshly picked wildflowers."

"Newman! Close the door!" Rachel yelled. "I'm going to barf if I have to keep hearing this dribble."

I blushed, embarrassed. Danny laughed. He hugged me more tightly. Whatever we now were to each other, he was enjoying it as much as I was.

After trudging to the dining hall, Danny brought me my lunch and settled in across from me. Eating was difficult because Danny wouldn't take his eyes off me. They sparkled like blue diamonds and the intensity of his smile was high-wattage. My insides tingled. I couldn't take my eyes off of him either. Is this how it would be when we became a couple?

"Hey, Newmans," Shane announced. He took the chair beside me and placed his plate and cutlery on the table. "What's going on?"

"Not much," Danny answered. "I'm trying to understand why m'lady's beautiful smile has down-turned."

"Maybe she realized who she woke up with this morning."

"Not funny, Shane," Danny snapped. Then he turned his attention back to me. "What is it, Eli? Does your ankle hurt?"

"Danny, I heard from the Dean," I frowned. "I have to drop my dance classes."

"Can't you just observe for the two weeks until you're better?"

I shook my head. "It's not that simple." Tears started down my cheeks. I wiped them away with the back of my hand. "The doctor said I could walk in two weeks. He didn't say anything about dance. My ankle has to be strong before I can go back on pointe."

"Baby, I'm so sorry."

"I know." I tried smiling but couldn't. "Dance was going to be my major. Now...."

"Danny, are you still coming to rugby?" Shane interrupted.

Danny frowned. "Eli, I have practice at two. I thought you'd come."

Shane and I exchanged confused glances. Then we glanced at Danny. Was Danny nuts? The field had to be a muddy mess from the rain.

"I'm on crutches," I blurted out, not believing I had to state the obvious.

"I was going to bring a folding chair," Danny said defensively.

I was appalled, but his offer was so thoughtful.

"Danny, the only girls who attend practice are girl friends," I said crossly.

"Eli, you can come. The guys won't care."

"I will care. Danny, if I show up, it looks like I'm your girlfriend."

"You're not?" Shane asked.

"No, I'm not. I don't want it to look that way either."

Danny frowned. "I don't agree."

"You know I'm right."

"Elizabeth is right," Shane interjected.

Danny ignored him. "You're not right, Eli. I want you there."

"It's not happening, Daniel." I said in frustration. When would he learn that the spoiled, petulant act did not work with me? If anything, it made me more stubborn.

"Please get me my crutches. I want to go back to my room," I insisted.

Danny and I left the dining hall in silence. Once away from the building, Danny stopped.

"Eli, what's going on? You've never cared if anyone thought you were my girl."

For the first time, I cared because becoming his girl seemed within reach. Danny shouldn't see me in the role until he was ready to cast me. I wouldn't tell him this, though. Instead...

"You're being very self-centered. I just told you how upset I am at having to change my major, and like a spoiled child you keep going on about rugby. My major is damned more important than rugby," I scowled.

Danny frowned. Then he flushed.

"Eli, you're angry with me?" he asked in disbelief.

"Yes. I am, Daniel."

Danny looked as though I'd slapped his face. He was at a loss. Danny was not used to anger from girls. Most were afraid to challenge him, grateful that he even spoke to them. I was not one of his worshippers and he knew it.

Danny sighed, resigned. "Eli, you're right. Your major is more important. And I don't want you at rugby unless I'm ready to go public."

I smiled at Danny and kissed his cheek. "Thank you. It's difficult for someone as pig-headed as you to apologize."

"I am not pig." Danny began to protest. "Okay. I am pig-headed," he relented. I touched Danny's lips with my finger and smiled.

"Even if you are pig-headed, I'll still be your best friend."

"Come here, best friend," Danny ordered, and he pulled me to his chest.

I smiled at him as he hugged me. "This is why I don't have a love life," I complained while Danny's hand lingered on my cheek."

"Oh, poor you," he said in a soft sarcastic voice. "Let me really ruin your love life." With that, Danny moved his hand from my cheek through my hair to the nape of my neck, while he sensuously kissed my lips.

My eyes sprung open. The color rose in my cheeks. I was livid. I wanted to slap Danny more that I had ever wanted to slap anyone. Anger, not pleasure was my reaction.

But I was paralyzed, unable to move. If I raised my arm to slap him, my crutch would fall and so would I... into Danny's arms, because he would catch me before I fell. I'd be back at square one – being held by Danny in public.

"This is your plan, isn't it?" I snapped. "Let people think we're together so nobody will ever ask me out."

I was furious with rage. I twisted out of his hold and abruptly turned toward Berkeley Hall. Danny's stunned expression told me I'd made my point.

I started as fast as my crutches would go, looking straight ahead at the nearby dorm. Tears obscured my vision. I didn't see the buckled pavement, uneven from the thick root of an ancient oak tree.

An ear-splitting scream bellowed from deep inside of me. I hit the pavement with hard force. Crutches went flying. I couldn't control the impact.

"Eli!" Danny shouted. Right away he was on the cold ground beside me, supporting me in his strong arms.

"You bastard!" I cried as I pounded my fists against his chest. The pain was unbearable. I feared losing consciousness. Danny cradled me protectively to stop the shaking that accompanied my sobs.

"Eli," he murmured. Danny's voice trembled with fear. "Baby, I'm so sorry. It's my fault."

"I hurt so much," I cried.

"I know, baby," Danny replied while stroking my back for comfort.

A small cluster of students formed around us.

"I called EMS, Danny. They're on the way," a male student said. The intensity of the pain was so extreme I gripped Danny's arms with all my might.

"Is your girlfriend okay?" a girl asked.

Girlfriend! There was that assumption again. Oh, hell! Except for the formalities like dating and sex, I supposed I was, for all intent and purposes, Danny's girlfriend. So why wasn't I happy about it?

CHAPTER 17 - DANIEL

"Eli, we're home." I nudged her when the taxi stopped in the Berkeley Hall parking lot.

Elizabeth's heavy eyelids struggled to open. The long afternoon of doctors, pain, and fitting her now fractured ankle with a boot cast had worn her out.

"We're home, hon."

Eli didn't move. I didn't comprehend what I had said.

Deja-vu. It was yesterday all over again, with Elizabeth passed out in my bed and me stuck babysitting. Only today I was not happy with my part in the play. It had turned into a nice afternoon and I'd missed rugby practice.

The team would survive, but I had pent-up energy to release. I needed to be physical. Pacing my room did not help.

I was so incredibly frustrated. Why did Elizabeth have to fracture her damned ankle? And why did I feel responsible for her well-being?

I knew the answer all too well. Elizabeth. I cared for her more than anyone else and far more than I cared to admit. Guilt also played a part. It was my fault that it happened. I would never admit it to her though.

The walls were closing in. I had to get out.

Elizabeth stirred. I returned to the bed and sat down beside her. Sleepy eyes opened, and she smiled. The drugs were working. I took her hand and smiled back.

"How are you doing, baby?" I murmured. "Are you in pain?"

"I don't think so."

"That's good," I said, and I kissed Eli's smooth cheek.

My heart skipped a beat as she snuggled against me, laying her dainty hand across my chest. There was something so comfortable with Eli's perfectly shaped body cozy against mine.

Eli jerked up to sitting, alert now, her demeanor radical, possessed. Lucid, Eli scrunched her face, trying to focus.

"You broke my ankle!" she exclaimed.

"I didn't break your ankle," I answered defensively. "You didn't watch where you were going."

"I was so watching," she persisted.

"No, Elizabeth or you would have seen that tree root."

Elizabeth was getting me angry; mostly at myself because she was right.

"I hate you, Danny!" she screamed. "Now I'll never dance again."

"You don't hate me. And yes you will dance again!" I shouted back.

"No, I won't!"

"Yes, you will. You'll dance," I insisted.

"I hate you!" Eli cried again. "I hate you more than anything!"

"Shut up, Elizabeth!" I shot back.

I grabbed her shoulders and crushed my lips against hers for a powerful kiss that shot bolts of electricity through both of us.

Our eyes shot open, wide. Stunned! We were both utterly stunned. Elizabeth stared at me, no longer angry.

"Can we do that again?" she asked shyly.

I smiled at Eli's innocent request. Then I eagerly complied.

This time I kissed her, caressing my Elizabeth. Our lips moved together, my tongue teased hers. This is what we wanted. Pure sweetness.

My heart beat with urgency, wanting to leap out of my chest. Elizabeth's heart beat just as rapidly as we remained glued together. When we parted for a breath she smiled. Elizabeth's warmth spread throughout me. This felt so right.

Eli pulled me to her and this time she kissed me, plunging her tongue into my mouth, challenging me to match her unbridled passion. Never had a kiss felt as wonderful as this one. I experienced every drop of love Eli now gave me. I hoped I reciprocated.

Eli was glowing. She could have lit up a dark room. I began kissing her again. Eli was the sweetest tasting girl I'd ever kissed. I wanted to spend the rest of the day doing nothing but kissing her.

But where did I want this to go? Eli lay quietly in my arms. Her full pink lips upturned in the loveliest smile. Gentle green eyes sparkled in my direction. Thick, auburn waves scattered in all directions across the forest trimmed white pillowcase. Eli was a portrait of utmost contentment that I dared not ruin.

We could not spend another night together. It was too dangerous. Until I made my decision, Eli and I needed time apart. I wasn't ready to become her lover. Another night together, hell, even another hour, and I would succumb.

CHAPTER 18 - ELIZABETH

"Let's go to the library," Danny suggested after class on Wednesday. I didn't want to go to the library, but I wanted to be with Danny, so I said, "yes."

After Saturday's afternoon of bliss, Danny became distant. We spent time alone only when Danny drove me home early from The Cellar. Danny had waited in the living room while I changed into pajamas. After taking my medication, he departed with a quick hug and a platonic kiss. The message couldn't be clearer.

Sunday afternoon I learned that Danny later accompanied Duncan to a party at The Village, a housing enclave for upper-classmen with the reputation as the place where drugs and sex flowed as freely as tapped beer. Cam divulged that Danny had partaken in all that had been offered including the affections of a girl whose name he didn't reveal.

Knives pierced my heart. My suspicions confirmed. Drugs and easy sex were Danny's antidote to his new affections for me.

That evening, using my ankle as an excuse, it was easy to cancel our study date. I couldn't face Danny. I was embarrassed, and I felt used.

Monday afternoon I cancelled Danny again when I met with my advisor. Tuesday, I avoided him.

Wednesday we spoke for the first time since I'd cancelled on Sunday.

"How was your meeting with your advisor?" he asked.

Danny sounded sincere, but if he cared, why had it taken two days to ask? I had only a moment to decide if I wanted an argument.

I brushed it off, though I answered curtly. "Fine. The meeting was fine."

"Eli?" Danny asked, morphing into Mr. Emphathetic.

"It's too late in the term for me to add a class. I'll need to take maximum credits through next year."

"Oh, baby," Danny acknowledged, understanding my disappointment. He cradled me in his arms. "I'll help you, Eli. I'm always here for you."

"Are you?" I asked, raising an eyebrow.

"Always," Danny said in an emphatic tone that challenged my doubts.

I let him hold me. The worn denim of his jacket was soft. It held the faint aroma of his cologne; warm, musky and masculine. Danny was cozy too; a sharp contrast to the blustery day. I smiled, content as a kitten.

The girl from The Village would never have this.

At the library we settled into adjacent seats at a corner table. Danny wanted to get an early start on his economics term paper and needed space to spread out. I was at a loss over what to do. The library had been Danny's plan, not mine. I opened a notebook hoping for inspiration.

"Hey," Danny said in a hushed voice. He leaned so his lips were beside my ear. His breath brushed my cheek causing my spine to tingle. "I'm off to the stacks."

"I'll come too. The computer lab is downstairs, too." I decided to read optional articles for Professor Denison. With my laptop in my room, I needed to print hard copies today.

My ankle made taking the elevator from the third floor to the basement mandatory. Few students used the library elevator that crawled like a tortoise.

I leaned back against the interior railing and the silver metal doors slowly closed. Danny towered over me and pressed his hands against the wall at my shoulders. He gave me the sexy, impish smile that always made my heart flutter and I blushed.

Danny's smile intensified. His eyes twinkled at maximum intensity. He bent toward me, his hand skimming my cheek to tilt my face upward. I covered his hand with my own. Then Danny's lips met mine, and we shared a furtive kiss.

As the elevator settled into its landing, our lips parted. We shared a smile, enjoying the moment. Our hands slipped apart. Another private smile and we stepped out of the elevator. Danny's infectious little boy grin made me giggle as it sent my heart soaring and I kept my eyes glued to him as we went in opposite directions.

Danny knew he had me. He knew I had him too.

I was elated. I glowed, both inside and out. Every inch of me tingled in anticipation.

Taking a step backward, I nearly lost my footing.

"Watch where you're going!" A male voice jarred me back to reality as I bumped into something that was both soft and hard at the same time.

I pivoted and care face-to-face with the student the voice came from. Embarrassed, heat rose in my cheeks.

"Sorry," I muttered.

"No wonder your foot's in a cast. You're too busy watching your boyfriend," he snarled.

"I said I'm... boyfriend?" He must have seen me come off the elevator with Danny. "He's not my boyfriend," I clarified.

"Well it looked that way," he answered. Then his voice and demeanor softened. "I'm Greg Alexander."

When he smiled, soft brown eyes peeking out from straight brown hair that needed a trim, crinkled in delight. Greg wasn't handsome, but a dimpled smile made him appealing.

"Elizabeth Jacobs," I replied. "Nice bumping into you," I added with a giggle.

I found Danny pouring over musty leather-bound books when I returned with the two articles I had printed.

"It must be crowded in the computer room," he commented without looking up from his work.

The room was not crowded, but I had spent nearly an hour with Greg. Upon learning that Danny was not my boyfriend, Greg had become friendly and talkative.

"I did some socializing too," I answered, and I flushed.

Why did I feel guilty? All I'd done was engage in a casual conversation. I glanced past my reading materials, across to Danny who was taking notes. He'd had sex with a girl on Saturday night. Danny did feel guilty.

What the hell was wrong with me? I deserved better. No self-respecting heroine in a Miranda Jordan movie would put up with this. Why should I?

I stared at Danny with new resolve. No longer would I allow him to touch or kiss me. No more of this ambiguous nonsense. If Danny wanted these privileges, then he should be my boyfriend. Until then, I was a single girl and I would broadcast it to the world.

Danny caught me starring and raised an eyebrow. Amused, he flashed his megawatt smile. Butterflies flitted in my stomach. I couldn't help it. That smile always melted my heart.

Be strong, Elizabeth. Without thinking, I returned my own megawatt smile. Instantly I regretted it. I already felt like a failure.

CHAPTER 19 - ELIZABETH

Early Saturday evening found me in my room primping when a quick knock came upon the suite door.

"Come in," Rachel shouted and the suite door opened and closed in quick succession.

"Who is it, Rach?" I called. I was not able to discern the voice of our visitor over the volume of both my hair blower and iTunes.

"It's him," she answered.

Oh, no! I snapped the blower off.

"Give me a few," I called back. "I'm almost ready."

I needed to put on make-up and jewelry. Greg was picking me up to go to a movie. Yes! I was going on a real life, genuine date. What better way to demonstrate that I was single than to go out with a man who wasn't Danny? What better way to show Danny, too!

"Almost ready for what?" Danny asked, appearing in my doorway. Lately he had developed the habit of showing up unannounced. Usually I welcomed him; not tonight.

My heart skipped a beat, both relieved that it wasn't Greg, and uneasy that Danny was watching me primp for another man.

"I have a date," I answered as I looked in the mirror and applied mascara.

"A date! Eli, what kind of date?" Danny asked, taken by surprise.

"The kind where I go out with a man who isn't you," I answered. Then I reached for my necklace. "It's really not your business, Daniel."

Flustered, I fumbled with the simple gold chain I was trying to clasp around my neck.

"Here, let me," he offered.

Danny came up behind me and took the chain from my hands. He sharply inhaled my light floral cologne while his fingertips brushed my neck. Danny expertly fastened the clasp, and I shivered from his touch. Bastard! He knew that I would. Danny's smirk reflected in the mirror.

"Anyone I know?" he asked.

Danny might be playing with me, but clearly he was shaken. I felt guilty. No! I shook my head to free it of emotion. That's what Danny wanted. I couldn't let him ruin my evening.

I took Danny's hands and kissed his cheek. "You're always telling me to find a boyfriend. This is a first date. I have to start somewhere," I smiled sweetly.

"Danny." Rachel had entered the room. "Let's go out," she said. "Give Elizabeth her space."

CHAPTER 20 - DANIEL

Rachel was right. I needed to get out of Elizabeth's room and fast. Part of me wanted to see what kind of guy Eli would have a date with, but a much larger part wanted to throttle him.

I was ill thinking some guy I didn't know might be touching Eli and maybe even kissing her luscious lips.

Of course I was a hypocrite. Since the start, I had been telling Eli to find a boyfriend, but the thought that she might actually get one tortured my gut.

I had deliberately embraced her. I could have said, "see you tomorrow" from across the room, but it was important to touch her. I crushed Eli against me and held her hands. I left her no choice but to inhale my scent, imprinting it in her memory.

"See you tomorrow," I whispered, my breath purposely stroking her ear.

Eli gasped and shuddered as I knew she would. Then, despite the glare she was attempting, I delicately brushed my lips against hers. The pleasure was apparent in her eyes.

"Have a good time, Sweetheart," I tossed out while arrogantly smirking. "Let's go, Rach," I said triumphantly.

I had just ruined any chance Eli had of enjoying her date. Eli would be spending the evening with mystery man and all her thoughts would be of me.

As the elevator door slid closed behind us, my smirk turned into the wildest grin. "I am one sick puppy," I said.

"I'm glad you know it," Rachel responded.

Eventually Rachel and I found our way to The Cellar. Earlier, we had attended a program of silent films being sponsored by the film department. As a major, I'm supposed to be interested in the history of the art form I am now presumably devoting my life to. Having already devoted every moment of my life since birth to the industry, I feel entitled to proclaim that I do not, and probably never will, like silent films, Charlie Chaplin and Harold Lloyd excluded.

To make matters worse, professors were in attendance. I had to actually pay attention when I really wanted to zone-out and spend the time quietly contemplating life. Even Rachel would have agreed if I'd run it by her.

My life badly needed contemplating. Alas, deep thinking would have to wait. The family reputation was on the line. Steven Newman's son had to be properly impressive during the Q&A that followed the screenings. It was expected.

At The Cellar, I quickly downed two beers while Rachel nursed her first. A cute blonde in tight jeans walked by our table and smiled at me.

"Hi, Danny," she said with a musical lilt and blew me a kiss.

"Hi," I responded lethargically, and she walked by. "Rach, do I know that girl?"

"How would I know? She certainly seems to know you though."

My brain kicked into high gear trying to figure out how the girl knew me. It was impossible. I knew too many girls and lately they all seemed to be blondes.

Rachel observed me thinking and laughed. "If you want to be with her I won't be offended. It's not like I'm your date."

"Rachel, are you, of all people, encouraging me to pick-up some strange girl?"

"If it gets your mind off my roommate, go ahead. I won't tell."

"I can't. I'm too busy thinking about your roommate."

"Elizabeth isn't your sister anymore, is she?"

I took a sizable gulp of beer three, afraid to confront what had become painfully obvious. From the moment we'd reunited, it felt different. The pleasant surprise of Eli's curvy body in my arms as we embraced that first day had filled me with conflict.

Why couldn't Eli be an unattractive, skinny, flat-chested girl with bad hair? Life would have been so easy. Eli and I could have remained best friends forever. I never would have found myself with desires I could no longer deny.

I took another gulp of beer. The buzz was coming.

"You're right, Rach. Eli's not my sister anymore," I finally confessed.

Instead of being cathartic, weirdness and a sense of "what happens next?" overwhelmed me. I finished beer three and ordered another.

Rachel was smiling. In my state this surprised me. Then she took my hands from across the table. This was puzzling. Rachel usually disapproved of my wasted lifestyle.

"That's great! You and Elizabeth belong together."

"We're not together, Rach. I'm here with you and Eli's on a date."

"Danny, you'll work it out. Admitting your feelings is half the battle."

"Eli's on a date, Rach," I repeated.

"Only because you didn't ask her first. Elizabeth did it to avoid thinking of you. We both know you ruined that option."

CHAPTER 21 - ELIZABETH

Shortly after Rachel and Danny left, Greg knocked on the door. In sharp contrast to Danny's entrance, Greg's seemed reticent. He smiled shyly, pleased by my appearance.

"Ready in a minute," I called out. Greg quietly seated himself in the living room while I brushed my hair one more time.

Normally Greg wore jeans torn at the knee and his flannel shirts hung loosely on his slender frame. Tonight Greg wore chinos and an oxford shirt. His trademark hiking boots and down vest marked him as being Greg. He had cleaned up nicely.

In the short time I had known the sophomore, I found Greg to be the antithesis of Danny. Greg was from a small town in Massachusetts. His father was a veterinarian and his mother was a high school principal. Both believed in the importance of serving their community.

A product of rural New England, low-key Greg was a double major in Physics and Environmental Studies. He planned on pursuing a Masters degree in Environmental Engineering.

I was nervous. I hadn't had a date since last summer, and that one, ugh, never mind! Greg and I were going to go to a movie. Perhaps later we would end up at The Cellar, a very public way of showing that I was not Danny's girlfriend.

What was wrong with me? Life should not revolve around Danny. Greg was a nice guy and pleasing to look at. I should enjoy this evening because it was enjoyable, plain and simple. Its effect on Danny should not enter into my dating satisfaction.

Stop thinking of Danny! But it was impossible. The scent of his cologne remained strong in my nostrils. I couldn't shake his presence. It was exactly what Danny had intended.

Danny would not ruin my good time with Greg, I vowed.

The movie, a big-budget action-adventure, was perfect for a first date. Neither romantic nor scary, there were enough plot twists to hold my attention.

Greg and I shared a large bag of plain popcorn and individual water bottles.

"Don't you want butter on it?" I asked while standing at the concessions stand.

Movie popcorn wasn't movie popcorn unless slathered with butter.

"Please, no," Greg answered. "Elizabeth, do you understand all the chemicals in that stuff? You shouldn't pollute your body with that crap. It'll give you cancer. Melted organic butter would be different."

Once we consumed the popcorn, Greg tentatively reached for my hand. I had grown accustomed to Danny's confidence. He would never be tentative about taking my hand. He wouldn't be tentative about taking any girl's hand. Danny would just take it. It would never cross his mind that a girl might not want him to.

Greg's hand felt warm, but not quite right. His fingers were shorter and stubbier than the ones I was accustomed to holding. They were rough from calluses.

Unlike Danny, Greg worked with his hands. He repaired his truck. He worked at Donnelly's organic garden. Physical labor, not sports, was part of Greg's life.

Argh!! I had to stop comparison Greg with Danny!

Different did not mean bad. I had to get it through my head that men's hands feel different from one another. It was no different than having twinkling sapphire eyes or soft brown ones. Both should be considered equally good.

Then why did I sit in the theater longing for twinkling sapphires?

Danny had certainly messed with my head. Why did everything lead to thoughts of him? I knew the answer, and it made me cross.

Eventually I became accustomed to Greg's hand. It was nice, I decided. I smiled, leaned over and kissed his cheek, a soft, quick kiss. He smiled and squeezed my hand.

Instantly I regretted it. What did Greg think by this act? Did he assume I had feelings or expectations that as far as I knew I didn't have?

This was not a dilemma when I kissed Danny's cheek. If Danny thought it might mean I wanted more, so be it. He would have been right.

Danny! Danny! Danny! Get out of my head! I wanted to scream.

Later, Greg and I returned to Donnelly after dessert at the organic bakery near the theater. Greg insisted on walking me to my door. I did not invite him inside my room. That would send a message I was not ready to send. Instead, I agreed to see Greg again, and he pecked my cheek good-night.

Greg's kiss did nothing to me. It was pleasant but tentative. There was no steam and my heart rate remained constant.

I was spoiled. I only knew Danny's kisses, ones that sent me soaring to the moon and back, kisses that left my heart wanting to leap out of my chest. I needed to get over it. Otherwise, I would set myself up to be disappointed for the rest of my life.

CHAPTER 22 - ELIZABETH

Tuesday a small group of us gathered at The Cellar to enjoy a low-keyed evening.

"Dance with me Eli," Danny said, his request more a command than a question.

I rose and followed him to the dance floor. "This is a slow dance," I pointed out giving him ample opportunity to back out.

"That's why it's perfect." Danny glanced down at my boot cast.

"Good point." I wasn't capable of dancing to a faster beat.

Danny hooked his arm around my waist and took my hand. My pulse quickened. As Danny pulled me closer, my heartbeat increased even more. The light scent of his cologne was intoxicating. I shivered.

Danny's smile met mine. His entire being lit up, and he pressed me even closer as the next song began. Danny leaned into me, and inhaled a sharp intake of breath.

"You smell nice, Elizabeth," he whispered. Danny's breath, light on my ear, sent more shivers radiating throughout me.

Moments later Danny whispered again, "Do you have any idea how good you feel?"

"No," I answered, somewhat terrified by his remark.

Danny gave me the most electric smile I'd ever seen, and I mirrored it.

"I don't want you to feel this good," he said, and frowned.

"Is something wrong with me?" I whispered. "Should we stop dancing?" I didn't want to stop. I was enjoying Danny's hands and the warmth of his body too much.

"No. This is too good. Elizabeth, you're perfect."

Soon the song ended.

"I want you to leave," Danny whispered.

I looked at him like he was crazy. Danny and I were having such a good time together.

"Why should I leave? It's early."

Danny's beautiful smile had been replaced by sad confusion.

"I'm afraid if you don't leave I'm going to do something I'll regret. Damn! This is too perfect tonight, Elizabeth."

I was depressed seeing Danny's conflicted emotions. Staying would in effect be an ultimatum. I couldn't do that to him. I cared too much.

The next morning Shane and Cam were alone at breakfast when I arrived. After last night, I wondered if Danny was avoiding me.

"Where's Danny?" I asked, trying to sound as casual as possible.

"Sleeping it off," Shane offered. "After you left The Cellar, Danny got blitzed."

"Why would he do that?" Danny was sober when I had said 'good-night'.

"So he could numb his brain enough to go home with the flirty blonde, instead of going with the brunette he really wanted. But she had already left," Cam said with brutal glee.

"Oh." I didn't know what to say. So that's why Danny told me to leave.

I took a couple of nibbles of toast, washed them down with a gulp of juice, then grabbed a banana and left without saying another word.

Too early for class, I walked back to Berkeley Hall, and nearly collided with Danny who was dashing out the door.

"Hey, Eli," he greeted me as though he didn't have a care in the world.

"Don't 'hey Eli' me, Daniel," I scowled.

Danny stopped in his tracks, keeping me from proceeding.

"E, what's got you this early in the morning?"

"I know why you made me leave The Cellar." I frowned.

"Shit! This is just what I wanted to avoid. You're hurt."

I couldn't answer. It was the obvious truth. Danny gripped my shoulders. "Eli," he said, "You've got to find a boyfriend so you won't care what I'm doing."

Furious, I pulled myself out of his hold.

"So I won't care what you're doing!" I exploded. "How about if you don't care what I'm doing. I had a date Saturday night, and you did everything to sabotage it."

Danny smirked. "I didn't sabotage your date. I said 'have a good time, Sweetheart.'"

I rolled my eyes in defiance, outraged. "Sweetheart? You're asking me about my date with another man and you're calling me Sweetheart! Unbelievable Daniel! I am not your Sweetheart and I never will be, so you've made it more than clear! And yes, I had a lovely time."

"Will you be seeing him again?"

"Trying to assuage your guilt, Daniel? Yes, I'm seeing Greg again, but don't come to my room first."

"Guilt?"

"Do you even remember last night? The part you spent with me?"

"Of course I do. It was the best part." Danny smiled. "We were dancing. I was holding you in my arms."

"You told me I was perfect," I stammered. "What should I think when you say something like that?"

"I was stupid, Eli. I've got to keep my hands off of you."

Danny took my hands and kissed my cheek. "Can you forgive me, Eli?"

he asked in a hurt little boy voice. "I'll be crushed if you don't."

"Daniel, you're impossible."

Why did I always give in to him?

Saturday evening I went out with Greg to an on-campus jazz concert, this time without Danny's interference. That was just as bad. I was distracted, wondering about his whereabouts, fearing an unannounced appearance.

When the time came to part, I decided that I didn't want a third date. Greg was nice, but we had no chemistry. The electricity generated by Danny's eyes, his touch, and his lips, ah, those lips, had me wanting more than Greg could deliver. Had Danny set me up to have expectations that no other man could ever fulfill? I couldn't let myself believe that. I had to believe it was just Greg and my realization that he was not the right man for me.

I had to believe that somewhere out there was a man I would want to get involved with who was not Danny. Otherwise, I was doomed.

CHAPTER 23 - ELIZABETH

"I'm meeting Rach to prep our film." Danny said as we left Professor Dennison's class the following Wednesday. "I hate to do this Eli, but I need a rain check today." Then Danny took my hand and gave me his biggest smile. "I'm sorry. You know I'd rather be with you."

He would? After our recent conversations, I had been following his no expectations game plan, so I answered, "I know. Class work comes first."

I tried sounding cheerful. I'd miss Danny, but it was just one afternoon. Still, I felt lost. For two months, every Wednesday afternoon had been filled with Danny. It was as though a part of me was missing.

How to spend the afternoon? I didn't want to return to the dorm. Boring! I would think about it over hot chocolate at the Cafe. Maybe I'd run into a friend and we could hang out.

I was putting my change away when two students doctoring their coffees at the condiment station stopped me.

"Are you a freshman?" asked the pleasant looking blonde.

"Yes," I answered with uncertainty.

The sandy haired girl noticed my cautious reaction. "I'm Sasha and this is Joely. We're the yearbook editors and we need a freshman to join our staff."

Then Joely added, "The freshmen editor takes pictures and lays them out. Do you have a camera?"

"Uh, yeah. I'm a decent photographer."

"Excellent," Sasha continued, "We're having a staff meeting now. Come on up and check it out. The editors are a great group. You'll like them."

And I did. This was exactly what I needed; an engrossing activity with a good group of students to take my mind off Danny.

As I was leaving the yearbook office after the meeting broke up, a pleasant, dark blonde upperclassman, all preppy in an oxford shirt and Topsiders, approached me.

"Hi," he said. The guy's soft blue eyes were nearly level with mine. He couldn't have stood more than five foot seven. "I'm Jackson Shaw, one of the Associate Editors," and he reached out his hand to shake mine.

"Elizabeth Jacobs, Freshmen Editor as of today. What does an Associate Editor do?"

"I'm in training to become next year's Editor-in-Chief. Mind if I walk with you? I also live in Berkeley. I've seen you in the building."

"You have?" That was a surprise. I hadn't noticed Jackson, but I had rather been walking around with blinders on.

"I live on the third floor. I've seen you with the freshmen on my hall."

"Shane, Cam and Danny are my friends."

We'd arrived at the dorm and continued chatting.

As we parted, Jackson said, "I'll see you at The Cellar this weekend."

"I'm sure I'll be there," I replied.

CHAPTER 24 - DANIEL

Rachel and I entered Berkeley Hall steps behind Elizabeth and some short preppy guy. Engrossed in conversation, Eli appeared at ease. The guy seemed familiar, but I couldn't place him. I frowned. Eli was smiling, even laughing at what must have been his jokes.

I motioned Rachel to stop once we were inside the entrance. I didn't want Eli to see us. I wanted to observe what was going on between her and whoever.

"What's with your roommate?" I finally whispered to Rachel.

"How's that?" Rachel cocked her brow seemingly confused, which was odd.

"Eli's changed. She had two dates last week with one guy and now she's with him. Who is that anyway?"

"Jackson Shaw. Junior. Lives on your hall."

"That's why he looks familiar."

Rachel smirked, barely hiding her amusement. "What?" I asked.

"Danny, you're funny. Everyone should recognize you, but you can't be bothered knowing who they are, even if they live down the hall from you."

I ignored her. Rachel had hit a sore spot. Besides I was too busy watching Elizabeth who seemed to be enjoying my neighbor's company.

As they parted I turned so I wouldn't be seen. I'd forgotten that Eli wouldn't be passing this way and Jackson had no reason to look at me. This was not lost on Rachel who gave me a wicked grin.

"Danny, you're jealous," she smirked.

"No I'm not," I snapped, averting my glance from Rachel.

"Yes, you are," she answered with certainty.

Rachel's eyes were laughing. She was enjoying my discomfort.

"Why would I be jealous? I have no claims on Eli. She's a free agent."

Rachel burst into muffled laughter. "Oh come on, Danny. The way you play with her? Elizabeth's no freer than a prison inmate."

I grimaced. "Jackson's not her type anyway," I groused. Observing Eli talking and laughing with Jackson had been enough for me.

Rachel laughed again. "How can you be so certain?"

"Because I know what her type is," I scowled. Because I am her type, and Jackson Shaw is not like me.

"Well, if you don't do something about it, that will make no difference." I hated that Rachel saw right through me.

"I can't date Elizabeth," I protested, albeit a bit weakly, I admit.

"I am so sick of it! Danny, you are so frustrating! You spend almost all your time with Elizabeth! The only thing you don't do is date, and if you don't hurry…"

"Okay. Enough already. Point made, Rach."

"I hope so. Danny, it's only a matter of time before somebody worthwhile figures out that you're not a couple and they'll ask Elizabeth out. And when she says, "yes," because she's tired of waiting, you'll be the sorry one."

"Thanks for the cheery thoughts," I said sourly.

Elizabeth had already said, "yes" to someone else, but he hadn't been Mr. Right. I couldn't risk the next one being more her type. As Rachel said, I would be the sorry one.

"Danny," Rachel began more gently "If I didn't care so much I wouldn't be nudging you. I don't want you to get hurt any more than I want Elizabeth to get hurt. If you keep going this way you're both going to get hurt."

"I'll think about it." I hated admitting it, but Rachel might be right.

"I don't know how Elizabeth puts up with your bullshit. She must see something I've missed because she tolerates it. Elizabeth more than tolerates it."

"Maybe Eli's a masochist?" I said sarcastically. Rachel rolled her eyes. "Joking, Rach."

"Maybe Elizabeth's not. Perhaps she realizes what you don't. You and Elizabeth are too connected. Danny, you share too much history. It may be that the only way you can get out of each others' systems is by getting together."

I understood why Eli put up with me; for the same reason I spent all my time with her. I had wanted to deny it and so I had. Rachel's confrontation made me realize I couldn't continue living in this state of denial any longer. And now I had Jackson Shaw and that other guy to consider.

Rachel was looking at me, trying to read my thoughts.

"I've got to make a phone call," I told her "I'll be up in five minutes."

CHAPTER 25 - ELIZABETH

"Guess what?" I called to Chloe as I disappeared into my room to find my camera. "I'm now on the yearbook staff."

"How'd that happen," Chloe called back as Rachel entered the suite.

"Right place at the right time. They named me Freshman Editor. My job is taking photos of freshmen doing things."

A knock came on the suite's door. Rachel opened it.

"You look nice," I heard Rachel whisper to Danny.

Danny walked in to find me sitting on the bed examining an SD card. Rachel was right. Danny did look nice. He had changed from jeans to chinos, added a baby blue cashmere sweater that set off his eyes, and brushed his hair.

"E, I missed you today," Danny said before plopping down beside me.

"How's your project going?"

"Off to a good start, but it's going to be crazy busy. How was your afternoon?"

I snapped the SD card slot closed, carefully placed the camera on the desk, and turned my full attention to Danny.

"Awesome. I'm now Freshmen Editor for the yearbook," I boasted.

"That's great, Eli. It's perfect for you," said Danny. "How did that happen?"

Then I gave Danny the run down on my chance encounter with Sasha and Joely.

"Now you'll be too busy for me," he teased.

"Never," I flirted, "I always have time for you."

"You'd better." Our eyes met and Danny kissed my hand. That was different.

"Let's celebrate. Ready for dinner?"

"Dinner?"

"Sure. Do I need an excuse to take my lady out to dinner?"

His lady? I grinned like a giddy fool. Then I bounced up from the bed. "Okay. I'm ready."

"You're not changing?" Danny exclaimed.

I considered his clothing. Danny's chinos and sweater were at least a couple of notches up from my jeans on the formality scale. We must be going to a real restaurant.

"Then Shoo! Go in the other room. I'll change."

Five minutes later I emerged wearing a pale blue silk chiffon shirt over a coordinating camisole. A black skirt, leggings, and boots flat enough to work with my cast replaced my jeans and sneakers. I had applied blush, brushed my hair, and spritzed on perfume.

"Better?" I asked, and I gave Danny my brightest smile.

"Much. Let's go." Danny grinned, pleased with my appearance.

"It's so early?" It was four-thirty.

"It won't be when we get there." And Danny flashed me another wicked grin that left my pulse racing. How mysterious!

Danny guided me out the door to the Berkeley Hall parking lot and his car.

"Let's get a move on. The reservation is at seven."

"Where are we going?"

"To the beach."

"The beach? There aren't any beaches for at least…"

"A couple of hours. That's why we have to leave now," Danny answered.

I was intrigued and up for the adventure.

Two hours later we were driving down what would have been a picturesque country road if the sun hadn't already set. I was aware that we were in the Adirondacks. Unfamiliar with the region, and with Danny not revealing anything, I had no idea where we were.

Danny turned onto a smaller road that soon dead-ended. Before us was an impressive white clapboard-sided inn trimmed in forest green and lit in a warm welcoming glow. Everything about it was perfect, as though it were the lead article in a travel magazine. A small sign announced, "The Lake House Inn."

To the right, a similar, but smaller, building connected to the Inn. Danny followed its separate driveway to the valet stand at the end. A matching sign proclaimed it, "The Beach House." Danny said we were going to the beach. Now I understood.

The resort was on the shore of a large lake, surrounded by a stand of majestic trees. I imagined the pine and fir trees soon being decorated with lights for the holiday season. The setting was spectacular.

"Where did you find this place," I gasped as we walked to the front door.

Danny smiled at my delight.

"New York Magazine, but I needed the right girl," Danny explained as he took my hand and we entered the restaurant.

Electricity shot from his hand through to my heart. So now I was the right girl. I was also a very happy girl.

Inside the décor was as beautiful as the grounds. French doors overlooked the lake and there was patio dining for the warmer months.

Decorated in upscale rustic, fireplaces scattered about created a warm, intimate ambiance.

The hostess lead us to a table with a banquette facing it's own fireplace, the ultimate in privacy. It was as though we were the only couple in the restaurant.

"This is amazing." I whispered to Danny who squeezed my hand. "Is there an occasion I don't know about?" I asked cautiously.

"I've been wanting to come here, and I thought you would like it."

Danny lifted my chin and gazed into my eyes. The effect was immediate and hypnotic. "I thought the Lake House was the perfect place for our first date."

"Our what! But…" Stunned, the words stuck in my throat.

Danny cupped my face in his hands, leaned in, and kissed me. I was trembling from both the power of his kiss and the unexpected turn the evening had taken.

I smiled at Danny, my head, my body, my soul, floating as though I had ingested a very pleasant and potent narcotic.

"A date? You never asked me," I stammered.

"Miss Jacobs, would you please go out with me this evening?" he chuckled.

"I'd be honored, Mr. Newman." A megawatt smile lit my face.

"Your other beaux won't mind." Danny teased.

"No. I'm not seeing anyone exclusively."

"Elizabeth, you are now. I expect my girlfriend to be exclusive."

"You're making a lot of assumptions, Daniel."

"That I am," he grinned. Then Danny kissed me again.

The waiter, a pleasant young man wearing the restaurant's uniform khaki trousers and denim shirt came to take our drink order.

"Would you like a bottle of wine, sir," he asked Danny.

After a moment Danny responded, "Let's make it champagne."

Champagne! The perfect drink for this now very special evening.

Soon the waiter returned with our champagne and took our dinner order. Danny and I decided to split a Caprese salad, and we each selected filet mignon. With Juliette gone from his life, Danny was back to being a carnivore.

When the waiter left, Danny turned this attention to me. My heart beat rapidly. Danny raised his flute, and I followed. I blushed. I melted. Danny was so intense.

"Elizabeth, my best friend and now my girlfriend," Danny began. "You're not only beautiful, you're compassionate, smart, funny, and most important, you tolerate my BS. Thank you for waiting."

A tear escaped my eye as we gently tapped our glasses together and Danny delicately brushed it away. Then we took our first sip of the wonderfully dry champagne.

"This is excellent," I said softly. I didn't know how else to respond.

Finally, I raised my glass, my hand trembling, "Daniel, I would be proud to be yours exclusively. Thank you for this magical evening."

The food was as wonderful as the atmosphere and that wasn't because I had consumed too many dining hall meals. The Beach House rivaled the best of New York and Beverly Hills.

A few sips into his cappuccino Danny put down his cup and took my hands. He was unexpectedly serious. His deep blue eyes held sadness I couldn't comprehend.

"Is something the matter?" I asked tenderly.

My stomach turned nervous flip-flops as I mentally replayed the evening. It had seemed perfect and Danny quickly confirmed my interpretation.

"No. It's been a great evening," Danny smiled.

I was even more confused, but Danny continued. "I've been sending you a lot of mixed signals lately." He paused for a breath. "This is hard. I'm not good at discussing my feelings. The truth is, Elizabeth you've become the most important person in my life. But the rapidity scares me. Hell, we weren't even on a date when we left Donnelly. Now you're my girlfriend."

I felt drunk with joy. Danny had meant what he said earlier.

"Elizabeth, you have no idea how much I wish we were staying here tonight." Danny's sapphires darkened with intensity. "But I'm not ready. I can't give you the commitment that would require. I'm afraid of hurting you and I want to be more certain that I won't."

I was shaking. Danny massaged my knuckles to calm me.

"Why do you think you would necessarily hurt me?"

Danny inhaled deeply. "I've seen it with my parents," he quietly admitted.

"But they're happy, right?"

"Mostly, I think. They are now. But Dad has caused my mother much pain over the years. My parents don't know that I know, but Dad has cheated on Mom."

Danny's voice quivered as he told me this family secret. I squeezed his hand in support.

"Is that why they once separated?" I asked in a near whisper.

Danny nodded sadly. "I overheard my mother crying to yours. I'm sure that's why they sent me to Bromley. With me at boarding school, Mom could go on location with Dad." Years later, his parents' marital problems still affected him.

"I'm so sorry. I can feel how hurt you are." I brushed his cheek with my fingertips. Danny took my hand and kissed my palm.

"I'm okay, but I'm determined not to hurt you like that. Eli, you know I never make any promise that I'm not one hundred percent certain I can keep. I don't think I can promise to be true to you. I'm asking a lot, but I need to work it out for myself. I don't want to hurt you. I'll understand if you tell me to go to hell."

Holy shit! I wanted Danny so badly, but I didn't want him being unfaithful.

"I could never say that to you."

"I'm glad. Part of me would die if you did."

"Maybe you're being honest in a way that most men never are. Should I do the same? Not promise to be faithful?"

"No. I told you before you are mine exclusively. If there's a guy you've been dating, Eli you're not anymore. You're through with him. That's how it has to be."

I gazed intently into his eyes. Danny's sincerity was palpable. I took his face in my hands and kissed him. Danny knew he was the only man for me.

It had taken him over eighteen years to take me on a date. Then he had declared me his girlfriend. Danny was overwhelmed. Settling down with me was in complete contradiction of his carefully crafted self-image. The lift of an eyebrow, a simple smile, those damned sapphire eyes, could land him any girl in the room and often did.

So here we were. What about today had been different? Was it as simple as us spending the afternoon apart? I had no idea. Something had made Danny take himself out of the game for the one girl whose very existence spelled permanency.

Danny was petrified. If it made him feel better to have invented a twisted out-clause we both knew he would never use, I would go along with the fiction. I was in it for the long haul.

"Let's get the check," I suggested. "I want to see the beach."

After Danny paid, we strolled the resort's grounds. The night was considerably colder now. Danny wrapped his arm around me, holding me close as we found the shore.

The lights from the inn illuminated the beach enough for us to see how pretty it would be by day. The moon reflected off the lake's smooth glass-like surface. Of all the places I had been, none compared to this.

Danny pulled me tighter. The electricity between us was so powerful I was trembling. He thought I was cold and held me even closer. Our eyes met, followed by our lips, and Danny transported me someplace magical.

A teak bench situated where the patio met the sand provided a private sanctuary. I settled onto Danny's lap and snuggled in his welcoming arms.

Danny and I were so into each other, content to enjoy the feel of our arms locking us together. Sharing kiss after kiss denied us all year was more potent than any spell.

"I could do this all night," I sighed as Danny's hypnotic eyes smiled at me.

Then he laughed nervously. "Eli, you have no idea how petrified I am. I don't even know what I'm supposed to do with a girlfriend. And you're even less experienced."

"Don't think so much," I said tenderly, and I nibbled Danny's lips. "We'll be the same best friends we were this morning, only now we can have sex."

"Sex with Elizabeth Jacobs," Danny pondered. "Do you realize the enormity of what I've done? You're the one girl I'm afraid to have sex with."

"Let's just get it over with. Then you won't have to worry anymore about me being Elizabeth Jacobs."

"You make it sound so simple."

"It is, Daniel," I said breathlessly. "It is." I reached around his neck and brought his lips to mine for another kiss. My poor honey; so full of conflict.

Later, Danny and I sat starring at the full moon caught between two tall pine trees. I frowned knowing our evening would soon be coming to an end.

"Before we go public, I want to give us time to become solid as a couple."

"You don't want the attention, do you?" Danny asked.

"Yeah," I said quietly, summoning my confidence to say what had been gnawing at me. "You split with Juliette, but have you been seeing anyone else?"

"Yeah."

"What!" I sat straight up and glared. How did I not know?

"You asked me a direct question. I promised to always be honest with you, Eli."

I glared at Danny, but he was smiling which puzzled me.

"There's this beautiful, wonderfully neurotic brunette from Santa Monica. I think you might know her." And he shut me up by kissing me again.

"Are you as happy as I am?" I asked.

Danny grinned and looked straight into my eyes.

"Yes. And relieved," he finally answered. "Eli, I've been conflicted from that first day in the dining hall. When we hugged... I told myself it was the surprise of seeing you again and how I'd forgotten you'd become a woman. I wasn't expecting it."

"I felt it too. It frightened me. I didn't want to become a twelve year old with a hopeless crush again."

Danny hugged me and laughed, "I loved when you were a twelve year old with a hopeless crush. It was so cute."

He hugged me again and continued. "We were together so much it frightened me. I didn't handle it well. I wanted you, and at the same time I wanted to keep the line drawn. That's sort of why I hooked up with Juliette."

I smirked. "You hooked up with Juliette to stay away from me?"

Danny laughed. "I thought if I had a girlfriend it would inoculate me. Obviously, it didn't work. I spent more time with you than with Juliette. I was hoping I could get to Christmas before breaking up with her."

Now I was laughing. Juliette was such an obvious mismatch for Danny.

"No, Thanksgiving," I choked. "You're spending the holiday with my family."

"That's right. All the time I was with Juliette, I was craving you. I need a girl I can be myself with. It's great that Juliette's a vegan, but it's not me."

I thought of my two hapless dates with Greg.

"Like if we were to go to a movie Friday night, you and I would share a big bucket of popcorn. And I would slather it with as much butter as I wanted, because of course that's the only way to eat movie popcorn."

"Yeah," Danny answered. "What other way is there?"

"You would never complain that we were about to ingest 'butter-flavored chemicals' and forbid me."

"Did somebody do that?" Danny asked in surprise.

"Yes," I answered earnestly.

"It probably is butter-flavored chemicals, but so what? We don't eat it every day. Movie popcorn has to be buttered." Danny paused for effect, and then twinkled his sapphire eyes at me. "And then I would kiss your buttery flavored lips."

"I would expect nothing less," I flirted back.

"All because of buttered popcorn. Let's see what's opening Friday night."

"I'm available."

"You'd better be or I'll have to break up with you." Danny answered, and he playfully rubbed his nose against mine. I giggled in delight.

"Your busted ankle was the turning point for me. The moment I received your text, making everything better consumed me. Those two nights were amazing."

"But we didn't do anything."

"Didn't matter. It was so incredibly intimate. Especially when the storm frightened you." Danny smiled at me. "Holding you while we slept felt so right."

"We can do it again," I said eagerly.

"I told you, I'm not ready."

"If you sleep with me you won't want to sleep with anyone else, not ever."

"You certainly are confident," he laughed. "What if you don't like sex?"

I looked Danny straight in the eyes as I brought my face to his and kissed him.

"Impossible. I'm with you."

CHAPTER 26 - ELIZABETH

Saturday dawned bright and warm for early November. Following a perfect Friday evening movie date, spent sharing a bucket of saturated buttered popcorn with Danny, it was going to be a great afternoon for rugby.

Chloe accompanied me to the field. "I don't understand anything about rugby," she giggled. "I just love watching cute guys run around in shorts."

Rachel refused to be a hypocrite. "Count me out," she declared. "I don't care if it is Danny and Cam. Rugby's a waste of my time."

Despite having attended several games, I still didn't understand the sport. No matter how many times Danny had explained it, rugby made no sense. Football, soccer – those I understood. Rugby, forget it, but I could still cheer for my man.

My man! Today marked my first appearance on the sidelines as Danny's girlfriend, though I didn't think anyone yet knew.

"Hey, look at you! Elizabeth Jacobs, photo-journalist." Danny teased when he spotted me, my camera hanging from my shoulder, standing with Chloe.

"Be nice or you won't get in the yearbook," I teased back.

"Great lens," Cam noted, referring to the high-powered zoom I had purchased on Thursday for this purpose. Cam was an avid photographer. He could teach me a thing or two.

Chloe and Cam left to talk privately, leaving me with Danny.

"Be careful," I cautioned. Our eyes locked, and we shared a lovers' glance while our fingertips touched. Electric!

"Don't worry," Danny smiled, "It's not as dangerous as you think."

"Newman." Duncan appeared from out of nowhere. I jerked my fingers away from Danny's. "I see you have your own publicist," he sneered.

I held up the badge dangling from a lanyard around my neck. "Yearbook staff," I answered curtly.

"My mistake, Lois Lane," he sneered.

"Duncan!" Danny admonished.

"I didn't mean to offend Malibu Barbie," Duncan smirked.

"You are too low on the food chain to offend me. Plus it's Danny who has a house in Malibu. Not me," I retorted.

Danny shook his head in frustration.

"Elizabeth, Duncan, put away your claws," Danny said in a stern, commanding voice. "I'll be with you in a minute," he told Duncan.

"Right." Duncan knew he'd gone over the line and left to join the team.

"Can't you two be civil?" Danny asked.

"Ask him," I answered. I sounded like a petulant little girl. I had disliked Duncan from the first and the sentiment appeared to be mutual.

Danny sighed. "Got to go, babe." He laced his fingers with mine. "Game time."

"Play well," I said, and I rose to full height to kiss his cheek. "And safe," I added. Danny grinned, and kissed me back. Then he headed to the team.

"Did you see that?" a girl standing behind me gaped to her friend. I smirked, stifling a giggle. Yeah, ladies, he's taken.

My new lens was awesome. I got great shots, and the zoom put me in the action without getting clobbered. Not so Danny. I cringed every time he was tackled.

"Rugby is safer than football," Danny had explained. "The rules are stricter and it's illegal to hit the head. There are rarely any concussions, Eli."

I didn't buy it then or now. There was something comforting about football players encased in aerospace-grade plastics.

The game was close until the final minutes. A Donnelly player got possession of the ball coming out of the scrum. As he was about to be tackled, he lateraled to Duncan. Duncan picked up a few yards and as he was tackled, he passed the ball to Danny.

Danny's speed enabled him to reach the goal after outrunning several opposing players. He scored!

"They won!" I screamed, and I jumped up and down hugging Chloe.

Moments later, the game was over. We sprinted down the field where the athletes were already celebrating. I threw my arms around Danny from behind and he spun around to greet me.

I stared in horror. "Your face!" I exclaimed. Danny's right cheekbone was bruised and puffy. I touched it cautiously.

"Ouch!" he grimaced.

"Get an ice pack," I barked at Cam.

"It hurts that much?" I asked in my gentlest voice.

Danny tried smiling but cringed. "I'm okay. I'll just be ugly for a few days."

"You could never be ugly," I empathized.

Cam ran over with the ice pack. I grabbed it and pressed it against Danny's battered cheek.

"Sonofabitch! Eli, that hurts." Danny grimaced, and he grabbed the ice pack. "Get any good shots, babe?" He asked as he held the ice to his face.

"I think so. I'll show you later. Can I get one of your face?" I smiled. "I've never seen you ugly and probably never will again. I want to remember it."

"Fine," he scowled. "Just don't blackmail me." I rolled my eyes. Like I'd ever do that. Danny complied and lowered the ice pack. The bruise was already turning purple. I snapped a few photos. "Perfect."

"Don't send that to my mother," he warned.

"Not a chance," I agreed. Ellen would freak.

"Newman!" Oh great –Duncan! "C'mon. It's party tine." Then he looked me up and down and smirked.

"E, the team's going to The Cellar. You and Chloe coming?" Danny asked.

"Lois Lane," Duncan sneered, "Rugby parties are not for amateurs."

"I can hold my beer." I glared.

"Eli, you don't drink beer," Danny reminded me.

"I do now," I responded stubbornly.

"This should be fun. Let's see how plastered Lois can get," Duncan smirked.

"Elizabeth," Danny cautioned, "This is a bad idea."

"We'll see. Elizabeth Jacobs does not back down from a challenge."

"I'm going to clobber both of you." Danny sighed, exasperated. "Elizabeth," he said crossly, "let's go." And he grabbed my arm.

"Lois, leave the camera home." Duncan ordered. "Paparazzi makes me nervous."

I burst out laughing. What did Duncan know about the paparazzi? His father was a Louisiana oil executive.

"Duncan, we'll catch you at The Cellar," Danny said.

"Looking forward to it Lois," Duncan sneered, and I glared as we walked away. Slime! Total slime.

Danny and I strolled over to my Range Rover. He didn't take my hand. Crap.

When I reached for the ignition button, Danny grasped my hand to stop me.

"You are not giving in to Duncan," he warned. "He's baiting you, Elizabeth. You are not getting drunk with Duncan today or any other day."

"It's not your decision. I can do what I want, Daniel," I said defiantly. "I'm tired of Duncan laughing at me. Lois Lane. Yeesh!"

"Not today," Danny insisted. "Elizabeth! Listen to me," he demanded. Then Danny winced. "Ouch, my face hurts so much."

"Honey, I'm so sorry." I lifted the ice and saw the even deeper purple Danny's cheek had become. I pressed my lips to the bruise. "Does that help?"

"Not really, but it's nice," Danny smiled as best as he could. "That's why you're not drinking this afternoon. I need you, baby."

"You do, don't you?" I smiled. I liked being needed.

"I hurt more than you realize. You getting into a drinking match with Duncan… You'll lose big time and I'll have to babysit you."

"Okay. I get it. But when do I get to have any fun?"

"Tomorrow. If I make it." Danny squeezed my hand. "I hurt so much, I can't even kiss you," he complained.

Everyone at The Cellar applauded Danny's grand entrance. We strode in, holding hands aloft and bowing. Like a decorated hero returning from war, he ate it up.

Pitchers of beer were already at the table. I ordered Danny into a chair while I went to the bar for ice. When I returned he had already chugged his first beer and was pouring a second.

A girl wearing a tight green sweater had taken up residence in the chair next to Danny and was fawning over him, batting her long eyelashes. Would it always be this way?

"Thank you for saving my seat." I smiled at her and I applied the ice pack to Danny's face. He winced from the cold, but he kept his hand over mine. Tight sweater got the hint and left. I dreaded the long night ahead.

By seven, I felt like a failure. I had no idea how much beer Danny had consumed, and despite being blitzed, his face still hurt.

We had danced a few times, but in Danny's inebriated state this meant he held me as tightly as possible while we swayed to the beat. His hand rested unwelcome on my rear, but I was powerless to remove it.

I felt tawdry and cheap, but I had promised to take care of Danny so I couldn't do what I wanted to do – flee. I was fed up with Danny, but most of all I was fed up with myself.

I would never put myself in this position again. After tonight, if Danny wanted to get blitzed, count me out. This was not the Danny I loved. This Danny I didn't know, and I didn't like. If we made it through tonight, I knew I wasn't ready for a committed relationship with him.

Somehow we adjourned to Duncan's suite in Daughtry House for part two of the never-ending evening. If it wasn't enough to be drunk, why not follow it up by getting wasted. Oh joy!

As the only person not partaking I was bored. So while everyone else shared joints, I sat on a bed propped against a wall and contemplated life. Danny had warned me, but talk had not prepared me. It tortured me trying to reconcile the two Danny's. Tears that none of the besotted souls in the room noticed, trickled down my cheeks.

Soon Danny had had enough of smoking pot and remembered he had a girlfriend. He climbed on the bed, kissed me, and laid his head in my lap. Then Danny took my hand and played with my fingers while I stroked his sweat-dampened hair.

His cheek looked awful although the swelling had stabilized. Wasted Danny was mellow. He gazed up at me with contented, angelic blue eyes and smiled. Danny was in no pain, but he was clueless about mine.

Duncan appeared and squeezed in beside me. Danny's glassy eyes acknowledged him and in a dreamy voice he said, "Eli's my best girl." Then he kissed my lips and added, "She even tastes good."

"Let me try," Duncan said in his wasted stupor. He grabbed my face between his hands.

"Get away!" I exclaimed, and I shoved Duncan who toppled over on to the mattress. I moved Danny aside more gently and jumped up. "I am so out of here! Danny, let's go."

Danny was too wasted to object. I grabbed his hand and pulled him out the door, leaving a room of stunned, wasted people in our wake.

When we reached Berkeley Hall after walking across the quad in stony silence, Danny embraced me for a kiss. I pushed him away. Ew. Vile. Danny still wore dirty rugby clothes. The stench of old sweats, stale beer, and pot was a nauseating combination.

"What's wrong?" he asked, oblivious to reality. "Are you angry?"

In his state, I decided to focus on the issue that required less of an explanation.

"Danny, you reek. You're wearing a soiled rugby uniform."

The usually fastidious Danny looked at his clothes and frowned, clueless.

"I'll shower upstairs."

"And brush your teeth." Danny grinned, a mischievous little boy grin. "I'm serious," I added with icy regard.

Danny wobbled up the front steps. He clung to me. I helped him to the elevator, praying his larger size wouldn't knock me over. Stumbling through the hallway, I cautioned him to be quiet. Then I realized it was 10:30. Nobody was sleeping. It was Saturday night.

Once inside Danny's room, I found clean sleep pants, a t-shirt, and underwear in his bureau. I pushed Danny into a chair and pulled off his muddy cleats and socks.

"Ugh! This is gross." I scrunched up my face. He smirked. I scowled. Then I threw the socks in Danny's face and he sniffed them.

"You're right. These are gross," and he threw them in the corner.

I pulled Danny up by the hand. "Shower," I announced, and I marched him down the hall to the bathroom.

I handed Danny the clean clothes and turned on the water. "Do not come out until you smell sweet again," I ordered.

Danny reached for his towel and soap, and before pulling the outer curtain closed issued me a challenge, "Join me, Eli? You can tell me when I do."

"No way," I laughed and I pulled the curtain closed. Not tonight.

Ten minutes later Danny emerged sparkling clean, wearing fresh clothes and smelling of Bumble and Bumble.

"Better?" he asked.

"Almost." And I handed him his toothbrush and toothpaste. Then he went to the sink and brushed. Danny didn't even glance up.

"Have you even looked in the mirror?" I asked.

Danny glanced up and examined his reflection. His eyes opened wide in shock.

"E, have I looked this bad all day?"

I nodded yes. Then I added, "The swelling's stabilized, but it's more purple now. Why do you think I've been so worried?"

"I didn't know…" For the first time he was concerned.

"Of course not. You were wasted."

Danny tapped his cheek with his fingertips and winced. "E, that's wicked. Do you think anything's broken?"

"Let me see. I'll be gentle." My fingertips skimmed his cheekbone, but Danny grimaced. Even my light touch hurt.

"Enough! Ouch!" Danny exclaimed and he yanked my hand away.

"I think it's just bruised."

I rummaged in my purse and found an Extra-Strength Advil bottle. I shook out three caplets and handed them to Danny.

"The only drug you should have taken."

"Point made, Elizabeth."

Danny swallowed the caplets and washed them down by cupping his hands under the spigot. Then he patted me on the head like a good puppy.

"Thanks, Mom… Mom." He stopped short. "My mother will freak. Promise me you will not tell your parents. You know they'll tell mine," he pleaded.

"I promise. I won't say a word."

Danny remained unsteady as we returned to his room.

"E, I don't feel well," Danny said with slow deliberateness.

"Are you going to barf?" I asked.

"I don't think so."

"Too bad."

"You're angry."

"Disappointed." I sat down on Danny's bed. "You put me in a compromising situation today. You exposed a side I didn't like. I've had to tolerate girls hitting on you, and then us hanging with wasted people. And Duncan tried kissing me!" I wept.

Danny wrapped his arm around me. "Was it that bad, baby?"

"Yes," I sobbed. "I don't even like you anymore."

"Yes you do."

"No, I don't." I wiped my eyes with my hand.

"Then why are you here?"

"I owed it to Ellen."

Danny let out a whoop of laughter and winced from pain. I sneered.

"If it helps any, even for me I was bad today. I tried everything to stop the pain. You were right. I should have taken Advil. It's starting to work."

"Good. Shift over. I'm going." And I rose.

"Don't go. I feel awful," he pleaded. Danny pulled me to the bed and started tickling me with my hair. "C'mon Eli. Don't be mad. You're my girl. You kept me safe."

"I don't know about that."

Danny lifted my chin and kissed me. "How about now?"

"I'm angry." Danny kissed me again. "You're making anger difficult." Danny trailed kisses down my neck eliciting shivers of arousal. "That's not fair."

"I don't play fair," he flirted.

"You're impossible." I succumbed and kissed him.

Then Danny shoved me aside and bolted for the door. He returned a while later looking white as a ghost.

"Are you alright?"

"I think so." Danny lay down on the bed, shaking. I covered him with the comforter. "I'm so sick, hon."

"I should go. You need to sleep."

Danny took my hand. "Don't go, Eli," he pleaded. "I hate being alone when I'm sick. It scares me." Danny quivered. How had he managed all those other times?

I removed my sweatshirt, slipped on his shirt that came down to my knees, and shrugged of my jeans. After turning off the desk light, I climbed in beside Danny. He wrapped his arms around me, a human blanket, and kissed my shoulder, holding me closer.

Soon, Danny fell asleep, but sleep did not come easily for me. In his condition nothing was going to happen between us, but this was Danny. Even with him sleeping it off, the electricity generated between us was potent.

When I drifted off, my sleep was shallow, not restive.

CHAPTER 27 - ELIZABETH

"Hey sleepy head." A happy voice greeted me upon waking.

I blinked. Sunlight flooded the room. Danny and I had forgotten to pull the shades down last night.

"I thought it was a dream, but you're here," he said

Those gentle words, like magic seduced my ear and touched my heart. Danny's easy smile warmed me. His soft hand skimmed my face.

"Yeah, I'm here. Like I promised."

"I'm glad," Danny whispered, and he kissed me, sending my head spinning.

"How are you doing?"

Danny touched his cheek and winced. "I need more Advil."

"After breakfast or it can hurt your stomach."

"Then we better get some food."

I yawned. "Not yet."

Danny pulled me even closer and grinned. Our lips joined while he stroked my thigh.

Danny's finger traced the contours of my jaw and lingered on my lips.

"I know what else will wake you up," he suggested.

"Daniel, I am not some girl you picked up at a bar. You're the one who wanted to wait. After yesterday, I have to agree. Before you ever have a chance at loving me you have to commit to getting your act together."

"Ouch. Elizabeth, you've ruined my day."

"No I didn't. You knew my answer before you even asked."

I rose from the bed and put on my jeans, hoodie and shoes. Danny followed me to the door and he kissed my hair.

"Ew, babe. You smell like a party," Danny laughed. I frowned and left him.

Danny was right. The stench was not confined to my hair. My clothing reeked of pot. The fabric had absorbed yesterday's pungent odors. In my room, I stripped, threw everything into the laundry bag, and showered, lathering my hair twice.

Overnight it had cooled considerably. Indian Summer over, I chose a snug-fitting marine blue V-necked cashmere sweater. It looked great over skinny jeans.

Soon Danny arrived to accompany me to brunch. He took my breath away. Dressed in a cotton shirt the color of his eyes, worn over faded jeans and topped off with a heavyweight denim jacket, its simplicity revealed perfection. I was speechless. I kissed Danny's cheek before grabbing my jacket and keycard.

I got a funny vibe as we waited in the hot food line.

"I feel everyone starring at us," I whispered to Danny. He furtively glanced around while I mindlessly loaded my plate with waffles, bacon and eggs.

"It must be your mountain of food. Eli, you can't possibly eat that much."

Danny speared my waffles and put them on his plate. To this he added eggs and bacon. I glared and retrieved one of the waffles.

At the fruit station I again whispered to Danny, this time with urgency, "Why are people starring at us?"

"I don't know that they are," he whispered back, "If so they're probably wondering how a guy with a mottled face could land a babe who looks like a model."

"A model?" I was a lot of things, but definitely not a model.

"Babe, you must never look in the mirror, because I see a model." I blushed.

Danny and I cleared check-out and went to our usual table which was oddly empty.

"Well, if I'm a model, then you're looking rakishly handsome this morning," I smiled as we sat down next to each other.

"Rakishly? Like a pirate?" Danny asked, surprised.

"Yep, my own personal outlaw. Waffle-thief."

I lifted a crispy waffle to my lips, and Danny squeezed my free hand as I bit in.

I blushed as Cam, Shane, Chloe and Rachel suddenly appeared with their plates.

"Danny, your face!" Rachel exclaimed as she sat down.

"You look awful," Chloe agreed.

"Danny does not look awful," I defended. "He's rakish."

"Ah, love is blind," Rachel teased.

"Danny does look awful, Elizabeth," Shane clarified.

"You'd better take good care of Danny," Cam added. "We wouldn't want him getting more bruises."

"You too, Danny," Chloe added. "Take of Elizabeth."

Chloe's eyes focused like lasers on the neckline of my sweater

Even Danny could not stifle his laughter. I frowned.

"Nothing happened," I said forcefully. "Danny was ill. I took care of him."

"Nothing?" Chloe giggled. She pointed to my collarbone. "Vampire attack?"

Cam and Shane couldn't hold back anymore. They burst into raucous laughter. Even Rachel joined in.

"Hickey?" I asked, embarrassed.

CHAPTER 28 - ELIZABETH

Three weeks later we left for New York to celebrate Thanksgiving. Danny and I planned on arriving before lunch to spend Wednesday afternoon together.

Our parents were arriving later. It had been so long. Just the same, I was anxious. Several times Danny and I had discussed what we thought our parents suspected about us, and when we would tell them.

"Mom will take one look at us and she'll know," I had fretted.

"Randi will approve. She's known me all my life," Danny pointed out.

"Which is exactly why she won't approve. Mom knows everything about you."

"Eli, your parents love me."

"Not this way. Mom and Dad have never once said, 'Elizabeth when are you and Danny hooking up?'"

Danny laughed. "Eli, you're embarrassed. You don't want your parents thinking that you're, that you and I are... Eli, you're almost nineteen years old!"

"Enough! Okay. You're right!" I had protested.

Danny couldn't stop laughing. He'd hit a sore spot. Danny and I had been together for nearly a month. Why hadn't we had sex yet? I certainly wanted to, and I feared what Danny might do if we didn't.

All the staff at The Regency knew Danny and I. Whenever we were in New York, the Jacobs and the Newmans stayed at the elegant hotel on Park Avenue.

The expertly professional staff greeted us warmly. My favorite bellman that I'd known since toddlerhood hugged me as he took our bags. The front desk manager who had known us even longer was equally happy. She embraced us and squealed, "How great to see you! Your suites are ready."

Our parents had each reserved spacious two-bedroom suites. The bedroom with the two queen-sized beds was mine. Mom and Dad would take the large master. The Newman's had the identical set-up down the hall. It was childhood all over again.

My cast had been removed on Monday. I could wear matching shoes again! I felt so free slipping my hand in Danny's while we playfully strolled the avenue me in flat black ankle boots. It was cathartic.

Our first stop was Bergdorf Goodman's. I loved their cozy restaurant where you could order the Gotham salad, their take on a Cobb.

"I know where you can get the best Cobb Salad in every city in America," I boasted and Danny laughed good-naturedly.

"So who makes the best one, Eli?"

"The Polo Lounge, of course!" I declared.

Next up, the fifth floor where the trendy designers are sold. Danny attacked a section of blouses with gusto and pulled several off the rack.

"Size zero, right hon?" he called to me.

I was a few feet away deciding between two sweaters. "Or extra small," I added.

"Try these," Danny suggested, and he thrust hangers at me. The sales girl promptly took them to start a dressing room. I loved shopping with Danny! He made it fun!

Then it was on to Barney's where I enjoyed selecting clothes for Danny. I was pleased that he liked my taste. With his physique, everything looked exquisite, though Danny's bruised cheek was the one feature that kept him from being truly perfect.

When we returned to The Regency, it was time to unpack and wait for our parents.

Luggage emptied, I crossed the hall to Danny. He was calmly lying on his bed reading a book. Danny smiled and took a swig of beer. I sat down on the edge of his bed and held my head in my hands. Danny put down the beer bottle and rubbed my neck and shoulders. His firm kneading ordinarily relaxed me, but not today.

"Eli, your knots have knots," Danny said softly. "Have the rest of my beer."

"I'm a wreck," I pouted and swatted the proffered beer away. "So what if your parents find out about us? We're telling them tonight. At dinner."

Before I could object, the door to the suite opened.

"They're here!" I quivered, and we ran into the living room.

"We thought we'd find Elizabeth here," Dad chuckled. "Our suite was empty."

"Daddy!" I exclaimed. He looked so handsome in his navy blazer, light blue button-down shirt and pressed chinos. How I missed him.

Everyone embraced, happy to see each other!   Until Ellen noticed Danny's face.

"Daniel, your face!" Ellen exclaimed and touched his bruise.

Danny winced and jerked his head from her touch. "Rugby, Mom. I'm okay."

"Have you seen a doctor?" Ellen demanded.

"Yes, Mom. Nothing's damaged. It's a bruise. It's going to take time."

"You should have seen him. Danny's face was swollen and purple," I added.

"Thanks, Elizabeth," Danny snarled.

"You're welcome," I answered sweetly, and I flashed him my most charming smile.

"It looks rakish, doesn't it?" Danny said and grinned at me.

CHAPTER 29 - ELIZABETH

The girl my parents had tearfully said good-bye to in August was not the same one sitting between them in the Town Car. And they didn't know it.

I was a fidgety mess. As a diversion I scanned my camera looking for the photos I had taken of Danny's bruised face directly after the game.

"Dad," I said handing him the camera, "Do you think I should show this to Ellen?" I smiled mischievously.

Dad grimaced. "Hmm. But it might calm her to see the improvement."

Mom reached across to take a look. "Ouch! I wouldn't show that to Ellen."

Dad retrieved the camera and leafed through the other photos.

"Are you Danny's personal photographer?"

"No, Dad," I flushed. "These are of my friends. I'm compiling flash drives as gifts."

"Elizabeth," Mom demanded eye contact, "I hope you're not copying Daniel's bad habits. We know you've had a crush on him since you were little…"

"Mom, I'm not twelve anymore. I don't have a crush on Danny," I interrupted. For the first time this was the truth.

"Sometimes girls want to fit in with a boy who's special to them," she lectured.

"Mom! I thought you trusted me," I protested.

"When you were younger Daniel often influenced you."

"Danny won't let me do anything," I snapped angrily. "He's very protective."

"Elizabeth, I love Daniel," Mom said gently. "Dad and I don't want you getting dragged into his world."

Dragged into his world? If only she knew how eagerly I had entered that world!

And Danny wanted us to tell them we were a couple? I had to stop him.

Simultaneously both cars arrived at the restaurant and our families entered together. Inside, Danny helped me remove my jacket. I noticed he was wearing the baby blue cashmere Burberry scarf we'd purchased at Bergdorf's. It matched his eyes perfectly.

"It's off," I whispered.

"Eli, we agreed," Danny whispered curtly.

"I'll explain later. We can't tell them," I insisted through gritted teeth.

Mom smiled at us, a complete turnaround from only minutes earlier.

She didn't blink an eye at Danny's good manners. Mom expected it.

The owner gave my parents a warm welcome and showed us to a quiet table in the back. Whenever my parents visited New York they dined at this small Upper Eastside Italian restaurant. Understated and elegant; the perfect neighborhood restaurant if your neighborhood consisted of multi-million dollar apartments housing New York's foremost citizens.

Dinner passed comfortably and in the end, I shared the photo of Danny's injured face with Steve and Ellen.

"Danny, why didn't you call me?" Ellen exclaimed. "Elizabeth, why didn't you?"

"Mom, I wouldn't let Eli call you. I knew how upset you'd be, and I knew it would fade before you saw me."

As the busboy cleared the table, and the waiter brought dessert menus, Danny asked, "Do you mind if I take Eli to see the balloons being filled?" Danny was referring to the giant balloons for tomorrow morning's Macy's Thanksgiving Day parade.

Danny hadn't shared this plan with me. I'd never seen the balloons being filled!

We kissed our parents good-night, and stopped to get our coats. Danny held mine open as I slipped my arms into the sleeves. We smiled at each other and buttoned up. Then I pulled on my gloves while Danny unfolded his scarf beneath his coat lapels.

"Am I dressed warmly enough?" I asked.

Danny removed his scarf and tied it loosely around my neck. "You are now," he said, and he kissed my forehead. Then Danny wrapped his arm around my shoulders and led me through the glass door to the street. I was certain my mother had not missed this intimate moment.

"What happened?" Danny asked as we hailed a cab to take us to the Upper West Side. He frowned as I explained. "Elizabeth, we're telling them tonight. No more secrets!"

Soon we reached Central Park West in front of the magnificent Museum of Natural History where the giant balloons were being inflated. What a sight! It was like being invited to an exclusive gala, where people of all ages gathered in the cold. Everyone was giddy, having a good time. It was like arriving at a winter carnival. The festive atmosphere filled us with joy and spontaneity. Danny and I felt like kids again.

Thankfully street vendors were also out. Danny bought me a navy knit cap that I immediately donned. I didn't care how funny it looked. Brrrr! It was cold!

Though gloves made photography difficult, I managed to take a lot of shots. I was photographing Danny hamming it up, when a tourist family approached us.

"If you'd like, I'll take photos of you," the husband offered.

Danny and I struck several poses. Then Danny approached the man and spoke to him so I wouldn't hear. Danny returned to my side and lifted my chin. Gazing into each other's eyes our lips met and "click," the camera captured the exact moment of our kiss.

Danny and I continued south, holding each other close for warmth.

"Let's see those pictures," he said.

A tingle went up my spine as we looked at the viewfinder. The photo of the kiss was incredibly romantic. These were the photos capturing the night we fell in love, even if we couldn't admit it quite yet.

Stopped under the street light, with Central Park as our backdrop, we turned to each other. With his gloved hand, Danny lifted my chin upwards.

"It will be good," he reassured me. "Mike and Randi will be happy for us."

For punctuation, Danny kissed me. His warmth spread throughout me. Danny's confidence made me believe anything was possible.

Danny's strong arms holding me close radiated love. Through his jacket I felt the rapid beating of Danny's heart and I knew we both felt the same.

"You're shivering, baby. Let's go back and order hot chocolate?"

Mmm. Hot chocolate! I didn't even need to drink it. My hands wrapped around the steaming mug would be sufficient.

I gazed at Danny with dreamy emerald eyes. The warmth of his smile stopped my shivers. Another powerful kiss melted me.

Danny and I returned to the hotel shortly after eleven, still somewhat frozen, because it had taken several blocks, before we found a cab. At the bar we ordered a pot of hot chocolate to have delivered to my suite. Freshly whipped cream and a plate of cookies completed the order.

That left enough time for the unavoidable - speaking with my parents.

My parents sat in the living room, relaxed and drinking coffee from fine china cups when we entered the suite. Were they waiting up for us? Did they suspect our agenda? I was getting paranoid.

"Let's see your photos," Dad requested. "I always went home for Thanksgiving."

Automatically I handed Dad the camera. Danny smirked. Huh?

Very politely he asked Mom, "Is it alright if I hang out with Eli for a while? We ordered hot chocolate from room service."

"Elizabeth needs warming up, Daniel?" Point made, Mom. The scarf and kiss at the restaurant had not been missed.

Dad returned my camera and locked eyes with me. "Excellent photos, Elizabeth. Interesting subject matter," he added. Dad's green eyes twinkled mischievously.

Damned digital camera and damn my own stupidity. Now I understood why Danny smirked when I handed Dad the camera. I'd forgotten the pictures of us.

"Thanks, Daddy. I'm going to change," I quickly announced, and I kissed his cheek before disappearing into my bedroom, grateful for the respite.

While I slipped into pajamas, I heard the hot chocolate being delivered.

"I'll bring it to Elizabeth," I heard Danny say.

"I don't think so," Dad answered.

"I'll get her then," Danny grumbled.

Danny knocked and entered my room. "We are so busted," he whispered.

"And it's all my fault," I moaned.

The hot chocolate waited in the living room. With my parents sipping their coffee, there was something so nineteenth century about the scene. They knew we didn't have chaperones at Donnelly.

With the tray placed on the low coffee table, Danny and I sat cross-legged on the carpet beside it rather than on the couch.

"Have a cookie, Sweetheart." Danny placed the small chocolate rugelah in my mouth and handed me a steaming whipped cream topped mug. With that small gesture, he told my parents what I feared sharing.

The buttery rugelah was delectable, but didn't relieve my stress. I took a tentative sip of the cocoa and placed the mug back on the tray.

"Dad showed me your photos, Elizabeth," Mom said. "He's right. These are excellent photos. Of a young couple on a date."

Why was I so uncomfortable? Of course, Mom had made her disapproval of Danny clear to me earlier. That might be a factor.

"I don't like deceptions, Elizabeth," Dad added.

I stared at the tray, wanting to drown in the hot chocolate pot. Then Danny protectively wrapped his arm around my shoulders. His love buoyed me.

"Eli's my girlfriend now," he confidently announced.

There, it was said. I furtively glanced at my parents for their reaction.

"We can see that," Mom answered. She hadn't formulated an opinion.

"When did this happen?" Dad asked. His smile stoked my confidence.

"It just sort of happened," I stammered. Explaining my love life was awkward. "From the moment we found each other at Donnelly we've been spending a lot of time together. Then when I busted my ankle, Danny took care of me."

I couldn't help smiling. Danny squeezed my shoulder.

"It's been about a month since our first real date." I added.

"I'm not really surprised," Mom said. "You've always been so close, but you were kids. Now Elizabeth has become a beautiful young woman and Danny, you're an attractive young man. It makes perfect sense."

"You didn't think we'd approve. Are you happy?" Dad asked.

I looked at Danny. "More than I've ever been. We know each other so well. It's so easy for us," I conceded.

"I've never felt this way before," Danny confessed.

"We've always loved you, Danny." I nodded my agreement with Mom. "You were inseparable as kids. We'd watch you at the beach. Danny would snap a towel; you'd splash him. There was always a lot of playful teasing. Ellen and I would sometimes speculate, 'wouldn't it be funny if?' Now 'if' seems to have happened."

CHAPTER 30 - ELIZABETH

After a late Saturday evening of downtown clubbing, Danny and I enjoyed brunch with our parents before driving back to Donnelly on Sunday. I was drained. What a weekend! Breakfast at editor Jasper Willis' Central Park West apartment provided the most amazing view of the parade. Thanksgiving dinner with the mayor at Gracie Manson followed. With theater on Friday evening, we had packed the entire New York experience into four short days.

At noon the valet brought my car around and Danny and I kissed and hugged both sets of parents before setting off.

Danny was driving. I could turn my brain off for the duration. If I closed my eyes, Danny would assume I was sleeping. He could listen to the Giants-Redskins game on the radio. That was fine by me.

Once we entered the New York State Thruway in Spring Valley, Danny took my hand.

"What's up, Eli?" he asked, seeing through my rouse.

"Nothing," I answered too quickly, my eyes opening.

"E?" he gently pressed. Then Danny lifted my hand and kissed it. "Elizabeth, you are a terrible liar. I know what's up. We've just spent an incredible weekend together," he smiled.

I smiled in return and nodded, "Yeah, we did, didn't we."

"Our parents are happy for us. Now you're wondering what's next."

I turned toward the windshield. I would not like whatever Danny said next. Good news does not require such long build-ups.

"I've been doing the same. I don't have an answer." Danny's explanation came slowly and deliberately. "And I won't during this car ride. I may not have one soon."

"Oh," was all I could say. I was unable to face him.

"You're angry?"

"No. I'm disappointed." I wanted to move forward, not stagnate.

Danny gave my hand a quick squeeze. "Elizabeth, bear with me. Finals start in two weeks. We both want to do well." He smiled. "Lovely as a distraction as you are, it's not the time to obsess over each other. We need to keep our heads clear."

All too soon, Danny was parking in the Berkeley Hall lot. Then he effortlessly removed our luggage from the car.

Despite my protestations, Danny insisted on accompanying me to my room. By the elevator was a poster advertising Saturday's winter formal. My roommates were going. So far I didn't have a date.

I stood with my hands on my hips and glared.

"The formal is Saturday," I blurted. "Are you taking someone else?"

Danny looked at me as though I were nuts.

"Someone else? Of course not, Eli. Are you waiting for me to ask you?"

"I thought I was your obvious choice. I am your girlfriend." His lack of response spoke volumes. "Everyone is going, even Rachel," I said bitterly.

Danny sighed. "So you want me to take you?"

I was furious. My friends who weren't dating anyone were going, but me, I didn't have a date. It made no sense.

"I don't know. It might be nice."

"Elizabeth, will you go with me to the formal?"

"No, Daniel. I won't go with anyone I have to demand an invitation from. It should have been your idea. You should have asked me weeks ago if you really wanted to go. I could have bought a new gown while I was in New York!"

I was disappointed, and I wanted Danny to know. It was the formal, damn it!

The elevator ride was silent. Entering the suite, Danny dumped the luggage on the floor of my room. He practically threw the Bergdorf bags at me. Why was he so angry?

Danny grabbed my shoulders, looked fiercely into my eyes and seethed; "There's another formal in the spring. Consider this your official invitation. That's more than enough time to get your hair and nails done."

Then Danny pulled me close and crushed his lips to mine. My pulse raced. My lips parted, welcoming him. I was angry at my response.

The door to the suite opened. Rachel entering abruptly ended our kiss.

"Hey, Rach. Welcome back," Danny, still holding me, smirked.

Rachel rolled her eyes and replied, "Why am I not surprised to find you here?"

"Don't you know? I've asked the Dean if I can be your fourth roommate."

"What!" We laughed. Danny was so obviously teasing her.

"C'mon Rach. They're not that liberal. Yet." She flushed red with embarrassment.

Danny picked up his case and backpack. "I'll see you later," he said, and he kissed my forehead. "Rach, I reserved the editing bay tomorrow afternoon." And Danny left.

CHAPTER 31 - ELIZABETH

When we returned from dinner, I stopped inside the lobby of Berkeley Hall to confirm with Danny that we were studying tonight. Before answering, he pulled me into the stairwell.

"Not tonight. I need to decompress."

"Decompress?" What did that mean?

"It's been a stressful weekend," Danny explained.

"It has?" I scrunched my face, puzzled.

Danny smiled and kissed my head. "Not you. Being around our parents."

I had already put it behind me. Surprising, Danny had not.

"I'm staying in tonight to read and play guitar." Danny kissed my head again.

"I've never heard you play."

"You haven't?" I shook my head no. "Then come by later. After nine. I need to do class work first. I'm not ready to headline, but I think I'm fair."

At about twenty after nine I knocked softly on Danny's door. He greeted me with his guitar in one hand and a joint in the other. Danny had changed into faded jeans and a well-worn chambray shirt that matched his eyes and showed off his physique. The effect was hypnotic.

"Where are your roommates?" I asked as I tentatively sat down on the bed.

Danny took a long drag on the joint and replied, "They went to The Cellar."

"Why didn't you go with them?"

Danny took another drag. "I don't feel like being social tonight."

"Should I go?"

"Of course not. I didn't mean you."

After another drag Danny said, "Here, hold this," and he handed me the joint.

Danny sat down beside me and began to play his guitar. I stared at his graceful fingers dancing across the strings. The most beautiful melody came off the instrument as he played, "For the First Time," and Danny gave me a flirtatious grin that melted me.

The first time? Our first time? Now I was the one who needed something to take the edge off. I glanced at the joint. What the hell? I brought it up to my lips, inhaled, and …broke into a coughing fit.

Laughing, Danny put down his guitar and rubbed my back. "Easy, Eli.

Don't inhale so deeply until you're used to it."

"Right," I choked out.

Danny handed me a water bottle. I took a few sips. Then Danny took another drag and handed me back the joint so he could continue playing. I took another, albeit smaller, hit and didn't choke this time.

The combination of music and pot; I couldn't help smiling. After a few more hits, Danny took back the joint. Then he tapped it out in a ceramic ashtray.

"Why'd you do that?" I asked in a dreamy voice.

"Eli, you're enjoying it too much," Danny smirked. "I don't want you wasted."

Danny turned his attention back to the guitar, but I started giggling, unable to stop.

"See what I mean?" Danny laughed, "I'm turning you into a delinquent, Eli."

"No you're not. I'm not. I'm just feeling..."

"Me too," Danny replied, and he put down his guitar.

Then Danny took my face in his strong but gentle hands and crushed his lips to mine. His probing tongue entered my mouth, tangling with my own, exploring.

Two hearts beat rapidly as one. Danny's hands moved under my sweater, gripping my back. Skin against skin; this was hot. I'd wanted this all day.

"What am I going to do with you?" Danny whispered by my ear and I shivered.

"Whatever you want, I'm yours." I wanted Danny so badly.

"This was not in my plans," Danny said softly, withdrawing his hands.

I turned away, unable to hide my disappointment and quietly cried.

"Eli, don't cry." Danny said gently, holding me in his arms.

"What do you expect? Because I don't know what your plan is. Neither do you. I was just going along and once again I've made wrong assumptions and I'm getting hurt. Maybe I shouldn't have come here tonight. Sorry I intruded."

"Don't say that. Eli, you're never an intrusion. You're the most amazing girl I've ever known." Danny sat up straight. His sapphire eyes masked deep conflict. "Damn it, Eli! I didn't want this to happen. I'm falling in love with you and I don't want to be."

Danny was falling in love with me! He didn't want to be. I was as confused as Danny. Tears fell again. Danny held me and let me cry. When I wouldn't stop, he held me closer and stroked my hair.

"C'mon, Eli," he said tenderly, "Don't cry. I thought you'd be happy hearing that I'm in love with you."

"I am. It's what you said next. You don't want to be."

"I want to be. Just not yet."

"I always thought when a man told me he was in love with me it would be followed by, you know, love."

"And all the problems of the world would be solved? You've been watching too many Miranda Jordan films, Elizabeth. We're not fictional. I'm a real man and you're a real woman. It's more complicated in real life."

"No, you're what's more complicated. I have never met anybody as complicated as you."

Danny lifted my chin up to look directly at me. "It keeps me from being boring, doesn't it." I smiled. "You wouldn't want a boring boyfriend anymore than I want a boring girlfriend."

"What I'd really like is a boyfriend who's consistent and makes sense."

Danny cuddled me to his chest. "I know," he said softly. "I just can't make promises yet."

"Daniel, what am I going to do about you?"

"Love me?" Danny gave me an impish little boy grin. "Love me despite my flaws?"

"Why do you have this power over me?" I blurted out in frustration.

"Because you love me?"

"It's so unfair." I adjusted myself onto my knees so I looked directly into the deep blue eyes that always melted me. I reached for Danny's hands.

"Danny," I trembled. I'd never confessed my love to a man. "You are the most infuriating man I have ever met. You drive me insane. I should tell you to go to hell, but I can't, because I love you."

I'd never seen Danny smile so brightly. His upturned lips quivered. The effect was electric.

Then Danny stared into my eyes with power and depth I had never experienced. "Elizabeth, you are the most beautiful girl I have ever known, both inside and out. You have the patience of a saint for putting up with me. I'm glad you haven't told me to go to hell, although you probably should have. Please don't, though. I'd be miserable without you honey, because I love you. More than anything."

Danny pulled me by my hands on top of him and tumbled me to his side. My hands clasped around his neck and he held me as close as possible. Our lips parted, joining us together, bound by love.

Danny and I kissed unlike any other time, his mouth forcefully claiming mine. Our hearts beat with an uncontrollable intensity. When we finally broke apart to breath, Danny whispered, "I love you, Eli."

"I love you too, Danny."

"I love how that sounds," Danny smiled, relieved that he'd finally confessed his true feelings for me.

Danny's kisses intensified. His hands crept beneath my sweater, touching every inch of my body with purpose. I gasped from the excitement, and I thought I would die when Danny lifted my sweater over my head and dropped it on the floor.

My fingers were shaking. I clumsily unbuttoned Danny's shirt. Then his fingers deftly unhooked my bra and pushed it off my shoulders. I finally removed his shirt.

I had seen Danny without a shirt before, but this was overwhelming. The sight of Danny's sculpted chest and the realization that it belonged to me, made me shiver. My bare skin against Danny's tingled. Never had I felt these sensations.

Danny's hands were all over me. There was no stopping. I didn't want him to. Danny had one hand around my back, holding me, and his other hand cupped my breast. I arched my back pressing against Danny's hand, encouraging. I'd never felt such electricity.

Danny's forehead nearly touched mine as I held his face, masculine with stubble. He looked at me in a way I had not seen before; pure love.

Powerful emotions had overtaken us. Without words, I knew how he felt. It was the same for me. It was impossible to contain the love I wanted to share with this incredible man.

"Tonight's our night, babe," Danny whispered.

Danny stretched his arm across me to reach a drawer in the nearby desk. I giggled as he crushed me while his fingers found what they were searching for; a foil condom packet.

"It might hurt a little the first time, but I'll be gentle," Danny promised.

I was soaring with happiness and shivering in fear. I wanted this so badly, but the unknown frightened me.

Our lips smashed together again, increasing our desire, while in the distance we heard Cam and Shane return to the suite.

My inexperienced hands struggled to open the button of Danny's jeans while his expertly opened mine. While I fumbled with his zipper, Danny pushed my jeans off and I eagerly lifted my hips, making removal easier.

Danny grinned as he stared at me lying on the bed, now wearing only a pale pink lace thong. "God, you're gorgeous, Eli," he whispered. I smiled brighter than ever, before kissing Danny again.

Finally, I had Danny's jeans open. He took my hand and guided it to him. I couldn't believe I was doing this. My heart beat even more rapidly. I freaked, but in a good way. I'd never seen a naked man before! Or felt one! I had no idea Danny would be so large, or so hard. How would he fit? This was going to hurt.

Without knocking, Shane bounced into the room. "Hey Danny, you should have..."

Danny collapsed on top of me, shielding my nakedness from Shane's view.

"Don't you know how to knock?" Danny scowled.

Shane turned crimson realizing for the first time that it was me laying beneath Danny.

"Sorry. I didn't ...," he stammered.

"Can't I make love to my girlfriend without you barging in?" Danny snapped.

"Girlfriend? I ... It was unlocked," Shane answered awkwardly, and he quickly backed out of the room.

Our mood had been broken. Danny lifted himself off of me so I could breath again. He propped himself on one elbow and clasped my hand. I enjoyed watching Danny's eyes take in my unclothed body, enjoying me fully, while I stared at his.

"Why didn't we do this last night when our parents were at the theater?" Danny asked.

"You were still being stupid?" I teased, and I pulled him to me for a kiss.

"Tonight isn't our night after all, baby."

"I guess not." I smiled at Danny. I was disappointed, but I didn't want Danny to think I was disappointed with him.

Danny kissed my hand and held it to his heart. "Eli, it will be our night very soon. I promise. And I will make it perfect for you. We've waited so long. What's another few nights to get it right?"

CHAPTER 32 - ELIZABETH

Saturday dawned as the most awkward day in what had become the most frustrating week. To my dismay, Danny had not found a time when his roommates were sure to be out of their suite. Worse, after declaring our love, I had barely seen him.

Danny hadn't dined with our group more than a couple of times. I hadn't seen him in the library. I hadn't seen him in The Cellar, either. He hadn't come to my room, or invited me to his. It was all very strange.

Danny sent me text messages. All they said was, "I love you" or "I have your car." Nice to know, but not insightful.

I couldn't exactly ask Shane or Cam what was up with their roommate. How would it look if Danny's girlfriend didn't know where he was? Cam and Shane would assume something was seriously wrong between us. And in the back of my head that concerned me the most.

After that magical evening, I wondered if there wasn't something already wrong in our nascent relationship. Had Danny changed his mind? Was he having second thoughts?

I could have called, but it was important for Danny to know I would give him his space when he wanted it. He shouldn't think I was one of those clingy girlfriends.

Tonight was the formal. It was absurd when you thought about it. Chloe was going with Cam as friends. Shane was going with someone I didn't know, and Rachel was going with a group of film department friends.

I, the only one with the boyfriend who sent love text messages, was home with no plans. Forget the formal. It was Saturday night. Danny should at least have made other plans with me, if for no other reason than as a peace offering.

Faced with watching everyone primping, I decided to go off-campus. The nearest decent mall was an hour away, near Albany. Retail therapy would do me good. I could jump-start my Chanukah shopping.

When I arrived in the snow-dusted parking lot, my car was gone! "Daniel!" I growled. Angry, I speed-dialed him.

"Hi baby," he answered cheerfully.

"Where is my car, Daniel?" I demanded.

"Don't you want to know where I am?" Danny asked innocently.

"I know where you are. You're in my car, which I want back. Now!"

I sounded like a spoiled brat, but I was desperate to leave Donnelly.

"I'm running an important errand. I'll be awhile," Danny explained.

"Great!" I answered sarcastically. "What am I supposed to do? I've got to get out of here, Daniel."

"Eli, calm down."

"I can't. All anyone is talking about is the formal. Then you're not with me. I don't even know where you are." My voice was rising to near hysteria.

"Take my car," he suggested.

"Why didn't you take your car? Then I would have mine."

"There's three inches of fresh snow in the parking lot," Danny pointed out. "Uh, yeah Eli, you can't take my car either then."

"We're in upstate New York! Why don't you get a car that's not so useless?"

"Eli, chill, honey."

"I will not chill! It's Saturday! Did you ever think I might want to use my own car on a Saturday, Daniel?"

"I did. But this is important. You'll see tonight."

"Tonight? You never asked if I was available, Daniel."

"Elizabeth, you're my girlfriend. It's Saturday night."

"You never asked me to keep myself free."

Danny took an exasperated breath before continuing.

"I didn't know I needed to. I thought it was a given that my girlfriend spends Saturday night with me," he pointed out.

"I'm still angry about the formal."

"I know, babe. I'm trying to make it up to you."

"You are? Then I can't wait to see you," I said gleefully.

"That's my girl," I could hear his smile. "Thanks, Sweetheart. I love you."

"I love you too, Danny."

An afternoon spent in the library was preferable to watching Chloe and Rachel primp. Neither had been sympathetic when I bemoaned not attending the formal

"What does it matter?" Rachel said in an uncharacteristically harsh tone. "Everyone knows you're with Danny. So what if you don't show him off one time."

That hurt. I didn't think I went around "showing him off."

"Danny isn't any boyfriend," Chloe added. "He's the hottest guy at Donnelly and he's crazy about you. That's all that matters."

They didn't get it. All the other girls at Donnelly who had boyfriends were spending the afternoon getting their hair and nails done so they would look perfect tonight. I had never been one of them. I wanted to be one.

The library was relatively empty, and I settled into a distant cubicle wanting to keep hidden. Distracted, I concentrated on tonight's date with Danny instead of my books. Once I got past my disappointment over the formal, Rachel and Chloe were probably right. In the long run what did it matter?

It mattered when I heard a girl whisper to her friend, "Look. It's Elizabeth Jacobs."

"Then maybe it's just a rumor, and she isn't dating Danny Newman," her friend replied in a hopeful whisper. "He might be available."

Enough! With uncharacteristic boldness, I strode over and tapped on the cubicle wall to get their attention. When the girls realized it was the object of their gossip, they froze them in place. Yeah girls, you're so busted.

"Excuse me," I said politely. "I couldn't help but overhear. Since you wondered, I'm here studying. Finals start next week, and I expect to ace mine. As for my boyfriend, he's definitely not available." And he wouldn't want you if he was.

I returned to my cubicle, smirking over their embarrassment and armed with renewed resolve to make tonight's date unforgettable.

There was under an hour left to prep for Danny when I returned from the Library. I had no idea what we were doing or what I should wear?

After examining my wardrobe and rejecting several choices, I selected a short denim skirt and the yellow and white print silk top Danny selected at Bergdorf's. I pulled my hair into a ponytail held by a yellow ribbon. It would accentuate the drawstring neckline I would enjoy having Danny untie. Finally, I dimmed the overhead light and lit some candles. There! Ready!

Seven o'clock came and went and I found myself pacing. I knew Danny wouldn't stand me up, so why was I such a bundle of nerves?

Danny said he was making up for us missing the formal, but how? There was only one way I could think of. But what was he planning that required an all day disappearance?

The knock on the door that I had been waiting all day for finally came. My heart caught in my throat and I grinned. Taking a deep breath, I opened the door. There was my love, looking like a G.Q. model; male perfection in a ski jacket.

Danny, his backpack on his shoulder, was carrying a large shopping bag. He entered, closed the door and locked it. Danny was wearing the biggest grin ever. I threw myself into his arms. His glee was infectious.

Danny's rosy cheeks were cold from the December air and smarted as I took them in my hands. "I missed you so much," I murmured, and I kissed him.

"This is the welcome I was hoping for." Danny grinned.

"You're ice cold," I said, and he shrugged.

I lifted Danny's cashmere scarf from his collar, pressed the length against his cheeks and kissed him again. Danny smiled as the fringe tickled. "How's that?" I asked.

"Baby, I feel warmer already," he answered.

Danny kissed me and moved into the room. I watched as he gently placed his backpack on the desk, barely avoiding a candle. That was not the fire I wanted to start tonight.

Meanwhile, the sizeable shopping bag remained on the floor.

"Petrossian? You went to New York?" I asked in disbelief. I was dumbstruck by the shopping bag from New York's finest caviar purveyor.

"Sorry I'm late. There was traffic," was all Danny answered.

He was so nonchalant, as though it was a typical weekday commute.

"You went to Petrossian?" I repeated as Danny removed his jacket and scarf and hung them on one of the colorful metal hooks affixed by the door. Underneath he was wearing a white dress shirt with jeans and loafers.

"Preppy looks nice on you," I said as I touched his softly stubbled cheek.

Danny pulled me into his arms and brushed an errant lock of hair off of my face.

"And Santa Monica socialite looks beautiful on you, Elizabeth," he quietly laughed as our lips met for another kiss.

When Danny released me, he returned to his backpack and grinned like the Cheshire Cat.

"I have something for you," he said playfully.

I moved closer, anxious to see. Danny opened the backpack and reached in without looking. His hand moved around, searching. For what?

"No, that's not it." Danny's hand searched around again. "Neither is that," he teased.

"Danny!" I squealed.

"Patience, young lady," Danny laughed. It was like waiting for Santa Claus to find the gift buried at the bottom of his sack.

Danny reached in once more and found what he was looking for. He eagerly handed me a small light blue box tied with white satin; it's origin unmistakable.

I gasped. "Tiffany's," I said excitedly.

"A little something to apologize for being a jerk and not taking you to the formal. You would have been the prettiest girl there."

"This is not a little something. You drove almost seven hours!"

This was love.

"Aren't you going to open the box?" Danny laughed. I blushed.

At this point, I didn't care what was inside. With my hands shaking, I pulled on the white satin and the ribbon came undone. Inside the light blue box was a small, darker blue fabric-covered box that I removed. Nervous with excitement, I could barely open it, but I did.

Inside was a medium-sized gold Peretti heart on a slender gold chain. My breath was taken away.

"It's beautiful," I gasped.

"Let me." Danny reached for the box and his hands lingered on mine. "You're shaking. Hasn't anyone bought you jewelry before?"

"Only my parents. Maybe, Grandma," I answered awkwardly.

"Then I'll have to shop for you more often."

"Have you ever bought jewelry for a girl before?"

"No. There hasn't been anyone I wanted to buy jewelry for."

I was his first! I couldn't help grinning.

Danny removed the necklace from the box. From behind, he clasped it around my neck while I lifted my ponytail. His delicate touch almost made me faint.

Next Danny removed the ribbon from my hair and my waves tumbled down past my shoulders. As hoped, he untied the neckline of my shirt revealing my cleavage.

"You look perfect," he declared.

"No, I don't. I'm too short."

I pressed myself tightly against Danny. Like a parent measuring their child for a growth spurt, I flattened my hand and ran it from the top of my head to his chest. The top of my head measured just below his shoulder.

"I like having a petite girlfriend."

"Danny…"

"And she has to have magical green eyes and wavy auburn hair," he grinned.

"Danny!" I squealed.

Danny reached his hands to my face and lifted my chin. Our lips met, then they parted for our tongues to explore. It was intoxicating. My head spun, like being drunk.

"Look in the mirror and see how beautiful you are," Danny murmured.

I stumbled into the bedroom and stared at my reflection. Was that really me? The girl starring back was flushed and glowing with newfound confidence.

Danny was opening Petrossian packages, and I wrapped my arms around his waist.

"I love it," I told him, "and I love you."

Danny grinned. "Tonight is all about you babe," and he kissed me. Swoon!

Danny was well prepared. He had even purchased a mother-of-pearl spoon to properly serve the caviar for the blinis we assembled by layering caviar, crème fraiche and chopped egg.

Finally, Danny reached into his backpack, pulled out a bottle of champagne and a larger Tiffany box, this one not gift-wrapped. He opened the box and removed two elegant crystal champagne flutes. Danny had left no detail unaccounted for.

"Moet," I noted as Danny picked up the champagne bottle. He smiled, pleased with himself. Then Danny released the cork. Pop!

My eyes opened wide, startled by the explosive sound, before Danny carefully poured. We held up our flutes, and he said, "To you, baby."

Then we tapped the flutes together, Danny's sapphire eyes connecting with my emeralds, melting me.

I took a big gulp of the champagne. Nerves threatened to derail me.

"Elizabeth! It's champagne. Little sips." Danny cautioned.

I shrugged playfully. "Oh well!" I giggled.

Danny cued his iPhone. "My Elizabeth playlist," he announced.

Specially compiled for this evening, the music floated out of the docking station's speakers. Then Danny blew out the candles, leaving the weak desk lamp to light the room. He turned the fixture to face the far wall, creating a soft, dim effect.

"There's only one fire I want to start this evening," Danny said, and I gasped.

I was floating. All my senses were heightened. An electrically charged atmosphere surrounded us as we ate the tantalizingly delicious blinis, drank more champagne and made and ate more blinis.

The champagne had the desired effect. I relaxed enough to enjoy what the evening ahead was certain to hold.

Slow, romantic melodies filled the air. I drank more champagne while Danny held me against his muscular chest and we swayed in each other's arms. It was not really dancing; more an excuse to hold each other; our own private formal.

Danny reached for my flute and placed it on the table. I was buzzed and his strong arms steadied me. I gazed at Danny's perfect features. My heart thumped wildly.

Our eyes did not leave each other as Danny cupped my face for a long, blissful kiss. My hands gripped his hair pulling him even closer. I trembled as Danny's hands moved down my side and pulled me into his body. Pressed against the wall, I gasped as his hardness probing against my skirt.

"What are we doing out here?" Danny whispered. His breath on my ear made me shiver. "We both know what we want."

My insides quaked in tremulous excitement as Danny verbalized the obvious I had been waiting all my life for but was now petrified to experience.

Danny's strong arms lifted me by my waist, our lips glued together. My legs wrapped around his hips as he carried me to the bedroom, and closed and locked the door in one fluid motion. With everyone at the formal, Danny's plan became apparent. Privacy!

With desperate urgency we ripped our clothes off; Danny pulling my blouse over my head and tossing it aside while I struggled with his small shirt buttons. Danny lowered the zipper on my skirt and pushed it down.

As I stepped out of it, I gave up on his buttons and pulled the shirt over his head.

"Babe, do you have any idea how gorgeous you are?" Danny whispered as he stared appreciatively. I wore only my white lace bra and matching thong.

I smiled shyly, uncomfortable with being stared at by a man while unclothed, but pleased by Danny's undeniable enjoyment. I began to shake. I didn't know if I was cold, or if it was from excitement laced with fear.

Danny gathered me in his warm embrace. His broad chest with its sculpted muscles felt secure, and infused me with renewed confidence. I reached around his neck and brought his lips down to mine. He unhooked my bra and slipped it off.

Danny gently squeezed my breast, now cupped in his large hand. "Hey, these are real," he teased, and I blushed. "Eli, you're amazing," he whispered, filled with delight.

I quickly undid the button and zipper on his jeans. Danny pulled a foil packet out of his pocket. He had planned everything. He had even brought condoms.

"We don't need that," I whispered.

"We don't?" He asked, puzzled.

"I took care of it; birth control pills."

"You did that for us?" Danny lit up, touched by my preparation.

I nodded, smiling, pleased that this small gesture had such impact.

"I love you, Danny," I whispered.

"I love you, Elizabeth."

Then I pushed Danny's jeans off his narrow hips. My eyes popped open wide in surprise. Danny wore no underwear! His eyes twinkled at my innocence.

Danny held me to his chest for another embrace. He pressed my rear with his hands, rubbing his front against mine. Then Danny's squeeze dissolved, and his hands took my face and brought our lips together. The force of our kiss carried Danny and me to the bed. I held out my arms reaching for him and Danny joined me, leaning over me, poised.

"You're sure about this? We can wait, if you're not." Danny asked in a gentle whisper.

"I want you so badly."

"I want you too. I love you, baby."

Danny deftly removed my thong, and I gasped, overwhelmed by emotion, suddenly uncertain. Danny was hard, pulsing against me. His hand ran up my thigh with quick, feathery strokes. My pulse quickened. Danny's fingers stroked me where no man had ever touched me before and then they entered me. My breath hitched. Yes, this was what I wanted.

Our lips met again and our bodies entwined. Danny carefully parted my thighs, and I wrapped my legs around his hips. I clutched Danny's back and inhaled deeply as I prepared for him to enter me. Danny glanced at me once more, wanting confirmation.

"Just do it," I whispered. We exchanged smiles. "I'm scared," I admitted.

"I love you, Eli," and Danny crushed his lips to mine to silence me.

Danny slammed into me and I felt a quick thrusting pain, immediately forgotten as the joy of knowing we were now truly one registered. Then I held on tightly as Danny's continued thrusts took me to heights of pleasure I hadn't known were possible.

Afterward, we lay silent and spent in each other's arms. I snuggled close against Danny and he gently pushed an unruly lock of hair off my face. Then he moved his hand to my hip and delicately traced patterns with his fingertip. The warmth of Danny's love radiated through me.

"I hope I didn't hurt you," he whispered.

"Only a little. You were amazing." Then I kissed Danny's cheek.

"Hey, Eli. Guess what? You're not a virgin anymore." We dissolved into laughter. "I've never been with a virgin before."

"You haven't?" That was surprising. Danny was only nineteen and the girls he'd been with were all experienced?

"No," Danny shook his head. "Knowing that a girl as incredible as you wanted me to be her first, that is just so awesome. And without a condom. I've never done that before, either."

"Why not?"

"Besides the obvious?" Danny sat up, troubled. "Dad warned me, 'Pregnancy is the easiest way for a girl to sink her claws into you. Until you want a girl's baby, always use a condom.' Dad must be right. I don't have any half-siblings."

"Danny, I'm sorry," I empathized. "Hey, how come tonight was different?" I asked, upbeat again. I didn't want Steve's foibles ruining our evening.

"I trust you. Eli. You don't want a baby. You want a diploma. Besides, there's nothing for you to gain by having my baby. You're Eliz...Oh my god!" Danny collapsed back against the pillows, laughing.

"What? Danny, what?"

"I just had sex with Elizabeth Jacobs!" Danny exclaimed, suddenly filled with the realization of what the evening had been about.

"And you survived," I scowled.

Danny pulled me into his arms. "I more than survived. This is the best night of my life. Eli, you can't believe how much I love you."

Danny tenderly kissed me. "When can we do this again?" I giggled.

"Whenever and as often as you want. I'm all yours, baby" Danny laughed.

I sat up, suddenly energized. The sheet slipped to my waist. "Danny, you are the most incredible boyfriend!" I exclaimed.

"I'm glad you think so, honey," he chuckled.

"I sure do." I blushed.

"You taught me something valuable tonight," Danny pulled me into his embrace.

"How could I do that?" I didn't know what I was doing.

"I've never been in love before. It makes a big difference, a very big difference."

Danny pressed his lips to mine for a long, passionate kiss. He was as happy as I was, and soon we dozed off, twined in each other's arms.

Not more than an hour later I abruptly woke. My head was pounding. Bile was rising in my throat. I struggled to sit, and that woke Danny.

"Eli, what is it?" he gently asked.

I could hardly speak. I was shaking. "I'm don't feel well," I whimpered.

I bolted from the bed and barely reached the bathroom in time before throwing up.

Danny followed me. Kneeling beside me on the floor, he rubbed my back.

"I'm so cold," I whimpered. My body was shaking.

Danny found my robe hanging on the back of the bathroom door and draped it across my back. I sat on the hard tile floor, poked my arms through the sleeves, and cried. Danny sat behind me, holding me close.

"I've ruined our perfect evening," I wailed.

"Shh, shh," Danny said softly, "No you didn't. This has been the best night I've ever had. It's my fault. I shouldn't have let you drink so much champagne."

"I've had champagne before," I whimpered.

Danny thought a moment. "What did you eat for dinner?"

"I didn't. I had a cookie at the library. I thought we were going out."

"You never had dinner?" Danny exclaimed. "Oh, Eli! No wonder you're sick. You can't drink champagne on an empty stomach."

My lower lip quivered, and I bit it. I couldn't help crying. I'd ruined everything.

"My head hurts so much," I wailed. It was furiously pounding.

Danny kissed my forehead. "I know it does, honey. I'll find some Tylenol."

Danny left for my room. When he returned, his jeans now on, he found I had been sick again. Danny sat back on the floor and held me. He stroked my hair. "You'll be okay, baby."

I threw up one more time and then I did feel better, but my head was pounding.

Danny led me to my room, dressed me in his shirt, and climbed into bed next to me. He held me in his arms and whispered, "I won't leave you, baby. I'll always stay the night."

CHAPTER 33 - DANIEL

Once Elizabeth was sleeping I tiptoed into the living room. As I cleaned up, I reflected on our evening. It had been the capstone of the best day of my life.

While I had been running around New York City, I imagined how excited Eli would be. I had spent the day smiling like a fool and had been rewarded with her love.

Lately I realized how much I'd grown to love Elizabeth in a romantic, adult way. Eli was no longer the girl who'd grown up with me. The incredible beauty lying in bed sleeping was so much more. I hoped I wouldn't blow it.

Rachel entered the suite dressed in her gown and carrying a small clutch. Her usually frizzy hair was blown out straight. I stared. I barely recognized her. I'd never seen Rachel in anything but jeans. Rachel looked good. I realized for the first time she was attractive.

"Rach, you clean up nicely," I said.

"Thanks. What are you doing here? Why don't you have a shirt?"

"I'm cleaning up. Eli is wearing my shirt."

Eagle-eyed, Rachel spied the packages and the crystal flutes. "Petrossian? Tiffany's? Danny, you went to New York!" Rachel was stunned.

"Yeah, so?" I shrugged. "I was making up for not taking Eli to the formal."

"Danny, you are amazing."

"Thanks," I answered as I threw the plates away. "Eli thinks so too."

"That wasn't a compliment. I meant amazing, as in what chutzpah you have."

"At least I'm not boring."

Rachel rolled her eyes. Where she was going with this?

"Look at this. Danny, you're uber-boyfriend, like someone out of a romance novel. No wonder Elizabeth is crazy in love with you."

"What's wrong with spoiling your girlfriend?" I asked innocently.

"Nothing. Except you're the biggest cheating cad at Donnelly. Kate approached me tonight," she whispered.

Kate? I was so busted.

"Kate was disappointed not to see you. She told me she'd enjoyed a couple of 'dates' with you earlier this week. Kate thinks you're hot." Rachel glared at my grin. "Wipe that smug expression off your face Danny

Newman and come back to reality."

Reality. My reality was the angel sleeping in the next room who would be devastated if she heard this conversation. I was thoroughly embarrassed.

"Sorry. One last fling before the wedding," Then I shrugged.

Rachel scowled. "Kate seems to really like you, though why I can't fathom."

"Unlike you Rachel, most girls find me desirable."

"Kate at least has better morals than you. She said she sees you hanging around with as she put it, 'Miranda Jordan's daughter' and wanted to know if anything was going on. I told Kate she should write you off and move on."

"Danny?" Elizabeth called and, I ran to her side.

CHAPTER 34 - ELIZABETH

Danny knelt beside me. My heart fluttered seeing his bare chest. Kindness, or maybe it was love, filled his eyes. Then he clasped my hand and kissed my cheek.

"I thought you had gone," I whispered, my voice cracking from dryness.

"No, never Eli. I promised. I was cleaning up. Then Rachel came home. How are you?"

"My head is killing me." Danny reached for the bottle of Tylenol from my desk. He shook out three caplets and grabbed a glass of water.

"How's your stomach?"

"Better." I smiled as Danny helped me sit and handed me the glass and the Tylenol. It was nice to beloved.

"E, you look awful," Danny smiled and he kissed my forehead, "But beautiful."

"Danny, my head is pounding like jackhammers at a construction trade show."

"I know. I've been there." Danny kissed me again. "I'll get a cold compress."

Danny was back from the bathroom in what seemed an eternity but was probably only moments with a cold, damp washcloth covering a Petrossian ice pack. He applied it to my forehead, and then took my small hands in his strong ones.

The cold felt good. Danny's hands felt better.

"I want to change into sweats. Are you okay if I leave Rachel in charge for a few minutes? I'll be right back."

"Okay," I smiled weakly, and with a kiss to my cheek, Danny left.

I had never been hung over before. It felt completely gross.

Slowly, I rose to my feet. Unexpected wetness between my thighs made me blush. Danny! I grinned and stumbled to the bathroom where I brushed my teeth and washed my face. Despite Danny's reassurance, I was embarrassed. This would either become one of those stories you share a good laugh over or it would mark the end for us.

It wasn't long before Danny returned. My headache was subsiding and Rachel was by my side. Now that she knew I'd enjoyed the evening, she felt free to discuss the formal.

"Rach, how's my girl?" Danny asked as he entered.

"I think she's on the mend."

"Hello! I can speak," I teased them.

"Right. How are you doing, princess?"

"Better. The Tylenol kicked in." Danny smiled. Rachel thoughtfully rose to leave.

"Great necklace. Danny, you certainly know how to treat your girlfriend." Rachel glared at him and left the room.

I lifted an eyebrow, confused. Had Danny and Rachel been fighting while I slept?

Danny locked the door, turned off the light and slid into bed. Wrapping his arms around me, Danny kissed my hair and whispered, "You smell nice. Let's get some sleep."

My earlier vulnerabilities vanished. I loved how secure he made me feel.

"They're gone," Danny whispered the next morning, waking me.

I blinked hard. The cold sun filtered through the border of the window shade was glaring in contrast to the warmth of Danny's limbs tangled around mine.

"What?" Huh?

"Chloe and Rachel. We're alone."

It took my sleepy brain a moment to digest this news. Then I understood exactly what Danny meant. My heart started thumping wildly and I grinned.

"How are you feeling?"

"Good as new," I assured Danny.

"How about if I make you feel better than new?"

"Oh, yes!" I giggled and Danny's lips devoured me as he climbed on top.

This was even better than last night. I knew what to expect and I wasn't frightened or in a champagne-induced fog.

After, we lay in each other's arms silently reveling in the pleasure of being together, enjoying gentle kisses and caresses.

"I want everyone to know you're mine," Danny said as he fingered the gold heart.

"Last night changes everything, doesn't it?"

"That it does," Danny replied.

Our fingers entwined and we made love again. Yesterday I had been alone and cranky. Today I was with the man I loved.

CHAPTER 35 - ELIZABETH

The first substantial snow storm came during study week. There had previously been a few dustings but this time nearly a foot was predicted!

Overnight the snow began falling. When I woke, I peeked under the window shade. My eyes danced in delight, thrilled to see the clean white blanket below and more thick flakes coming down. My first real snow storm!

I threw my old ski bib on over long underwear and a turtleneck. Then I shoved my feet into snow boots, grabbed my parka and flew down the stairs to Danny. I had seen snow before, but only in Aspen. This was different.

A sleepy-eyed Shane responded to my urgent knocking.

"Where's Danny?" I asked breathlessly.

"Asleep. Like me," he snarled.

"Sorry." In my excitement I had ignored the fact that it was only just past seven. I dashed into Danny's bedroom, letting my jacket drop to the floor and approached his sleeping body. I shook his arm.

"Danny, wake up!" I urged, and I sat down on the bed. One eye slowly opened and attempted to focus.

"Eli? Are you going skiing?" Danny asked in a sleepy haze.

"No! It's snowing! A lot. Danny, we need to make a snowman!"

"Thanks for the weather report. By the way, I finished my history paper."

Oops! Awkward. In my excitement over the snow, I forgot the reason I had slept alone was Danny's need to complete this paper.

"When did you get to bed?" I asked with new concern.

"I don't know. About four."

"Oh." I was disappointed. "I wanted to play," I pouted.

"Is it still snowing?"

"Yes. A lot," I brimmed with excitement.

"The snow will still be here later." Danny closed his eyes again. "Take off that snow bunny costume and get into bed," he ordered while moving over to make room.

I should have known Danny wouldn't find the snowstorm as exciting as I did. He had gone to prep school in New Hampshire. Snow wasn't new to him.

I sighed and pulled off my boots followed by the bib, the turtleneck and the long underwear. Then I unhooked my bra, flung it onto the pile of clothes, and climbed into bed. Danny swiftly removed my bikini and folded his arms around me. Comforted by my closeness, he fell back to sleep. I merely dozed.

By ten o'clock I was restless. Listening to Danny's steady breathing against my neck as he continued in a deep sleep was not all that interesting.

I gazed at his perfect face. Danny's disheveled hair was completely sexy. I gently moved a lock away from his eye. Danny needed to get it cut, but I did like its longer, shaggy length. I smiled. Danny was so beautiful.

I spotted a dribble of drool on his chin and carefully blotted it with the top sheet. What was he dreaming about? Danny was smiling. Me, I hoped.

Contentment filled me as I watched him. I thought of the girls I always saw starring at Danny and how I was the only one he wanted beside him as he slept. I felt at peace in the security of our love.

My resistance finally wore down. Danny's allure was too powerful. I pressed my lips to his sleeping ones and kissed him. He immediately responded by devouring mine.

"Elizabeth, this better be you," Danny murmured. He hadn't even opened his eyes. Did Danny think some other girl was naked in his bed kissing him?

"If it isn't me, you're in big trouble with both me and whoever it is that you just called Elizabeth."

"It's you all right. If it wasn't, I'd have been slapped in my face by now."

"I could do that if you'd like," I teased.

"And ruin my wake-up?"

Danny opened his eyes and cradled my face in his hand. "I knew it was you all along. Nobody tastes as sweet."

"Right answer," I murmured. "Can we play in the snow now?"

"No."

"No? Don't you want to fulfill my childhood fantasy?"

"I thought I already had," Danny grinned, sapphires twinkling full strength.

I blushed. "My other childhood fantasy."

"Oh, that." Danny pulled me even closer than we already were and kissed me hard. "Let's fulfill my fantasy now and we'll fulfill yours this afternoon."

By the time we rose and made ourselves decent, it was mid-afternoon and we were hungry. After a bowl of soup, I was ready to tackle my books. Playing in the snow would wait. I spent the remainder of the day drafting my political science take-home final.

Danny and I made a date to go traying that evening. Traying was a tradition at New England schools where snow was plentiful, hills were commonplace and nobody had enough room for sleds, but everyone had access to old dining hall trays.

At ten o'clock Chloe, Rachel and I bundled up and met the guys at their suite. Giddy, we walked across the quiet campus to the hill. The steepest hill at Donnelly led to a crystal-clear lake on the distant end of the campus.

What a magnificent setting! The clean, virgin snow blanketed the smooth, tree-less expanse. The remaining sides of the lake were surrounded by majestic pines and firs stretched tall against the horizon. Scattered among them were leafless maples and oaks that would have shared incredible displays in October. The natural beauty made me tingle. I squeezed Danny's hand. His smile told me he understood and felt similarly.

Already other students were careening down the hill. I carefully studied their technique, noting how they did a planned fall off their trays just in time to avoid landing in the icy lake. I made a mental note to bail even earlier; sunbelt risk management.

"Ready to give it a try?" Danny asked.

"Definitely," I answered, and I flashed a big grin.

The walking path had left us off at the top of the hill. We dropped our trays to the snow, seated ourselves with bent knees, and pushed off. My cheeks stung from the cold breeze. Soft powder flew up around me and I barreled down the hill. I glanced at Danny. He was grinning like a kid. What fun!

The lake was rapidly approaching, and I bailed to my right. Danny bailed to his left at the identical moment and our trays went flying, landing nearby with soft thuds. Danny and I fell into each other, a playful collision of lovers on the soft snow. Our arms and legs splayed out in all directions and we burst into laughter.

I lay back on the snow, swishing my out-stretched arms and legs, making an impromptu snow angel. Danny reached over and grabbed me in a bear hug.

"Daniel," I squealed in delight and he laughed. Then Danny's gloved hand reached for my face and we kissed.

"I love you snow angel," he whispered, and we kissed again.

Danny stood first and extended his hand to me. I took it, but as I went to stand Danny let go and I landed back on my rear.

"Danny!" I exclaimed, and he chuckled.

"I couldn't resist. I'll be a good boy this time." But Danny was laughing as he extended his hand. Did I trust him?

Reluctantly I gave Danny my hand. This time he helped me to my feet and dusted me off as we righted ourselves for the trek back to the top of the hill.

At the peak, a party atmosphere prevailed. Cam and Shane were passing around a thermos bottle filled with rum and coke. I passed. Danny didn't take the thermos either.

I was proud. During the last two weeks, when studying and paper writing had become intense, Danny had barely consumed more than a couple of beers and had stayed away from getting wasted. Maybe he was changing.

The wind picked up, making it colder.

"I can't stay much longer," Rachel complained. Her arms were tightly folded across her chest in an attempt to stave off the shivers.

"It's not that bad," I replied. Danny's arms were securely wrapped around me.

"You have Danny keeping you warm."

Danny was the best blanket. Soon Rachel and Chloe left for the warmth of Berkeley Hall.

Traying was the release we needed from the pressures of studying. Laughter filled the hillside. Impromptu snowball fights broke out.

Danny held me between runs and I gazed into his molten eyes, full of love. I smiled, at peace.

Later, when everyone else had gone, it was magical standing on the snow under the moon light, wrapped in each other's arms.

"I love you, Elizabeth," Danny whispered.

I reached my hands around his neck. "I love you, Daniel."

Against a backdrop of a cloudless, starlit evening we kissed.

CHAPTER 36 - ELIZABETH

Two weeks later, after a long limo drive to Kennedy Airport, Danny and I settled into First Class seats to prepare for takeoff. In five hours we would land, having completed our first semester of college.

I yawned and Danny reached for my hand, kissing it.

"Get some sleep, babe," he said.

Before drifting off, I thought of what a remarkable few months it had been. When I left home last August, a boyfriend was not on my to-do list. But here I was, on a cross-country flight with Danny. Who would have thought it?

Assuming Lincoln Boulevard is clear, it takes no more than 25 minutes to get home from LAX. For the first time, I found myself wishing I lived in the valley instead of Santa Monica. The advantages of the neighborhood paled in comparison to extending my time with Danny.

All too soon the driver entered the gates to the Jacobs' San Vicente compound.

Surprisingly my mother opened the door. Miranda Jordan never answered the door. "They're here!" she screamed and Mom embraced us both warmly.

"Elizabeth!" Dad exclaimed. He hugged me, excited that his little girl was home.

"Daniel," Dad embraced Danny. "It's always good to see you, son."

"Good to see you too, Mike," Danny replied. "I'll take Eli's bags upstairs." Then he went to retrieve my suitcases from the chauffeur.

On his second trip, I followed Danny up the long curving staircase and down the lengthy hallway to the end. My bedroom seemed as though it belonged to someone else. I felt so removed from the girl who only a few years earlier had worked with the decorator to create a dream teen sanctuary.

"Elizabeth, you look lost," Danny interrupted my thoughts.

"I feel lost," I answered.

Danny took my hands. "It'll pass." He'd been through this while attending prep school.

"This is different. Danny, you won't be at breakfast with me."

Danny took me in his arms, brushed my hair off my face, and kissed me.

"The car is waiting. I'll call you in the morning, but I'm seeing Chad and Eliot tomorrow night before they leave for Hawaii," Danny said apologetically.

Danny's Brentwood posse. I shuddered thinking what he might do out with them.

"When will I see you?" I hated having to ask.

"Saturday. And I know the perfect place to spend the afternoon before we go to Ali's."

"I was hoping you'd forget. Ali never invited me."

"I'm sure it was just an oversight. Besides, you're my girl, so who cares."

Danny kissed me, holding me as tightly as he could. Every insecurity vanished.

Mom knocked on the open door. I turned crimson.

"Daniel, the driver is waiting." Mom scowled.

"I'll be right down, Randi," Danny answered calmly. Then Mom left.

Danny turned back to me. "I'll speak to you tomorrow. I love you, baby," he smiled and kissed my forehead.

CHAPTER 37 - ELIZABETH

Flora responded to the rich tones of the doorbell. Through the intercom Danny's voice was unmistakable. I ran downstairs to greet him. What was he doing here at barely past eight?

A few steps from the bottom of the staircase and we were face-to-face. Danny had cleaned up nicely, wearing freshly pressed chino shorts and a polo shirt. His shaggy hair was brushed perfectly into place. My hair was wet from having just stepped out of the shower and I was wearing nothing but my short terry robe.

Joyously I threw my arms around Danny's neck and kissed him.

"What are you doing here?" I asked breathlessly.

"You said you'd miss not having breakfast with me," he answered with a twinkle in his eyes and an impish grin on his lips.

"You're here for breakfast?" I laughed.

"Why not?" Danny shrugged. "I missed you."

"So you said to Ellen 'bye Mom, I'm eating at Eli's?' What? Do we have better eggs?"

Danny laughed. "More or less. Mom wants you happy and so do I. View's better here too." He fingered the neckline of my robe to sneak a peek.

"Daniel!" I playfully scolded as I swatted his fingers away.

"What's for breakfast, anyway?" Danny asked.

"I don't know." I hadn't even thought about it.

"Maybe you are." Danny drew me into his arms for a kiss.

"Good morning, Daniel." Dad interrupted, surprised to find an unexpected guest.

"Hey, Mike," Danny answered as though it were normal for him to be here, holding me in a clinch.

"Danny's here for breakfast," I chirped.

"Elizabeth, put some clothing on," Dad sternly ordered.

I blushed as I noticed my robe had slipped and was half-opened. I yanked it closed while Danny's eyes and beaming smile never left me.

Dad shook his head. "I hope you're being smart," he called as he passed. "I'm too young to be a grandfather."

Once upstairs, I quickly threw on sweats, a v-necked tee, and flip-flops, finger-fluffed my hair and hurried down to the patio.

Flora had already served my parents and Danny. She offered me fluffy scrambled eggs while Danny rose and pulled out a chair for me to sit between him and Dad.

I helped myself to a croissant from the basket while Danny poured me fresh-squeezed orange juice from the crystal pitcher. It was a beautiful day; warmer than one would expect this late in December.

I smiled at my parents, hoping that would diffuse the tension threatening to envelope us like the June fog. It didn't.

Danny reached for a second croissant. Otherwise the silence was deafening. If breakfast at the Jacobs' home was like this, I would seriously consider dining at the Newman's tomorrow.

"Daniel, are you moving in?" Mom finally broke the silence. I stared, first at her and then at Danny. Dad nearly choked on his coffee.

"No," Danny stammered. Even he was flustered.

"It's my fault, Mom," I started, "We always have breakfast together and…" Too late I realized how that must sound. "… and I told Danny I would miss him," I hurried to complete before I stuck my foot further into my mouth.

"Yeah, Randi," Danny added, "I thought I would surprise Eli since I can't see her today. I didn't mean to be presumptuous."

Mom sighed, exasperated. "Daniel, you know you're always welcome here."

Danny didn't stay much longer. He had golf with Steve and the Newmans take their golf very seriously. Disappointed, I walked Danny to his car.

"Be good," Danny teased while standing by the side of his shiny, black Porsche convertible. Our arms wrapped around each other and we kissed before Danny climbed in and sped away.

I spent the remainder of the day with Dad at his office on the Sony Pictures lot. Later Mom joined us to attend Dad's annual corporate Christmas party.

The well-attended gala was intended for families. There were activities for all ages, including a hill of trucked-in snow to play on. The caterers were the best in Hollywood and a popular DJ provided the entertainment.

Mom, as always, looked chic in designer trousers, a sweater, and black leather boots with stiletto heels that made her taller than Dad.

The evening was immensely enjoyable. Dad could relax now. He was closing the office until after New Year's. Enjoying family time was all that mattered now.

CHAPTER 38 - ELIZABETH

When Danny picked me up late the next morning, my parents had already left, relieved not to have had an unexpected guest for breakfast.

The weather had turned cloudy and cooler, but Danny greeted me in the carpark with a warm embrace, stroking my cashmere V-necked sweater.

"Eli! I missed you, babe," Danny said before kissing me.

"It didn't feel right. A whole day without you." I sounded like an addict and I didn't care.

Danny opened the passenger door to the Porsche and helped me in before climbing into the driver's seat and turning the ignition.

"I brought a picnic basket. We're going to the beach," he said.

What a delightful choice! The Newman house in Malibu was so obvious. Less than an hour away, it was like going to another world; our own private idyllic world.

As children, Danny and I had spent a considerable amount of time there. Summer days found us under the watchful eyes of our nannies, building sand castles and frolicking in the surf. Our families sometimes even spent weekends together.

I giggled at the fond memories. Danny gave me a sideways glance, and having reached the straighter Pacific Coast Highway, he took my hand again.

Soon enough, we turned onto Malibu Road. The exteriors of the older beach houses are unimpressive and the Newman's fit the rule. Architectural conformity made the house difficult to find unless you'd visited before. It was ordinary light blue clapboard with a level of porthole-sized windows rising above the three-car garage.

Danny punched in the security code on the keypad by the door leading into the house from the garage. My heart fluttered in anticipation. It had been so long.

"You are such an incredible romantic," I said as we entered the house with Danny carrying the wicker picnic basket. "I always hoped I'd find a man who was romantic."

The brief hallway from the garage led to the Great Room, a combination living/dining room and sizable open kitchen. The pickled hardwood floors were just as I remembered. The furniture I was less certain of.

"Has Ellen redecorated?" I asked.

"New sofas," Danny answered. "E, you never heard about the infamous

121

party my first year at Bromley when I invited five classmates for Christmas?"

"I must have missed that one."

"You were definitely not on the guest list. Six preps, a keg of beer and uh, other stuff," Danny admitted sheepishly. "Not the place for a 'nice girl' like Elizabeth Jacobs."

"Not fair! I miss all the fun." I pouted.

"You would not have found it fun. Trust me, E. It was not the place for you. When my parents arrived the next morning," Danny shook his head, embarrassed. "Let's just say, I've never seen them so angry. It was ugly."

The new sofa was a pale turquoise sectional with matching pillows. The seating areas were quite deep. Snuggling with Danny would be cozy indeed. Getting up would be impossibly difficult.

Through the wall of glass sliders was an enclosed deck leading to the beach. The perimeter enclosure served as a barricade between the Newman's private paradise and the public. Designed with several seating/dining areas, chaise lounges, and an outdoor kitchen, there was even a hot tub and a gas powered brick fireplace.

"Let's have our picnic," Danny suggested.

Then he grabbed a chenille throw from the sofa and we strode through the doors, to the patio and beyond to the empty beach, hand-in-hand with our basket.

Reaching a flat piece of sand, Danny laid out the blanket, and we sat down to enjoy our lunch. Danny had packed simple fare; strawberries, wrap sandwiches, chips and cookies. He had even packed two champagne flutes and a bottle of sparkling cider.

"I would have brought champagne but I couldn't take a chance," Danny teased.

"Am I ever going to live that down?" I asked.

"Probably not," and he kissed me. "You're an adorable drunk," Danny added, "Even when you get sick."

"Thanks. I think."

Danny laughed and poured the cider and handed me a flute. Then we lifted our glasses, and he toasted me.

"To the girl who always puts a smile on my face." And of course, I smiled.

Then I kissed Danny's cheek, and we drank to his toast.

"My turn," I declared. "Danny, you've made me so happy. I love you. Always."

After eating, I nestled into Danny's strong arms and we sat silently watching the waves. The warmth radiating between us as Danny held me against his chest was as relaxing as a day at the spa. We were so content.

My thoughts drifted. Was there a connection between tonight's party and that party from year's ago? Had Ali been a guest? Could jealousy be the reason for her snub?

"Danny," I hated interrupting our mood. "Was Ali at that party?" I stammered. I didn't know if I wanted to learn the truth.

"Yeah, Ali was there," Danny said contritely.

That sinking feeling in the pit of my stomach formed.

"Did anything happen between you and Ali?"

"I was so wasted. All I remember is my parents arriving in the morning."

Danny held me tighter and gently stroked my shoulder.

"Must we discuss this? It's in the past, baby." Danny sighed uncomfortably.

Even I wasn't that naïve. "Danny, you slept with Ali!" I gasped, horrified.

This bothered me a great deal though I knew it shouldn't. It had happened five years ago. I knew Danny had been with other girls. It wasn't as though I'd thought he'd been a virgin. But Ali Hayes! Ali was vile!

Danny felt my revulsion. I couldn't look at him.

"Eli," he spoke softly. "It was years ago. I was only fifteen. I've never gone near Ali again. This has nothing to do with us."

"This probably explains Ali's animosity toward me." I frowned.

"You don't really think that, do you?"

"I don't know. I'm the only one she didn't invite."

Danny was silent. Finally I sighed. It was up to me to rescue our day from this funk. I smiled into Danny's sparkling sapphire eyes. He lifted my chin and kissed me.

The sun was setting now, creating a glorious display of pink, purple and gray across the horizon. There was a chill in the air.

"Let's go inside," Danny whispered.

I nodded and picked up the picnic basket. Danny slung the throw over his shoulder. Then he picked me up by my waist, swinging me in a circle.

"Danny," I laughed.

"Eli," he smirked.

Danny carried me all the way to the house before setting me on my feet.

"Now I'll show you your old room," Danny said after he laid the throw back on the sofa and I placed the basket on the kitchen counter.

"I'd like that," I responded breathlessly.

I grabbed Danny's hand and pulled him up the stairs. My old room was the back one. It had a large window on the side where if you stood just-so you could catch a glimpse of the Pacific. Smaller, portholes looked out on the road. The master was the only upstairs room with an ocean front balcony and full view.

I stopped short in the doorway. Ellen had been at work here too.

"It's so different," I said, surprised to find navy-bordered Frette linens on an untouched king-sized bed.

"Mom wanted a change," Danny answered. The room was so pristine it looked as though no one lived there.

"Has anyone ever slept here?" I wondered aloud.

"I have. A few times," Danny replied.

"Alone?"

"Yes, alone. I'm banned from having overnight guests."

I laughed. "Are you kidding?"

"Actually, no. I need explicit permission before I can bring friends and then a parent or Graci stays over."

I giggled. How embarrassing.

"What about me? Do they know we're here?"

"No," Danny answered sheepishly. "I didn't tell them."

Hiding my smirk, I jumped backwards onto the bed. My body enjoyed the luxurious mattress and extra plump down pillows. I reached out my arms to Danny and he gently jumped on top of me. I giggled and we kissed.

"You're sure you can have guests who are girls?" I asked with a wry smile.

"Probably not. But you, yeah," Danny answered, "After all, you're not a real girl. You're only Eli."

Danny grinned, and I kissed him. Then he urgently removed my clothes. Danny enjoyed letting me show him that I was indeed a very real girl.

Snuggled in Danny's arms, my hand tracing patterns on his taut shoulder, I sighed, content from our lovemaking. Danny's scent, a heady mixture of salt air, perspiration and faded cologne was intoxicating. The strength of his muscles provided a masculine counterpoint to my soft femininity. I looked up at him and couldn't help but smile.

"Maybe we could skip Ali's party and stay here," I thought but I didn't dare voice. I knew I would lose the argument, so why bother.

"What's up, baby?" Danny asked softly.

"You. You and how happy you've made me." I pressed my body into him. Danny took a handful of my hair and tickled my cheek with it.

"Stop that!" I playfully protested.

"Not until you tell me what you're thinking."

Danny kept tickling me. I squirmed and giggled until I couldn't take it any more.

"All right, already!" I exclaimed and Danny dropped my hair. "I'm uncomfortable about tonight."

"Ali's not going to throw you out or cause a scene. You're with me." The most popular guy in Brentwood whom the social scene revolved around, that fact went unspoken.

"It's not just Ali. I haven't told Steff and Emma about us."

"How do your best friends not know who your boyfriend is?"

"I'm shy?"

Danny stopped, and stared at my naked body.

"Shy? I don't think so, Eli," he laughed.

"Not with you," I giggled. "With showing up in Brentwood with you. Everyone always thought I was your pet, following you around."

"You're an adorable pet and you can follow me anywhere you want. Elizabeth, you're being really weird. What is your problem?"

I shrugged, embarrassed. "I am being weird, aren't I?"

"Yes. But you're cute, sexy and I love you, so snap out of it."

"Danny, how do you think our friends will react when we walk in together?"

"The girls will turn green with envy and claw your eyes out. The guys will gawk and say, 'What a hot babe! Lucky Newman,'" he responded flippantly.

"I'm serious, Danny."

"I don't care what anyone thinks. I'm confident that I'm with the most desirable girl on earth. If someone doesn't like it, that's their problem, not mine."

I studied the perfect mouth these words had come from. More importantly, I thought of the loving heart beating against my palm and its genuineness.

This crowd considered me an awkward geek and Danny the coolest guy in town. Arriving at Ali's with Danny would be my vindication. If Danny could be this confident, so could I.

I threw my arms around his neck and enthusiastically kissed him. Danny crushed me into the pillows and devoured my lips. My body tingled as I felt him harden against me. We were drunk with love.

CHAPTER 39 - ELIZABETH

Fortunately nobody arrives at a nine o'clock party until at least ten. By the time we pulled ourselves out of bed and showered it was already past seven. Then Danny insisted we eat dinner.

It was after nine by the time we arrived at my parent's house for me to change into a denim miniskirt and Danny's favorite silk blouse. With the drawstrings open, my Peretti heart rested perfectly on my chest for all to see.

Indeed, we made a very handsome couple as we skipped down the stairs holding hands, smiling and laughing.

"Have a good time kids," Dad said as he and Mom bade us good-night.

"I can't wait to see everybody," I lied.

"I'll bring Eli back tomorrow," Danny told them. "We'll spend the night at the beach."

Danny quickly ushered me out the door before my parents could react.

"I can't believe you," I scolded Danny as soon as we were in the car.

"Elizabeth, you're an adult." Danny laughed.

I smacked his arm with my fists and he kept laughing. Danny could hardly speak.

"Oh hell, Liz! Enjoy! Where's your party face?"

After parking, we followed the path behind the Hayes' spacious home to the pool house where the party was in full swing. Music pulsated through the open doors.

Danny smiled, and he squeezed my hand. Then he kissed my cheek. I smiled back. It was expected.

"Danny!" Ali exclaimed, ignoring me as we entered. Her face lit with joy.

Ali reached for Danny's hands and deliberately kissed his lips. If Ali's goal was to make me uncomfortable, she had more than succeeded. I hoped I hid it well.

For Ali, an ordinary looking girl, despite a nose-job and chin implant courtesy of Beverly Hills' finest cosmetic surgeon, she looked good tonight, as good as Ali could ever hope for. Her hair and make-up were professionally done, and she was wearing a very short fashionable dress that clung to all the right places on her slender frame.

"Elizabeth?" Ali greeted me with a sneer. "I don't remember inviting you."

"You didn't," I replied with confidence.

Ali looked down her sculpted nose with disdain.

Meanwhile, Danny's hand settled possessively on my waist.

"Elizabeth's with me. Ali, you don't mind me bringing my girlfriend, do you?" Danny asked in a voice that challenged our hostess.

"Your what?" Ali asked, taken aback by the news.

"My girlfriend," Danny answered, grinning.

"Right," Ali answered dismissively, and she left to greet other guests.

Danny whispered in my ear, "Our hostess is not happy."

"Ali should have invited me."

Danny nuzzled my neck, and I squirmed. "Today was great," he whispered.

"Elizabeth!" Shrieks interrupted us. Danny and I snapped apart, and there they were.

"Emma! Steff!" I squealed in response.

My two closest friends embraced and kissed me, our first time since August.

"Steff, your hair!" Her long blonde hair now barely grazed her shoulders, and she wore bangs for the first time. "I love it!"

"I got it cut this afternoon. Bobs are more D.C.," Steff, a student at The George Washington University, explained. "What about you? Au naturel, I see."

"I don't have time in the morning to fuss." Danny's closeness made me blush.

"I like it," said Emma, a student at Duke.

"I do too," Danny chimed in. "Hey Steff, Emma."

"Danny Newman? Oh my god! It is you!" Steff exclaimed, and they embraced.

"Did you come together?" Emma asked as she embraced Danny.

"Eli's my designated driver."

"Danny's my bodyguard," I added.

"I'm guarding her body from Ali."

Steff and Emma looked at us with questioning eyes.

"Ali didn't invite me, so I'm Danny's date."

"How convenient," Emma laughed. "Just like you both ending up at Donnelly."

"Have you been keeping Danny out of trouble, Elizabeth?" Steff teased.

"Actually, I've been too busy getting Eli into trouble, so I haven't had time to get myself into any," Danny responded.

"Yeah right," Steff said, "Elizabeth in trouble. That's a good one."

"Why does everyone think I never do anything?"

"Because you don't," Steff immediately answered.

"Elizabeth might have changed," Danny suggested.

"Yeah, right."

"Has anyone seen the white lace yet?" Emma whispered to me. "You've been off the grid for so long, Steff and I thought maybe…"

Why must she ask this in front of Danny? Of course she didn't know, but was the thought of us together so preposterous it never entered her mind?

Thankfully Steff was distracting Danny. Or was she? Danny turned to Emma and whispered, "I've seen it. Good choice."

I frowned. This was not how I wanted to break our news to my friends.

"I understand you picked out the lovely ensemble, Em."

I wanted to sink through the ground and disappear but I couldn't. Danny had wrapped his arms around my shoulders and was grinning.

"Elizabeth is breathtaking in them."

"What!" Steff gasped.

"Eli's modeled for me." Danny said nonchalantly.

I stared at Danny not knowing what he was going to say next. Instead, Danny took my stunned face in his hands.

"Of course they didn't stay on for long, did they baby?" Danny brought his lips to mine and kissed me, pushing his tongue into my mouth. I was in shock, unable to resist him. My tongue joined with his. Electricity fused us together.

When we parted, Danny's arms remained around my shoulders. Steff and Emma stood glued in place, gaping.

"How long have you been together?" Emma stammered.

"A couple of months," I answered with guilty discomfort.

"I can't believe it. Elizabeth, you never said anything."

"I thought you wouldn't approve."

"Emma and I have always liked Danny. Of course we approve," Steff said.

"Eli and I figured we knew each other well enough," Danny said, and we smiled at each other. Then he turned me into his arms. "I love you," he said, and he tenderly kissed me.

As if on cue, Ali appeared, drinks in hand, ending our kiss.

"Danny, Elizabeth, I've brought your drinks." Plastic smile turned to maximum, Ali handed Danny a bottle of Corona beer with a lime in it, and for me a colorful concoction.

"Thanks, Ali," Danny said.

"What's in this?" I asked, glad she'd gotten over her earlier snit.

"Rum and fruit juice. My secret recipe."

I took a sip of the cold, fruity beverage. "This is good," I exclaimed. Then I took a larger sip. Ali walked away. I was thirsty and quickly drank about half.

"Danny, you should try this. It's really good." I held up my cup, and he sipped.

"Do you know what's in this?" he asked as I gulped more punch.

"Ali said rum and fruit juice," I answered, slurring a little.

"Try rum, fruit liqueurs and minimal fruit juice."

I was confused. I felt buzzed.

"There's less fruit in your drink than in this." Danny indicated the lime in his beer.

Well, it tastes good," I laughed, and I finished it off. Danny rolled his eyes.

"There goes my designated driver," he groaned.

I leaned into Danny. His shoulder supported my tipsy weight.

"I feel great," I slurred while smiling dreamily up at him.

"I'm sure you do, baby." Danny smiled with a twinkle in his eyes.

"Elizabeth never got drunk when we were at Archer. Does she do this often now?" Emma asked Danny.

"Only when I have a special evening planned," Danny answered.

"You have something special planned?" I gushed.

"We were going to the beach," Danny reminded me.

I sighed. "I love the beach. Let's dance." I grabbed Danny's hand to lead him to the pool deck where everyone was dancing.

"Later, ladies" he said to Steff and Emma and bowed.

Danny's strong grip kept me from falling as I stumbled to the patio. I kept my hands clasped around his neck and his hands held my hips while we danced. My legs felt like Jell-O as I tried to keep up with the fast-moving music.

"This is awesome!" I exclaimed and I gave Danny a very affectionate kiss.

"You are a most delightful drunk, Elizabeth." Danny smirked.

"Danny!" A man's voice called.

Danny abruptly broke apart from me and I teetered for a moment before regaining my equilibrium.

"Bobby! Hey, how are you?"

Danny embraced his friend, clapping his shoulders.

"Jason!" he greeted the second guy. "I can't believe how long it's been." Danny and Jason embraced. "Where's Zac?" Danny asked, referring to the fourth member of their tight-knit group who had met in Kindergarten at Crossroads School

"He's in Europe with Gibby," Bobby answered.

"Damn! We leave for Aspen on Tuesday. I wanted to catch up with him."

"We?" Bobby asked.

"You remember, Elizabeth Jacobs."

Jason and Bobby gave me the once over and exchanged curious glances.

"No," Jason answered while Bobby nodded his agreement.

"You don't?" Danny was surprised.

"Danny and I are going to Aspen," I giggled.

"Is she related to that Leelee Jacobs who used to hang around you?" Bobby asked. I giggled at his ignorance.

Before Danny could answer, Jason added, "She was that kid who followed you around like a poodle. Even looked like one with all that frizzy hair."

"I remember," Bobby exclaimed. "Skinny little thing with glasses."

"Shame she didn't look like her mother," Jason added.

"Miranda Jordan. Now that's one hot babe," Bobby smirked.

I crinkled my face in confusion. Mom was not a hot babe! She was Mom. I wanted to protest, but my mouth felt glued shut.

"I'll let her know she's the object of your wet dreams," Danny laughed. "Miranda will love that."

Danny wrapped his arms around me from behind. This was so weird, and he knew it. "Uh, guys, Leelee Jacobs has grown up since you last saw her. And she's called Elizabeth now."

I giggled at Danny's cryptic response as he pointed at me.

Their jaws dropped. Jason was speechless.

"But she's beautiful!" Bobby stammered.

"And she's mine," Danny gloated. "So put your tongues back in your mouths. We'll catch you later. My lady wants to dance."

I smiled as Danny led me back to the pool deck.

"I hate when people call me Leelee," I complained. Then I wrapped my arms around his neck and Danny kissed my forehead.

"I'm really hot," I whispered.

"I know," he smiled. I giggled at the double entendre.

"I mean I'm thirsty."

"That wasn't so obvious, baby. I'll get you a drink."

Danny took my hand and led me off the dance floor. Ali approached carrying drinks on a small tray. "Want one?" she asked. Danny reached for a Corona while I took the last cup of punch and quickly gulped down half.

"No more, Elizabeth," Danny said sternly and he grabbed the cup.

"This punch is so good," I exclaimed.

"What's the matter, Dan?" Ali said emphasizing the diminutive name. "Can't Elizabeth have a drink?"

"Cut the crap, Ali," Danny replied.

"You and Leelee, who'd have thought? My sources were wrong then."

"What sources?" Danny asked.

"I have friends at Donnelly," she snapped.

"You have friends?" I giggled.

Danny gripped my shoulder. Ali snarled.

Ignoring me she sneered, "Everyone assumed she was one of your flings."

Ali's venom sobered me.

"Ali, you don't know squat." Danny said angrily. He protectively reached for my hand. "Is that why you didn't invite Elizabeth? You wanted on that list?"

"No," Ali quivered. "I thought you'd see what you were missing and..."

Danny's eyes were on fire, incensed. I hoped this wouldn't come to blows.

"I'm not missing anything." Then Danny smiled at me. "Let's go, baby."

"Curfew for Leelee?" Ali couldn't resist hurling one more barb.

"Elizabeth and I have better things to do than listen to your tirade, Ali." Then Danny looked directly into Ali's eyes. "We're off to my house in Malibu for the night.

CHAPTER 40 - ELIZABETH

A gloriously sunny day greeted us as I woke entwined in Danny's arms. We cherished every moment, luxuriating in the privacy.

After a short, barefoot walk on the cold sand, we warmed up in the hot tub. A languorous soapy shower after making love on the chaise, and we were ready for the drive home.

"Elizabeth, Daniel, in here," Mom called from the sitting room as we entered the house.

The casual sitting room was decorated in overstuffed sofas and chairs of peach, cream and pale green fabrics. It was a comfortable room to cozy up in to read and that was how we found Mom. She was seated on the sofa, her feet curled under, with a screenplay on her lap.

Mom set the script on the table. Danny and I slowly sat down on the love seat across from her. Taking my hand, Danny set it on his thigh and held it with both of his.

"Randi," Danny began, "I take complete responsibility for last night. Elizabeth didn't know my plans. Please don't be angry."

Danny's sensitivity warmed me and I smiled proudly.

Mom's lips upturned, almost laughing. "Daniel, I'm not angry." Mom even smiled.

Danny and I sat a little further back, the tension vanquished.

"It may be hard for you to believe, but I was once young and in love."

I blushed. Danny smirked.

"It's hard coming to terms with my little girl being a woman in love with a terrific young man. I'm trying my best," she explained.

"We know, Randi," Danny said "We appreciate it."

Mom uncurled her legs. I rose, and she welcomed me into her arms.

"I love you Mom," I said, and we kissed each other's cheeks.

"All I want is for you to be happy, Elizabeth."

"I'm the happiest I've ever been," I assured her.

Soon Mom left for the kitchen. When she wasn't working, Mom loved to roll up her sleeves and whip up elaborate dishes. Her favorite times were holidays, and tonight was the first night of Chanukah featuring Mom's special potato latkes.

When we were all in town, the Newmans always celebrated with the Jacobs. Ellen would supply dessert, probably baked by Graciela. Ellen's kitchen had been featured in magazines, but she could barely boil water.

Meanwhile, I stretched out on the loveseat, resting my head on a pale green pillow placed against the armrest. My feet rested on Danny's lap and I yawned.

"Am I keeping you up?" he asked as he typed a text message on his phone.

I yawned again and stretched my arms like a cat. "It must be the rum. Or you. I'm so sleepy," I purred. Then I closed my eyes.

"Why don't we go upstairs?" Danny asked, "I can text anywhere."

It took every effort I could muster to right myself and stand. I leaned against Danny, and he helped me up the stairs. My head felt so heavy, my legs so wobbly.

At the landing, Danny picked me up and carried me down the hall to my room where he placed me on the bed. Danny lovingly covered me with the pink cotton blanket. Then he kicked off his shoes and sat down beside me.

The last thing I remembered was Danny leaning against a pillow propped against the headboard. He had been about to send a text message.

In my dream I heard knocking and then it stopped. It was so cozy under the soft blanket with Danny's warm, familiar hand resting on my hip. I heard knocking again. It wasn't a dream.

"So he fell asleep too," I thought. Danny's phone was on the bed, not far from his other hand. He must have dropped it as he fell asleep.

I fought to become more fully awake. The door opened. Dad! He smiled as he noticed me with half-opened heavy eyelids, and Danny cuddled up beside me. Dad tried to stifle a laugh.

"Hey, sleepy-heads," he said in a soft voice. "Dinner's about ready."

Danny stirred.

"Dad, is it really that late?" I asked.

"Yes. You're still jet-lagged. Mom says you've been out for a while."

"Mike?" Danny yawned as he tried raising his head, not comprehending where he was.

"Kids, you have fifteen minutes." Dad smiled warmly. "You're both adorable," he added with a chuckle. Then Dad closed the door, and left.

I loved holidays at home! Celebrating with the Newmans made it even better.

Grandma Margie was also coming to dinner! It was an easy drive from Sherman Oaks for Mom's mother to make, and I couldn't wait.

"Grandma!" I exclaimed when she entered the sitting room. We were gathered for informal cocktails. After last night, I was content to nurse a Diet Coke.

I ran over and hugged her. For Grandma, dressing for the holiday meant a flowing figure obscuring caftan over leggings. Tall like Mom, she could carry it off. As always, Grandma wore Birkenstocks and colorful chunky beads adorned her neck. I loved Grandma Margie!

"How's your new boyfriend?" she asked.

"Mom told you?" As the only child of a single mother, Mom and Grandma were very close. I didn't think their closeness extended to my love life, though.

"No, you did. I took one look at you and I thought, Elizabeth's in love, she's glowing. He must be someone wonderful."

"He is, Grandma." I nodded for Danny to join me. Once he was by my side I said, "You've met Danny Newman."

"Steve and Ellen's Danny Newman?"

"Guilty," Danny answered, and he wrapped his arms around me.

"I haven't seen you since the bat mitzvah," Grandma said in wonder. "You're taller. And you're in love with my Elizabeth. Lucky boy."

"I certainly am." Danny's chin rested on my shoulder.

"You'd better take good care of her."

"Of course he does. Danny treats me like a princess."

"A very high maintenance princess," Danny added with a wry smile.

"Elizabeth," Grandma warned, "I hope you're taking birth control pills."

"Grandma!" I was mortified. It was awkward enough coming from Grandma made even more so by Danny having his arms around me.

"I don't want you ending up like me."

"Don't worry, Grandma," I stammered. "It's taken care of."

"Margie!" Dad called from across the room. Thank you Daddy.

"Looks like Michael wants me." Grandma kissed us and sought out Dad.

Danny laughed at my discomfort.

"What did Margie mean, she didn't want you ending up like her?"

"Grandma never graduated from high school."

"Then you can't be like her. You're in college."

"That's not exactly what she meant," I said with urgency.

I pulled Danny out of the room to the foyer in search of privacy. Danny stood close, and I leaned against the wall. Our voices wouldn't carry

"Danny, Grandma's only fifty-six years old. Didn't you know that?"

"Margie's only fifty-six! No wonder she looks so great," Danny answered. Grandma's face was unlined and her thick brown hair had no gray. "Wait," he continued, puzzled, "Isn't Randi in her forties?"

"No. Mom turns forty in April."

"Your grandmother was sixteen when Randi was born!" Danny exclaimed, his voice getting louder.

"Shhh. Keep your voice down," I cautioned.

"I thought Margie looked young for a grandmother, but I never thought she was that young. Some of our friends have mothers older than that."

"I know. It's embarrassing."

"It shouldn't be."

"Mom's never said anything, but I don't think there ever was a Grandpa Margie. I think Grandma had too much fun at a rock festival. She has tickets framed and hanging in her den. They're dated July. Mom was born the following April. Do the math."

Danny counted nine months on his fingers.

"Okay, it adds up," he admitted. " I always heard your grandfather deserted them when your mother was a toddler."

"That's just a story; the official Miranda Jordan biography. It sounds better than Grandma spent the weekend wasted when she was fifteen, got knocked up and out popped little Miranda."

"So that's why Randi's so strict." Danny tried hard and failed at muffling his laughter. I smacked his arm.

"It's not funny! Supposedly 'Grandpa' was a very attractive redhead from Greenwich, Connecticut, although that part could be a stretch. Grandma was wasted."

Danny hugged me, burying his face in my shoulder to muffle the sound of his laughter. Then he twirled a lock of my auburn hair around his finger.

"So that's where this comes from, mystery grandpa," he choked.

"Daniel, this is not funny," I scolded while maintaining hushed tones.

"I'm sorry, Eli. If it wasn't that Randi has always been so proper," Danny said before pressing his lips against mine for a playful kiss. Then he ran his finger down my cheekbone and I shivered.

"You're impossible," I sighed.

"At least I've met all my grandparents," Danny laughed

"It's one of the reasons why I'm glad it's you I love."

"The Newman pedigree?"

"You do not have a pedigree. But you do know who all your relatives are and none of them are mine. I always wanted to go to an east coast college, but once Donnelly accepted me I worried that I'd fall in love with a redheaded boy from Connecticut. He could be my half-uncle."

Danny let out a loud whoop. My hand flew up to cover his mouth. Danny was consumed with laughter. He pushed my hand away and hugged me tightly to control his shaking.

"You're half-uncle? Eli, I love the way you always make me laugh," Danny choked and wiped tears from his eyes. I frowned.

"Daniel, this is not funny. I revealed my vulnerabilities to you. You are not supposed to laugh," I sniffled.

"Oh, babe, I'm sorry. You have to see the irony in this. Everyone thinks you and I together is incestuous and all this time you were worried about the real thing."

"It's not funny!"

"I'm sorry. You're right." Danny fought to regain his composure. "But you can stop worrying. Nobody in my family ever had red hair. You're safe, honey. Can we kiss and make-up? I love you, even with your checkered past."

"I do not have a checkered past!" I seethed.

Danny's strong hands circled my waist and pressed me against the wall. His hypnotic sapphire eyes stared into my soul.

"I'm serious, Elizabeth. I love you. You will never become like your grandmother. I would never desert you. If you got pregnant, and you didn't want an abortion, I would proudly stand by you. That baby would be mine too."

"You really feel that way?"

"Of course I do. I love you, baby."

"It won't happen until I'm at least twenty-five."

Danny dropped his hands, relieved.

"Good, because I won't be ready until then either so keep taking those pills. Why didn't Margie abort your mother?"

"Grandma's grandparents were Holocaust survivors. Her parents are orthodox. They disowned Grandma and even sat Shiva."

"Incredible. Margie looks like an old hippie. I never pegged her as religious. I guess I can understand why Margie couldn't get an abortion."

"That's why Mom became a model. Stage mother was one of the only things a teenaged mother without a high school diploma could do to make money legally. Mom has supported Grandma since she was an infant. She still does."

"See, that could never happen to you. Mike and Randi would never disown you. And I have a trust fund. But it's never going to happen because you're not getting pregnant and I wouldn't desert you if you did."

"I love you, Daniel." I clasped my hands around his neck and kissed him.

After filling ourselves with Mom's delicious roast chicken and latkes, Danny and I excused ourselves. We were off to go to a club in West Hollywood that had a reputation for showcasing unknown talent. A new band was performing this evening.

The club was already crowded when we arrived, not an empty seat in sight. As we waited for the waitress to bring Danny change of a fifty for his beer and my Diet Coke, I spotted my friend, Grant Barnes.

Only twenty-four, Grant had become an overnight sensation two years earlier. Dad, at my urging, had convinced his director to cast Grant to star in a major film he was producing.

Anticipation grew. By the time filming began, poor Grant could barely go out in public so I invited him to stay at our house.

Public disclosure of my houseguest could have made me very popular except Dad swore me to secrecy. That the hot young star was spending his evenings playing Guitar Hero with a high school student sounded so preposterous, even bloggers wouldn't have believed it.

"Lizzie J!" Grant called out. Danny glared at Grant, all sexy tousled brown hair and pale sea-green eyes.

Grant always called me Lizzie. He was the only person who did. I hated it, but he was Grant Barnes. He could call me whatever he wanted. With his posh London accent, it was music to my ears.

Grant threw his arms around me and kissed my cheek. "I didn't know you were in town!" he exclaimed.

"I got home the other day. Grant, I live here, remember?"

"Yes, I've been there. How is university?"

"Amazing. What are you doing in town?"

"Leaving. First flight home tomorrow. Mum can't wait and neither can I. I'm tired of living out of a suitcase. I haven't been home in over a year thanks to you." We both laughed.

"Do you know how many actors would kill for your life?" I asked.

"Don't get me wrong, Lizzie," Grant explained. "I'm living the dream, but I'm exhausted. I've just been stuck in Utah for three months. It was good coming to L.A. for ADR just to see my mates."

Danny, not pleased with the warm reception I had received from the terminally attractive actor, stood with his arms possessively around my shoulders, but he laughed at Grant's story.

"Boyfriend?" Grant asked. I nodded yes, and then introduced them.

"I'm glad you're Lizzie's boyfriend," said Grant. "You look right together." Then he added, "When I was staying with your family, I always wondered why a girl as attractive as you are didn't have a boyfriend."

"Elizabeth was waiting for me to return to her life," Danny answered. I blushed and turned to gaze into his sparkling sapphires.

"That's pretty close to the truth," I told Grant.

"I'm happy for you Lizzie." Grant turned to Danny. "Why were you laughing about Utah? You've spent time there?"

"My Dad worked there years ago. Let's just say it's my family's least favorite state. Dad was so lonely he developed a drug problem."

"Steve had a drug problem?" I never knew that and I was family.

"It was years ago. We don't discuss it, Eli." But he was.

Then Danny turned back to Grant. "Dad's fine now, but he's never gone back. Mom won't let him."

"I don't blame her. I won't let you work there either, " I declared.

"What does your dad do?" Grant asked.

"He's Steven Newman," Danny answered knowing the name said it all.

"Of course. I'd love to work with him. He's brilliant."

Later, paparazzi were staking out the sidewalk as I left the club flanked by Danny and Grant. We lingered, talking by the side of the Porsche. Grant warmly embraced me before Danny and I got into the car for our drive to Malibu. By morning, pictures of Grant embracing me would be all over the internet.

CHAPTER 41 - ELIZABETH

Flying from Santa Monica to Aspen in our Gulfstream takes only about two hours, which was good because today I was an inexplicably nervous flyer.

Danny, Teddy and I sat apart from our parents. Teddy had the right idea. During take-off, his iPad earbuds were in place and he concentrated on reading a book.

Seated beside me, Danny tried putting me at ease by talking into my ear about an item in the morning newspaper. Then in mid-sentence, Danny leaned over and kissed me. "We're up, baby," he said and smiled.

Then it hit me. "You were boring me so I wouldn't think about the take-off?" His guilty smirk answered my question. Then I reclined against Danny, resting my hand on his chest, while he settled into reading *The Grapes of Wrath* on his iPad.

Set against a snow-covered mountain, the large, mission-style lodge beckoned. Danny, Teddy and I approached in the car we were sharing. The house was surrounded by a stand of evergreens, seemingly cut off from civilization. Smoke rose from the multiple chimneys against the clear blue sky. The household staff had prepared for our arrival.

Keeping our excitement tamped down, Danny and I carried our luggage to the private downstairs suite. The spacious room was decorated in warm, southwestern hues. The bed and bureau were made of rustic thick cut pine. A deep-seated studded leather love seat with matching ottoman faced the sizable window with its views of the majestic mountain. An overhead antler-styled lighting fixture made this the perfect spot for curling up with a book, though I doubted I'd have time to indulge.

Best of all, on the wall opposite the king-sized bed was a wood-burning fireplace. The staff kept it stocked and ready to go. All we needed was a match to light the kindling. Nothing would be better after a day on the slopes than a hot whirlpool bath followed by snuggling by the fireplace with Danny.

Dinner at the lodge was a casual, raucous affair with seven of us at the table. The cook had prepared an old-fashioned barbeque as our welcome meal with platters of ribs, warm homemade potato salad, a green bean casserole, and the most delicious cornbread.

Later, Teddy joined Danny and me in the lower level playroom to shoot pool. The over-sized room also contained air hockey and foosball tables. There was a large screen television, cozy seating areas and a bar. Sliding doors led to a patio where the hot tub was discretely hidden by landscaping.

Pool does not work with three people. I offered to play for both Danny and Teddy to even the sides, but they both declined my offer. After warming up, it was clear why. Elizabeth Jacobs sucks at pool!

If Teddy would disappear, Danny and I could play and then I might improve. I felt like the stereotypic jealous lover only it was my brother whom I was jealous of.

Instead I amused myself by throwing darts. Grant Barnes had taught me proper British pub techniques. I'm good at darts. In fact, I excel, but neither Danny nor Teddy noticed the bulls-eyes I was throwing.

You can throw darts without competition for just so long. Tired of being ignored, I called it quits. Saying good-night would be safer, as I was tempted to throw a few darts at painful places neither my boyfriend nor brother would be pleased with.

I approached Danny and hugged his waist.

"I'm going to bed," I whispered. "Don't be long."

I kissed his cheek promising more to come. Danny rested his cue, against the pool table. Hint received.

"Teddy," he said, "I'll be right back." Danny turned to me. "Let's go, Eli."

His arm around my shoulder, we walked into the bedroom. I grabbed Danny's shirt collar, pulled him to me, and planted a warm kiss on his lips.

"Get rid of Teddy," I urged.

CHAPTER 42 - ELIZABETH

Visions of bumping off Teddy filled my brain. Admittedly, this was not healthy. Saner was turning my attention to the handsome bare-chested man sleeping beside me.

I had no recollection of Danny coming to bed, so it must have been late. What could have been so fascinating about Teddy to keep Danny from me?

I touched my hand to Danny's stubbled cheek and gently kissed his full lips.

"Good morning beautiful," he whispered, so content.

All evil thoughts vanished as Danny responded with his own kisses. I was happy all over again that we had been given our own private suite.

"You didn't wake me when you came in," I complained.

"I didn't want to disturb you. You were sleeping so soundly."

"Do you think anyone is up?" I felt compelled to whisper though nobody could hear us. Our families were at minimum two flights up.

"I don't know," Danny answered.

I smiled wickedly. Danny grinned. Then I threw my arms around his neck and kissed him. Danny tightened his hold and returned the kiss. My leg wrapped around his and he urgently pressed against me, hard, ready. Our hearts were pounding. I was breathless.

Danny worked open the buttons on my shirt. I took a deep breath as Danny pushed it off my shoulders and tossed it aside leaving me naked. Electricity radiated between us. Pressed against the pillows with Danny poised above me, his fingers feathered down my side and he prepared to enter me.

A quick, loud knock came on the door, followed by Teddy's entrance. I gasped, horrified. Danny jerked his fingers back and collapsed on top of me, shielding me from Teddy's view. I hastily pulled the sheets up around us.

I couldn't look at my brother. I didn't know if ever could again. The thought that fourteen-year-old Teddy had caught us naked in bed was mortifying.

Teddy was equally shaken. "Mom wants to know when you're coming to breakfast?" he stammered.

"Tell her we'll be right up," Danny answered. Teddy flushed and hastily retreated out the door.

Danny moved off me so I could breath again. He held me and stroked my back. I was shaking.

"I'm going to kill that kid," Danny said, more annoyed than angry.

"I have first dibs. Teddy's my brother."

"Poor Teddy!" Danny laughed. "He's probably traumatized. Walking in and finding your sister..." Danny kissed my forehead. "We better get upstairs before a parent shows up next."

Teddy accompanied Danny and me to the slopes. I felt inappropriately dressed for skiing with my brother. My new Bogner jumpsuit clung to every curve. I had purchased it with only Danny in mind. The Bogner had seemed sophisticated. With Teddy at our side, and Danny gawking at my every movement, I felt like an expensive slut.

The mountain air was crisp and fresh. The powder was pristine and perfectly groomed. It was cold, but not uncomfortable on this sunny day. Perfect conditions for starting a ski trip!

Disembarking from the gondola, I noticed several girls my age wearing similar attire. Now I was glad to be wearing my Bogner. The hell with Teddy! Danny's eyes would have no reason to stray today.

I adjusted my helmet and lowered my goggles. Danny and Teddy did the same. I sidled up to Danny and playfully smiled.

"Race you to the bottom," I challenged before taking off.

The wind flying through my hair was invigorating. The quality of the snow was exemplary. The mountain wasn't crowded this early; perfect conditions for a friendly race.

I had the early advantage. Still, after skiing about halfway down the run, neither Danny nor Teddy had caught up. I anticipated them passing at any moment because I was losing steam. Rustiness and the thin Rocky Mountain air, were taking a toll.

The tortoise and the hare; I definitely related to the old yarn. Forced to stop, and out of breath, I was the arrogant hare. The tortoise would soon catch up and gloat.

I moved to the side, practically asthmatic, and attempted deep breathing exercises. Danny made a dramatic entrance, stopping beside me, spraying me with soft powder. He starred through my goggles to my eyes.

"Hey, Eli. Are you okay, hon?"

"I'm a little out of breath. I'll be okay," I answered with a wheeze.

"Babe, you're not okay. You're not used to the thin air."

I nodded, embarrassed.

"Same. No more racing. We'll go slowly. Together." Danny smiled warmly. His love was reassuring.

"Okay," I whispered, and Danny and I took off, this time at the same slow pace.

Teddy was at the base waiting.

"I beat you!" He exuberantly announced.

"Good going, squirt," Danny responded enthusiastically. Teddy beamed.

"Juice break," I announced.

Outside the base lodge we propped our skis. Then we removed our helmets and gloves, and entered the building to find a table.

"Large cranberry," I told Danny. As I put down my gloves and my helmet with goggles attached, I added, "I'll be right back. I'm going to the restroom."

As I turned to go Danny grabbed my arm.

"You're okay now?" He asked.

"Yeah. I can breath again." I smiled and gave Danny a quick kiss before leaving.

Men stared at me as I walked toward the restroom. How unusual. It was quite disconcerting. I missed not having my sunglasses shielding me from uninvited eye contact and I quickened my pace.

While returning to the table, I was stopped three times by men who wanted to buy me a drink. Of course I politely declined, but the unsolicited attention stunned me. I purposely bestowed an affectionate welcome back on Danny so they would see that I was taken.

"If this is the greeting I get, next time I'll pay men to hit on you," Danny teased.

"Can you stop doing that?" Teddy complained.

"Sorry." Then I turned to Danny. "You saw?" I gulped down my juice. The thin air was dehydrating.

"Who could miss?" he laughed.

"They're very bold here. Why are those men bothering me?"

"You are kidding, right?"

"No," I said. "Can you please order me another?" I indicated my empty glass.

"Sure," he replied. "Have you looked in the mirror today, Eli?"

"When I got dressed this morning."

"Baby, you're like Snow White in spandex."

Teddy rolled his eyes, took his iPhone from his pocket, and inserted his earbuds.

A waitress passed and Danny ordered me another large cranberry juice.

"When you bought this, didn't you notice how it clings to every luscious curve on your body?" Danny grinned.

"I thought you'd like it," I said n a flirty voice.

Danny smiled, almost laughing, and hugged me. "Of course I like it." He released me and held my gaze. "It's amazing on you. And with your coloring, well you do look like Snow White if she skied."

"I wanted you to like it."

"Why do you think I didn't pass you on the mountain? I liked the view." Danny laughed. "It never entered your mind that I'm not the only man who would be looking at your 'ass-etts?'"

I rolled my eyes at his attempt at humor. "No. Why would I think about people I don't know?" Danny wrapped his arm around my neck and playfully gave me noogies.

"Elizabeth you lovable knucklehead. I love how naïve you can be."

There was enough time for one more run before lunch. This time, even Teddy took it easy. When we finished, I was beat. I hoped eating lunch would revive me.

Delicious, hot food was what my body craved, but it wasn't enough. I was history, and it was obvious enough that Danny took one look at me and without asking, called the house caretaker to come and get me.

CHAPTER 43 - ELIZABETH

The sound of spraying water greeted me when I woke. Crackling wood and the scent of pine permeated my senses. Someone had lit the fireplace. It was cozy under the comforter and my limbs felt heavy. I didn't want to move. So I didn't.

The shower ceased leaving the sound of the fire. I wouldn't be alone much longer and that made me smile.

Moments later, Danny emerged from the bathroom wearing a bath sheet wrapped around his waist. Droplets of water glistened on his sculpted chest. I sighed. His damp, shaggy hair was tousled and something about its wetness and the way it fell, was so arousing. I couldn't help but grin from ear to ear. May I never grow bored with this view.

Danny rewarded me with his shy smile. "What?" he laughed.

I decided to feed him back the line he had used on me this morning. "Have you looked in the mirror today?" I asked.

Danny climbed onto the bed behind me tickling my neck with my hair. Droplets of water fell on my face and I giggled. "Not since I got dressed this morning," he said.

Now facing him, I ran my fingers from his cheekbone to his chin and back up the other side. All smooth. "Liar!" I laughed. "If you hadn't looked in the mirror since this morning your face would be a bleeding, scabby mess."

I turned to my side. Danny leaned over my shoulder, his fingers gently moving my shirt collar aside. The wetness from his hair as it brushed my neck, and his breath touching my ear, caused me to gasp.

"You've got me on that," he replied.

The slowness of his enunciation against my ear caused uncontrollable tremors. I squirmed, but I wanted to stop. My back and legs were already sore from skiing.

"My muscles hurt," I complained.

"Here. Let me," he answered.

Danny rolled me onto my stomach. He tried massaging my back but the fabric of the shirt was bunching up. He yanked it over my head.

"That's better," he declared.

Danny was right. What did I have to be modest about anyway? Danny's fingers adroitly kneaded my back, pressing all the right places. I hoped he would go on forever.

Then Danny's skillful hands moved down to my thighs that he expertly administered to. When Danny reached my inner thigh, shivers coursed through me. Soon this would stop being therapeutic.

Cold droplets of water fell on my lower back. Danny's hair was dripping. The coldness made me startle. Reflexively I rolled onto my back, bucking Danny who was on his knees leaning over me ready to continue the massage.

"You're dripping on me," I complained.

A mischievous grin played across his lips. Danny whipped off his towel and rubbed his hair with it.

"Better?"

I stared at his magnificence. I was mesmerized. There, Danny was, his perfect body naked. Danny grinned as a dare to take him. He expected me to reach out and pull him into my embrace. Painful to resist, but I had to.

Instead, I smiled and kissed his shoulder. Danny smirked and pulled me into his arms, pressing his lips against mine for the kisses Danny knew I'd be powerless to resist.

"Danny!" I squealed, and he grinned.

Danny kissed me again, urgently this time. His power pushed us into the pillows. Our hearts beat rapidly together as one. My head spun as we kept our lips locked together. His kisses, and his touch, drove me to an unparalleled frenzy. Danny wanted me so badly and I wanted him as much. I lost all control when he entered me, and I didn't care.

"Shower time," Danny murmured to me a while later. We had been lying peacefully in each other's arms. He was gently playing with my hair and I was absent-mindedly tracing abstract patterns on his chest with my finger.

"You sure know how to ruin a girl's good time," I pouted. I clasped my hands around his neck and delicately kissed his lips.

Danny smiled, his eyes twinkling. "I love you, Miss Eli."

His gentle hands held my cheeks as he kissed my impatient lips.

CHAPTER 44 - ELIZABETH

Following a long noisy dinner, Danny and I hung out downstairs watching the 84-inch 3D television Dad had installed earlier in the fall. Peace, quiet and the hot tub awaited as the perfect antidote.

Danny and I waited impatiently to see if anyone else planned to use the hot tub tonight. Fingers crossed – nobody would want to. Meanwhile, we watched an old romcom while listening to the rhythm of the house.

"I keep expecting Teddy," I whispered to Danny.

"Don't sweat it. Teddy's not going to bother us," Danny said with certainty.

"How do you know?"

"Because I threatened him. If Teddy dares to come down here without my permission he'll be skiing alone tomorrow."

Tomorrow. I was dreading it already. I had serious reservations about my ability to get out of bed in the morning. Usually it was the day after when being charley-horsed set in. If I was this bad tonight, I didn't want to think about tomorrow.

Worse, Danny wouldn't allow me to sulk in bed. Danny would twinkle those sapphire eyes I couldn't resist. Then Danny would smile that special smile he reserved for me, the one that lit his face and sent my head swirling. The pain would be unbearable, but those eyes and that smile. The promise of a day with them would motivate me past the agony.

I didn't want to listen to the comings and goings of our household members any longer. I wanted my evening to begin.

"Help me up?" I asked Danny. "I want to change."

Danny, graceful as a gazelle, stood, reached out his hand and pulled me up.

"Ow, ow, ow," I grimaced.

"Eli, you're not playing. You really do hurt."

"Yes," I hissed. "Finally he believes me!"

Danny was waiting by the time I changed into my new bikini. Silver-colored rings held the navy swirl confection together. More revealing than my usual, it was intended for the most private of parties.

I sauntered over to Danny and confidently tilted my chin toward him. His mouth was agape, his eyes popping. To get this reaction, the bikini was worth every penny it had cost and then some.

I ran my fingernail across his lower lip and smiled. "Glad you approve."

Danny swept me into his arms and kissed me. His warm touch against my exposed skin threatened to cloud my mind. I didn't want that, so I pulled away and took Danny's hand. "Hot tub," I commanded.

"That can wait," he answered with a sly smile.

"I thought you understood. I am in serious pain. I need bubble therapy."

"Elizabeth, you're killing me, love." I gave him a flirty shrug. "Did you ask your stylist to only choose clothes to torture me with?" Danny laughed.

"Of course not. I pick my own clothes to torture you with. Let's go."

Danny picked up two thick white terry robes from the bed and tossed one to me. "Eli, you'll want this. We're not in Malibu," he said while putting on the other.

"Thanks." And I dramatically blew Danny a kiss.

Danny was right. We needed the robes. While the hot tub was only a few steps from the door, the air temperature had to be down to the teens.

Bubbly steam rose from the ground in front of us. I let my robe slip off my shoulders to the heated floor tiles.

Danny watched my every move. For his benefit, I vamped it up. I smiled at him and then winked while shimmying my shoulders. I hadn't been thinking. This was not the weather for flirting while wearing a bikini. I dashed for the hot tub. It was sooooo cold out!

I lowered myself into the welcoming bubbles and settled on the tiled seat by a jet. Danny joined me. Without hesitation, he wrapped his arms around my shoulders and kissed the side of my neck. I smiled and removed his hands. Danny frowned, disappointed by this rebuff.

"Daniel, you don't get it. I am in pain." I emphasized the word 'pain.'

"Where do you hurt the most?" he asked tenderly.

"Everywhere but here." I indicated my heart.

Danny eyed me skeptically.

"Okay. Mostly my shoulders, back, butt and thighs."

"I don't understand," he laughed "For a girl who's always exercising, how can you be so out of shape?"

"I am not out of shape!" I protested.

"Wrong word. E, your shape looks great. It's your muscles that suck."

"Thanks a lot, Daniel. Must I remind you, I was in a cast for a month."

"I'm sorry. I wasn't thinking."

I didn't want to bring up my ankle. An argument would be counterproductive.

Danny sighed and softened his voice. "Let me take a look."

I turned my back toward Danny and he began to knead my shoulders and back.

"Baby, you are really tight. Your knots have knots."

Danny kissed my neck, sending shivers through me despite the heat of the water. Then he swept my hair around to one shoulder and again began

148

expertly massaging my neck and shoulders. Danny's strong hands knew exactly what they were doing. Soon the tension left my body. This was great!

"Where did you learn this?" I purred. I was practically in a trance.

"I have to keep some secrets from you, babe."

"This should not be one of them."

Danny kissed my neck again which unleashed a new round of shivers.

"They don't do that at the spa," I observed.

"They better not."

Danny untied the bow at my neck. The small fabric triangles fell forward. My massage continued for another few minutes. Total, heavenly bliss.

"I'll do better when we go in," Danny said as he stopped. I couldn't imagine it being any better, but if he said so.

Then Danny effortlessly lifted me onto his lap. In the hot tub, I was weightless. He cupped my face in his hands and kissed me. My breath was taken away.

My arms laced around Danny's neck and his wrapped around my shoulders and back as I sat sideways, my feet playing in the wake of the nearby jet. Our eyes locked on each other's with unmatched intensity.

"I love you, Elizabeth. More than anything," Danny whispered.

"I love you too, Daniel. Always."

Danny and I pressed closer and closer like two magnets that couldn't defy the laws of physics. Our lips never separated. We were oblivious to everything but each other as the jets created a hot, pulsating swirl that enveloped us.

Soon I felt Danny's hardness probing, wanting to enter me. We exchanged knowing smiles, and I nodded. Danny peeled back the fabric of his swim trunks, freeing himself from its confines. My insides clenched in anticipation.

Then he lifted me, my back against his chest. As he did so, he moved the fabric of my bikini bottom aside and settled me on top of him. I gasped at his entrance and moaned. With his hands on my breasts and his lips feathery on my neck, the fullness was exquisite. My hands pressed on his thighs and I began to move rhythmically, losing myself in his love.

"Ahem," a throat cleared from behind us. Shit! Steve!

"Dad!" Danny exclaimed.

Danny and I abruptly stopped, looking at each other in panicked fear. His hardness wilted and slipped out. Danny pulled me into his chest, shielding me from view while he re-tied my bikini top.

Had Steve seen us? Had he recognized our movements and heard our moans? Thankfully our backs were toward him. Neither Danny nor Steve could see the shade of crimson I had turned. I wanted to drown myself out of embarrassment.

I kept my face buried against Danny. This was so much worse than Teddy's interruption.

"Sorry. I didn't see… The landscaping…" Steve stammered.

"Dad. It's okay," Danny cut him off.

It was painful. Steve was as uncomfortable, and nothing shocked Steve.

I shyly turned around. "Hi," I said tentatively.

"Red looks good on you, Elizabeth," he said sternly, having regained his composure.

"Dad, we're sorry," Danny apologized. "We weren't really doing anything."

I felt myself blush worse than before, knowing what a lie that was.

"Really? Then I'm glad I didn't show up when nothing became something." Steve said pointedly, seeing through Danny's lie.

"We thought everyone was sleeping," Danny explained, further putting his sizeable foot in his mouth.

"That's why it's called a common area. Anyone can use it. Any time." Danny and I fell silent, chastened like naughty children being disciplined. "You have a bedroom. Use it."

CHAPTER 45 - DANIEL

Aspen was great. After we had acclimated, my days spent on the slopes with Elizabeth were bliss. Of course Teddy usually tagged along, but we devised ways of losing him for at least part of each day.

Evenings were quiet, family times. Randi planned a different activity each night, but with only three days remaining, Eli and I were going out tomorrow. She hadn't wanted to hurt Randi's feelings, but I was insistent and had approached Randi privately.

"Of course I don't mind. I've been wondering why you were home every evening. Where are you taking her?"

"I made a reservation at Matsuhisa." We hadn't eaten sushi since we arrived.

"Perfect! Tomorrow's a great day too. We're doing girls' day at the spa."

The men countered with father/son day, but Mike was fighting a cold and begged off skiing. Teddy, feeling guilty, stayed behind. It would be me alone with Dad.

Conditions were perfect when Dad and I arrived at the base. Clouds cut the sun's glare yet there was no threat of snow. The temperature had moderated to the twenties, with no wind.

Dad clapped me on the shoulder as we entered the gondola.

"Great day, Danny!" he eagerly exclaimed.

"Too bad Mike isn't feeling well," I said, though I was glad to be alone with Dad.

"Don't tell Michael I said this," Dad laughed, "But I'm glad he and Teddy didn't come. I never get to spend time alone with you anymore. I miss you, Danny."

"I miss you too, Dad."

"I'm looking forward to this summer; you and me working together for an entire shoot. Vancouver will never be the same."

"Can they handle us?" I laughed. "Two Newmans in one town."

I was going to be Dad's assistant on his next film. Scheduled for production this summer, I was thrilled for the opportunity.

Soon the gondola reached the summit. Through the windows I could see the snow blowing. It would be colder than I thought.

"Danny! C'mon!" Dad called. As soon as we disembarked he turned and began his descent down the mountain.

My goggles needed adjusting. "I'll be right there," I shouted back.

I quickly caught up. Despite his grandstanding, Dad wasn't that far ahead.

"Hey, slowpoke," he said good-naturedly. "You're not going to let your old man beat you to the bottom, are you?" And off Dad went, carving turns through the powder, leaving me frustrated and alone. So much for togetherness.

Dad turns everything into a competition, and skiing was no different. He insists on skiing only the most difficult terrain, and it's important for him to beat me down the mountain. It's like some sort of middle-aged test of virility.

By the end of a morning spent keeping up with Dad, I was weary. Needing time to recover, I decided to eat lunch with all deliberate slowness. A thick, juicy burger covered with mushrooms was exactly what I craved, and the one I ordered arrived cooked to perfection. Plus, it came with my favorite, extra crispy fries. Dad ordered the same.

"It's a treat spending time with you, Daniel," Dad said after taking his first bite.

Daniel. In one word Dad telegraphed his intention to have a serious discussion. What was it with parents? They showed their hand so easily. But what now? This better not be about the hot tub incident.

"I agree. This is great, Dad. We should do it more often. Maybe this summer."

"You've changed this year," Dad began. "Elizabeth has been a good influence."

Now I knew. This was about Eli and me.

"Yes, she is. I can't get into trouble when I'm with Elizabeth."

"Is that what you want? Someone to keep you out of trouble?"

I hadn't thought about Eli that way. Did I want her keeping me out of trouble? If Dad meant had I sworn off partying, the answer was no. Between needing a clear head for finals and being on break, it had been weeks.

Over the last few days I had begun looking forward to hanging out with the guys when we returned to Donnelly. Trouble. Yeah. I was getting ready for some trouble.

"No. Not really. I love Eli, but I'm not ready to change yet," I answered. "Some trouble would be fun. I'm in danger of becoming too domesticated." I laughed trying to keep it as light as possible.

I spied a passerby trying not to be noticed as he starred at Dad. I hated when we were engaged in regular family activities and strangers recognized him. It was so rude. Couldn't a man eat lunch with his son?

Now that man was going to report to his companions that he had spotted Steven Newman dining with someone who must be his son. How sweet! Depending on his previous opinion of Dad, it would either confirm that he thought Dad was a nice guy or, if he didn't like Dad, it might leave him thinking differently.

I preferred being on the slopes where Dad's goggles left his face obscured and unrecognizable. On the mountain, Dad was one more anonymous man with his son.

"Does Elizabeth know?"

"That I'm in the mood for some trouble? We haven't discussed it. Eli doesn't like when I party, but she knows it's who I am." I said. "I don't want to reform yet. I'm only twenty, Dad. Eli knows I still want to have fun. It's not like we're married."

"You look it. For two weeks I've felt like an intruder on your honeymoon."

"Dad! Don't be ridiculous," I stammered. He was embarrassing me.

"You don't see it, Daniel. You're always touching each other. She leaves, you kiss her. She returns, you kiss her. And in between your eyes follow her to the door. When she re-enters, you light up and your eyes follow her until she's by your side again."

"Dad! You're exaggerating! I know Eli and I are always together. We love each other. Maybe we'll end up together. Maybe we won't. I don't know. We're young."

"You are young. You shouldn't be this serious about one girl."

"You were. You and Mom got your first apartment when you were nineteen."

"And we were too young. I'm sure I would have married Mom eventually, but I never had the chance to think about it. It was New York. What student could afford his own apartment? We both needed someone to room with. It was practical."

"Dad, don't worry. I'm not you. I've never told Eli she's my life partner."

"As long as Elizabeth knows. I wouldn't want her to get hurt because you keep the truth from her or avoid the difficult discussions."

"I would never hurt Eli. We're always honest with each other." After a pause I added, "All right. I'll bring it up tonight. In case she's forgotten."

CHAPTER 46 - DANIEL

For Aspen, I felt dressed. I wore a sport coat over my jeans and shirt. Somehow that made the evening seem more special.

I watched CNN while waiting in the playroom for Eli. She had kicked me out of our room saying it was more date-like if she made a grand entrance.

Elizabeth was right. My jaw dropped when she entered the room. Flustered, I rose from the sofa and embraced her.

"Babe, you take my breath away. I love you, lady."

Eli smiled shyly, and I kissed her luscious pink-stained lips.

For her part, Eli's outfit was in keeping with her theme for this trip. Skinny jeans that showed off every curve were tucked into Uggs. A tunic length, scoop-necked cashmere sweater with broad cream and peach colored horizontal stripes worn belted, emphasized her tiny waist. All eyes would certainly be on Eli tonight.

All eyes in the dining room were as we stopped by before leaving the house. Every parent starred as we said, "good-night."

Before even biting into the first piece of sushi, I was happy all over again about my choice of Matsuhisa. I had not realized until I read the menu how sick of cowboy food I was. Once we left Aspen, I did not want beef for a long time.

I could almost hear Juliette snickering. That was a name I hadn't thought of lately. Once she got over our break-up, Juliette had been cordial whenever Eli or I had run into her.

Tonight Elizabeth looked even prettier than usual. The dim ceiling lights reflected off her shiny, well-groomed hair. Eli's deep emerald eyes were like multi-faceted gems and her skin glowed from her spa treatment.

I lifted a perfect, manicured hand. It felt like satin. When I kissed it, it even smelled nice, fresh but light. The perfume Elizabeth wore was also fresh and light, with citrus undertones. Eli was intoxicating.

Our eyes met, and we exchanged smiles. It was so good to be alone. I kissed Elizabeth's hand again. With no parents watching, I could hold it all night.

The first course of sashimi was placed before us. I expertly picked up a piece of salmon with my chopsticks and raised it up toward Elizabeth.

"Here," I said, and I brought the fish to her lips. Eli blushed, giggling at my gesture. Then she bit into the salmon. I smiled in delight.

"Danny, you're not going to do that all night, are you?" Eli giggled.

"No." I grinned and popped the remains into my own mouth. Then I leaned over and kissed Eli's salty lips before we continued dining.

As the meal progressed, Elizabeth was unusually quiet. I could see through her sparkling emeralds that she wanted to say something, but so far couldn't. That was all right. I was having the same problem, only as far as I knew, Elizabeth hadn't yet guessed.

After sharing broiled black cod with miso, I lifted a strand of hair off Eli's face. As our eyes met, I quietly asked, "What's up, hon?"

Eli blushed. I was right. There was something. I reached over and reassuringly squeezed her hand.

"One more week until we return to Donnelly. I can't bear the lack of privacy," she complained. I smiled and pulled Eli close for a kiss.

"We'll figure it out," I promised.

It pleased me knowing how important our physical relationship was to Eli. It had only been a month, yet she was always eager to be with me. Then the perfect idea hit me.

"When we get home, let's go to Malibu for a few days."

"I love you, Daniel," Eli answered with a wicked grin followed by a very warm kiss on my lips. I took that to be an emphatic yes.

Dad would not be happy. It was easy to give advice. It was not easy to follow that advice when seated beside Elizabeth. I would wait until we returned to Donnelly before having any state-of-the-relationship discussions.

Three days later we deplaned into sun-drenched Santa Monica Airport.

"I'll pick you up in an hour," I told Eli as we kissed good-bye.

Back in Brentwood, Dad followed me to my bedroom. I hefted my suitcase onto the bed and opened it to unpack. Graciela had to get my laundry done.

"Why are you taking Elizabeth to the beach?" Dad barked.

I stopped emptying the suitcase. "Dad, I listened to everything you said. I spent a lot of time thinking. I appreciate your concern, but when I went to dinner with Eli, I took one look at her eyes. They were sparkling like diamonds. Eli loves me. Unconditionally. She knows my flaws and she knows what I'm about. Yet Eli loves me, all of me. And I love her too."

CHAPTER 47 - ELIZABETH

Snow blanketed the majestic Donnelly campus when we returned. A deep freeze greeted us, providing as sharp a contrast to Malibu as you could find. Melancholy was unavoidable.

It wasn't entirely surprising that I didn't see Danny much the first week back. Danny was anxious to see his friends and party. Part of me, a large part if I was completely honest, wished he would grow up.

For now I was the understanding girlfriend, giving Danny free rein. If it meant remaining silent while he got wasted, the rewards of our relationship far outweighed this blip and Danny appreciated the lack of pressure. We registered for another political science class together and Friday Danny was a body in motion with non-stop fidgeting. I kept glancing at him with question marks in my eyes, but received no answer. Finally, I typed him a note, "What's wrong with you?" but all Danny did was smile.

When class ended, Danny was anxious to leave, excited about something, but he wouldn't tell me what. He was full of manic energy. "C'mon, Eli. Let's go."

"Go where?" I asked.

"You'll see."

Danny pulled me along, crossing the campus. Despite his grip, I slipped on an ice patch, but Danny caught me before I fell. He frowned at my stiletto leather boots.

At the far end of the Student Center was a large multi-purpose room known as The Stage. With capacity of a couple hundred, this space was used as an independent performance venue. It was here that Danny stopped.

"Look!" Danny pointed at the outside bulletin board where they posted flyers promoting upcoming events.

Halfway down a blue flyer with black ink, printed in a large font, but not the largest, was his name along with Duncan, Ron and Kirk.

"That's you!" I squealed, my excitement matching Danny's. It wasn't clear what it meant though.

"That's me!" he responded.

"That's you!" I squealed even more loudly. Danny's smile was huge. He grabbed me around my waist, lifting me off the ground, and hugged me. "What does this mean?" I hated sounding ignorant.

Danny kissed my cheek and released me. "Battle of the Bands. Round One is next Friday. And we're in!"

I knew Danny played bass with his friends, but he hadn't told me that they had formed an official band, nor that they were any good.

"Awesome! When did this happen?"

"Auditions were yesterday. I wanted to surprise you if we made it."

"So you've been rehearsing. I thought you were just getting wasted with Duncan."

Danny laughed. "We were doing that too, Eli."

"When's your next rehearsal?"

"Tonight."

"Can I come?"

"You want to come?" I didn't understand Danny's surprise. I loved him and this was important. Of course I wanted to come.

"But it's Duncan. And you hate the Village crowd."

"I can deal with it," I said confidently. "I'm a big girl. It's you I want to be there for. This is important to you, so it's important to me."

Ron and Kirk lived in The Village, a collection of fifty semi-attached dwellings at the far end of Donnelly. The Village was the perfect place for heavy partiers to live. The increased privacy afforded by its distant location, lack of resident faculty and RAs, meant you could pretty much do whatever you wanted with impunity. However, even by Village standards Ron and Kirk's place was notorious.

When Danny and I arrived, the house was already rocking. A section of the living room was cleared of furniture and turned into a makeshift stage. Ron's keyboard, Duncan's drums, Kirk's guitar and Danny's bass guitar waited. There was even a microphone. Along the wall facing the 'stage' were two well-worn sofas, and pillows were scattered across the floor as additional seating.

Duncan was downing a beer, not his first, when we entered the dimly lit room. Danny joined him, picking up a long-neck. The recessed lights had their bulbs removed, and instead there were a couple of low-wattage lamps plus the glow from the nearby kitchen.

The pungent aroma of pot assaulted my nostrils. I was definitely outside my comfort zone. Then I scanned the room and realized Duncan was the only person other than Danny whom I had ever met. Not a comforting thought.

Two skinny guys in t-shirts and jeans, one with three-day stubble on his chin, approached us. They smiled, friendly enough.

"Ron, Kirk, this is my lady, Elizabeth." Danny kept one hand around my back and held the beer with his other as he introduced me. I wasn't keen on being referred to as 'my lady.' Danny did not speak like that. In this environment, identification as Danny's possession made me feel safe. Tonight I wouldn't protest.

"I can't wait to hear you play," I told them. I had never met Ron, Kirk or their roommates. Despite my discomfort, I smiled at them.

Because we hadn't been together all week, and I wanted Danny to regret it. I had dressed in black leggings tucked into high-heeled leather boots and a long Stella McCartney sweater with a plunging neckline, my version of upscale rocker chic.

Tonight Danny didn't mind me wearing those boots. He was enjoying the overall effect way too much. His friends were gawking. Let them see who Danny's lady was.

"Who's the model with Newman?" I heard someone remark.

Danny heard it, too. He beamed with pride as he squeezed my shoulder and kissed me.

After making the rounds, Danny handed me a beer and led me to one of the sofas.

"We're going to start now, baby," he said.

I smiled at Danny and he kissed me hard, bruising my lips. At this party, the guys were not shy about aggressive public displays of affection. It was as though the girls were marked so the men would know who was taken. Demonstrating possession, not love, counted as cool. It was a place you brought your mistress, not your wife.

Except that she was leaning over a thrift-shop issue coffee table rolling joints, I never would have noticed the ordinary girl seated on the sofa. Wearing torn jeans and a tour t-shirt from an unfamiliar indie band, unkempt dirty-blonde hair fell across her face. A black rose was tattooed on her upper arm below the hem of her short-sleeved shirt. The flower looked dead. Why would she want a wilted flower permanently inked on her arm? Did she feel wilted?

The girl looked up from her task as our embracing bodies cast a shadow over her workspace.

"Dan, who's your date?" she asked in distracted curiosity.

Dan? Nobody called Danny 'Dan.'

"Phoebs, this is my lady, Elizabeth," Danny boasted, his hand around my waist. She handed him one of the joints. Danny lit it and inhaled deeply.

"E, this is Phoebe."

"Nice to meet you," I told her.

I didn't know what else to say, although I had a feeling it was not at all nice to meet her. She was definitely not my type.

"Phoebs, this is good stuff," Danny said as he took another hit.

"It should be," she answered, "You bought it."

Of course he did. Who better to invite to the party than Danny and his bankroll?

"Danny, c'mon. Let's do it," Ron said as he passed on his way to the stage.

"I've got to go, hon," Danny said. Then he squeezed my waist and kissed me.

After one more long pull on the joint, Danny handed it to me.

"Hold this for me, Eli." I nodded, surprised by the request.

"Phoebs, take good care of my girl," Danny said, and he left to join his band.

I took the seat beside Phoebe. Glancing at my hand holding the joint I wondered what Danny wanted me to do with it? Would he be coming back after each song? Or would Danny wait until the band was taking a break? Was there an ashtray to rest it in? A quick glance at the table provided an answer; no.

Phoebe had finished her handiwork and lit her own joint.

"I didn't know Dan had a girlfriend," she scowled. "Are you new?"

Phoebe starred straight ahead as she spoke. How did she not know?

I took a small hit from Danny's joint. I needed it.

"I'm not new," I answered indignantly. "Everyone knows I'm with Danny."

"Not here we don't," she responded coldly.

I looked at her incredulously as I took another hit of the joint. Was this an alternate reality? How did they not know about me? I frowned.

"When did Dan take up with you?" Phoebe's sneer made it sound like some casual hook-up or at best, a tawdry affair.

I wasn't about to reveal my life story so I opted for the abridged version.

"We've been together since October," I answered confidently.

For the first time since Danny left us, Phoebe turned and stared at me. Her wide-eyed expression spoke volumes. But why the surprise?

"You've been with Dan since October? Unbelievable."

"Why is that unbelievable?" I took a much needed large hit.

"He doesn't seem the type."

What did that mean? Just what 'type' did she think Danny was? Or me? I wasn't going to get into it with her. Phoebe was insignificant. She meant nothing, so why bother. The only one in this room who meant anything required my undivided attention at this moment, and attention was getting difficult for me to do.

Warm-ups over, the band began playing. Rock music thumped loudly, vibrating. I sat back against the cushions, focusing on Danny. "He's mine," I thought smugly. Then I grinned. Danny only had eyes for me.

With my feet propped on the table, I was feeling mellow. Was this being wasted? I wasn't sure. I just knew Phoebe wasn't my concern anymore.

Danny smiled at me from the stage while he sang. The lyrics became our private conversation. I smiled back and took a longer hit of the joint. Eyes lingering on Danny, I couldn't help myself. I winked.

Danny burst into laughter. What was so funny? I didn't know, but I started laughing too. Danny's laughter was infectious.

"From the top," he choked out, tears filling his eyes, his laughter uncontrollable.

Nearly doubled over, laughing, Danny couldn't play.

Frustrated, Kirk stepped in, "Take five, everybody," he snapped.

Near hysterical, Danny laid down his bass and sprinted over. He knelt beside me, cupped my face in his hands, and kissed me hard. Mmm. That felt good. And I looked at him with dreamy eyes.

Danny reached for the joint and inhaled deeply. Then he climbed over my legs and onto the sofa beside me in one quick motion. Danny cradled me in his arms and smoothed some hairs off my face.

"You're so wasted Elizabeth," he laughed.

"Am I?" I asked dreamily.

"Yes. And you're adorable," Danny answered, his breath on my face. With Phoebe sitting on the other end of the sofa, Danny was practically on top of me. Excitement percolated throughout my body. I tingled.

In this closeness I reached for Danny and smashed my lips to his. Danny's hands were in my hair, pulling me so close. My body pressed against his, nearly joined. I was frantic. I wanted Danny so badly. I wanted him now and he knew it.

"Later hon," he whispered, "We're in public."

"I don't care," I giggled.

Danny grinned, his face lit up. "You are so wasted," he said again.

"Yeah," was all I could answer.

Danny ran his index finger over my lips and I kissed it. We looked at each other with lustful eyes. Then Danny's lips were on mine again, so possessively, so passionately. I could only contain myself because he was still in control.

"I am so hot," I whispered.

"You sure are," he chuckled, "But we'll have to wait. We don't have a room."

"Find one. I want you now," I whispered.

"You would hate yourself tomorrow."

"No I wouldn't," I protested.

"You would hate me too. I want you to still love me tomorrow."

"Do they have any food here?" I asked, still whispering. "I'm starving."

Danny grinned as he pondered my request. "Oh, Eli," he laughed.

All I could do was smile, a dreamy, lustful smile. Damn his good breeding!

"Phoebs," Danny called. "Time to order pizza. My lady's got the munchies."

"Order it yourself," she snarled.

"C'mon, Phoebs. I don't even know who we call. You always order the pizza. The number's on your speed dial.

Grumbling, Phoebe reached for her phone.

"Thanks. They have my card on file." Of course they did.

Danny turned his attention back to me. I wanted him so badly.

"Time to rehearse. I'll keep this," Danny plucked the stub of the joint from my fingers.

A quick kiss, and he returned to his band. I sighed, thrilled with the rear view of his snug jeans as he walked away. That would have to suffice for now.

Phoebe completed the pizza order. She was impressive. She knew exactly what to do. I marveled at how prepared she was. Keeping the pizzeria phone number on speed dial, knowing they would have Danny's credit card information, now that was efficient.

I knew only one person who could pull off a feat like this so effortlessly, and that was Dad's secretary. Danny was only a college student, but he enjoyed many accoutrements that no other student had. Did that mean? Did Danny have..."

"Are you Danny's secretary?" I blurted to Phoebe in my state of giggles.

Phoebe's response was the nastiest glare I'd ever received. If looks killed, Danny would soon be a widow. Mom and Dad would be heartbroken. Teddy would be crushed. Didn't Danny pay Phoebe well enough?

"Are you kidding me?" Phoebe snarled.

"You don't have to be rude," I exclaimed. "I just thought because..." My voice tailed off.

"Sorry, princess," she responded sarcastically, "I'm not Dan's secretary or anyone else's. Why? Are you his wife?"

I thought about this and grinned. Danny and I spent virtually every night together. He loved me, so yeah, maybe I was.

"Sort of, yes, I guess," I answered, still giggling.

Phoebe glared again. "How did I get saddled with Newman's wasted date?" she muttered.

I may be wasted, but I knew I didn't want to engage Phoebe in any more conversation. I turned my attention back to Danny where it counted.

Danny was excellent on the bass. He had an intoxicating singing voice, too. His melodic tenor danced on my ear. Danny could perform all night, and it would not be long enough.

The sway of his hips, and the strength of his grip on the bass were raw masculinity. Danny's eyes sparkling for only me, were overpowering. Other girls were starring at his every move. I smiled smugly; I was the girl Danny was taking home.

Soon the pizza arrived, and I struggled to stop at two slices. I desperately wanted a third. Just because we paid for it didn't mean I should be a hog. I really did crave that third slice. Stella McCartney said no.

Gradually the buzz wore off. I was sleepy. Despite the loud music and the lumpy sofa cushions, I dozed. When I woke, the music had stopped and through my eyelashes I could see Danny and Ron in tense discussion.

I kept my eyes closed. Two girls were talking to Phoebe, about me.

"Who is she?" the African-American girl asked. Before Phoebe could answer, the washed-out preppy blonde asked, "Why was Dan making out with her?"

"She's a stuck-up twit. Says she's his girlfriend," Phoebe tersely explained. "Since October."

"Dan has a girlfriend. That makes no sense," said the African-American.

"He always said he was a free-agent," the blonde added.

"Pru, maybe that's so you'd be content as a friend with benefits," the African-American said caustically.

"Jazz, it's been a while since I enjoyed benefits," Pru snapped. "I'll ask Amelia."

"She might be an import," Jazz suggested.

"From where? Teen Vogue?" Pru laughed at her own joke and Jazz joined her.

I'd grant them another minute of speculation before 'waking'.

"Why has Dan kept her hidden?" Jazz asked.

"Maybe he hasn't," said Phoebe. "Look, we're the ones who are hidden. We're always up here. We rarely go to The Cellar and we never do dorm parties. Look at how Dan dotes on her. They were all over each other."

"But Amelia told me…." Pru stopped mid-sentence as Danny approached.

"Phoebs, how's my lady doing?"

"Looks like she's sleeping," Phoebe answered curtly.

"I'll wake her," Danny replied with a grin in his voice.

I readied myself for his touch as Danny settled onto the sofa beside me.

"Time to go home, sleepyhead," he said softly as he lifted my chin and grazed my lips with his. I opened my eyes with a big smile as I met Danny's sapphire gaze.

"Hi," I whispered back. I wrapped my arms around his neck and returned his kiss with ardor.

Those awful girls were watching. I happily put on a show. Then Danny took my hand, and I turned on my megawatt smile.

"I love you Daniel," I whispered as I gently moved a lock of hair off his face with the intimacy reserved only for a serious love.

"I love you too, Elizabeth. Ready to go?"

"More than ready." I squeezed his hand.

Danny playfully pulled me up. He retrieved my jacket from the back of a chair and helped me into it. Danny's arm around my shoulder, our eyes locked on each other, we strode out passed the three gawking girls.

CHAPTER 48 - ELIZABETH

Tuesday was damp and dreary. Despite Rachel's insistence that a day when the temperature reached fifty degrees constituted a thaw, the rawness of the thick clouds left me chilled to the bone. By nightfall I even put on socks with my Uggs.

I was flying solo tonight. Rachel and Chloe didn't want to go to the library, and Danny was at rehearsal. The guys wanted no distractions. They insisted rehearsals be closed, even to girlfriends.

A similar desire led me to occupy a carrel in the basement of the library's original nineteenth century building. The musty stacks created a cozy, comforting environment.

Solitude virtually guaranteed, I prepared for Political Science. With his grueling rehearsal schedule, Danny was relying on me for tomorrow's class.

Sometime later, footsteps caused me to look up from my note taking. I recognized Pru and Jazz. They hadn't struck me as library types. They must be at a loss for what to do this evening.

The pace of their steps indicated that they were looking for someone. I was relieved that they did not recognize me when they passed by. I was not dressed for a date with Danny tonight. I was not even dressed for public consumption. All I had wanted was warmth and comfort.

My face was make-up free. My hair was pulled back into a thick braid, and Danny's navy knit cap covered my head. Donnelly logo sweat pants were tucked into Uggs. A zippered hoodie over a long-sleeved t-shirt was cozy. Danny's Burberry scarf around my neck was the only luxury.

When we weren't together, I liked wearing an article of clothing that belonged to Danny. The faded scent of his cologne on the swath of cashmere brought me instant pleasure. Lifting it to my nose and inhaling, I fantasized Danny's presence. And I could enjoy a dose any time I wanted!

"Amelia. There you are," I heard Pru's voice nearby.

My ears perked up. Friday, Amelia's name was mentioned several times as though she held the key. But to what?

"When did you get back?" Jazz asked.

"Late last night. What's so urgent, Jasmine?"

"You missed an interesting party Friday. Didn't she, Pru?"

"Yeah. Where were you?"

"At my own interesting party. I was visiting James, remember?"

"Now it makes sense," Jazz said.

"What's your status with Dan?" Pru asked Amelia. My stomach fluttered uncomfortably. Fear gripped me.

"We've hooked-up a few times. So?" Amelia answered.

My pen slipped from my grasp, my muscles unable to control its weight. It made a gentle thud on my open book.

"Recently?" Pru pressed.

"Mostly very recently," Amelia answered matter-of-factly. "Dan's sweet. I'm thinking of dropping James. I'm tired of driving to Hanover."

Recently! What the hell? My stomach lurched as horror consumed me.

"Don't shred your gas card yet," said Jazz.

"What don't I know guys?" Amelia asked.

"You should have seen Dan at Ron and Kirk's Friday night," Jazz began.

"He showed up with a model," Pru added.

"Phoebe said she's his girlfriend. They've been together almost all year."

"Impossible," Amelia said, her voice tinged with hurt. "How did Dan keep that a secret?"

"The girl's a freshman," Pru stated. "She lives in a dorm."

"What was she like?" Amelia asked scornfully.

"Her name's Elizabeth. She's gorgeous, like an actress. Everything about her was couture, like she stepped out of the pages of Vogue," said Jazz.

"Or Beverly Hills. Doesn't Dan come from there?" Pru added.

"I think so," said Amelia. "Was she up from Vassar for the weekend?"

"No," Pru answered. "Phoebe says Duncan knows her and he doesn't like her."

"Amelia," Jazz advised, "Stay with James. They were all over each other and Dan said, 'I love you.'"

Enough! Nauseas, I crammed my laptop and books into my tote bag and jammed my arms into my jacket before I threw up. I shook so badly I risked dropping everything. "Keep it together," I urged myself.

Once outside, I inhaled large gulps of frigid winter air. I didn't know what to do. I stood in front of the library clutching my bag, immobile, unable to move.

I needed to think. What was there to even consider? It was obvious like a slap in the face. Danny had cheated, and recently. Recently. There was that word again.

I didn't need the calendar to verify that it had to mean last week, when I naively granted Danny free-reign to party with the boys.

Recently. The word echoed in my brain. Sobs wanted their release, but I stifled them. I was in public. I needed my room if I could get there quickly enough.

I ran most of the way, breathless from gulping the painful January air.

Dashing into the suite, I startled Chloe, sitting in the living room reading. Not stopping, I continued to my bedroom. The door slammed closed, and I buried my head in the pillows and wept. Great, body-wracking sobs overwhelmed me. I was shaking. Uncontrollable.

Was something wrong with me? I thought Danny and I had a great relationship. He told me he loved me. Had he lied? Did he say those words because I wanted to hear them, no, needed to hear them? I had given him everything, and more. What was I lacking? How blind was I?

Danny made me believe I was everything to him. He made me believe I satisfied his every need and then some. I recalled this weekend. Danny and I had been together continuously since Friday afternoon. It had been great, as always. At least I thought so.

We had spent passionate time alone. We had made love numerous times. Danny couldn't take his hands off me and I couldn't take mine off him. And now I learned that for Danny it had all been a lie. He wanted Amelia? That wasn't possible.

Was Danny playing a part? Why be so cruel? I hadn't pursued him. I hadn't asked him to become my boyfriend. I had been content with being friends until it became apparent that we both wanted more. If Danny couldn't properly love me, then let me go. Let me be free to fall in love with someone who would love me.

Exhaustion finally claimed me and I fell into a fitful sleep.

Waking in the middle of the night, curled protectively in fetal position, I cried again. Still dressed from the library, I clutched myself tightly, trying to literally hold myself together.

A fresh wave of nausea swept through me, this one too strong. I ran to the bathroom and threw up. I did not feel any better. I threw up again, but my empty stomach produced dry heaves. Collapsing onto the hard tile floor, I wept.

I willed myself off the floor and back to bed. It wasn't even five o'clock. I glanced at my desk. The glow from my phone distracted me. Perhaps I should call home. No. Bad idea. Mom would assume someone had died or been hospitalized if the phone rang at this hour. It was one something at home.

Somebody had died. Me. My heart had shattered. I wasn't certain it would remain beating by daybreak.

There was a text message in my in-box. When I pressed the touch screen my swollen eyes read: "E – I love u – D." I broke out in sobs all over again. How could he!

How could Danny text that? It was so obviously false. How much could one person lie?

Fitful sleep reclaimed me once more.

A knock on the door woke me. Rachel.

"We're going to breakfast. Are you coming?" she asked, oblivious to my pain.

"No. I don't feel well," I answered. "I'll see you later."

"I'll bring you some Cheerios."

Rachel was the best, but I couldn't confide in her. Rachel had always suspected Danny would hurt me this way. I couldn't tolerate her "I told you so," even if unvoiced.

As soon as Rachel and Chloe left, I pulled myself out of bed and staggered to the bathroom. A hot, steamy shower would do me good.

The reflection in the mirror looked like death, with red, swollen eyes. I would need an entire hair and make-up crew to look presentable today. Unfortunately, I was not on a movie set.

I skipped morning classes and ate the Cheerios for lunch. Avoiding Danny was not an option. We had Political Science today. After class we had to talk. Then I would break up with Danny. It was better that way. Let Danny know he couldn't break my heart with impunity.

Sunglasses on, I took my seat in the classroom. I barely controlled my trembling. Which had me more nervous; Danny sitting next to me, or what the professor would say about my eyewear?

Soon, Danny entered, taking his seat beside me. He had no idea, not a hint, of the hell he was responsible for causing.

"Hey, babe," Danny said.

He quickly kissed my cheek. I knew where those lips had been. It took every ounce of strength not to show my revulsion.

"Hey," I answered quietly.

"Your roomies said you weren't feeling well." Danny's genuine concern surprised me. How could he act the same as usual?

"Yeah," I answered lethargically.

Professor Dennison approached the lectern.

"We'll talk later," Danny said, and he squeezed my hand. We certainly will. "You're sunglasses, Eli."

I shrugged him off, ignoring him.

"Miss Jacobs," Professor Dennison looked directly at me, "It isn't particularly sunny in here today." The color rose hot in my cheeks.

"I need these today," I stammered. Danny cocked his head toward me.

"Did Mr. Newman give you a black eye last night?" he asked drolly.

"Of course not! Danny would never do that!" I was appalled. How dare the professor accuse Danny of spousal abuse. Danny was gentle, kind and sweet.

What was I thinking? The man had broken my heart. I had spent the entire night crying. I should be twisting the skewer. But I couldn't. Danny would never hit me.

"Miss Jacobs, I wasn't serious. If I thought Mr. Newman had given you a black eye, I would meet with you privately and refer you to a social worker."

I turned a deep shade of scarlet, humiliated.

"I'm sorry, professor," I finally answered, "Please, I have conjunctivitis and the fluorescents are bothering me. My eyes are very sensitive."

"Just for today, Miss Jacobs. Next time bring a doctor's note."

"Thank you professor." I was so relieved. My puffy red eyes would stay hidden.

The professor might have bought my story but not Danny. He spent much of the class watching me.

At dismissal, Danny helped me with my jacket. His manners left me chillier than the weather. The thaw had ended. Winter was back, mirroring my emotions.

"We have to talk," I said somberly when we reached the path to the quad.

"Something's wrong." Danny said just as solemnly.

"Not here."

As usual, Danny unfolded his arm around my shoulders. Normally it felt warm and comforting. Today I shrugged him off. What if we passed those girls? It would be even more humiliating than it already was.

I let him hold my hand. That wasn't quite as intimate or possessive a gesture.

I was quiet until we entered Danny's room. Then I sat down on the edge of the bed. Danny joined me. He lifted my Ray-Bans, unveiling my eyes. Shock followed by concern filled his face.

"You've been crying. Baby. What's wrong?"

Danny sounded so kind it was hard to reconcile this gentle, loving man as the cause of my pain.

Danny took my hands and massaged them. The speech I rehearsed in my head all morning escaped me. I was silent. With his hands clasping mine, and being face-to-face with those beautiful sapphires eyes, I couldn't remember the words.

"Elizabeth," Danny nudged me, "What is it, baby?"

Be brave. Don't cry.

Without emotion, I replayed what I overheard at the library. When I finished, I broke down sobbing. Danny was crestfallen. He enveloped me in his strong arms, a place I used to find comfort.

Stroking my hair while I cried, Danny murmured, "Baby, I'm sorry. I am so sorry."

Danny held me until I regained my composure enough to speak.

"Are they right?" I asked. "Did you cheat on me?"

"I wish that wasn't a direct question."

"Since December?" Danny couldn't look at me. He understood the reference. "Yes," he answered in a near whisper, ashamed.

I tried to keep myself in check but failed miserably. My insides froze like ice. I shook uncontrollably. I shivered. Bringing my knees up to my chest, I hugged myself. Danny wrapped his arms around me.

"Don't touch me," I hissed. He didn't listen. Danny knew I needed his warmth.

Soon, I calmed enough to speak again.

"Why? How could you? I thought you loved me."

"I do love you. You're the best thing that's ever happened to me," he said. Then he paused. "This wasn't about you Elizabeth."

"How is this not be about me?"

I glimpsed sadness in his eyes. "Winter break scared me. Our parents accepted us. We had a great time. I was as excited as you were to share our news with our friends at Ali's party. My date was the most beautiful, girl whom I love very much."

Danny stopped for my reaction. I sniffled, blinking back tears. hat had been a wonderful night. The entire break had been great.

"I was so happy because I'd spent the break with you, Eli. Then the guys discussed their vacations. When I recounted mine, they teased me about staying at my in-laws house. They called you my wife and mirrored what Dad had said."

"What did Steve say to you?" I was furious. How dare Steve interfere!

"Dad loves you, but he thinks we're too young. He doesn't want us to be like him and Mom. He thinks I shouldn't commit to never dating other girls yet."

"So the minute you had the opportunity you had to prove him right?"

Tears tumbled down my cheeks.

"Eli, I'm ashamed of what I've done. I panicked, baby. I'm an idiot. I wanted to prove I was still single. I should have handled it more maturely. I shouldn't have cared what they said."

"You flaunted our relationship to the people that count the most! Our childhood friends. Our families. You spent two weeks in my parents' home sharing my bed! I thought that meant something." Tears spilled again.

"It did. It does," Danny said contritely. "You're all that matters to me, Eli."

"But it wasn't enough. Not that you asked, but I'm not ready for marriage either. I'm only eighteen! But I thought you were committed to us. Why else would you share my bed in my parents' house? How can I ever face them? I'm so embarrassed."

"You've done nothing to be embarrassed about. You're as much in love with me as I am with you."

"How can you say that? You don't know what love is. I was so naive. I thought if I were the one sharing your bed you'd have no reason to stray. The thought of you with another girl makes me ill. I threw up last night."

"I'm sorry, Eli. I'm so sorry. I do know what love is, because love is what I feel for you. This wasn't done to hurt you."

"I turned a blind eye for so long. I pretended it didn't exist. But those girls."

"Eli, how can I make it up to you? How can I make it better?"

"I don't know that you can. It's happened. It's out there. I feel so empty."

"What do you want to do?" Danny whispered.

"I'm so confused."

"You're not breaking up with me, are you?" Danny asked tentatively. "I know I deserve it, but please don't." He panicked as he considered my options.

"I haven't decided. Maybe. Probably." I sniffled loudly.

"Baby, no! I can't lose you. I love you, Eli," Danny pleaded.

"I don't want to, Danny, but. I have my pride."

"I hurt you. Just what I didn't want to do."

"Yeah, well guess what? Elizabeth Jacobs is breakable."

"No. You're just young and inexperienced."

"What does that mean? If I'd had five other boyfriends first this wouldn't hurt?"

"Yeah," Danny smiled, "Because then you wouldn't even be my girlfriend."

"Daniel, you're a hypocrite."

"Absolutely," he smiled again and kissed my head.

"Don't do that! I have not forgiven you!"

"Yeah. I wouldn't forgive me yet either." Danny smiled then added, "Better this happened now than in fifteen years."

"You are not your father, Daniel."

"I'm just like Dad. Find the most wonderful girl in the world, have her fall in love with you, then break her heart. What's wrong with us Newman's?"

"Danny, you're not Steve," I said firmly. "You told me the risks of loving you. I chose to ignore them. I was having too much fun."

Danny grinned. "Me too. I was having too much fun."

I slapped his face. Hard. Danny winced at the sting and rubbed his cheek.

"With you, Elizabeth. You're the only one I have too much fun with."

"I have to go. I need my space."

"You do. I deserve whatever you throw at me."

Danny took my hand again and looked at me with pleading eyes. "Eli, if you do break up with me, can you tell me by Wednesday?"

What the hell? "Wednesday? I can't put a timetable on my decision." I frowned.

"I'll need to cancel our plans for next weekend."

"Next weekend?" I paused. "Right. Valentine's Day." I frowned.

It would have been my first time having someone to celebrate with. I had imagined the roses, at least two dozen red ones that Danny would have bought. We would have gone somewhere romantic for dinner, perhaps The Beach House. Maybe this time we would have stayed at the Inn. That would have been just like Danny. He could be so sentimental.

"I had a great weekend planned. I'll cancel it. There's always next year."

"That's so unfair," I sniffled. Tears ran down my cheeks. "You've probably planned the most romantic time."

"Of course I did. I love spoiling you."

"You're impossible," I sighed and wiped the tears away with the back of my hand. "I do believe you love me, just in your own peculiar way. That's what makes this so difficult." I rose from the bed.

"Will I see you later?"

"I doubt it."

I took two steps toward the door before coming to a screeching halt.

"Shit!" I exclaimed. "I have to see you at dinner or everyone will wonder. I don't want you saying anything to anyone, especially not our roommates."

"We have to keep talking, Eli. As long as we're talking we can work this out."

"I doubt we can," I said sadly.

"I love you, Eli. Remember that."

CHAPTER 49 - ELIZABETH

Everywhere I went the next morning my eyes darted in all directions, certain that Danny was lurking somewhere at the edges of my peripheral vision. The predictability of my schedule was the problem. Danny knew where I should be if he wanted to 'run into me.' Sanity demanded I shake things up for the afternoon.

I stopped at The Café for lunch. I did not want to relive last night's debacle at dinner. Forced to smile and act as though nothing were the matter, Danny sat by my side, the ever-adoring boyfriend. Our friends never suspected that all was wrong in the Jacobs-Newman household.

It was a deplorable situation made worse because in spite of my anger and hurt, I found myself enjoying Danny's attention. I did not want distractions like this while I was so vulnerable.

After my sandwich, I returned to my room where I packed a gym bag and headed to the swimming pool. An hour of laps was the perfect outlet for my energy. The solitude would let my mind drift and hopefully I'd see things more clearly.

By three o'clock I was spent and mentally only marginally improved. I showered and changed to sweats. My damp waves fell down my back creating a wet spot on the back of my shirt. I even wore my fuzzy pink slippers. Nobody was going to get me to leave the comfort of my secure cocoon.

Rachel and Chloe had late classes. Their well-intentioned concern was not what I wanted. I needed to be alone. Peace and quiet! It felt so good.

While I sat at my desk pretending to read French, I was exchanging Facebook messages with Steff. As far as I would tell her, all was well. No need to alert her until I had concrete news to report. I hated this.

An unexpected knock came on the door to the suite. The interruption jarred me. Someone must be looking for Chloe. "BRB" I messaged Steff . "Let me see who it is and get rid of them," I thought.

I shuffled to the door and opened it. Danny! What was he doing here? I frowned. Then I giggled. There Danny stood, smiling shyly and carrying the largest bouquet I had ever seen. Danny must have purchased every stem the florist had in stock.

"I'll be right with you. I'm on with Steff."

I returned to my computer, typed "g2g. DN," and then I logged out.

Danny had followed me into my room. I sensed hesitation.

"Elizabeth, I'm so sorry about everything," Danny said quietly. "These are for you," he added, and he handed me the vase.

The vase was quite heavy, and I placed it on my desk. "They're lovely," I said.

I felt unusually timid. I had nothing to say and Danny was silent, awkward. What did he expect? I certainly wasn't going to jump into his arms.

Danny fidgeted. His eyes were downcast while he mindlessly picked at a cuticle. I had never seen Danny insecure before. Did he not know what he wanted to say, or did Danny fear my rejection? Were Danny not the subject of my ire, I would have felt sorry for him.

"Eli, baby I miss you," he began in a soft uncharacteristically tentative voice. "I don't want to be without you. Baby, what can I do to make everything right?"

"Danny, beautiful as these flowers are, if you think this is how to make things right, you're wrong. I trusted you. I loved you with all my heart. I gave you everything I had."

"E, I've learned my lesson. I'm miserable, baby."

"I'm miserable too," I admitted, "But you betrayed me. If I can't trust you, what do we have? Trust is what's most important and flowers won't earn it back."

"You're right, Eli." Danny removed a plastic card from his shirt pocket. He placed it in my hand and wrapped my fingers around it. "Perhaps this can be a start."

I looked curiously at the plain, unmarked white credit card.

"What is this?" I asked.

Danny smiled, pleased with himself. "It's my room key. I told security I lost mine so I could get one made for you."

"Your room key?" Why? I was on the verge of breaking up with him.

Danny wrapped his hands around mine. His hands filled me with their unwelcome warmth.

"I want you to come and go whenever you want," he explained. "Twenty-four/seven. My room is your room, Eli."

I gaped at him. The implication was clear. Danny would not give me his key unless I could trust that he would be there alone every evening. A tear escaped my eye.

"Danny, are you sure about this?" I was so vulnerable.

Danny hugged me tightly.

"Yes, I'm sure. I love you, baby."

I looked into his eyes. The sapphires were filled with depth and sincerity.

"I love you too, Daniel."

I walked Danny to the door. Standing on toe I kissed his cheek.

Last week I would have been thrilled to pieces if Danny had given me a key to his room. Now I was conflicted. My anger at his betrayal was strong, but if he was trying to demonstrate trust, there was no more powerful a way than this.

I wanted so badly to trust Danny again. Was I gullible if I accepted his key? Was I letting my need to love Danny cloud my judgment?

I needed a confidante. Ellen had lived through worse, and it placed her in a unique position to provide council.

When I reached her at home, Ellen was happy to hear from me, but she sensed right away that this call concerned her son.

Without hesitation I explained the situation.

"Oh, Elizabeth," she empathized, "What does your heart say?"

"My heart? My heart says I love Danny."

"And he loves you. Elizabeth, it sounds as though you want permission to give Danny another chance. That's why you didn't call Miranda."

I considered what Ellen was saying. "I suppose," I answered sheepishly.

"You love Danny very much Elizabeth and you don't want to give that up. That's okay. What he did was despicable, unforgivable even. Is Danny aware that you're hurt?"

"I haven't been shy. Danny knows how hurt I am."

"Elizabeth, he won't do it again," Ellen said, confident.

"How can you be so certain?"

"Years ago, Steve hurt me similarly, only there was more to it. Danny knows part of it. You can't keep secrets from someone living in your house. Danny heard us arguing. He heard me crying. We sent Danny to Bromley so we could work things out."

"I'm so sorry, Ellen."

"It's okay, dear. Steve and I went to counseling and our marriage is much stronger now. I sincerely believe that."

"I can't imagine you and Steve divorced."

"Neither could we. That's what saved us. That and the devastating affect it had on Danny. He's very sensitive."

"Danny doesn't want anyone to know that, but I know."

"Of course you do. That's why Danny will never do this to you again. Danny feels as badly as you do. Part of him died seeing you so hurt. He's devastated. Danny loves you. He's crazy about you. He feels terrible knowing he's violated your trust. But Elizabeth, you can trust Danny. If you want permission to patch things up, you have it. Tell him you want to work it out if that's what you want."

"That's what I want. I can't imagine not being with Danny."

"I know, dear. I can't imagine it either."

"Ellen, how do I get past the humiliation?"

"You are Elizabeth Jordan Jacobs. Act it!" Ellen admonished. "Those who may want to hurt you will realize they don't stand a chance. You need to give yourself back the power."

Ellen was right. I had been playing the victim. No more.

"Danny must be trying everything to win you back," Ellen laughed.

"He is, Ellen. Danny brought me a huge flower arrangement. Then he gave me my own key to his room."

"Then hang up and use it Elizabeth. Danny wants to do the right thing. He loves you very much. Remember, you have to follow your heart."

Ellen was right. I had the power. I was Miranda Jordan's daughter. Steven Newman's son expected no less from me. I owned one of the most recognizable faces in America; time to let it show. Danny always said I should. The new me would be formidable like Mom. Danny deserved the best girlfriend I could be. No girl should be more desirable.

Twenty minutes later I emerged looking like a proper girlfriend for Danny. I dressed in my favorite jeans tucked into Uggs and a stylish low-cut sweater. My Peretti heart rested just where I wanted Danny's eyes to alight.

I wasn't going to make it easy. Danny needed to win me back. At the same time, I had to show Danny that with me he would have no reason to look elsewhere.

Standing in the hallway outside Danny's suite, I regarded my new keycard. Danny had told me to use it, but did his roommates know? I starred at the keycard again. If Danny's roommates were taken by surprise, I would leave it to him to explain.

Taking a deep breath, I inserted the card into its slot and pulled it out.

Miranda Jordan's daughter let herself in and found Danny pacing the room, all nervous energy and on a phone call. I waved the card at him. Danny smiled, pleased to see me, and motioned for me to sit. I remained standing.

"I've got to go," Danny spoke into the phone. "I've got company. See you at eight." He placed the phone on the desk.

Danny studied my face, my posture, and my cleavage. Noting the heart, he smiled, a shy smile.

"Hey," I said quietly. "The card works."

"I'm surprised to see you, Eli. I wasn't expecting you." There was pain in his eyes and hope in his voice.

"It's been a long afternoon." Then I paused. "I've been doing a lot of thinking."

Danny took my hands and massaged my finger tops. The warmth of his touch began melting my resolve. I couldn't help smiling. In return, he smiled back.

"I spoke to Ellen," I confessed. "She's very supportive. She's been through this."

"I know," he answered curtly. "Did Mom tell you to tell me to go to hell?"

"Not at all. She provided insight. Ellen wants you to realize you're not Steve."

"I know. I called her too. Mom's very disappointed and thinks I'm a schmuck."

"What do you think?"

"She may be right," he answered and pulled me to his chest. "I'm sorry, baby." Danny stroked my hair. "I really am so very sorry. I want to make it up to you so badly."

"I believe you."

"You do?" Danny loosened his hold on me to look into my eyes. I nodded. "You do." He tilted my chin up and gently kissed me.

Danny held me very closely, as though he were afraid to let go.

"I love you so much, Elizabeth. I promise I will never hurt you again."

We kissed again. All would be good.

CHAPTER 50 - ELIZABETH

"Band rehearsal tonight," Danny announced as we were nearing the end of dinner. "I want you to come."

"I thought rehearsals were closed."

"Not to you, baby."

I didn't want to go, but…

"Okay, I'd love to." I smiled, and I kissed his cheek. Ha! Village girls.

After dinner, we stopped at Berkeley Hall so I could grab a book. I wasn't sure I would have the opportunity to read, but just in case.

On the way out, Danny kept his arm snuggly around my shoulder. I was convinced he wasn't going to let go of me for even a moment tonight.

Outside on the landing, Danny took my hands and smiled. His grin was so infectious I couldn't help giggling. Completely engrossed in each other, we practically skipped down the front steps.

"Won't the guys get angry when I show up?"

"If I say I need my girl, too bad on them. Besides, you're an asset."

"How am I an asset?"

I hadn't planned on doing anything at the rehearsal except stay out of the way.

Danny stopped and gazed into my eyes. "Your presence will make a big difference even if all you do is sit on the couch."

I laughed. "That sounds so hokey."

"It's true, Eli," Danny laughed. "You're right. It does sound hokey, but it's true."

We both laughed, and Danny hugged me.

"Eli, I'm worried about Friday," he said, his chin leaning into my shoulder. "Ron, Kirk, even Duncan, they're serious musicians. These guys are so much better than me. I'm bass by default. And my voice; I'm lead singer when I'm a serviceable tenor at best. I'm not confident."

Danny burst into laughter, hearty and uncontrollable. He wiped a tear from his eye. I didn't know what he was laughing at, but now I was laughing at his laughter.

"Eli, these guys are awful. Ron and Kirk can barely sing back-up. If I wake up with laryngitis on Friday, we're screwed."

"Don't even think that way. And you are not a serviceable tenor. I love your voice."

"Thank you, baby," Danny said and he hugged me. "I think you may be more than a little biased, my number one fan."

"I'm being perfectly objective. I've heard you sing. Danny, your voice comes through with power, clarity and passion. I feel the lyrics when you sing."

"Eli, you were wasted."

"Danny, you're an excellent singer." I was adamant. "I felt the passion."

"Of course you did. It was directed at you. And you were wasted. Kirk says I've been lackluster this week."

"Because we've been fighting?"

Danny shrugged. "But hey, that's over. Now I have my passion back."

"That's why you want me at rehearsal?"

Danny drew me close and held me in his arms. His eyes locked on mine. My heart skipped a beat.

"It's much easier to perform with passion when the object of your passion is in the front row."

"I'm there for you. Always," I said breathlessly.

Danny pulled me closer. His lips pressed into mine, and I eagerly responded, parting my lips for him as my hands entwined in his hair.

"Dan?" A female voice interrupted.

Our lips parted yet we continued in our clinch. I giggled before I dropped my hands to Danny's waist while he continued cradling me against his chest.

"I thought that was you," Phoebe said.

On their way up the steps of Berkeley Hall were Phoebe and another girl I didn't recognize. The pink streak in her otherwise medium-length blonde hair distinguished her from the blandness her preppy clothes and looks would have otherwise been assigned to.

Pleasant looking in that way a man might find attractive but women didn't, the girl smiled at Danny, naturally. She must have been at least five foot eight and large boned. I felt so petite, but I was well protected. Danny's arm remained holding me as though I required shielding.

"Phoebs, Amelia, what are you doing here?" Danny asked.

Amelia. So this was Amelia. My face had better not betray the queasy sensation brewing in my stomach. Danny's arm tightened. He felt the shudder of revulsion I was trying to hide behind a plastic smile. I could do this. I had the power.

For her part, Amelia was scrutinizing me as much, if not more so. She was way too obvious as she sized up her opposition in the competition she was never in.

"Party on Five." Phoebe answered. "Aren't you late?"

"We're heading to rehearsal now. Phoebs, you remember Elizabeth?"

"Elizabeth, yes. Your girlfriend," Phoebe emphasized for Amelia's benefit. "The one you kept secret until last week. You're bringing her to rehearsal? Isn't it closed?"

"Not to Elizabeth. She's with the band."

"We should go. I don't want the guys angry with you," I told Danny.

"You're right. Later, Phoebs, Amelia."

"Right, Dan," Phoebe answered curtly with a deadly stare.

Smiling sweetly was the best response as was Danny planting a kiss on the top of my head as we walked away toward the parking lot.

CHAPTER 51 - ELIZABETH

"Lois Lane!" Duncan sneered. He was well on his way to becoming wasted when we entered Ron and Kirk's house. "What's she doing here, Newman? Rehearsal's closed." He handed Danny a joint. Danny inhaled deeply.

"My girl's always welcome," Danny retorted, and he kissed my cheek. Then Danny took another hit and glanced at me. "None for you, young lady. It's a school night," he teased.

In contrast, Ron and Kirk were pleased to see me.

"Hey, you've brought your lady, Newman," Ron said enthusiastically. "What do you see in him, Elizabeth?" he laughed.

"We can use you," Kirk added. "Elizabeth, we're getting down to the wire. I think we sound pretty good, but if you'll critique us, we might be even better," Kirk explained. "So pay attention to everything Elizabeth, and stop us whenever we're not perfect."

Rehearsal progressed nicely, though the first time I stopped the guys it was awkward.

"Wait!" I called while raising my hand. This was power.

The instruments immediately went quiet, even Duncan's drums. I tried not to laugh, but Danny had made the mistake.

"Danny," I hesitated and I couldn't help but smile, "You came in a little late on the second chorus. Sorry." I blushed, feeling bad criticizing him in front of the others.

"Thanks, Eli. Good ears." Danny grinned.

Then rehearsal resumed. I stopped the band only a few more times. With two days to go, they were in good shape.

"Newman, much improved," Kirk said as rehearsal ended. "You brought the heat tonight."

"It helped having my muse here," Danny laughed.

"Elizabeth, you cannot miss Friday. Our voice needs you."

Upon entering the Berkeley Hall lobby, Danny pulled me into his arms.

"My place?" Danny asked. Sapphire puppy-dog eyes tugged at my heart.

"Not tonight. It's been an emotional day," I answered sadly.

"I'll walk you upstairs then," Danny answered, disappointed.

"Danny, you knew I was going to say no or you wouldn't have asked."

"Eli, you know me too well," Danny laughed.

"No, you know you're still in the doghouse."

"Not for long, I hope."

Friday, I was a jumble of nerves. Getting through my morning French class was impossible. While confident of Danny's performance, my anxieties over who would share my table had me obsessing.

Yes, I was with the band, but who else was? I feared tonight would find me sharing a table with Phoebe or worse, Amelia.

No! Let Amelia be tortured by me. I had what she would never get. I was the girl going home with Danny.

Danny was waiting outside the dining hall when I arrived with Cam.

"Has Eli been a good girl this morning, Cam?" Danny asked and kissed my head.

"Your girlfriend's a wreck. Elizabeth almost spoke Spanish in French class."

Once seated, Danny's nerves were evident to everyone. Danny picked at his food. His usually hearty appetite was missing.

"Daniel, you've got to eat something," I said when I noticed how little he had consumed. "I don't want you passing out from low blood sugar later."

"What about you, Eli? You've hardly eaten a thing."

"I can eat later. I'm not performing."

Danny did a little better after that but soon we decided we'd had enough of pretending to eat lunch and I accompanied Danny to his room.

"E, you're sure you want to be here with me?" Danny teased."

"I'm quaking," I answered sarcastically.

Danny's hands circled my waist. "I know what would quash my nerves."

"Class. We have class."

"We can miss it. I'm too antsy to sit through class." Danny pulled me close.

"Danny! I didn't say I wanted sex. I'm not ready. I'm still angry."

Danny pressed his lips to mine and consumed me. The electricity was overwhelming, and I felt him hard, pulsating against me. My traitorous heart thumped wildly. Danny's did the same. I could barely breathe as his hand pressed me closer and closer as we continued kissing.

Finally, Danny declared, "You're ready."

"No I'm not," I answered breathlessly. "I was waiting for after the show."

"Eli, you just said you were still angry."

"I'll be over it by tonight."

Danny grinned. "If you can predict you'll be over it tonight, then you're over it now."

"Tonight," I protested.

Danny pushed me down on the bed. As his lips again crushed mine I fell back into the pillows. In one fluid motion he lifted my sweater over my head.

"Now, Eli. I want you now, babe."

Danny unfastened my jeans. I could no longer resist the power of our lust.

"Now is good." I smiled and Danny continued undressing me.

As I lay in Danny's arms afterwards, he felt warm and comforting. In Danny's strong arms, I was home. There was nowhere else I would ever want to be. I had followed my heart, and I knew I made the right decision.

Danny continued holding me, kissing my lips, my cheeks, my neck, and my shoulders. We let our eyes, our lips, our fingertips do the talking. Danny had followed his heart too, back to mine. Nobody could come between us. Our bonds were too strong, our love too deep. Once again we were sharing two halves of the same heart.

I didn't want to move. We had missed class, and I had no place to be for at least five more hours. I would stay right where I was until then.

I looked into Danny's deep, reflective sapphire eyes and smiled. I reached for his face and I kissed his warm, full lips. Then I climbed on top of him. I wanted Danny again so badly.

Completely spent after making love again, we fell asleep in each other's arms.

The ringtone jarred us back to consciousness.

"Newman! Where the hell are you?" I heard Duncan's screech coming through the speaker when Danny answered.

"What time is it?" Danny asked groggily.

"You're not awake? It's three-thirty. You're late!"

"Shit! We didn't mean to fall asleep."

"We? Let me guess, Lois Lane is with you."

Danny ignored him. "I'm on my way," he answered and ended the call.

Danny jumped out of bed and grabbed his jeans.

"I've got to go, honey. I was supposed to, well you heard."

Danny pulled on his jeans, leaned over, and kissed my forehead. "I hate leaving you, but if I don't get to my band, we know who they'll blame."

"Guilty"

"You sure are," Danny laughed, and he kissed me again before pulling a clean shirt out of the closet.

CHAPTER 52 - ELIZABETH

"C'mon already," Rachel urged me. She was frustrated by the care I was taking with getting ready for the evening.

After I left Danny's room I took a quick shower and set about doing my hair and makeup. No matter what I tried, my hair wasn't falling into place. This would not do. Wrong night for a bad hair day. Danny Newman's girlfriend must look perfect. I felt far from perfect.

My outfit for the evening was perfect, however; black-wash skinny jeans, a low-cut cream and black silk blouse, and a wide silver belt, all ordered from Neiman Marcus earlier in the week. My high black boots completed the look. But my hair – total frizz!

"Your hair looks great," Rachel moaned as I brushed it yet again, this time spraying my hairbrush with Static Guard. "We have to go. Danny is expecting you."

In disgust, I slammed down my brush. "Do I really look alright?" I asked.

"Elizabeth, you look great. You're perfect." Rachel said, exasperated.

"Are you sure?"

"I'm sure! You resemble a friggin' cover girl. Let's go!"

"I hope Danny likes what I'm wearing." I had to outshine Amelia.

"Why are you so insecure? Danny only has eyes for you."

"He does, doesn't he," I thought of this afternoon spent in his bed. "I'm being silly. Danny always likes my appearance. My hair looks fine, doesn't it?"

"Yes. Let's go already. You may have a reserved table, but I don't and Danny's fan club is counting on me." Rachel insisted.

With more than an hour before show time, Rachel and I arrived at The Stage. Amidst a flurry of activity, musicians were arriving and unloading their instruments. We entered through the front door where a student working the door had a list of those with reserved tables. I gave him my name.

"Elizabeth Jacobs should be on there, even twice," said Rachel. "She's doing photos for the yearbook and she's Danny Newman's girlfriend."

"Newman plus one?" he asked, sounding doubtful

"That's me. Plus One Jacobs. Catchy." I said in a friendly voice.

"I need Danny to confirm you're the plus one." What!

"Do you think I'd make this up?" Do people really lie about this?

"Danny has only one girlfriend, and Elizabeth is her." Rachel was even more indignant than I was.

"It's not my job to keep track of his love life." The door keeper picked up his walkie and summoned Danny.

Within moments Danny arrived. "There's my ladies!" he exclaimed.

Danny's face lit up and he kissed me on my lips.

"E, you're stunning!" Danny exclaimed while taking in every inch of my body with his eyes. "You too, Rach," he hastily added.

"Even her hair?" Rachel asked, and I rolled my eyes.

"Her hair?" Danny shrugged, confused. "Your hair always looks good, Elizabeth."

Danny picked up a few strands and twirled them as proof.

"Danny, he won't let me in. Would you please tell him who I am?"

Danny studied the list. "You're right here. Danny Newman, plus one. What's the problem, babe?"

"We're not at the AMC CityWalk." I tossed out the name of the popular theater where premieres were often held. "Next time leave my name."

Danny turned to the doorkeeper. "May I?" he asked, and he took his Sharpie. Danny crossed out the "+1" and wrote in "+ Elizabeth Jacobs".

"I'll take them to their tables," Danny said. He wrapped his arms around my shoulder and Rachel's. We were his girls.

Danny guided us to a stage front table with a reserved sign in the middle. Rachel grabbed the non-reserved table immediately behind it for our friends.

"I'm glad you're here. I need you," Danny said, and he took my hands. His gaze was mesmerizing. His love melted my heart. "You're so beautiful, E," he whispered.

I squeezed Danny's hands and smiled just for him. "I had an amazing afternoon," I whispered, and I blushed.

"I did too," he answered just as softly. Danny kissed my lips. "I love you so much, Elizabeth."

It was more than words to him. Something about Danny's declaration clouded my brain and left me floating on air. I knew he meant it. Tonight it was truly heartfelt.

"I love you too, Daniel," I whispered. Danny rested his hands against my face and held me for a long, passion-filled kiss. He knew I always meant it.

"Newman," Kirk interrupted. "We need you." Then he added, "Hi, Elizabeth."

"Hi, Kirk. I'll let you have Danny now."

"I'll be with you in a minute," Danny answered.

Kirk nodded and left for backstage.

"Rach, take good care of my girl," Danny instructed.

"Right," she sneered, "As though anything's going to happen to

Elizabeth while she's watching you sing."

"I don't like leaving Elizabeth."

"Danny, I'll be fine," I insisted.

"What is with you today? You're worse than usual, Danny," Rachel remarked.

From behind, Danny wrapped his arms around my shoulders and hugged me.

"Rach, maybe I am. I'm a blessed man. Eli and I had a big blow-up earlier in the week and she almost dumped me."

Rachel's jaw dropped open, registering surprise at the newly released secret.

"Was that the day you wouldn't leave your room?"

I nodded.

"Chloe and I thought you were sick."

"Elizabeth was sick; heart sick," Danny answered. "It was my fault, but we've worked it out. I don't want to imagine if we hadn't."

"I'm glad we don't have to," I replied.

Danny gave me one more hug and kissed my cheek.

"I'd better go ladies. I'll see you later."

I watched Danny as he walked toward the backstage door. After a handful of steps, he abruptly pivoted and returned. Danny pulled me into his arms and hugged me tightly. He leaned his chin into my shoulder to whisper.

"Eli, I'm so glad you're here," Danny said, his voice laced with emotion. "I couldn't go on tonight if I didn't have you."

"I'm always here for you," I whispered as I rubbed his muscular back.

One more kiss and Danny was gone again.

Soon the doors opened. People filed in. The venue was buzzing. From the corner of my eye, I picked up Amelia entering with a preppy guy I hadn't seen before. At this distance he appeared pleasant looking, but in a patrician way, wearing the uniform pinstriped oxford shirt under a crewneck sweater. I turned in the opposite direction to exchange a few words with Chloe now seated at the table behind me.

I wouldn't put it past Duncan to give Amelia seats at my table, though nobody but Danny knew I was aware of their fling. I reminded myself of this now. If Duncan placed Amelia at my table, then he was doing it to get to Danny. Why would he want to sabotage Danny's psyche tonight of all nights? I hated Duncan all over again.

Not unexpectedly, when I turned back from speaking with Chloe, who should be sitting beside me but Amelia's date, with her on his other side. Thankfully Amelia was engaged in animated conversation with Phoebe and Jasmine, seated at the table behind her.

Not intending to do so, I made eye contact with Amelia's date. His small brown eyes were partially hidden behind round wire-rimmed eyeglasses. Reflexively I smiled, then instantly regretted it. He looked me up and down. Snarky. For a man with a date, he shouldn't have been looking at me that way. It gave me the creeps.

"You're not from here, are you?" he asked in a clipped New England accent.

What did that mean? "I'm a Donnelly student," I answered succinctly.

"I'm not. I go to Dartmouth," he boasted. "I'm here with Amy."

Amy? Lovely. This must be James. I would keep conversation to a minimum. Amelia must not think I was hitting on her date.

"James Brower McKenzie. The third," James announced himself as though he assumed I would recognize his name. Then he offered his hand.

"Elizabeth Jordan Jacobs. The first, and only." I shook James' hand. It was cool to the touch, not firm.

James laughed, thinking I was trying to be funny. I wasn't.

"We don't use titles in Santa Monica."

James smiled. Was he the type Danny had encountered at Bromley Hall? My poor honey! Now I understood.

"Why is a girl as pretty as you alone tonight?" James asked.

"I'm not alone."

As though on cue, I spotted Danny frantically pushing through the crowd toward me. Danny had changed and was now wearing a grape-plaid shirt, sleeves rolled up, worn open over a grey t-shirt.

"I'm with him," I exclaimed.

I jumped out of my chair to warmly receive the emotional hug Danny delivered. Why was he out here? Danny should have been backstage preparing with his band.

"Nice shirt. Purple," I said as I fingered the soft cotton.

"Babe, I need you," Danny said with urgency, his lips against my cheek.

I pulled back and appraised him. Danny was always confident and secure. Now he seemed frightened like a little boy, my little boy.

James used this opportunity to stand and extend his hand to Danny.

"James Brower McKenzie, the third," he said.

Danny glared. I could guessed what he was thinking. Instead he politely shook James' hand, "Daniel Martin Newman, the first," and turned away. Danny led me by the shoulder a couple of steps away.

"E, who the hell is that?" Danny resented James' intrusion.

"Amelia's boyfriend." That said it all.

"Great! Sorry he's next to you." Then Danny switched gears. "E, I'm a wreck."

"Sweetheart, don't be," I said, and I hugged Danny. My heart went out to him. This wasn't like Danny.

"I've never performed in front of so many people."

"You're not. You're performing for me. Block out everything and focus on me."

"All I have to do is pretend you're the only one here. You are, Elizabeth. You're the only one that matters."

"Danny, you'll be great, but even if you're not, I'm here for you. You can forget every chord and every lyric and I will still love you. No matter what happens on that stage Daniel, I will be going home with you tonight."

I reached my hand to his face and brought his lips down for me to kiss.

"Now get back to your band, before they get angry with me."

I watched as Danny left for backstage and I sat back down.

"What's going on?" Rachel asked from her seat at the table behind me.

I was glad to have an excuse to turn away from James.

"Danny's very anxious," I fretted. "He enjoys music, but Danny's never performed on stage before a large crowd before. That's not his aspiration."

Rachel squeezed my hand. "He'll do fine," she assured me. "He's Danny."

I turned my attention back toward the stage, willing the concert to begin. Amelia had stopped talking with Phoebe and Jasmine. She sat holding James' hand. Perhaps he would leave me alone now.

"Boyfriend?" James asked.

"Yes," I said and I grinned. I loved that word when it applied to Danny.

James dropped Amelia's hand and turned all his attention on me.

"What's it like living in L.A.? Know any stars?"

"Yeah, I dine with some every night," I answered flippantly, but I smiled. Let my facial expression make him think I was lying.

James' face lit up. Ugh! Backfire! He was enchanted.

"No shit! Do you really? Now don't go pulling my leg," he exclaimed.

"Would I do that?" I answered and grinned. It was fun playing him.

"Isn't Dan enough for you? Now you're going after my boyfriend too," Amelia snapped. Her scowl startled James too. Crap! This was exactly what I hoped to avoid.

"Now Amy, Elizabeth's just telling me what it's like living in Hollywood."

"Danny requires my full attention," I said to Amelia, emphasizing Danny's complete first name. "I don't have the time or inclination to pursue yours or anyone else's boyfriend."

Thankfully the first band began to play, and I turned my attention to the stage. I could concentrate on Jackson's assignment to take pictures of more than just Danny.

During the break after the second band, I left the table to shoot pictures of my friends and I also took some long shots of the venue. That would please Jackson.

Upon returning to my seat, Chloe tapped my shoulder.

"They were really good," she said.

Chloe was right. The second band had been exceptional.

"I hope Danny didn't hear them," I told Chloe. "He's enough of a wreck without sizing up the competition."

"I was thinking the same thing."

"Fingers crossed," I said, and I held my crossed fingers aloft.

Finally Danny's band was announced. I turned my complete attention to the stage. He was why I was here and my support was sorely needed.

Shane tapped my shoulder and I turned to him.

"Let me do this," he suggested as he reached for my camera.

I appreciated Shane understanding my need to give Danny my full attention.

Three songs. The band only had to get through three songs.

Danny, Kirk, Ron and Duncan took to the stage. My eyes were riveted to Danny. He strapped on his bass with fluidity and grace, the jitters seemingly gone. Confidence defined him again.

I took a deep breath and released it slowly. I took another deep breath, and the tension left as I exhaled. My shoulders returned to their normal position. If Danny could be this confident, so could I.

The guys launched into their first number. As he hit his first chord, Danny made eye contact with me and grinned. I smiled back, my eyes glued to his every movement. Danny's eyes darted through the audience, but kept coming back to mine. Whenever they did he grinned. Rock star handsome, Danny's sapphire eyes were mesmerizing. He didn't miss a note. One down, two to go.

The band began their second song with even more enthusiasm and confidence, playing off the audience's energetic response.

My heart jumped as I heard unfamiliar chords rise up from their instruments. This was not the song they'd rehearsed on Wednesday. How could they perform a song they hadn't rehearsed? The song they had planned had a few problems on Wednesday, but nothing yesterday's rehearsal wouldn't have solved.

Now I understood Danny's earlier trepidation. He knew they were giving their biggest performance ever, and they were unprepared! My heart beat rapidly. My jaw clenched and my sweaty palms locked together. I dug my nails into the tops of my hands, nearly drawing blood.

Danny smiled. He appeared confident and in control. How could he be under these circumstances? Danny nodded at me. His eyes twinkled as if to say, "E, don't worry. We know what we're doing."

Okay. If he wasn't concerned, then I supposed I shouldn't be either. But of course, I was. Danny would be devastated if they didn't do their best.

This song had a slower tempo than the one originally planned. It contained soulful, romantic lyrics. It also contrasted to their first song, which had been pure rock. If their aim was to play three completely different songs to showcase their versatility, they were succeeding. We'd find out later whether the judges agreed with this tactic.

For this dreamy love song, Danny's eyes locked on mine. They didn't move. The emotion in his rich tenor voice reached through to my heart as only Danny could do. The deep expression in his eyes touched my core. Tears filled my eyes from its beauty. I flushed as my heart pounded rapidly. From behind me, Shane squeezed my shoulder, silent acknowledgement that he understood.

Danny slid to his knees for the second chorus. Now just a few feet above my eye level, he leaned toward me. Holding the mic with both hands, it was obvious he was singing to me.

"When you find your love, always remind your love,
When you find your love, never let her go."

It was also apparent to Amelia. Her chair pushed back from the table and she walked out. She might have James doting on her every word, but it was clear the only man she wanted belonged to me. Too bad!

The emotions and love I experienced threatened to overwhelm me. Danny's passion was incredible, like nothing I had ever felt before. I wanted him to know, so I kissed my palm and blew him a kiss. His renewed smile told me he'd caught it.

Danny understood. I wiped a stray tear off my cheek. Danny smiled; pleased with the affect he had on me. The two hundred other people in the club didn't exist.

For the finish, Danny was on his feet again. His eyes remained locked on mine. This was our song he was saying. After our near split, this was Danny's way of letting everyone at Donnelly know he only had eyes for me.

The roar of applause startled me. I was shaking to find our song was over..

"Amzaing!" Chloe whispered. "I can't believe how much Danny loves you."

"Yeah," I answered in a trance. It was as though I were in a dream state.

And that was most amazing of all. Danny was never shy with showing affection, but this performance was more of a public declaration.

I had to emotionally settle. There was one final song in the set. A fun, up-tempo anthemic rock song was a complete change of pace for both the band and the audience. It was perfect for bringing me back to planet Earth.

The final chord played. I jumped to my feet, put my thumb and middle finger in my mouth, and let loose. Wolf whistle! Everyone in my vicinity turned and stared. Danny laughed. I shrugged and wildly applauded.

Once the curtain closed, my friends gathered around me, embracing each other, thrilled for Danny.

"He was great!" Chloe exclaimed.

"I can't believe that song," Rachel added. "I thought Danny was going to jump off the stage and maul you. Talk about bedroom eyes."

Shane took my hand. "You're shaking."

"I'm a wreck," I laughed. "They didn't rehearse that song."

"Everyone's going to be talking about it all week," said Chloe.

"People have better things to do than talk about a song," I laughed.

"It's the passion they'll talk about, not necessarily the music," Chloe added.

Toward the end of the next set Danny eased into the chair beside me. My heart fluttered, and I smiled as he kissed my cheek. Danny's hair brushing my face was damp from perspiration, and he smelled of sweat, Danny's sweat.

Danny reached for my hand and kissed the top of it. I hugged our joined fingers to my cheek, then set them in his lap for him to caress.

When the set ended, Danny said, "E, let's get some fresh air."

I nodded, but we didn't get more than a step away when friends deluged him.

"Great job!" Cam said, and he clapped Danny on the back.

"Elizabeth, here's your camera. I got great shots of you, Danny," Shane said.

"Keep the camera, Shane. We're going out for some air," Danny responded.

Chloe reached up and kissed his cheek. "Beautiful song, Danny. Elizabeth's a lucky girl," she whispered.

"Thanks, Chlo," Danny answered. I beamed with pride.

Then Rachel embraced him. "You were great," she exclaimed.

"Thanks, Rach." Danny grabbed my hand. "We'll be back. C'mon, Eli."

Danny led me through the packed club to the exit, ignoring the considerable crowd vying for his attention.

Once outside, Danny took a deep breath and spun me into his arms. The air was crisp and cold, a shock after the heat of the club.

"Oh my god! It's freezing out here!" I exclaimed.

Danny tightened his hold on me and vigorously rubbed my arms.

"Did you enjoy it?" I asked. Frost was on every breath.

"Oh, Eli. Eli, Eli, Eli." Danny repeated my name with increased enthusiasm. "It's over, babe. It's over!" Danny was relieved and held me close, my face pressed against his sweaty plaid shirt. "How does Randi do it? This was awful!"

"Mom has more than one chance to be perfect," I laughed. "She's only live to the crew and they can do as many takes as they need. Mom has never done theater for that very reason."

"Now you tell me. I kept thinking if Randi can do this, so can I," Danny laughed.

"I'm sorry, honey. I thought you were wonderful."

"I'm glad I had you there, fan club chief."

"That second song was amazing!" I pronounced as I pulled back to examine Danny's face. "I loved it! But you scared me. Danny, you didn't rehearse it on Wednesday. When I heard the opening chords, I panicked."

"You did, didn't you?" He grinned.

I was puzzled. "Is that why Duncan was angry? Were you supposed to rehearse it today?"

Danny began laughing. That only added to my confusion.

"What's funny, Danny? You could have screwed up."

Danny laughed again and hugged me. "That was never a risk. Eli, I have a confession. That song was for you. We've been working on it since after break. I wanted it to be a surprise."

He really does love me!

"That's why you kept me away. I can't believe you did that!" I exclaimed gleefully. "Chloe was right. I am a lucky girl."

"No, I'm the one who's lucky."

Danny reached around my back and pulled me in with loving arms. Then he lifted my chin, his warm sapphire eyes locked on mine, and Danny tenderly pressed his lips to mine for a loving kiss.

"So, did you like your song?" Danny asked when our lips parted. His breath on my neck tickled and sent a shiver through me.

"Yes. Even more now that I know understand the trouble you went through," I whispered. I reached my arms around his neck and kissed him. "I felt your passion. It was as though I was the only person in the room."

"You were." Danny kissed me and held me tightly. "I love your passion, too."

"I can't wait to get home. Then you'll really see my passion."

Danny kissed me again. I wrinkled my nose as the breeze blew the scent of Danny's sweat toward me.

"First you'll have to shower," I giggled.

"You can scrub my back," he teased.

I looked at Danny with dreamy eyes. My pulse was racing from his kisses.

"I'd like that. As long as you scrub mine," I answered in a flirty voice.

Danny grinned and pulled me in for another kiss. I was shivering, this time from the bitter cold. Silk nestled against damp cotton was not sufficient for the weather.

We returned to our seats in time for the sixth and final band. Then it was time to wait. A panel would decide which three bands would move on in the competition. Duncan, Kirk and Ron gathered at our table. Nervous energy smothered us.

The buzz of the crowd abruptly came to a halt. The audience took their seats. Danny squeezed my shoulder. I gave him an encouraging smile and hugged him.

Danny smiled back. "Whatever happens, I'm okay, E."

Moments later came the announcement. Danny's band had come in fourth placing them out of the competition.

"Respectable," said Danny.

CHAPTER 53 - ELIZABETH

"Skiing in Vermont! When?" I was so excited.

So this was the Valentine's celebration Danny had hinted at when we separated. A ski weekend certainly was special. Still, Danny's announcement had caught me by surprise.

"What about Friday's classes?"

"We blow 'em off." Danny shrugged. To him that was no big deal. "I already told Professor Dennison."

"You told the professor we were missing his class to go skiing!"

Danny's audacity amazed me, but not as much as his response.

"Owen's cool with it."

"Owen?"

"Now that he's my advisor, he insists."

I was impressed by their new closeness. I didn't call Professor Dennison "Owen." He'd never given me permission.

After the break, Danny had made it official, declaring Political Science and Film as his double majors.

"You discuss us with a professor?" How disconcerting.

"Owen thinks we're great. Anyway, he brought it up. Owen asked what I was planning, so I told him."

Thursday afternoon could not come soon enough. I hated waiting for Danny's last class to end before we could set out for Vermont.

Darkness greeted us when we arrived shortly after six o'clock. The hotel was at once cozy and luxurious. Danny had reserved a suite. The pine-pole Adirondack style furniture was casual yet elegant. Large picture windows in the living room overlooked the slopes lit for night skiing. Both the living room and bedroom contained wood-burning fireplaces with copper barrels stocked with logs seated on the hearth.

Shutters separated the bathroom from the bedroom. Set on a platform, allowing for a view through the bedroom window, was a whirlpool tub large enough for two.

"This is perfect!" I exclaimed after completing my tour. Would I even want to leave this suite to ski?

We found the fireplaces readied, with additional wood waiting in the copper barrels, when we returned from dinner. Danny lit a match and the living room filled with the promised warmth and glow from the orange-yellow flames.

My hopes for an evening of romance were dashed when Danny pulled out a book. "Danny!" I protested. It was only eight o'clock, but I wanted the entire weekend, selfishly every minute, to be about us. Why did Danny have to be so conscientious?

After kicking off my boots, I plopped down on the plush sofa where Danny sat. I leaned against the armrest and settled my feet in his lap. If Danny assumed I was going to quietly comply with his plans, he didn't know me as well as he thought he did.

I wanted to play!

I tickled Danny with my feet. "Phew," he teased. Then I tickled him again.

"Cut it out," he said sternly and held up his book.

I stuck out my tongue. Danny ignored me. I didn't care. I was content to either cram when we returned or deal with being unprepared on Monday. But not Danny. Anyone who thought he was nothing more than a spoiled party boy did not know Danny.

There was a very good reason why Danny aced every class. He was able to expertly compartmentalize his life. It was why he could spend Saturday night wasted and come to class Monday brilliantly prepared.

When I thought about it, being Danny wasn't healthy. He tried to control every aspect of life, even spontaneous fun. I worried one-day he would crack. Nobody should be that in control. If I occasionally threw Danny a curve, it might prove therapeutic.

This had become my mission; teaching Danny that control was not an either or proposition. He needed to learn that you were not in total control at all times until you were completely out of control. There were varying degrees of control. Danny needed to live closer to the middle.

I removed my book from Danny's backpack, but I could not concentrate. I didn't want to read. I wanted to play.

I glared. Danny was infuriating! Desperate, I took aim and tossed my paperback, hitting Danny's thigh, but he threw it back without missing a beat or losing his place.

Restless, I walked to the window, staring at the night skiers without any of it registering. Speck-sized people schussing down the mountain weren't that interesting.

I crept up behind Danny, wrapped my arms around him, and peppered his neck and cheek with little kisses.

"Elizabeth, you're a pest tonight," he scolded.

"Yes, I am," I answered in a flirty voice. I reached for his face to kiss his lips.

Danny took my hands and pleaded, "Can't you give me an hour? I want to read this. I'm actually enjoying this book."

"I don't want to wait," I pouted.

"You sound like a spoiled little girl who isn't getting her way," Danny smirked.

I growled and gave him a dirty look. Danny laughed.

Frustrated, I announced, "I think I'll try the tub."

"Great idea," Danny said. He was probably glad to be rid of me.

I went to the bathroom and turned on the water. There was a jar of bath salts. I threw a scoop of the vanilla scented powder under the rushing water. It was going to take awhile to fill the large spa tub.

After undressing, I reached for the plush robe hanging in the closet. Satin on the outside, soft, thick cotton on the inside. It fell to my ankles.

Then I pulled my hair into a ponytail and clipped it high on my head. Checking the water level, I saw the tub was far from ready so I returned to the living room.

I sidled up to Danny and leaned over to kiss him. I let my robe loosen. Danny could not miss what waited if he gave up on that damned book already.

Danny reached around my waist and smiled. As I kissed him, the sash came undone. The robe slid open. Danny's eyes went straight to my breasts and lingered. From there they traveled to my hips and finally to there. He grinned, no longer neutral.

The robe fell to the floor. Lust filled Danny's eyes. I pressed against him for another kiss. The book fell from his hand and his arms enveloped my back. I quivered.

"You win, Elizabeth," Danny laughed. "You don't fight fair."

CHAPTER 54 - ELIZABETH

"Eli, time to rise and shine, sleepyhead."

Danny walked his fingers up my torso beginning at my naval and ending at my chin. Tenderly, he planted a kiss on my lips. I sighed. This wake-up call was one I didn't want ended. I smiled, satisfied.

"We don't have to ski. We could spend the day in the suite instead."

"Eli, we like to ski," Danny pointed out.

"It's so nice here. No roommates. No family. Just us."

"I love being alone with you too, babe. But we'll still be alone, even when we're on the mountain."

Danny tickled my neck. I squirmed, and he grinned, pleased with himself.

"I'll start our shower," Danny announced. As he rose, he kissed me once more.

When I emerged from the bathroom, Danny was signing the room service tab. Last night we had filled out the order form and placed it outside on the suite's doorknob. Now that I was energized, I was looking forward to the hearty breakfast.

Danny and I had ordered enough food to create our own mini-buffet. There were scrambled eggs, blueberry pancakes with locally produced maple syrup, bacon, whole-wheat toast and orange juice. Except for the bacon, there was one order of each item. Danny and I split the food, leaving each of us with a little of everything.

Last night I was delighted to find my white Bogner jumpsuit when we unpacked. "How did this get here?" I had asked when I discovered it.

"I called Randi," Danny answered with a self-satisfied grin.

"You called Mom?" That was surprising; Danny discussing his plans with Mom.

"Yeah. Randi had Aspen FedEx it. I wanted to keep my plans secret."

This morning I was even more pleased by his thoughtfulness. I remembered how much he had enjoyed me in this outfit in Aspen. "Snow White in spandex," Danny had called me then. I kept my hair loose to affirm his vision.

Danny warned me that skiing in Vermont was different than in the west. The mountains were smaller than the majestic Rockies or the Sierras. Runs were shorter and narrower. Instead of fluffy powder, the snow would be packed, possibly granular.

Bright sunshine greeted us as we made our way to the chair lift. The dusting of snow we had experienced at Donnelly earlier in the week had dumped over six inches in Vermont. Conditions were therefore excellent.

I squinted. The sun reflecting off the snow produced a sea of sparkling diamonds. I stopped to put my goggles on while taking in the natural beauty of our surroundings.

"Expect ice when you get off the lift," Danny cautioned, and he was right. I slipped, but quickly regained my balance.

"No racing today," I warned. "We don't know this mountain."

Danny laughed and made clucking chicken noises.

"You are not going to intimidate me, Daniel," I scolded.

Of course Danny grinned slyly and quickly set off. Soon he realized I wasn't rising to the challenge, and he stopped. After that Danny was content to ski at my pace.

Exhilarated, the day passed quickly. It was Friday, and we skied more runs than we would tomorrow when the weekend crowds arrived. We took full advantage, stopping only for lunch and a brief afternoon warming.

At dusk we ended the day as we began it, back in our suite. Once again, Danny lit the living room fireplace. While I took a hot shower, he ordered dinner. The steam felt good as the water cascaded over my sore muscles. Afterwards I donned cozy sweats and fuzzy pink slippers. Perfect for a casual evening in.

Danny was also showered and dressed in sweats by the time dinner arrived. After signing the tab, he turned down the lights, and we dined by the warm glow of the fireplace.

Saturday we spent much the same. Now familiar with the terrain, we chose our favorite runs to concentrate on as longer lift lines made exploring difficult.

"I hate the crowds today. There's so many kids," I complained as we waited for a table in the base lodge at lunch. On the slopes they scared me. The kids went racing down the mountain without considering the other skiers.

"Were we like that when we were kids?" I asked.

Danny laughed. "You probably not. Me probably yes."

If this was what vacationing with children was like, then I didn't want any for a long, long time.

Sunday came too soon, and we prepared to depart. Instead of skiing, Danny and I slept-in and enjoyed a leisurely brunch. But first we had to drag ourselves out of bed. Neither of us wanted to.

Upon waking, Danny had arranged more logs in the bedroom fireplace. The orange glow of the flames provided a warm contrast to the dull early morning sky.

Crackling wood and its enticing aroma filled our nostrils. Danny's arms were holding me, and my legs wrapped around his. Gentle kisses on my neck and shoulder sent electricity pulsating throughout me. This was definitely the way to start the day.

"Thank you for the best Valentine's Day ever," I whispered.

"This was the best one for me as well."

"This was your first one, too?"

"Yes," Danny laughed. "I've purposely stayed away from girls during February. Misunderstandings are too easy."

"What about me? Do you think I've misunderstood anything?" I flirted.

"No. I think we've enjoyed an amazing weekend and you're thinking that I must seriously love you. And that's fine with me, because I do seriously love you. Vacations with you are great."

"I wish we could do Spring Break."

"If I weren't already going to Florida with Shane and Cam I'd take you to Saint Bart's in a heartbeat. But I made those plans well before there was an us."

"That's fine. I don't want you to cancel. Danny, you need to do guy stuff. Besides, they'd get angry with both of us if you cancelled now."

CHAPTER 55 - DANIEL

One afternoon a few weeks later, while in my room studying, Dad called.

"Hey Dad," I answered cheerfully, glad for the interruption.

"Danny, David called me yesterday about an Amex bill and certain transactions I didn't make."

David was a junior member of the business management and accounting firm that handled our finances. If it were anything serious, the senior partner would have called.

"Was I a bad boy?" I asked while trying to make light of it. Dad never cared what I charged, so I couldn't imagine what he was referring to.

"Not really. David asked about $3,000 spent in Vermont. I assume you went skiing."

"Guilty as charged. It was Valentine's Day, Dad."

"Who was the lucky girl?"

"Eli, of course. Who else?"

"Danny, you've been back at Donnelly for six weeks and you haven't mentioned her. For all I know you could have a new girl."

"Dad! Of course I don't. What gives? You love Eli."

After a pregnant pause, Dad continued. "I do love Elizabeth, Danny. Dinner at a nice restaurant and flowers wouldn't have sufficed?"

"No, Dad. Eli and I wanted time alone. Eli is my girl. I wanted to take her someplace special. Randi didn't mind, so what's bothering you?"

Dad took a deep breath. "Danny, your mother speaks to me. I know you were having problems after New Year's."

Ugh! So that's why he was calling. Thanks, Mom.

"Any problems we had are in the past," I answered firmly. "Did Grandpa give you a hard time like this when you met Mom?"

"My parents were indifferent. The Slades weren't family friends. They didn't even meet my parents until the engagement party. Grandma and Grandpa liked Ellen, but they assumed she would be the first of however many girlfriends I'd have before I found the one. Junior year, when we announced our intention to marry after graduation, they weren't happy."

"At least your parents gave you and Mom a chance."

"Not exactly. My parents kept their mouths shut. Grandpa confessed years later that they assumed Mom and I would divorce before we turned thirty. He thought an early marriage would force me to pursue a more practical career."

"Boy, was he wrong!" I laughed. "Grandpa sure didn't know his own son."

"No, he didn't," Dad laughed. "The Slades were worse. They didn't know why Ellen wanted to marry 'an arrogant boy who has nothing to be arrogant about.' That was how they put it. The Slades were so against us marrying they wouldn't even pay for the wedding."

"But I've seen your wedding album. Mom looked so beautiful."

"I promised Ellen she'd never want for anything if she married me beginning with the wedding. Mom and I had money saved from our b'nai mitzvahs and summer jobs. Together it was almost $30,000. When the Slades saw we were serious, they gave in."

"I thought Grandma Naomi was crazy about you. She always makes a big fuss."

"Not at first. Naomi hated that we moved to L.A. the moment we graduated. Naomi hated it even more that Ellen was working at the bank while I was bringing in no income.

Naomi kept hoping Ellen would come to her senses and run off with Michael. She loved Mike because he was in law school. Naomi hated when Mike fell in love with Randi. She finally realized Ellen would never leave me for him."

"I can't believe it! Mom and Mike would have been the world's dullest couple."

Dad laughed. "Anyway, the day Mom stopped working Naomi changed. Your birth was what sealed things. Naomi took one look at you and was smitten. She said if I could produce something as amazing as you, then I had to be good for her daughter."

"Dad, Eli and I are happy. I want you to be happy for us."

"Danny, I'm your father and I know you better than anyone."

"Is this a lecture?"

"No, but after our talk in Aspen I thought you would cool it. When you hadn't mentioned Elizabeth in all these weeks, I hoped you'd gone back to being just friends."

"We can't, Dad. Eli and I are in love."

"I'm sure you think you are. Look Danny, I won't tell you what to do, but until you're certain, I'd turn down the heat a few degrees so nobody gets burned."

The door to the suite opened.

"Hi! I'm home." Eli! And she was carrying an armload of books.

"It's Eli. Hold on, she needs me." I tossed the phone on the bed and rushed to her side. "Hey, baby. I'll take those." I grabbed the books and my lips brushed hers.

Then I placed the books on the desk and fished around on the bed for the phone. Found it!

"Gotta go, Dad. Eli's home."

"Home? I didn't hear her knock."

"Eli used her key."

Carrying a water bottle she had taken from the fridge, Eli floated back into the room like a fresh breeze. "How was your afternoon?" she asked.

"Much better now that you're here." I pulled her into my arms and kissed her full pink lips. She even smelled like a fresh breeze.

"Danny! Danny!" Dad called through the phone.

I forgot I was holding it. I stopped kissing Eli, and she giggled.

"Sorry, Dad. Just greeting my lady."

"Danny, obviously you're busy. I'll speak to you later,"

"Right," I said, flustered. "Speak to you later." I pressed the end button and placed the phone on the desk.

Standing on tiptoes Eli threw her arms around my neck and kissed me. As I held her closer, I responded with my own kiss, parting her lips, entwining our tongues. I would consider Dad's advice later. For now, I was powerless to think at all. I scooped Eli up in my arms and carried her to our bed.

With Eli lying in my arms and me playing with her glossy hair, I came to the realization that making love to her had been the dumbest thing I could have done. Dad's advice crept into my conscience. Had this been revenge on Dad sex?

I loved Elizabeth. She was the most important person in my life. But as I mindlessly twirled her hair, and she kissed my shoulder, I had to admit that Dad had a point. I wasn't confident I could make the total commitment Eli deserved.

Perhaps it wasn't a good thing that in the past few weeks Eli had practically moved in. Shane and Cam called her their roommate. I was pleased by how well we all got along. It had made it so easy for Eli to spend night after night with me.

Dad's intentions were good, but little did he know, I could no longer live without Elizabeth in my daily life.

I glanced at Eli nestled in my arms. She responded with adoring emerald eyes that made me melt. Eli was as in love with me as I was with her. No man in my position could resist. I had no choice. I had to kiss her. So I did.

Reducing the time spent with Eli would be torturous. I didn't want to do it. Any time spent with Eli was a treat. Her presence even made studying enjoyable. With midterms followed by Spring Break, at least the school calendar was on my side. For the break, she was going home. I was off to Florida with Shane and Cam. That would buy me time.

Why was I letting Dad get into my head? I had been doing just fine without his well-intentioned fatherly advice. Still, Dad had a point. I would have to carefully think this through. I didn't want to hurt her.

Elizabeth eyes questioned me. "Is something wrong, Danny? You seem distracted."

I affixed my best smile before responding, "No, I'm just tired. I've been studying all afternoon and I have a lot more reading tonight."

"Do you want the night off from me?"

"You wouldn't mind?"

Eli kissed me. "I can endure it," she said. Then she winked, and we laughed.

CHAPTER 56 - ELIZABETH

After a couple of hours at the library, I called it an early night and returned to my own bed for the first time in weeks. It felt foreign, though I easily fell asleep.

The phone startled me awake. I answered on the second chorus, and noticed only fifteen minutes had passed since turning off the light.

"Hello," I said in a bewildered, drowsy voice.

"Baby, did I wake you?"

"Danny?" Nobody else called me "baby."

"Baby, I miss you, honey."

"I miss you too." I was a little more alert. "How's your studying?"

"I'm done. Can you come down? I want you, babe."

"Danny, I was sleeping."

"You're not anymore. Please, Eli? I can't sleep without you."

"Danny, it's late."

"Eli, I love you. You belong here with me. Are you going to make me come get you?"

"I love you too." Danny was impossible to resist. He knew it, too. "Let me get my slippers," I relented.

"Bring your key." Danny's glee perked me up.

CHAPTER 57 - DANIEL

"There's my girl!" I called as a sleepy Elizabeth entered the suite. I jumped off the sofa where my roommates and I were watching a DVD, to greet her. Smoothing hair off her tired face I said, "I missed you, babe," and I kissed her.

I no longer cared what Dad said. I did not want to turn the heat between Eli and me down by even one degree. Eli was hot, and I wanted her to stay that way.

"Danny, you said you couldn't fall asleep," she said, bewildered.

"That's what the DVD is for. I can't fall asleep without you, baby."

"Aw shucks," Cam said sarcastically. "Be quiet, Newman. Some of us actually are watching the movie."

Elizabeth yawned. "I'm sorry," she apologized. "Danny woke me."

Then she curled up like a sleepy kitten. Soon Elizabeth fell asleep, her head resting in my lap. I sat stroking her soft, glossy hair. Everything about Eli felt so right tonight.

When the movie ended, I carefully lifted her in my arms.

"Good-night," I whispered to Cam and Shane as I carried Elizabeth to my room.

Ever so gently, I placed her on our bed, careful to leave enough room for myself. Then I covered her with the comforter and kissed her head. In her sleep, Eli smiled.

While Elizabeth dreamed happy dreams, I sat at my desk prepping for my morning economics mid-term. I had lied when I told Eli I had finished studying. If she knew I needed a couple more hours, I doubted she would have come.

At three, I turned off the light, crawled into bed and cuddled Eli, wrapping my arm around her. Instinctively she turned toward me, searching out the comfort that I brought her.

Way too soon the alarm clock blared. I barely had time to shower, throw on clothes and get a cup of strong coffee before my exam.

Elizabeth was sitting up under the covers when I returned from the shower. Her smile lit the room like early morning sunshine. Elizabeth giggled, eying me wearing nothing except a towel draped around my waist, droplets of water falling from my head.

I took her in my arms. "Good morning, Miss Eli," I announced.

"Good morning, Mr. N.," she said playfully. "Now I'm wet too!" she laughed.

I pulled her face to mine and kissed her with all my heart.

"If I didn't have a mid-term in half an hour, I would never let you go," I told her.

Eli laughed. "I can see you later," she said.

"Yes, you can and you'd better."

Elizabeth gleefully pulled off my towel.

"Get dressed, Daniel," she ordered while laughing.

Elizabeth's laughter was golden music to my ears. "Yes, ma'am" I answered.

CHAPTER 58 - ELIZABETH

Winter slowly loosened its relentless grip on New York State. I was proud of having made it through my first one. March had come in like a lion, but there was hope. You could feel it in the air.

The ground remained covered in snow and ice; the sky often flat and gray. Yet today seemed different. Bright sunshine bathed the horizon. The temperature reached fifty degrees. Everywhere was puddles and slush. If you weren't careful, dribbles from melting icicles landed unexpectedly on your hair. Tonight it would all refreeze, but for a few hours we could enjoy a taste of spring.

My final mid-term was a take-home in History due on Thursday. With Professor Denison scheduling his mid-term for Wednesday, I wouldn't even get to touch history until that afternoon! But first, Psychology and French were both on Monday.

Lucky Danny! With Economics out of the way, his film mid-term being a cakewalk, and film history being watch some old movies and analyze them, the only studying Danny had was political science.

"Time to hit the books," Danny announced when we left dinner on Monday.

I stared in disbelief. "Are you daft? I took two midterms today. I'm taking tonight off. My brain is fried. I'm going to The Cellar."

"I'll let you go if we first strategize for tomorrow. If you don't ace Political Science your parents will blame me. Randi will say, 'I told you Danny was a bad influence. I don't want you spending so much time with him.'"

"Mom wouldn't," I answered but with uncertainty.

Danny raised an eyebrow. "Eli?" Was I that naïve?

"Alright. Mom would, but who cares? I'm an adult."

"I care. I want your parents on our side."

"I do too, but if they're not..." I sighed. "Let's go to the library until nine. We'll have earned an hour at The Cellar and we can still get to bed by eleven. I want my A."

Danny and I woke earlier than planned on Tuesday. Before my eyes opened, Danny's lips joined mine. His hands running down my body sent excitement through me. I was as eager as he was to continue where we had left off last evening.

Sometime while dancing at The Cellar, sadness had enveloped us. As I had completed a pirouette into Danny's arms, our eyes met and he held me close for the rest of the song.

"Two weeks apart," Danny said sadly. "I don't like it Eli."

Neither did I. Spring Break should be a happy time. For us, it wouldn't be.

Friday, Danny was driving me to Albany to begin my journey home. Saturday, he was travelling by train to New York with Shane and Cam to stay at the Reynolds' until Monday. Then they would fly to Miami where Cam's family had a beachfront condo in South Beach.

Focus Elizabeth. Dwelling on our pending separation was distracting. I needed an A on tomorrow's mid-term or Danny I feared would be right. Hell, I couldn't afford more than one B-range grade if I didn't want parental grief.

CHAPTER 59 - ELIZABETH

Winding my way through the terminal at LAX confused me, as though I were wandering aimlessly, following the signs to the luggage carousel, but not aware of my environs. It was just past noon, but I'd already logged long hours.

"Dad!" I called. There he was, standing tall and handsome, waiting with a luggage cart. I ran to his welcoming arms feeling the eyes of other travelers asking, "Is that Miranda Jordan's daughter? And isn't that her husband?"

"Elizabeth!" Dad hugged me tightly.

I needed his hug so badly. My heart weighed heavy with loneliness.

"Sweetheart, you look great," he said appraising my appearance. "Tired, but great. Doesn't Danny let you sleep?"

"Dad!" I scolded. "I've been up since midnight in this time zone." We hugged again. "Daddy, I'm so glad you're here."

Dad held me close and whispered, "I thought you'd need me. A part of you is missing today." Dad understood.

For the next few days, I went through the motions. Home was pleasant, but the combination of jet lag and missing Danny left me miserable and lethargic.

"Tomorrow let's have girls day out," Mom declared at dinner. "I've made us hair appointments. We'll go shopping and have lunch." There! Mom to the rescue!

Danny phoned later that evening interrupting my mindless web-surfing.

"How's my girl?" Danny asked cheerfully. His voice always put a smile on my face. "I can't talk long. It's late." It was ten o'clock here, one in Miami. "I love you," he added.

"I love you too, Danny." I missed him so much the words hurt.

"Are you alone?"

"Who else would be in my bedroom when you're not?" I laughed. Where was this going?

"What are you wearing?"

I looked down at my bathrobe and laughed. "I was about to bathe."

"So you're wearing nothing?" Danny asked with surprise.

"My robe is on."

"The short pink fluffy one? I can imagine what's underneath it."

"I'm sure you can, Daniel." I blushed.

"What are you imagining, Eli?"

"That you're with me," I stammered. "Can anybody hear us?"

"Cam and Shane are asleep," Danny answered. "If I'm with you babe, what am I doing?"

"Danny, you're holding me. We're kissing."

"Are my hands inside or on your robe?"

"Danny! You're embarrassing me."

"You're too proper, Eli."

"No I'm not. I'm your girlfriend."

"Eli, you've got me there," Danny laughed. "My hands are inside your robe by the way. Can you feel them?"

I blushed, relieved that my door was locked.

"Yes, I do." I really did. "They're all over me. I'm on fire." I tingled. My breath hitched.

"I know. Eli, you're soft and warm. Your kiss tastes sweet, too."

"Danny! This isn't fair." I squirmed, already damp between my thighs.

"I'm driving you crazy, aren't I?" he laughed. "I can guess what you're imagining, Eli," Danny teased.

"So are you."

"Tell me, Sweetheart."

"I can't. Okay. I'm so embarrassed, even if nobody is here."

Danny laughed at my discomfort.

"Danny, I wish you were here," I moaned, so aroused.

"I wish I were too, babe."

"We should both take cold showers," I said.

Danny laughed. "You're right. Weren't you about to run a bath?"

"Yes, but a warm one."

"Enjoy it, baby. I love you. I'll call you again tomorrow."

CHAPTER 60 - ELIZABETH

"Elizabeth, your hair looks absolutely perfect!" Mom raved as we entered the elevator after leaving the second floor salon.

"For once, it is perfect," I agreed. "Too bad nobody's going to see it."

"Be honest. You mean Danny. Must everything be measured by how it relates to him?"

"No, but it seems a waste my hair when it looks its best for Danny not to be here."

Mom sighed, "So you'll get it styled before the next time you're with him."

"Antonio doesn't have a salon in upstate New York."

"Elizabeth, you're hopeless. Danny loves you no matter what your hair looks like."

The elevator opened into a small lobby designed with the aura of a Mediterranean villa. Inspiration hit. The pale, stucco-covered wall would be a perfect backdrop.

"Take a picture of me," I said to Mom, and I handed her my iPhone.

"Elizabeth!" she groaned.

"Mom," I insisted, "It's the next best thing."

Mom snapped two pictures; one close-up and one full-body. Before we left the building, I texted them to Danny. I imagined he was swimming on what had to be a beautiful south Florida day. At some point he'd be back on land and open my message.

"Sending Danny a taste of what he's missing?" Mom asked as we rejoined the crowds on Rodeo Drive.

"You betcha," I responded. "I hate thinking nobody is going to see my hair looking this nice." I admit I sounded like a spoiled brat.

"Lots of people will see you, Elizabeth. You just aren't aware of it," Mom said, indicating the masses on the street.

"Mom, they see you, not me," a sorry fact of life that came with having a superstar for a mother. I'd long ago come to accept it, though I not necessarily enjoyed it.

Through my darkest sunglasses, I furtively glanced at the passing strangers. People glanced at us, some even starred. The pitfalls when your companion is Miranda Jordan.

This is why I hate Rodeo Drive. The street always teems with gawking tourists. Unable to afford anything in the shops, they came for stories to post on Facebook. Today's crop was earning their bragging rights in spades.

"Ahem," Mom whispered indicating a young couple in shorts and tees. You could always spot the tourists. Unless they were foreign, they rarely carried packages and their ubiquitous cameras were at the ready.

This young couple was giggling and holding hands. Honeymooners.

"That couple is thinking who is that beautiful young woman with Miranda Jordan," Mom continued. "Perhaps it's her much discussed but rarely photographed daughter, and that hair!" Mom teased.

"Mom!" I scolded. "And now they're thinking Miranda Jordan must lie about her age because her daughter looks awfully grown-up."

Mom and I both laughed. Mom had never lied about her age. She couldn't. She'd gotten her big break as a teen.

Near Brighton Way, Mom said, "Now that young man is definitely looking at you, not me." Mom was referring to an attractive young man with spiky brown hair wearing designer jeans, a t-shirt, flip-flops and most important, no camera.

"Zac!" I called out. I loved Zac!

"Elizabeth! It is you," he answered, excited.

Zac and I exchanged quick embraces and cheek kisses.

"Mom, you remember Zac Hartman?"

"Yes, of course. How are you Zac?"

"Great, Mrs. Jacobs. I'm home from Harvard for the break."

Impressive, it was even more so coming from Zac who grew up in the most dysfunctional family I had ever known.

Zac's father had played lead guitar in a legendary rock band for over thirty years. Gibby had multiple piercings, endless tattoos, and had been in rehab so many times nobody kept count anymore. At 50, the world marveled that Gibby Hartman was not only alive, but was able to perform on yet another world tour.

"How's your Dad?" I asked.

"Knock on wood. Eighteen months and he's still clean," Zac said proudly.

"Excellent news, Zac," Mom said. "I'll keep my fingers crossed."

"How's Steve Newman? I haven't heard from Danny since probably October. It's like he's dropped off the planet. I was afraid…"

"Steve is good," Mom answered. "He hasn't had any set-backs for years."

I looked at Mom, then at Zac and back to Mom, my mouth agape. Mom never discussed Steve's past substance abuse issues with me and I was family. Yet here she was, answering Zac as though it were common knowledge. Maybe it was.

"Elizabeth, do you run into Danny?"

I flushed. "We're roommates," I wanted to answer, but didn't. "Danny lives in my dorm," I responded. How did Zac not know about us?

If Danny hadn't told him, why hadn't their posse? We'd seen them at Ali's.

"Danny's not in any trouble, is he? I mean, that could be why I haven't heard from him."

Trouble? "Danny 's just been busy," I answered.

"That's what I figured. Danny's such a nerd." Zac joshed. "I was in Europe with Gibby's tour at Christmas so I'm sort of out of the loop."

"Of course," I nodded.

"Elizabeth, tell me if this rumor is true." Zach said with urgency. "If it were anyone but Danny... It just sounds too incredible."

"What rumor?"

Sequestered with our books in upstate New York, we'd been leading rather boring lives, certainly nothing to gossip about. If there were rumors about Danny, I would see that they were quashed. I fingered my iPhone hidden in my palm.

"I don't know the details, but I heard he's got a girlfriend, and it's serious. That doesn't sound like Danny."

Do not look at Mom! Do not look at Mom! Stay sober.

"Zac, you're right. It doesn't, but it's true. Danny does have a serious girlfriend."

Toying with Zac was fun. Could I keep a straight face?

"Danny's girlfriend is very bright and very beautiful. And she has great hair," Mom added. "Steve and Ellen just love her.

I bit my lip to avoid laughing. Why did Mom have to torture me by mentioning the hair?

"No shit!" Zac exclaimed. "The Newman's have met her!"

"His girlfriend comes from an excellent family," I added and gave Mom a furtive smirk. I would give it right back to her.

"Unbelievable. Danny Newman with a real girlfriend."

"Why wouldn't Danny have a girlfriend?" I frowned. Danny was so easy to love.

"I'm sorry. This must hurt. I forgot. Elizabeth, you've always had a thing for Danny"

The vibration of the ringtone against my hand startled me. I recovered my composure and noted the incoming number.

"Hi, Daniel," I purred into the phone and stared at Zac.

"Got your message, babe. It's not quite, but it's almost as good as having you here. I miss you, Eli."

"I miss you too." My heart was soaring and a big smile crossed my face. "Mom and I were at the salon."

"Baby, you look perfect, as always."

"Thanks, honey. Whatcha doing?"

"I'm sitting at the pool reading a book."

Zac starred wide-eyed while Mom stifled a laugh.

"Hold on a moment. Mom and I ran into Zac. He's trying to say something."

"It's you!" Zac stammered.

I grinned in response, giddy.

"Zac just figured out that I'm the girl in the who is Danny Newman's girlfriend rumor," I said to the phone. "Zac, you can close your mouth now." It was opened wide with disbelief. "He looks like a fish." Danny was now laughing. Even Mom couldn't help herself and was laughing.

I couldn't imagine how we must have looked to anyone passing. A movie icon, a young woman, and a cell phone all laughing while a young man stood befuddled, looking helpless. In the middle of Rodeo Drive, of all places!

"I'm sorry, Zac." I choked out while trying to regain my composure.

"Eli," Danny was also trying to stop laughing. "Babe, put me on speaker."

I held the phone up, so we were all facing it.

"Zac, you okay?" Danny asked.

"I don't get it. Elizabeth?"

"This is why we haven't spoken in months. I knew you wouldn't understand. Zac, are you looking at her?"

Zac turned toward me and I preened. "Yes, I'm looking at Elizabeth."

"Good. 'Cause she's the most beautiful girl you're ever going to set your eyes on and she's mine."

Zac rolled his eyes. I stood smugly holding the phone. Mom smiled.

"Danny, I want to invite Elizabeth to my party on Thursday. Can she come?"

"Elizabeth doesn't need my permission, Zac. E, if you want to go it's up to you."

"I know but Zac is being a jerk."

"He is, but by Thursday you'll probably be bored."

"Good point. I'll go."

"E, take me off speaker so we can have some privacy."

I took Danny off speaker and moved to the side of the building.

CHAPTER 61 - DANIEL

Having grown up with a beach house in Malibu, I didn't understand why I found the view of the clean sand and the Atlantic Ocean so impressive and so mesmerizing, but I did. Try as I did to analyze it, all I could think of was because it was different.

Malibu is quiet and private. It's rustic, a place for solitude. This condo pool deck was the opposite, urban and sophisticated. Three towers surrounded the enormous yet perfectly designed, pool. And lining the boulevard was an endless line of similar hotel and condo towers.

It was late in the day, but several dozen people remained at the pool. Music I had not selected played from hidden speakers. It pulsated, as did the well-tanned bodies. I might enjoy a week of this, but the beach I wanted for life was Malibu.

The book I was reading before I called Elizabeth sat where I'd left it, on the small teak table beside my cushioned lounge chair. In this environment I had only been able to read a few pages. I didn't feel guilty by deceiving Elizabeth into thinking I had actually been reading. What Eli didn't know wouldn't hurt her.

What I was guilty about, although not guilty enough or it wouldn't be happening, was the leggy blonde model I met earlier. At this point nothing had happened beyond flirtatious conversation, but it was only the afternoon.

Noticing a line at the bar, I sent Reggie for drinks so I could call Eli. Reggie. Her name even sounded like a model. Happy hour was starting early for me!

Reggie would soon be returning. I needed to wrap up my call with Elizabeth.

"Babe, you have a fun afternoon with Randi."

"I wish it were with you instead."

"I do too. We'd be at the beach planning an evil evening." I meant it too, even if my eyes were monitoring Reggie in her bikini as she paid for the drinks with the money I had given her. If Eli were here, Reggie would not even be on my radar.

"I wish." There was longing in Elizabeth's voice.

I felt a tinge of guilt. I was one hundred percent certain that Eli was not even contemplating finding a substitute for me while we were apart. A good thing too, for if she did, I would have to break up with her and I didn't want that.

I tried to cheer her up. "I can picture you in the bikini you wore in Aspen. Just the thought of it drives me crazy."

"I'm sure there are lots of girls in bikinis in Florida."

Shit! I hope I wasn't busted already.

"Baby, none of them are as sexy as you." And I meant it.

As if on cue, Reggie returned with our drinks. I took a large sip of the fruity rum concoction. I was on vacation in Florida, after all, and I placed it on the table. I motioned Reggie that I would be a moment.

"Danny, I love you. You always know what to say."

"E, I should let you go. I don't want to anger Randi."

Reggie perched herself on the lounge chair facing me. She smiled prettily trying to act as though she didn't hear the intimate conversation I was engaged in. I didn't really care. Reggie needed to accept that she would at most be a vacation fling. If not, c'est la vie. Either way, I was going home to Elizabeth.

"Okay. I can't strand Mom in the middle of Rodeo Drive."

"With Zac!" I added, and we both laughed. I love Eli's musical laugh.

"Poor Mom!" Eli laughed some more.

"I'll call you tonight. It'll be late. I'm going to a party with the guys."

"What should I wear?"

"Surprise me, darlin'."

"I'll buy something new." Eli was excited and that pleased me.

"For a phone call?"

"Danny, you'll see," she said seductively.

"Babe, what are you planning? Am I in trouble?"

"I sure hope so, Daniel."

"Baby, I'd better go. You have no idea what you're doing to me."

"I can imagine," she giggled. "I love you, Danny."

"I love you too, baby," And I pushed the off button.

I reached for my drink, taking a long sip of its frosty goodness. Reggie leaned forward exposing what her bikini top hid. In contrast to Eli, she had little to hide.

"Who was that?" she purred.

"My girlfriend," I answered.

It certainly wasn't my mother. When you end a call by saying, "I love you too, baby" it's pretty obvious you're talking to your girl. Reggie's smile dropped a fraction, taken aback by my frankness.

I saw the wheels spinning in her head as she rapidly processed this information. Perched by my side, Reggie had less than thirty seconds to reach a decision. Finally she smiled again.

"Dan, I appreciate your honesty. Most guys here for spring break don't tell you they have girlfriends at home."

"Reggie, I didn't come for fun. If it happens, it happens. If not, oh well.

If you don't like my status, my friends are unencumbered."

Reggie squinted her face, confused by my vocabulary. She didn't know, but had I been available, Reggie had failed the first test. A girl who couldn't keep up with me intellectually could never be more than a temporary diversion, no matter how beautiful they were.

"Whatever. It doesn't matter," she said.

"I'm glad that's clear." I smiled at Reggie. The girl might have peanuts rattling inside, but she was breathtaking to look at. My hand rested on Reggie's thigh leading her to smile in what she believed was triumph. I raised my glass to her.

"Here's to some fun in the sun," I toasted and we tapped our drinks together.

CHAPTER 62 - DANIEL

They certainly can party in Miami. What a wild scene! The DJ was first rate, the drinks flowed feely, and the girls were hotter than hot.

True to her word, Reggie brought a few friends to keep Shane and Cam occupied. Later, she and I slipped out to spend quality time at her condo. A glossy, ultra-modern one-bedroom with walls of glass leading to a wide ocean-view balcony, Reggie had been eager to show me her home. It hadn't disappointed.

I left Reggie at around one, content, sleeping under the covers, and returned to the party. It was going strong with wall-to-wall attractive, tanned young people.

After one more beer and a couple of dances, I was drained and needed my sleep. Cam, Shane and I staggered back to the condo.

"I'll be in soon," I told Shane. Shane and I were sharing a bedroom. Cam had his own. The master, belonged to his parents. "I told Eli I'd call her."

Shane stopped in his tracks. "Aren't you on the outs?" he asked.

Shane's question surprised me. "Of course not. Everything's great with Eli."

"Then what's with the blonde? Or do you enjoy living dangerously?"

"Reggie's a charming amusement for the week," I answered.

"Danny, you already have the hottest girlfriend. Why risk it?"

"There's no risk. You and Cam won't say anything. What happens in Florida stays in Florida." I was being arrogant.

"And if someone sees you?"

"I'm being careful. I won't do anything to hurt Eli. I love her too much."

"Do you have any idea how insane that sounds?" Shane exclaimed. "I love my girlfriend. I won't do anything to hurt her," he mimicked. "Except I'm screwing a gorgeous model which of course would most definitely hurt Elizabeth if she found out. Why are you doing this?"

"If you can't be with the one you love, love the one you're with?" I flippantly quoted the old song.

"This isn't funny, Danny. Elizabeth would be devastated."

"Eli will never find out. Besides, I never promised to be a good boy."

"I give up!"

Shane threw up his hands in frustration and went off to bed. I took out my Mac and set it on the dining table. Tonight I felt like Skyping.

CHAPTER 63 - ELIZABETH

"Ring. Ring! Ring!" I willed my phone to ring.

I didn't expect the phone to ring. Danny was at a party. He certainly wasn't going to glance at his watch and tell the guys, "Gotta go. Eli's expecting me."

The evening had been deadly quiet. Since about ten I had been reclining on my bed channel surfing. Nothing kept my attention.

My favorite singer! Danny! At the concert, Shane had recorded Danny's love song, and I had made it my ringtone. Now my phone was singing.

Tossing aside the remote, I snatched the phone. My love!

"Hey, you!" I answered cheerfully.

"Hi, baby," came Danny's beautiful voice. "Let's Skype."

"I was hoping you'd say that."

"Afraid you'll forget what I look like?"

"Sure. Like that's ever going to happen. No. I have a surprise to show you."

"Can't wait, darlin.' So get off the phone and get over to your laptop."

I crawled across the bed at warp speed and tore across to my desk. The laptop was waiting. All I had to do was access Skype, and I did so with alacrity.

"Much better," Danny said as I settled into my desk chair. "Eli, you're what's been missing from my day."

"I've missed you too."

Holy shit! I tried not to visibly react to Danny's appearance. But his eyes! They were puffy, and dark circles made them appear almost sunken. Had I not known, I would never have guessed at their usual brilliant blue. Danny looked exhausted, too.

"Oh, honey! What have you been doing?"

"It's two in the morning, Eli." Danny showed his annoyance.

"Danny, I've seen you at two in the morning." The haggard face on the screen was disturbing. What had he been doing?

"That's because when I'm with you at two in the morning, I'm snug in our bed cuddled up with you, dreaming of the fun we've just had."

"Danny, what's going on?" I demanded.

"Eli, they have wicked parties here. I was out misbehaving."

"Daniel!" I groaned, disappointed. When would he grow up and stop thinking it was cool to get blitzed?

"Please don't get angry, Eli. I love you, baby."

"I know you do. And I love you, which is why this worries me."

"I don't want you worrying."

"Please be careful, Daniel. You don't know the people down there. I don't want you getting into trouble."

"I won't. I miss you terribly, honey."

Danny sounded so sad. "Are you okay, Danny?"

"Elizabeth, I'm scared," he said forlornly.

"Scared? About what?"

"I'm afraid I'll do something stupid and you'll be disappointed."

"Danny, you could never disappoint me. I love you."

"Eli, every day since you left, I wake up feeling lost. I have to psyche myself up to believe I can be the man you want even though we're apart. I don't feel worthy."

"Danny, get it through your thick skull. I love you. There is no man for me but you."

"I have a hard time accepting that. Eli, you're too good."

"Are you drunk?" I asked.

"Somewhat, babe. But I really miss you."

That explained his melancholy.

"I miss you too."

"Are you angry?" Danny asked in a little boy voice.

"I never stay angry for long. Honestly, you're like an overgrown child at times."

Then Danny grinned, knowing I could never resist his smile.

"Eli, you're so beautiful tonight. That's a great color."

I was wearing a new deep orange polo shirt.

"Thank you, honey. I wanted to be beautiful for you."

"Baby, you never disappoint. What else are you wearing?"

I giggled, knowing what he would see. The hem of the cropped polo hung just above my naval. All I had on below was the navy thong bikini I wore in Aspen.

"Eli, you're not wearing anything!"

"Yes, I am." I laughed. "I'll show you." And I slowly turned, knowing he would be seeing mostly skin.

"Eli!" Danny gasped. I grinned. "Can I touch?"

"I wish," I answered. "Oh god, how I wish." My pulse quickened.

"Is anything on under your shirt?"

"Maybe," I giggled.

"Maybe not? Okay, Eli. I'm completely sober now."

I laughed. "You're such a man."

I pulled my shirt over my head revealing bare breasts.

"E, you're killing me."

I wanted him so badly.

"Glad you approve, Daniel," I purred.

"God, I wish I was with you."

"You're surrounded by girls in bikinis all day. I wanted you to see the one girl you're missing."

"Point made. I haven't seen any girl who can compete with you. Oh, babe! You're gorgeous." Danny's eyes glowed. "You know what I'm thinking about?"

"That night in Aspen?"

"You, me and the hot tub, our fantasies about to be fulfilled," he sighed.

"Until Steve showed up."

Danny laughed. "I need you, babe. I'm lonely here without you."

CHAPTER 64 - DANIEL

After a light rain had fallen, it had turned into another perfect south Florida day. It was so perfect, even my hangover was gone. The only damper was Cam and Shane's obvious displeasure that I was hooking up with Reggie for the day.

Cam and Shane had hit it off with a couple of Reggie's friends and were enjoying themselves. Why wasn't I allowed to have any fun?

The streets of South Beach were crowded with a mixture of colorful locals, flamboyant wannabees, and vacationing tourists. An occasional out-of-place businessman added a humorous touch.

Every inch of Reggie was evenly tanned making her long, blonde hair appear even paler. Her short blue shorts emphasized slender legs that went on forever. She had tied her crisp white cotton blouse above her waist revealing a flat torso. At 5'10" she didn't need heels to approach eye-level with me. I didn't necessarily like that.

After lunch at a patio bistro, I held Reggie close, my arm draped around her shoulder as we made our way to a bicycle rental kiosk. Heads turned. Reggie always attracted attention.

Then my phone vibrated in my shirt pocket. I quickly removed it. Eli was calling. Feeling guilty, I dropped my arm from Reggie's shoulder.

"I've got to take this," I said. Reggie nodded. "Hey, baby," I said into the phone. "You're up early."

"It's almost eleven, Danny."

"Right. So what's up?"

"I'm checking on you. Danny, you sounded awful last night."

"I did, didn't I, babe."

"Feeling better?"

I glanced at Reggie smiling so beautifully.

"Much better, Eli," I answered, but I smiled at Reggie.

"Danny, I hate when you're drunk. I couldn't fall asleep."

"Why didn't you call?"

"I wanted you to sleep it off."

"And I did. Baby, you worry too much."

"Can't help it. I love you, Danny."

Reggie had to be uncomfortable with the words she was hearing.

"E, I should get going. I'm on the street and it's noisy here."

"Okay. Remember. I'll be at Zac's later. Reaching me will be difficult."

I nodded. "Eli, have fun at the party. Take the Porsche."

"Seriously?" I loved the glee in her voice. "Danny, you're the best!"

I laughed, picturing the shock her arrival would cause.

"I love you, baby. Text me when you get home. I want to know you're safe."

I hung up the phone and shoved it into my pocket before turning to Reggie. Shit! If she didn't stomp off in a huff after listening to my end of this conversation I would rate her as the most tolerant woman I had ever met.

"Girlfriend?" she asked, already knowing the answer.

"Yeah." What else was there to say? It was so painfully obvious.

"Her name is Eli?" Reggie appraised my seemingly neutral reaction.

I had avoided revealing anything personal to Reggie, so I answered carefully.

"It's a nickname."

Reggie looked directly at me. "She must be very pretty to be your girlfriend."

"Reggie, don't ask me these questions. But yes, she's very pretty."

I made an immediate decision; today would be my last spent with Reggie.

If she were asking about Eli, her fishing expedition wouldn't end there. Reggie, knew little about me, which was just the way I wanted it. The last thing I wanted was for a fling to discover I was Steven Newman's son.

"Don't trust girls," was Dad's mantra. At times it seemed extreme, but I listened. Dad's implied warning was not to unintentionally father any babies. Too many girls had the goal of landing a wealthy baby daddy. Even if you wouldn't marry them, when the DNA tests came back positive, they'd be set for life.

CHAPTER 65 - ELIZABETH

What a night! It promised to be one of those rare moments where you get revenge on your entire high school circle all at once. How often did that happen? Almost never, I assumed.

I might be flying solo, but I wanted everyone to see that the shy, geeky Elizabeth they remembered was dead. I was the vivacious woman Danny Newman proudly called his girlfriend.

But first I was meeting Steff and Emma for dinner at the Cheesecake Factory in Marina del Rey.

"Oh my god!" Emma exclaimed when the valet brought the Porsche up after our meal. "Danny gave you his car!"

"I can't believe it!" Steff echoed. "You're like married?"

"I've been telling you," I complained. "I don't know why it takes a car for you to believe we're serious."

"Because it's Danny," Steff answered. "He's only LA's most notorious playboy."

The Hartman's lived in Santa Monica Canyon, one of those small, rustic enclaves that only locals know about.

The roar of the turbo-charged engine preceded me to the valet stand in front of Zac's tree-house styled home on a curvy, narrow road. Several recent arrivals stopped in anticipation. Even in this crowd, few owned a Porsche.

"Must be Newman," someone said as I stopped the car. The "DMN" vanity plates made identification obvious. Wouldn't they be surprised when I stepped out of the driver's side? Already I was having fun.

Dean was standing in the driveway, smoking a cigarette, a bad habit I had hoped he'd have dropped by now.

"Elizabeth?" Dean greeted me warmly.

"Dean!" I answered, and we exchanged air kisses. I wouldn't get any closer. Ugh, the stench of tobacco. He reeked. Did Dean realize what a turn-off that was?

"Isn't that Newman's most-prized possession?"

"No," I answered and a playful smile lit my face.

"But that's his Carerra," Dean said with authority.

"It's Danny's car, but Dean, it's not Danny's most-prized possession."

"Did his parents buy him a Cessna?"

"Are you kidding? Danny's blind as a bat," I laughed. "He could never get a pilot's license."

"Then what's more important to Newman than that car? It's all he talks about."

I looked at Dean directly. "The girl driving the car," I answered.

"So it's true? You and Newman. It's like an arranged marriage. There's something almost incestuous about it. It's like you're sleeping with your brother, Elizabeth."

"That is so gross, Dean! Disgusting, actually."

"So, Miss Prized Possession, where is he?"

"Danny's in Miami with his roommates."

"He trusts you to be here alone?"

"Of course he does," I laughed.

"Maybe we can change that." And Dean winked.

"Huh?" I was stunned. Was Dean coming on to me? That would be a first. He'd never even looked twice at me before.

I patted Dean's shoulder. "In your dreams," I said, and I skated past him.

What a raucous scene! Unlike Ali's party, this was my crowd, not Danny's. There was close to one hundred people, most of whom I'd grown up with; a fantastic reunion of the Westside's most elite youth.

Everyone was dancing as a celebrity DJ spun the best tunes. The bar was open and flowing. Delectable munchies from a premiere caterer were being served. I regretted having eaten dinner. I wanted to be hungry!

As the evening progressed, I was enjoying myself. Being among old friends was such fun. Every time I turned I found myself exchanging squeals and hugs. These were the people who knew me the best.

The girls hadn't changed much since last summer's parties. We reminisced and brought each other up-to-date with stories of our new lives. There were few secrets in this room. Soon I knew the minutiae of everyone's love lives. Mine intrigued the most, and the girls fawned over me, wanting to know every detail.

I was having a blast! Then Dean caught up to me.

"Elizabeth, let's dance," he said innocuously enough.

Before I could answer, Dean grabbed me around the waist and practically carried me out to the dance floor. He held me so close I couldn't push away. His tobacco-scented breath mixed with beer, was stale in my face and nearly made me ill.

I did not want to dance with Dean!

Dean had always been pleasant and well mannered. He was never a close friend, but when we crossed paths we had gotten along well enough. Not tonight. It was as though demons had possessed him.

"Dean, I don't want to dance anymore," I protested.

The song was over and I tried disengaging. Instead, as the next song began, Dean tightened his hold on me. He moved his hand to my bottom. I resisted, trying to pull away, but he pressed me against him. Was Dean drunk? Drugs? It didn't matter. Either way I felt violated and tried my best to wriggle free.

"Remove your hand!" I ordered.

"I'm sure you let Newman do this."

"Is that what this is about? Danny?" I said angrily, while trying to tear his hands off my waist.

"Newman's not here. We could have fun, Elizabeth."

"No, Dean we cannot!" More insistent, I tried pushing away again.

There were at least fifty people in the room. Why didn't anyone see my struggle and come to my assistance?

"Let's find a room," he said in a low, lascivious voice that nobody else could hear. His eyes were glowing, possessed.

"Dean, stop it! Danny will not be happy," I threatened.

Nobody here would want to incur Daniel's wrath. He was the alpha. Piss him off, you might as well start hanging out with the transplants, or worse, move to the Valley.

"Then don't tell him. C'mon, Elizabeth."

"Let go! I'm Danny's girl." Dean grabbed my wrist, holding my hand toward my chin. He laughed derisively and then squeezed my bottom.

"Dean!" I exclaimed. That was it! I felt the adrenaline rush and pulled my free hand back. With all my strength I unleashed my power and smacked Dean's face.

"Ouch!" he cried, startled. "Bitch!"

Glaring, Dean released me and I raced past him.

I ran to my car without saying good-bye to anyone, not even Steff or Emma. Shaking from the confrontation, I longed for Danny's protective arms. Dean would never have gone near me if I were with Danny.

At that moment I missed him more than I had all week. In Danny's arms I was safe. Frustration left me fighting for air. "Danny! I need you so badly." But I couldn't even call him. It was too late in Miami. The phone ringing would wake Cam and Shane.

Inside the Porsche, I inserted Danny's favorite CD and raised the volume. I felt surrounded by him. Then the floodgates opened. I sat parked, gripping the steering wheel, my head hidden against my hands while I cried my heart out.

CHAPTER 66 – DANIEL

"Look what the cat dragged in!" Shane exclaimed.

Disheveled from a night spent with Reggie, I straggled into the condo early the next morning. Shane was in the kitchen buttering a freshly toasted bagel as Cam was pouring coffee.

"I'll take a cup," I told Cam as I passed through.

The guys were a blur until I dragged myself into the bedroom and returned wearing my eyeglasses. It was a marvel that I'd found my way back to the right apartment. I hadn't planned on sleeping out. When I woke, my dried out lenses had to be thrown away.

"Thanks," I said on my return as I took a hot, steaming mug from Cam.

In sharp juxtaposition, my roommates were decidedly chilly. I took a seat at the counter where Shane was biting into his bagel, and I yawned. A hot shower would be very welcome after the coffee. A nap would be nice, too.

The silence in the kitchen was deafening. Had Cam and Shane had an argument?

"Danny, what the hell are you doing?" Cam's accusation startled me.

I nearly spit coffee back in the mug. Nobody ever talked to me that way. How dare he. And Shane looked as sour as Cam sounded.

"What are you talking about?" I shot back. "I'm drinking coffee."

"Did you and Elizabeth break up?" Shane asked more calmly.

"Of course not. I love Eli." Cam and Shane knew that.

"Then why are you with Reggie?" Shane asked.

"What's your problem Shane? I'm just having some fun. It's called vacation!" Jeez. What was his problem?

"What about Elizabeth?" Cam pressed.

"What about her? What she doesn't know won't hurt her," I answered crossly. "What happens in Miami stays in Miami," I warned them with a steely stare.

"When it was a one or two night fling maybe, but you've been hanging around Reggie like she's your girlfriend."

"Cam, it's not your business." They were pissing me off. Nobody ever questioned me.

"Danny, it is our business," Shane started in his calm, Zen-like demeanor, which I usually enjoyed but right now I hated. "You're our roommate and our friend. We care about you, and Elizabeth, too. Cam and I like her very much. She's a great girl. We don't want her to get hurt."

"I would never hurt Elizabeth."

"If Elizabeth finds out about Reggie, she'll be devastated," Shane said.

Damn, Shane! I pictured Eli, her head buried in a pillow crying her heart out. I shook my head to clear that vision. Eli trusted me and I had spent the break abusing that trust.

"I don't want to hurt Elizabeth. I love her. I miss Eli terribly."

Cam's laugh stung. "If this is how you treat people you love, don't ever love me."

"Cam!"

"I'm serious. Danny, you're treating Elizabeth like crap. You're a fool."

Cam was entirely out of line and he was entirely correct. No one but Elizabeth had ever challenged me like Cam and Shane were now doing. Usually my peers feared me. I was Steven Newman's son. No one dared risk losing my friendship.

A sobering thought crossed my mind. If Cam and Shane felt they could criticize me, did this mean they were my only true friends? I was not ready to accept that.

"If you miss Elizabeth, what are you doing with Reggie?" Cam asked.

"Trying to forget how much I miss Elizabeth."

"That's bullshit, Danny," Shane declared. "There's nothing wrong with missing your girlfriend. Sure you're used to getting laid every night, but is it that difficult for you to go without for two weeks? I'm sure Elizabeth isn't cheating on you."

"Of course she isn't. Eli would never do that. She loves me."

"You are such a hypocrite, Danny."

"Shane, ease up. I get your point. I'm an idiot who made a fool of himself."

"Glad you realize it."

"I'm learning. Anyway, Reggie left for Germany."

"Good," Cam said. "Reggie's poison."

"Don't say that. This was my doing. Reggie's a nice girl."

"Reggie's poison, Danny," Shane concurred with Cam. "Reggie knew you were taken. She heard you on the phone talking sweet to Elizabeth and it didn't stop her."

"Reggie's poison." Cam repeated.

I paused for a moment, glad to have the guys back. I smiled above the rim of my mug. "Reggie's poison," I agreed. "But Reggie's the sweetest poison I ever tasted," I smirked.

CHAPTER 67 - ELIZABETH

Danny was singing? In my sleep? It was the middle of the night. Oh, the phone! Without turning my head or opening my eyes, I reached for the nightstand and grabbed the phone.

"Hello," I mumbled in a sleepy stupor.

"Sorry I woke you, baby," came the beautiful voice that always put a smile on my face.

"Danny? What time is it?" I mumbled again.

"A little past six-thirty for you."

"Six-thirty!" I moaned. "I didn't get to bed 'til one."

"I really am sorry. The guys are getting an early start, and I wanted to Skype."

Danny's words made me feel his love. It was the perfect antidote to the memories of Dean and his abhorrent behavior.

"I look awful. The phone won't do?"

"Get to your laptop, Eli. Now," he ordered, but in a voice filled with longing.

Bleary-eyed, I obeyed, dragging myself to my desk and logging on.

Danny was on the screen. He must have just taken a shower. Danny was bare-chested, his hair was wet, and he was wearing his eyeglasses. I felt very unattractive wearing Danny's oxford shirt with my hair not even brushed. I hoped the mascara I had been too tired to remove last night hadn't smeared all over my face.

I smiled my approval at his bare-chested visage.

"Aren't you wearing anything?" I gasped in delight.

"I have a towel on," Danny laughed. "I just came from the shower, darlin'"

"My hair isn't even brushed."

"Elizabeth, you're as beautiful as you are every morning."

I blushed. "I am?"

"Eli, your hair is never brushed when you wake up. It's always a sexy mess."

I was drowsy, and I yawned. Danny laughed. "I'm sorry, hon." I shrugged. "Hey, are you wearing my shirt?" I could hear and see his pleasure.

"I wear it every night when you're not with me. It feels like you're here."

"I wish I had a piece of you with me." Danny said sadly though he smiled. "How about opening a couple more buttons."

"Daniel!" I exclaimed while obediently following his suggestion. The shirt was now open to my waist and falling off my narrow shoulders. I was completely exposed.

"That's better," Danny said, and I turned bright red. "I love when you blush, Eli."

"Daniel!" I protested.

"Now this is the girl I wake up to every morning."

"If your roommates walk in, I'm going to kill you."

Danny laughed. "Don't sweat it. Shane and Cam know I'm on with you."

"What are you doing today that you're up so early?"

"The clouds are moving in so we're going shopping. I have a hot babe to spoil."

"Me?" I squealed. That was just like Danny to buy me a gift.

Danny chuckled. "Hey, how was Zac's party?"

I recounted the evening, including my encounter with Dean. That last part left me shaking. I dabbed my moist eyes with a tissue from the nearby box.

Danny knitted his brows, seething with anger.

"Honey, if Dean ever touches you again, he will regret it. Nobody touches my lady. Except for me, of course."

"I wish you had been with me."

"This never would have happened. At least he didn't ruin your entire evening."

"Yeah. It was still a fun party. And I had the best car."

"I'll bet you did." Danny grinned. "I wish I could reach through cyberspace and touch you. I want so badly to take your hand."

I nodded in agreement. Smiling, I pulled my shirt back over my shoulders and reached my hand toward the monitor. Danny did the same. It appeared our hands were touching.

"Dean doesn't know what it means to be in love."

"No, he doesn't," I agreed.

"Honey, I'm glad I put your smile back on, but I have to go now. I want you to crawl into bed for at least two more hours."

"Can I call you later?"

"You can call me whenever you want. Bed, Eli," Danny ordered.

"I'm going." I threw a flirty kiss to the screen. "I love you, Danny."

"I love you too, baby."

I crawled back into bed, pulling the comforter over my shoulders, up to my chin. With a smile on my lips and warmth in my heart, I fell soundly back to sleep.

CHAPTER 68 - ELIZABETH

Friday morning I cursed the alarm clock. It was only 3:30, but the flight to Albany, by way of Chicago, was leaving Los Angeles at 6:15. At O'Hare I would have a two-hour layover before continuing. If all went as planned, I could collapse in bed by 7:30 tonight. Ugh!!

Had I been nuts when I booked this flight? It had been an incredibly tiresome day when I came home. Now I was doing it in reverse. An insane desire to prove my maturity by living with my decisions drove me.

This morning I was paying the price. What an idiot. As late as yesterday, I could have changed to a less grueling non-stop to Kennedy. Or I could have flown the Gulfstream. That's what Danny would have done.

I crept down the stairs and out the door to the car waiting to deliver me to LAX.

Arriving in Albany, I was exhausted. I had not slept on either flight. If my reflection in the restroom mirror was accurate, I looked like hell. At least journey was nearly over.

Apparently I fell asleep because it had turned dark by the time the Town Car from the airport approached the Donnelly gate. I called Danny to let him know I was almost home. I promised to call from my room and Skype. I couldn't wait for Sunday's reunion. I would look and feel good again by then.

CHAPTER 69 - DANIEL

I anxiously paced inside the back door of Berkeley Hall. Peering out the window, I waited for Eli's arrival. I couldn't wait to see her reaction.

A Town Car pulled into the lot. She was here!

Elizabeth stepped out of the car. In the dim lighting, I couldn't make out the details of her face, but her body slouched, exhausted as she had described.

The driver removed her suitcases, three in all, from the trunk, and proceeded toward the door, Eli leading the way. When she reached the top step, I opened the door and walked out.

"Danny?" she gasped. Elizabeth's eyes opened wide in complete surprise. A smile washed over her tired face as she realized it really was me.

"It's me," I answered, the biggest grin crossing my face. "May I help with your luggage ma'am?" I asked.

"I hope so," she replied breathlessly and launched herself at me.

My arms wrapped tightly around Eli's slender frame while her hands reached around my neck. My lips hungrily devoured hers.

"I thought you wouldn't be back until Sunday," she whispered.

"I couldn't let you sleep alone in an empty building. You might be frightened."

"I would be. I was dreading it," she answered, and we kissed again.

Elizabeth opened the door, and I carried her luggage across the threshold. Once in the elevator, as the doors closed behind us, I pressed Elizabeth against the wall and started kissing her all over again. Elizabeth giggled, delighted, as I kissed her lips, her face, and her neck. Her gentle hands held my face as her lips hungrily met mine.

Elizabeth unlocked the door to her suite. The empty suite was eerily silent and dark before she switched on the overhead light. I was glad neither of us would sleep alone tonight.

Releasing the heavy luggage was a relief. How much stuff had she brought? Before I asked, Eli jumped into my arms, wrapping her legs around my hips. Her warm hands brought my face to hers for our lips to meet. Pure sweetness. Total bliss

"I missed you so much," I murmured.

"I know," she smiled. "I missed you so much too."

As I held her face to mine, she deftly unbuttoned my shirt. I thought she would be too tired. I pushed her sweatshirt off her shoulders letting it drop to the ground. With Eli's help, my shirt fell to the floor. She ran her delicate fingers over my chest and held me close. My heart thumped loudly.

Then I pulled her tee over her head, unhooked her lacy bra, and let it fall to the ground. The feel of her bare chest against mine was overwhelming. Our lips locked, our bodies pressed together, we were on fire.

"Take me to bed," Eli whispered breathlessly. Her eyes filled with lust.

I effortlessly carried Elizabeth to the bed where we made love with the pent-up passions of two completely in love people who had endured a lengthy separation. God, she was amazing!

As Eli lay in my arms, the picture of perfect contentment, we exchanged gentle caresses and equally gentle kisses. I loved nibbling on her lips, her neck, and her soft, smooth shoulder. I knew this was what I wanted. Eli. Always.

I propped myself up on my elbow and smiled at her. Then I smoothed unruly auburn locks off her face and kissed her again. Eli rewarded me with the brightest smile as my fingers traced her luscious curves. Under my touch, Elizabeth squirmed in innocent delight.

Miami seemed a lifetime ago. I was lucky to have friends like Shane and Cam who cared enough to smack some sense into me. Eli would never know about Reggie.

Why had I risked jeopardizing everything I had with Elizabeth? She was perfect and perfect for me in every way. Elizabeth was the right combination of beauty, intelligence and sexiness. She was my best friend. I loved her more than anything. I vowed to never do anything to hurt or disappoint her.

CHAPTER 70 - ELIZABETH

"When do I see your dress?" Danny asked.

He had arrived at my room in time to see me pushing the air out of a Neiman Marcus garment bag as I zippered it.

"Tomorrow. When it's on," I answered and gave a flirty smile.

Then I turned to finish packing. I decided to add a pashmina. The theatre might be cool and the second week of April was early for strapless in New York City.

"There. I'm done," I announced as I zippered my case closed.

Danny folded the case in half and clasped it closed. He had already loaded his luggage, and a backpack filled with books into his car.

It felt odd to first be driving to New York City on a Sunday, but tomorrow was the East Coast premiere of Steve's latest film. Danny had worked on this film last year.

Steve was landing at Teterboro Airport later this afternoon. Ellen had a head cold and had stayed at home. When we'd spoken yesterday, she appointed me Steve's escort. I would be pulling double-duty at the premiere. Now I was even more pleased that Mom's stylist, Romey, had sent me a dress.

Earlier in the week, as I returned with Chloe to Berkeley Hall after lunch, two sizeable boxes were waiting for me at the reception desk.

"What are those?" Chloe had asked.

"The big one's from my stylist. I don't know about the other."

"You have a stylist?"

"Romey works for Mom, but for special occasion she shops for me too."

I flushed. Average Donnelly students did not have stylists.

I was expecting the box from Romey containing my dress and accessories for the premiere. The other box was a complete mystery. I had no idea what was in it, but Chloe instantly recognized the logo on the shipping label.

"Nola Lee!" she gasped. I shrugged.

Nola Lee was one of my favorite designers. Chloe's too. Her eclectic designs made of fabrics you loved to touch, were beloved by fashionable young women everywhere. Like me, Chloe bought several pieces each season.

I tore into the box. On top of the soft pink tissue paper was an envelope with my name hand-written on the front. The accompanying note was on

Nola Lee's personal stationary and I read it aloud.

"'Elizabeth, Romey tells me you're a fan. Next time you're in New York, please stop by the showroom. Meanwhile, enjoy the pieces I've selected for you. Best of luck with your studies.' And it's signed, "Nola.""

I smiled and put the card down.

"I can't believe designers send you clothes," said Chloe.

"It's good for her business. Now Nola is hoping 'Miranda Jordan's daughter' will be photographed wearing her clothes and her sales will increase."

To hold up my end of the implied bargain, I was wearing one of the Nola Lee outfits. Not only was comfortable for the three-hour car ride, I knew as soon as we met up with Steve, cameras would go off.

After checking in to The Regency Hotel, Danny and I unpacked and tried studying. Rather Danny tried studying. I had no interest, so I cuddled up beside Danny on the bed.

Danny's long legs stretched out, and he sat with his Economics text in his lap. I reached for his face and kissed him.

"E, c'mon." Danny sighed. "I'm studying and you should be too." It was like Vermont all over again.

I was in love with the coolest geek in the world! So I compromised. I let Danny study while I remained cuddled against him, enjoying the feel of his body against mine. And if he changed his mind… He didn't.

Monday was an exciting day, but first I was a good girl. After breakfast, I joined Danny at a quiet corner table in "The Library". Between meals, the bar was virtually empty, making it the ideal place to study.

At four o'clock, before the crowd filtered in, we returned to our room. Once I dropped off my books, I collected my Swarovski crystal encrusted hair clips. Then off I went to a nearby salon to have my hair styled. Tonight I wanted my auburn waves to tumble over my shoulders with the clips keeping them off my face. The stylist would ensure that my hair was soft and silky, not frizzy.

Back at The Regency, I found Danny showered and shaved. We had an hour until the limo would take us to the Ziegfeld Theater, more than enough time to primp.

"Perfection takes time," I teased Danny.

I gathered my lace-trimmed thigh-highs, shoes, pashmina and garment bag. Then I kissed Danny on the cheek and disappeared into the bathroom. He could get dressed in the main room.

Forty minutes later, satisfied with my appearance, I emerged from the bathroom.

"E!" Danny exclaimed as his eyes, wide as saucers, examined me from head to toe. His face lit up. His eyes twinkled like blue diamonds. A smile stretched from ear-to-ear. I did a full pirouette. Danny more than liked what he saw.

"Eli, you're gorgeous," he said breathlessly. I giggled and smiled shyly.

My form-fitting dress was elegant cream-colored silk shantung covered with scattered small magenta and light pink rose buds. Above the knee, but not mini in length, it featured a strapless sweetheart-style neckline. Not too revealing, the waist-nipping bodice only hinted at what lay beneath the fabric.

The back was cut only as low as where my bra strap normally crossed and my hair covered most of my bare skin. I wore high open-toed magenta Jimmy Choo pumps and carried a small Judith Lieber clutch. For the moment, my pashmina of lighter pink cashmere was sat low, nearly at my waist.

In my ears I wore medium-length gold hoops of carved roses. Around my neck of course, lay my gold heart. On my wrist was the gift Danny had brought me from Miami. The gold charm bracelet had only two charms, an Assistant Director's clapper, and a banana.

I had laughed when Danny gave it to me. Then he reminded me that I had told him to bring me back a plantain. A small, gold banana charm was his idea of a plantain.

Tonight was the evening I'd waited all my life for! I was the girlfriend of Steven Newman's son, and I was substituting for Ellen. Eyes would be on me as I entered on the arm of the most important man of the evening and his very impressive son.

Danny's appearance took my breath away. My heart did flip-flops. Seeing Danny every day, I almost forgot how handsome he was. With broad shoulders and slender hips emphasized by the well-cut suit, his hair brushed perfectly into place but still tousled, Danny could have been mistaken for a model.

I felt shy, as though it were a first date. I even blushed as Danny smiled and took my hand. His looks were intimidating.

Danny was dressed equally well in a blue-grey suit from Gucci. He wore a darker blue-grey shirt and a midnight blue silk tie. The blue-grey hues highlighted his sapphire eyes. Danny wore gold cufflinks, engraved with his initials "DMN" in italics. At his waist was a narrow black leather belt and Danny's shoes were black leather ankle boots. Both were Gucci.

The suit, his massive smile, and the killer twinkling eyes combined to thoroughly captivate me. I was speechless. It confirmed why I had fallen in love with this man so many years ago.

I plucked a microscopic piece of lint off his shoulder. I was beaming with pride that I was the girl accompanying Danny tonight.

Finally I recovered my ability to speak. "You're perfect, Daniel. Steve will be very proud, as am I."

The drive to the Ziegfeld Theater was short, but the inside of our limo was filled with nervous energy. Already the film was generating strong positive buzz from early reviews. Last week's Los Angeles premiere had been an unqualified success.

"What if I trip?" I fretted in anticipation of our red-carpet arrival. I did have a recent history of clumsiness.

"Don't worry. I'll catch you." Danny tried to reassure me but I could see he was trying not to laugh. Then he returned to his conversation with Steve and I sat clutching Danny's hand, only half-listening to them.

As the limo approached the theater, I was like a debutante making her entrée into society. Only instead of entering a ballroom dressed in a long white gown, I was entering a theater in a short cocktail dress. Which group would be more forgiving if I messed up?

Tonight I would be recognized as an adult. Hollywood would see that Miranda and Michael's daughter was no longer a kid. My reward for a good performance; inclusion on the A-list under my own name. Did I want that? Who wouldn't!

In front of the Ziegfeld was a swarm of activity. Uniformed police were controlling crowds and traffic. Muscular security personnel in business suits and wearing Secret-Service style earpieces were controlling the human traffic on the sidewalk.

Additional security contained crowds armed with cameras, paper and pens behind a low gate. Personnel allowed ticket holders to pass to the entrance via a narrow ribbon of sidewalk. A red carpet led from the theater halfway down to the corner. Protected from public view by tall panels, television crews and credentialed photo-journalists lined the carpet's perimeter where the celebrities would pass.

Complete sensory overload greeted us when our limo pulled up to the curb. Both Steve and Danny could sense my trepidation. Steve leaned across and kissed my cheek.

"You'll be fine, Elizabeth. Enjoy it."

"Remember, you're with us," Danny added.

He meant to be reassuring. Usually a reminder that I was under the protection of not one, but two Newmans, would be comforting. Not tonight. Being with the Newmans was what had me at the eye of the storm.

Showtime!

The driver opened the passenger door of the limousine. A beefy security man stood to the side of the door to keep away any unauthorized person who tried to approach. I heard the cacophonous fans and felt the stares directed our way as nobody could as yet identify that this was Steven Newman's car.

Danny kissed my hand, releasing my fingers. Steve confidently exited. At forty-five, Steven Newman cut an impressive figure in an impeccably tailored charcoal grey suit. Steve was as tall as his son, but not as slender, though he didn't have an ounce of fat. Steve had spent years working out with a trainer. With dark, straight hair mostly still on his head, he didn't look like Danny, but he did have those mesmerizing blue eyes.

Experienced from being at the top for nearly two decades, Steve was as relaxed as ever. Tonight was his night, but he'd been through this many times before.

Steve turned back toward the car and reached for my hand. I inhaled deeply and exhaled slowly. As I rose, Danny patted my rear. As he knew I would, I couldn't help but turn and smile. In return, Danny smiled and flashed me thumbs-up. I knew everything would be all right.

With Steve guiding me, I exited the limo. The warmth of his fingers, so similar to his son's, put me at ease. My confidence returned as I acknowledged that this was my night too, the first of many.

A television reporter pounced on us. I recognized her as a pariah from the gossipy cable program that always sought out the bad side of the industry and capitalized on scandal.

She starred wide-eyed, not recognizing me. Instinctively, Steve protectively cupped my shoulder. The reporter stopped short, blocking us in a well-practiced move. We had no choice but to stop.

"Steven, does Ellen know about your date?"

Her rudeness struck me as so absurd that I found myself giggling. Steve squeezed my shoulder and smiled at my immaturity, but hell, I am only eighteen. Biting my lower lip kept me from dissolving into full-fledged laughter.

"You think it's funny being with a married man?"

She shoved her mic in front of me. Steve removed his hand from my shoulder and grabbed it. My eyes searched for Danny. Thankfully he was just steps away.

"This is Elizabeth Jordan-Jacobs," Steve said with authority.

He merged my middle name with my last and created a very impressive hyphenate. The woman examined my face. Finally, recognition.

"Miranda Jordan's daughter?" she asked cautiously, in case I wasn't. She couldn't risk being incorrect on camera.

Danny was now at my side and I moved a step closer to him to take his hand.

Steve nodded. "And my son Daniel's girlfriend. Ellen is home with the flu. I'm flying solo. Sorry to deny you a scoop."

Steve led us past the dumbfounded woman to the sheltered red carpet as photographers stopped to our take pictures. For a father, Steven Newman was hot! It wasn't surprising that the reporter could mistake me for being his date. Steve was incredibly attractive and women often showered him with attention. Many starlets would die for the chance despite his marital status.

In front of a lit screen emblazoned with the film's logo, and those of the evening's corporate sponsors, Steve posed alone and then with Danny and me. We stood beside him as he answered reporters' questions about the film and then he introduced us.

The reporters were pleased to snap photos and capture us on video. The flurry with which they posed us barely contained their excitement over Miss Jordan-Jacobs being coupled with young Mr. Newman.

After the formal poses were completed, and we had walked a few steps away, Danny placed his hands on my shoulders and faced me.

"You were great, Eli," he whispered, and he gently moved his hand to cradle my face. I no longer felt insecure. "I love you, babe," and Danny leaned in to kiss me. Several cameras captured the candid of the night.

Upon entering the disproportionately long auditorium, an intern led us to the seats Steve had chosen on the left center aisle, two-thirds of the way back, the optimal location.

The large theater was nearly filled. There were executives in business suits and dresses. There were actors, including the film's leads and co-stars dressed to the nines. And there were assorted members of the New York film community. Just your typical industry crowd, but New York style. I'd never seen so much black clothing at an event that wasn't a funeral. It made my cream-colored dress an instant sensation.

As the lights dimmed and the curtain on the wide screen opened, Danny took my hand and kissed it. It was his first time seeing the film he had worked so diligently on.

What an amazing film! I was so proud of Steve. His month of filming in Africa had been challenging, but it was well worth it. The beauty and grandeur of Botswana became the third co-star of the story that was essentially an international intrigue adventure with secondary love plot.

Other segments of the movie had been filmed in Prague, London and New York, but they were inconsequential. Now I fully appreciated the importance of Danny's gap year. He had travelled to such marvelous locations. If only I could have joined them. I felt a tinge of jealousy.

Once the end credits began to roll, I quickly hugged Steve and kissed his cheek.

"Amazing, Steve! I loved it!" I told him with complete sincerity.

Danny leaned across and reached Steve's arm. Steve wore a huge grin.

"Dad, home run," Danny whispered.

"Thanks, Danny," he replied and then added, "Don't miss your credit."

Normally, Steve would have already left, but he wanted to share his son's big moment. The credits continued rolling. A big budget film such as this with its multiple international and visual effects crews had a seemingly endless list of credits.

"There it is! Danny, it's you!" I exclaimed.

Steve joined me in tradition by applauding Danny's credit.

"Stop it," Danny laughed as he put his hands over mine to stop my clapping.

"I'm proud of you." I pulled my hand away and touched his cheek. "I really am."

Danny pressed my hand against his cheek and kissed my palm. "I'm glad you're with me tonight, Elizabeth." Then he smiled.

As the credits concluded, Danny stood and brushed by me to reach Steve who was also standing. I enjoyed watching my men embrace.

"I love you, Dad. It was great," Danny said softly.

"Hey, Danny. I love you too, son. I couldn't have done it without all your hard work. I mean that."

They smiled at each other and embraced again. I filled with their love.

Soon we were back in our limo en route to the party. I leaned against Danny. His arms wrapped around me for the short trip to the venue, my rock supporting me.

On the outside, the Metropolitan Club appears to be a diplomatic outpost such as a consulate or United Nations mission, but in fact it had always been a private club. The building dated to the late nineteenth century. The Club was founded by New York City's elite businessmen of the time. It has the appearance of a Italianate mansion with its marble facade. Surrounded by modern towers, the proportions and grandeur of the property were unlike any I had seen that was not a museum.

The massive brass-topped, ironwork gates to The Metropolitan Club were open to ticket holders. Had I not entered on the arms of the Newmans, the premises alone would have intimidated me. My eyes were wide taking it all in. The cavernous two-story high main floor, its ceiling inlaid with marble, the walls and floors also marble and the sweeping staircases with carved banisters and trim, all magnificent.

At the same time, the Club was a pulsating swirl of humanity. I had no idea how many people were in attendance. This very large space was teeming with guests jockeying for social position and trying to find tables that were in short supply. Gloved wait staff were passing hors d'oevres among the well-dressed revelers.

We were ushered through several smaller rooms where endless lines formed by buffet stations, until reaching the less crowded VIP room. An elegant table set for eight with a card announcing "Newman" tucked amongst the floral centerpiece was ours.

The others at our table were New York area friends of Steve's. I was thrilled to spend the evening with them. As soon as Steve introduced me to Marc, his wife Paula, and their friend Ray, I knew I was going to have a good time. They had gone to NYU with Steve and Dad.

CHAPTER 71 - DANIEL

I didn't know which I was enjoying more, being at the heart of this throbbing social event, or studying my beautiful Elizabeth.

After returning from the bar with fresh drinks, I stopped inside the doorway and stared at her. I couldn't take my eyes off of Eli. Elizabeth always looked great, but tonight… Incredible. Brimming with confidence, she moved among the guests as though she had been born to work a room. In a sense, I suppose, she had been. We both had.

Dad's hand on my shoulder announced his arrival. He grinned watching me.

"Elizabeth's an amazing girl, Danny."

"Eli sure is. It's great how confident Eli's become."

"Thank yourself. It's your influence, son."

I took a sip of my martini. Dad's compliment made me uncomfortable.

"I was wrong," he continued. Dad admitting to being wrong made me stop mid-sip, and stare. This was a rarity, perhaps even a first.

"About what, Dad? I thought you were never wrong," I teased.

As we spoke, Elizabeth glanced my way and smiled shyly, having caught us starring. Dad and I smiled back. I flirted from afar by throwing her a kiss. Eli blushed and returned her attentions to the actors she was talking to.

"Steve!" a burley, older man in a black suit clapped Dad on the back.

"Ed! Good to see you, my son, Daniel. Danny, Ed Tegarten."

Ed Tegarten attempted to shake my hand but laughed when he couldn't because I was holding a drink in each one.

"Who's that pretty young thing you're both starring at?" he asked.

"Elizabeth Jordan-Jacobs; Mike and Miranda's girl," Dad chuckled, "and if my son doesn't blow it, she'll be my daughter-in-law some day."

"But Dad, you said…"

"I was wrong, Danny. You're not too young if it's the right girl. Elizabeth is the right girl. I can't imagine her not being in our family."

"Thanks, Dad. That means a lot to me."

CHAPTER 72 - ELIZABETH

Paula shared stories with me about Dad that I'd never heard before. Apparently Michael Jacobs had been quite the party boy in college before law school and Mom had changed him. Now I better understood his closeness to Steve.

"I need to borrow my date." Steve interrupted us with his sudden appearance.

"What's up, Steve?" I asked.

"A photographer from the Style Section of The Times is here. Please find Danny. I need you both in five minutes."

Danny had excused himself to go to the men's room, and now that I thought about it, he should have returned by now.

I began my search by heading toward the men's room, tucked under the sweeping staircase behind the bar, another possible destination. I hadn't left the VIP room since arriving and was relieved to find the crowds in the other rooms had thinned. I could move around.

Danny's height certainly helped as I readily spotted him across the room. He was engaged in conversation with an attractive, deeply tanned, tall blonde. In her very high heels, she even appeared taller than Danny.

I didn't move as I assessed them, my intuition on guard. My knees began shaking, and not from my Jimmy Choo stilettos.

What was she doing? Her fingers brushed against Danny. They touched his shoulder, his lapel, and then his face. And Danny didn't object! He smiled at her. What the hell?

Who was this woman? Her legs stretched on forever. Only the very top of her thighs was covered by her skin-tight mini dress. The clingy dress cheapened her appearance. Danny would never let me out in a dress like that. The strapless bodice covered by a shrug-like metallic jacket barely contained her A-cup assets. Why was I jealous?

My reaction ashamed me, and I composed myself by taking a deep breath. Danny was with me. We were here with Steve. He wouldn't dare flirt with another woman tonight. It would humiliate me and embarrass Steve. Danny would never do that.

This woman had approached him, I concluded. Who could blame her? She didn't know about us, and Danny was the handsomest man at the party. Alas, boyfriends, unlike husbands, do not wear rings.

This woman wasn't even his type. Danny liked brunettes with naturally occurring skin tones, not tanning booth blondes. He wanted his girl to have curves, not be built like a boy. This woman was too tall. Danny enjoyed teasing me about being only five foot three. Danny loved that I wasn't tall because he could tower over me and feel protective. That's what he always said. Even tonight while I wore stilettos, Danny towered over me.

CHAPTER 73 - DANIEL

Trying to extricate myself from Reggie while not setting her off took the skills of a neurosurgeon. At any moment, Elizabeth was going to seek me out. My trip to the men's room had gone on too long. The situation was tenuous at best.

I couldn't believe Reggie was here. How the hell had this happened? I knew the answer of course, in vague terms. Models always attended premieres. They dressed up the room. Ambitious managers had no difficulty securing invitations to high-profile events for their clients.

As Reggie had no idea who Dad was, I had to chalk this up to one unfortunate coincidence and deal with it as best as I could.

"Sweetheart, there you are!" Elizabeth purred, her megawatt smile flashing at me. Elizabeth leaned into me, placing her hand on my arm and sliding it into my hand. I had no choice but to pull her close.

"Steve needs us. A photographer from The Times is here," she added.

Though not unexpected, Eli's appearance caught me off-guard. Even with the lateness of the hour she was breathtaking. Eli's hair and make-up remained perfect, so elegant.

But what was going through Elizabeth's head? Had she seen Reggie's hands on me? Did she suspect anything? Was Eli's sunny greeting genuine, or an act? Eli might be an excellent actress. I wouldn't know until we returned to the hotel.

If my neck weren't on the line, it would be interesting to watch this unfold. When Elizabeth felt threatened, she became mama lion, subtly pulling rank. In this case, her message was loud and clear. Elizabeth was royalty and I was her willing subject.

Reggie understood. Eli was the girlfriend on the telephone, and her smile diminished ever so slightly. I ignored it and hoped that I seemed at ease. Elizabeth needed to remain ignorant.

"Eli, this is Reggie Ames."

"Nice to meet you Reggie. I'm Elizabeth Jordan-Jacobs," she responded and offered her hand to Reggie. Reggie complied and shook it.

I smirked. Eli's introduction was a power play. She rarely introduced herself by her entire name, but tonight Eli wanted to be recognized, so she was liberally using it. Most everyone in this room recognized the name, though I doubted Reggie did.

"Eli, how nice," Reggie answered frostily. Her eyes looked Eli up and down, sizing up the formidable adversary she never had a chance against.

Elizabeth cringed. Nobody called her Eli, except for me.

"It's Elizabeth, dear," she answered in a haughty voice I didn't recognize.

Reggie didn't flinch. Was she used to being the other woman, forced to speak to wives and girlfriends? Eli continued smiling.

"I'm sorry," Reggie began, "I thought Dan said…"

"Only Daniel calls me Eli," Elizabeth cut her off and smiled at me.

"Reggie lives in Cam's parents' building in Miami. We met at the pool."

Eli gasped, a staged response. "I hope you didn't hear our phone calls." The giggle in her voice dared Reggie to recall an awkward memory while she fished. Power play.

"I guess. Maybe," Reggie answered tentatively.

"Daniel, why didn't you excuse yourself from your friends and go someplace private?" Eli scolded with a lilt that kept her voice light and friendly.

"I was at the pool, Eli. There was no place to go."

"My apologies, Reggie," she said sweetly, "Having to listen to our conversations." Eli smiled at me and touched my cheek. "Those were R-rated, dear," she purred.

I had Reggie's feelings to consider. I took Eli's hand from my face and squeezed it. I warmly smiled at her. "Yes, they certainly were," I answered sheepishly.

"I wasn't listening," Reggie quickly added. "There were others there."

"You're from Miami. What brings you here?" Elizabeth changed the subject.

"I model. I'm in New York for work," Reggie answered more comfortably now that Eli had asked a familiar question.

"Daniel got you on the guest list?" Eli turned to me. "You didn't tell me friends from Miami would be here. We could have met up earlier."

How cozy that would have been. Not.

"I didn't invite Reggie. I didn't even know she was in New York."

"My agent arranged it," Reggie cooed. "Dan, you can get me on the guest list? Aren't you a college student?"

Elizabeth's expression told me she realized that Reggie did not know who I was.

"I am a college student, but I know some people," I answered evasively.

"Let me guess, Daddy's connected," Reggie said with a tinge of sarcasm.

"Sweetheart," Elizabeth's syrupy voice saved me, "We don't want to keep Dad waiting. It is The Times, after all."

"I have to go, Reggie. Good to see you." I hoped I sounded casual.

"Good to see you too." Reggie's disappointment was obvious to me but hopefully not to Elizabeth.

CHAPTER 74 - ELIZABETH

Danny guided me back to the VIP room. The tension between us was palpable.

"Danny, who is Reggie?" I frowned. Why did she call him 'Dan?' The use of Danny's diminutive reminded me of Amelia all over again.

"No one to concern yourself with. Reggie's just a girl the guys and I met at the pool."

"She didn't seem happy when I showed up."

"I was happy when you showed up," Danny answered playfully.

"Danny, you'd better be."

"I'm always happy when you show up."

"But she wasn't."

"What a tigress! I wouldn't want to run into you in a jungle. You're claws were showing, lady," Danny answered with a smile. "I think your point was well made."

"What point was that?"

Danny stopped short. He had a bemused but serious expression on his face as he placed his hands on my shoulders and leaned in close to me. Our heads nearly touched. We would not be overheard.

"Baby, you know what point. That I'm a happily married man with a stunning wife who's far more beautiful than any model."

My eyes opened wide, shocked by Danny's metaphor. "We're not married!" I exclaimed.

"Maybe not legally, but spiritually we are."

We are? Who cared about Reggie? I grinned stupidly. I was Danny's wife!

"Eli, we love each other, we're best friends, and we're lovers. We're married."

"Are you sure?" The conversation caught me so by surprise. I couldn't think of anything to make me think Danny wasn't being sincere. He was even sober.

"E, who spends every night with me and will continue to do so always?"

"This is heady."

Danny smirked. He held me to his chest. The fine-gauge wool of his jacket was soft against my bare shoulders. Danny's light musky cologne seduced my senses.

"I love you very much Mrs. Newman," Danny whispered.

My eyes opened wide at this salutation. Before I could speak, Danny was holding my face as his lips pressed against mine for a slow kiss. Shivers ran through me.

"I love you very much too, Mr. Newman," I whispered when our lips parted.

Danny's eyes brimmed with joy. My heart fluttered. I smiled shyly, afraid of crying. Our foreheads touched. Danny's breath on my face coursed electricity through me.

"Elizabeth, you are so lovely tonight," Danny whispered. "Can I kiss my bride?"

"Of course," I nodded. "Does this mean tonight's our honeymoon?"

Danny grinned. Then he placed his hands on my face to hold me as he once more brought his lips to mine. I held on tightly, my hands around his neck. My lips parted and our tongues entwined, full of joy, playfully savoring the moment. The power of our love left me drunk. My head spun. If we hadn't been holding each other so firmly I would have teetered on my Jimmy Choo's and stumbled.

When we parted, Danny held me close in his arms.

"Do you realize where we are?" I was suddenly aware of the guests in the room. Several tried to avoid being caught staring.

"But I love you, Eli," Danny whispered, and brushed his lips against mine, again sending bolts through me. "I can't wait to get you back to the hotel."

"Danny!" I was blushing.

"Eli, you know you can't wait either, so say it."

Danny waited expectantly, a devilish grin on his lips.

"I can't wait to…" I threw my arms around his neck. "Oh, Danny, when can we go? I'm dying to get back to the hotel already," I whispered.

CHAPTER 75 - DANIEL

"There you are," Dad greeted us. "Any longer and I was going to send out a search." Steve grinned. He wasn't angry at our delayed arrival.

"Sorry, Dad. I ran into somebody."

"They're here," Dad said to the impatient photographer.

The photographer used a floor-to-ceiling window covered by heavy red brocade drapery as the backdrop and took several pictures.

"Thank you, Mr. Newman," he said to Dad before taking his leave.

Elizabeth had lost her spark and teetered back to our table.

"Dad, can we go? Eli's tired."

"Sure, but remind the driver to come back for me."

"That's okay. Eli and I are walking."

Dad joined me at Elizabeth's side. "It's getting late. Why don't you kids head back to The Regency?"

"You're sure?" Elizabeth asked. I nodded.

Then Dad folded Eli in his arms. "Good-night, dear." And he kissed her cheek.

"It was great, Steve." Eli rallied her last ounce of enthusiasm. "Ellen can call in sick anytime she wants. I'll gladly be her substitute. But I hope she feels better."

"Of course," Dad laughed.

"I'm telling Mom what you said," I teased Eli, and she blushed.

"Daniel! Don't you dare!"

"Mom knows you're not trying to dethrone her. Chill, Eli."

"Get going," Dad commanded. He turned back to Eli and appraised her. "Oh, hell!" he said, and Dad pulled Eli in for an all-encompassing hug. "Just because you're a grown woman doesn't mean I can't hug you all I want. Elizabeth, you've been my daughter all your life."

"And you've been my second dad. I love you, Steve."

I took Eli's hand, and we made our way through the thinning crowd to the massive front doors. Relief. We exited to the gated driveway without running into Reggie again.

A crisp breeze was blowing from Central Park. It was noticeably colder now than when we'd arrived. Elizabeth unfolded her pashmina and wrapped it around her shoulders. The thin cashmere could not possibly be warm enough to protect her. I smiled. Why should Eli suffer?

"Here." I removed my jacket and gently placed it across her slender shoulders.

"Thank you," Elizabeth said and she tilted her head up to look into my eyes. The warmth of Eli's tired smile melted me. My arm slipped around her shoulder and drew her closer. I let my other hand lift her chin for our lips to meet for a slow, love-filled kiss.

"Feeling warmer?"

"Yes," Elizabeth answered in a near-whisper; her green doe eyes continuing to melt my heart. Having pushed her arms into the jacket sleeves, Elizabeth wrapped her pashmina around my neck as though it were a cashmere tallit and delicately kissed me.

"There," Elizabeth said. "I have to take care of you too. You've done such a good job of taking care of me."

"I've always taken good care of you, E. It's what I do best."

"What you do best?" Eli giggled. "Always? We've only been together for six months."

"My taking care of you predates Donnelly by years, Eli."

I took Eli's soft, delicate hand. It was only a few short blocks to The Regency.

"Remember the brush fire? You were thirteen, and I was almost fifteen."

"That was the scariest night of my life."

"Mine, too," I agreed.

"Danny, you were scared? I never knew."

"Eli, you were little. I couldn't show you my fear. I had to…"

"Take care of me." Eli quickly kissed me, the misty memory etched on her face.

CHAPTER 76 - DANIEL

That July evening six years ago had started normally enough. Sunday, with Los Angeles mired in a heat wave, Mom and Randi had fled to Malibu with Eli and I. Wednesday the menacing Santa Ana winds began blowing. By Thursday, a small brush fire started in Malibu Canyon. It wasn't far from our house, but it wasn't that close.

After five days in Malibu, the moms were restless and they left for Century City to see an early movie and enjoy dinner. Elizabeth and I were perfectly comfortable staying alone, and we enjoyed leftover fried chicken and a pan of frozen French fries.

By seven-thirty, we began a chess match, and sitting on the rug while playing, we devoured ice cream sundaes. Bowls of vanilla ice cream covered in chocolate syrup contained a sampling of every sweet we could find including Hershey's kisses, rainbow sprinkles, and whipped cream.

Elizabeth wrinkled her nose and inhaled. "The air smells awful," The heavy, acrid smell of burning brush had infiltrated our nostrils.

Dad called from Chicago, disturbed to learn we were alone.

"Danny, turn on the television," he insisted. " Malibu is burning."

That ended the chess match. KNBC had suspended regular programming to report exclusively from Malibu. This small brush fire had grown into an out of control inferno, consuming the canyon.

On edge, Elizabeth and I sat, eyes riveted to the television. She put down her ice cream bowl, clutched a pillow to her chest, and sat hunched over crossed legs. As we watched the news reports, Elizabeth chewed her lip.

"Eli, don't worry," I said, attempting to soothe her, "they'll be here soon."

"Danny, I'm scared." Elizabeth was trembling.

"I know, but I'm here." I tried to sound as confident as a frightened fourteen year old could sound. Nobody had to say it. I was older, and I was a boy. It was expected that Elizabeth would rely on me. I couldn't disappoint her or our parents.

A wind gust howled, causing the glass patio doors to shake. The smell of smoke temporarily intensified and Eli ran to look. The plants on the patio were blowing. Palm fronds danced across the usually clean-swept tile surface. In the distance, the Pacific was choppier than usual. Otherwise, on this side of the house the world seemed normal.

"I can't just sit here, Danny. I must see what's happening." Elizabeth's voice rose, nearing hysteria.

"There's nothing we can do until they get back. We'll be all right."

Elizabeth dashed to the front door. "Where are you going?" I called.

"I have to look." Elizabeth bolted out the door. I ran after her.

Standing in the driveway, our eyes focused northbound up Pacific Coast Highway. The sun was setting, but it wasn't dark. In the distance entire hillsides were ablaze, mountains of orange and red with thick billowing smoke. Elizabeth and I stood transfixed by the sight, so frightening but at the same time stunningly beautiful.

Grey-white ash floated down like a surreal mid-summer snowstorm. It left a thin layer on the driveway and stung the eyes of Elizabeth and me, two petrified kids holding each other for the only support available.

Fire trucks, lights and sirens blaring, raced past us. Elizabeth clutched my arm. Only wearing shorts and a tank top, she seemed so small.

"Danny, I'm scared," Elizabeth said breathlessly, her eyes wide.

Instinctively I draped my arm around her shoulders. Elizabeth was shaking.

"Let's go inside," I suggested, though I didn't really want to. The fire was mesmerizing in its ferocity.

Inside, Elizabeth began crying. "I wish we were home," she whimpered.

I gathered her in my arms and rubbed her back. Already five-nine, I felt like a giant holding my miniature best friend.

"Eli, don't cry. We'll be fine." I repeated over and over as a mantra. I hoped she believed me. I didn't.

The phone rang. Randi!

"Danny, they won't let us through. The police have closed Coast Highway."

In the background I heard Mom frantically pleading with an officer, "Our children are alone." "Ma'am, we're evacuating. All lanes are going southbound except for emergency vehicles." "Do you know who I am?" "Yes, and even you and Ms. Jordan can't enter Malibu tonight, Mrs. Newman."

"Listen carefully Danny. You're on your own. Go to the kitchen and find the flashlights. The electricity could go at any moment."

I walked into the kitchen and removed two flashlights from a drawer. Elizabeth watched my every movement. I was fearful for the first time.

"Do you see the car keys on the counter?" Randi asked.

"Yes. Why?"

"Put them in your pocket. Danny, can you drive a car?"

"I'm only fourteen, Randi."

"I know how old you are," she said crossly. "I'm not asking if you're allowed to drive, only if you can."

Was Randi really asking me to drive her Mercedes? Sweet!

"On a straight road. Probably if I don't have to park," I understood it was important for me to say I could.

"If the police order an evacuation that's what you're going to do. Danny, you only have to get as far as Gladstone's."

I was dumbfounded by Randi's request, but if it was an emergency.

"And Danny,"

"Yeah, Randi?"

"Take care of Elizabeth. She must be petrified."

I put the phone down. Anxiety was etched across Eli's face.

"Danny?" she asked tentatively. "They're not coming, are they?"

"PCH is closed, Eli. The police won't let them in."

"What are we going to do?" she wailed and burst into a fresh round of tears.

Elizabeth was so vulnerable she really was like my kid sister tonight. The eighteen-month age difference that was usually of little importance was an impassable chasm, a glaring reminder that I was the mature one and had to act it.

"We'll be fine," I said reassuringly. "If we have to evacuate. I can drive." I took the keys from my pocket to show her.

"You can drive?"

"I don't have a license, but yeah, I can drive," I confidently answered. I prayed we wouldn't have to find out.

Eli looked at me in awe. "I didn't know!"

I grinned. I had just passed an important milestone if you're a Southern California man – impressing a girl with your car.

"Let's watch a movie," I suggested, "Your pick."

Settled on the sofa for a Harry Potter marathon, our nerves were on alert. Every wind gust, and they were frequent, startled us. With each one came a temporary strengthening of the pungent smell of burning brush, leaving us staring at each other, waiting for the call to evacuate.

Intermittently, fire engines raced past, interrupting the steady hum of vehicles on the road. Elizabeth looked to me for reassurance and I provided it as best I could.

The back of Professor Quirrel's head morphing into Lord Voldemorte did not scare either of us anymore. Elizabeth and I had seen this movie so many times. The professor's head was nearly unwrapped now.

Lights flickered. The television flashed. Blackout!

"Danny!" Elizabeth shrieked, and she grabbed me.

"Shit!" I reached for the flashlight nestled against my thigh and flicked it on.

"What do we do?" Elizabeth cried, shaking.

I took a deep breath and exhaled slowly. Time to be the adult. Elizabeth was completely dependent. Time to be strong.

"Let's look outside." I wanted to gauge the wind's direction. The beam from the flashlight guided us to the front door.

The burning hillsides were an even more fantastic inferno than before. The conflagration appeared closer. Red and orange flames lit up the night sky. An eerie orange haze obscured the nearly full moon. But the wind was not blowing our way!

Emergency vehicles continued racing northbound. Luxury cars, SUVs and pick-ups with horse trailers attached, all filled with frightened people, their pets and as much cargo as could fit, marched southbound in an orderly double column.

Somewhere north of us, conditions were so bad evacuations had been ordered. Through it all, nobody noticed two kids staring fearfully at the horizon from the side of the road, armed with nothing more potent than a flashlight.

"The wind's blowing the fire away from us," I said. Elizabeth nodded. It wasn't clear that she understood. "Eli, we're safe. Let's go inside."

Elizabeth followed me like an obedient pet. Inside, I shined the beam on my wristwatch. Ten-thirty. With our adrenaline pumping, we weren't sleepy.

"Let's play chess again," I suggested. "We can see with the flashlight."

Eli tentatively went along. She was petrified, incapable of decision-making.

Chess was an excellent diversion. Our competitive desires to win took our minds off the inferno. Deep in concentration, we blotted out the chaos.

"Check mate!" Elizabeth proclaimed, a grin stretching across her face. She had bested me two out of three, and I would never let her know it had been deliberate on my part.

Eli was a good chess player, just not as good as me. We had a lively rivalry, but had I not let her win sometimes, she might have quit. If she kept at it, soon she would beat me honestly, then the fun would begin.

"Great match," I said. "Tired?"

"Maybe," she yawned.

"Me too." I shined the flashlight on my watch. "It's almost one. We should get to bed."

"Danny, I'm scared. What if we don't hear the police come when they come?"

"We'll hear them. The police will break the door down."

Elizabeth started crying again. I folded her into my arms.

"Let's go upstairs. If you're sleeping, you can't be scared."

The flashlights guided us up the stairs.

"This way, Eli," I said, and I led her to my parents' room. Through the windows we saw the waves breaking at the shoreline. "It's the biggest bed in the house. We'll feel more comfortable."

"That's silly," Elizabeth laughed. "We're kids."

"I'm almost fifteen, Eli. I'm not a kid. I'm a man."

"You're a man? Yeah, right." Elizabeth laughed.

With the beam from the flashlight focused on my face, she saw I was serious.

"Oh," she stammered as realization dawned on her. "When did that happen? You're not dating anyone."

"It's not your business. A gentlemen doesn't kiss and tell."

Elizabeth was dumbfounded, not knowing what to make of my revelation. I hoped I hadn't rocked her world too badly.

I opened the sliders and closed the vertical blinds. With the power out, it was getting uncomfortably warm. This was one of the few weeks each year when even Malibu required air conditioning. The breeze would hopefully cool us, though I doubted the salty ocean tang was strong enough to cover the acrid aroma of the fire.

I had to keep Elizabeth calm while now being scrutinized. In the soft flashlight glow I studied Eli's puzzled face as she sat cross-legged on the bed in deep thought.

"I know what you're doing," I lay down and propped myself up on my elbow. In the dim light, Eli's blush showed. She was embarrassed. "Little wheels in your head are spinning."

"They are not," Eli protested.

"Spin, spin, spin," I said while twirling my finger against her temple. "You're trying to remember every place and every person I've mentioned all summer," I laughed.

"Danny! C'mon, tell me. I'm your best friend. I won't tell anyone."

"Some things are private, even between best friends."

"If I were a boy, you'd tell me."

"Eli…" She was probably right, but I wouldn't admit it.

"Do your parents know?"

"Don't go there, Eli."

"Steve must know. But I wouldn't tell Ellen, either."

I grabbed the pillow and playfully swatted her. "Eli, cut it out! I'm never going to tell you so quit badgering me."

"That's so fair. I would tell you if it were me."

"You really think I would want to know?"

Eli's downcast eyes showed her hurt.

"I thought you would. What if you don't like him? Don't you care?"

"Of course I care, but I really don't think you'll want me to know. I doubt you'll call me the next morning. That would be awkward, wouldn't it?"

"Shut up, Daniel! You're just jealous 'cause it won't be you!"

I burst into uncontrollable laughter.

"I hate you!" she squealed. Eli grabbed the pillow and hit me. My hands shielded my face from her assault while I kept laughing.

"Eli, cut it out. You're gonna hurt me."

"Good," she answered curtly.

I hugged Elizabeth to the bed and smoothed her hair.

"You don't mean that. Eli, you love me."

"No, I don't." Elizabeth twisted out of my grasp and turned away, hiding. "Is this going to change our friendship?" she whimpered.

"Of course not. I'm just growing up sooner than you are because I'm older."

"Maybe you won't find it fun being with a girl you can only hang-out with."

I smiled. So that was her real fear. "Nothing's going to change. We're still BFFs. It's not like I have a steady girlfriend taking up all my time."

"Why can't I ever do anything first?"

"You're only thirteen, Eli. You better not have done this one first."

"It's still not fair."

"Someday, Eli. Someday," I sighed. I was propped up, Eli lying beside me. "You probably don't want to hear this, but you're a very special girl."

"Danny, you sound like my parents."

"I'll try not to," I laughed. "But you should wait until you meet the right guy to fall in love with."

"You still sound like my parents."

"If you became a slut you'd be unhappy, and I'd be disappointed." I laid my arm around her. "I expect better from my kid sister."

"I'm not your kid anything and you are such a hypocrite, Danny."

"You're acting like my kid sister. And I am not a hypocrite. Overprotective, maybe."

Elizabeth stuck out her tongue. "I promise I will never do anything to besmirch the Newman name."

"Funny, Elizabeth," I said sarcastically.

"I wasn't being funny," she pouted "You said I was your sister."

"Hey, Eli," I said softly, "You'll find the right guy. He'll have to be amazing or he won't stand a chance, but you're only thirteen. Eli, you have plenty of time."

"What if it doesn't happen?" she sniffled.

Elizabeth turned away, embarrassed again. That's what was bothering her. Eli might attractive, but socially she was an awkward geek.

"Eli, hey. I have an idea. I'm certain it won't come to this, but if you return home after freshman year of college still a virgin, I'll do it with you."

"Seriously?"

"Completely."

Already I regretted it. If I had to recruit and bribe a guy, I would. I couldn't imagine anything weirder than sex with Elizabeth. Waking beside Eli the next morning; no, that would be weirder. I had six years to find Elizabeth a boyfriend. It was doable.

Eli smiled. "Okay, it's a deal," she laughed.

"Time for bed," I announced, glad that this emotional crisis was over. Discussing sex with a thirteen year-old girl was very uncomfortable even if the girl was, no maybe because she was, Eli.

"Can I have a good-night kiss? My parents always kiss me before I go to bed."

I looked at her skeptically. "Here's your kiss."

Grinning, Eli turned her cheek toward me. Instead I leaned a little further and gave her lips a quick smacker.

"Danny!" she gasped while I laughed.

"Sweet dreams, Elizabeth." Then I rolled over and fell into a deep sleep.

When I woke, it was dark, too early to rise. Elizabeth was snuggled against me, an arm across my chest. How she had ended up in such an intimate position? Last night there had been plenty of space separating us in the king-sized bed.

My blurry eyes focused as best as they could. I felt guilty studying "my sister." Without her glasses, Elizabeth was stunning. Her thick auburn waves flared like the loveliest halo on a sun-kissed angel. A contented smile played upon her lips. I had never noticed how full they were, or the color that looked like permanent lipstick. Something about Elizabeth's petite frame felt so right.

I didn't want these thoughts. She was Elizabeth, my sister-like friend. Enjoying the feel of her body contradicted what our friendship was about.

Walking toward Park Avenue holding Elizabeth's hand I laughed at how only six years earlier I thought we might have to settle for each other when we were older. My logic had been sound. If I was thirty, and she was twenty-eight, we could both do a lot worse than agreeing to spend life with our best friend.

I smiled at my naïveté. One part was true. I was spending life with my best friend, but I never would have believed how. And it sure wasn't because I was settling.

Eli glanced at me and giggled. "You have the strangest grin, Danny."

I stopped and hugged her. "I was thinking how that night I never imagined that only a few years later we'd be in love; completely, totally, over-the-moon in love."

I traced Eli's jawbone with my finger. When it reached her chin I kissed her slowly and deliberately.

"I imagined it. I knew you'd come around," she whispered with a sly smile.

CHAPTER 77 - ELIZABETH

Waking, snuggled against Danny's warm body, reality struck. Grateful to be facing away from him, I kept my body still. I did not want to wake Danny.

What an evening! The excitement of last night had clouded my ability to think rationally and make accurate conclusions. In the quiet of early morning, that no longer applied. I couldn't risk Danny waking until I conducted a crucial analysis. Decision time, and not necessarily a happy one, was here.

My insides knotted. My heart ached. I replayed the encounter with Danny and Reggie over and over, beginning with the moment I first spied them talking. What I couldn't identify then, was now so obvious.

Danny seemed to enjoy Reggie's attentions far too much for her to have merely been a neighbor he'd met at the pool. Words and body language that seemed innocuous last night I now recognized for what they were. Only because I knew Danny so well did I expertly decode them.

Clarity led me to only one conclusion, one that I worked overtime to refute. Danny had an affair with Reggie. I knew that now with certainty. There was no denying it. My stomach churned. I swallowed hard, fighting the bile rising in my throat. Nausea threatened to distract me and I needed mental acuity.

Danny didn't have to admit it, but the truth was obvious. While we shared the sexiest phone calls and Skype sessions, Danny had been fooling around with Reggie. When? Where? Frequency? Even once was too often.

What kind of woman listened to our conversations, knowing Danny had a serious girlfriend, and yet still pursued him? That didn't matter. That was her sad life.

What was Reggie doing at the premiere? Whomever admitted her should be put to task. How dare she show up at my debut! This was my night! It was my night.

How could Danny do this to me? Why? Since I'd confronted him over Amelia, Danny had given me no reason to doubt his love. Who would doubt the sincerity of a man as devoted as he seemed to be?

Danny frequently professed his love for me, publically. Last night he declared us 'spiritually married' and began calling me Mrs. Newman. He kissed me in front of Steve and everyone. The guests, the press, they all observed us being a couple.

A confrontation would require a decision. There would be no getting around it once my knowledge of the affair was out there. I needed to make my decision now, before Danny woke. This was a game changer.

Tears filled my eyes. I couldn't wipe them away. The motion would wake Danny. I hated being in this position. It had been my night. Everyone received me enthusiastically. My dress was one of the loveliest. I looked great. Danny's eyes lit up when he saw me. Steve was so proud, too. Ruined now.

Absent Reggie's appearance last night, I would be blissfully ignorant. Blissful ignorance was not a bad place to be.

I was no longer ignorant or blissful. If Danny found this out, it threatened to create an insurmountable chasm between us. Unless there was another fluke like last night, neither of us would see Reggie again. We could easily pretend she never existed. Danny would follow my lead, relieved. Last night, Danny demonstrated how much he loved me. Perhaps Reggie had been that one last fling to solidify his decision.

Could I be selling myself a bill of goods? That was my real dilemma. I hurt, but I loved Danny, and I truly believed he loved me back. Danny would die if he were aware of my pain.

I didn't want to break-up with Danny, the most significant risk with confrontation. Danny and I would be forced to say good-bye. The thought of us separating was more painful than the idea that he'd been with Reggie.

Reviewing the time line minimized the impact. Whatever had transpired with Reggie during Spring Break must have been early on and of brief duration. Our conversations had escalated in emotional intensity as the break progressed. If I needed further proof of Danny's devotion, it occurred when he surprised me on my return to Donnelly.

Once or twice Danny had sounded wasted or hung-over when calling from Miami. Perhaps that's what happened. He was inebriated. Danny couldn't control himself. When Danny woke the next morning he was probably contrite.

We needed to have a serious discussion. Danny didn't seem capable of going out with the guys anymore without getting wasted. My patience had been wearing thin for weeks. Now my tolerance had reached its limit.

Danny declared me his wife last night. We even toasted to the new Mrs. Newman with a split of champagne from the minibar. The champagne had mostly been consumed by Mr. Newman. If I was now his wife, I was going to act like one.

When the time came, and it would be soon, I would put my foot down. I wasn't simply tired of Danny's partying, it frightened me. As this episode revealed, Danny's drinking encroached on our lives together. I didn't want to become Steve and Ellen.

For now I would keep silent. I didn't want our relationship to end. Danny wouldn't want that either. Last night was the proof. Danny's love would hopefully help me forget. I was willing to forgive. This time.

There was an annoying strand of hair on my face that I desperately wanted to brush away. I hadn't, knowing the slightest movement would have woken Danny. He would want to continue with our honeymoon. Now I knew I wanted it too.

Slowly, I lifted my hand to where the strand had stuck to my earlier tears. As I gently moved it behind my ear, an arm tighten around my hip. Then a hand gathered my hair and swept it to the side off my neck. Tender kisses nibbled my shoulder, and I squirmed.

I turned from my side on to my back. Sparkling sapphire eyes gazed into green with powerful emotion.

"Good morning, Mrs. Newman," Danny said in a scratchy whisper.

I swelled with pride. Mrs. Newman. I liked that.

"Good morning, dear husband," I answered in my own whisper.

I reached my hands around Danny's neck while his circled my back. Our lips met, our bodies pressed against each other, then joined. Fire ran through us until we exploded together.

Our love was a potent drug we were both addicted to. His behavior was inexcusable, but like a hapless junkie, I couldn't live without my fix. Lying amongst the crumpled sheets, snuggled against Danny holding me tight, I knew I'd made the right decision. In his arms, I belonged. Always. Danny was my life.

CHAPTER 78 - DANIEL

"Be downstairs at 6:15," I ordered Rachel and Chloe.

"We know!" they snapped.

I supposed I deserved it. I'd lost count as to how many times I had reminded them, but I was anxious and Chloe was always late.

Tonight we were seeing Dad's new film. I had purchased six tickets on Tuesday and I insisted we be early to have the pick of the best seats.

Tonight was a first. I'd never seen any of Dad's films in a public theater. I either went to screenings, or we viewed them in the screening room at home. At least this theater had stadium seating and a good digital sound system.

I was anxious, anticipating my friends' reactions and those of the audience. I expected a crowded theater. The predicted box office hit for this weekend was Dad's film.

"We're so early," Shane complained.

It pleased me that the spacious theater lobby was mostly empty.

"I don't care," I answered arrogantly. Eli glared.

"Sorry, babe, but I don't. We have to grab the best seats. Popcorn can wait."

Elizabeth rolled her eyes. In this less than perfect setting, I wanted to control what I had the power to control. Where I sat was about it.

"Why don't you let Rachel and Chloe save us spots on the line while Cam and Shane help us with refreshments? If the doors open, I'll finish getting the snacks and you can grab the seats."

I smiled at Eli's calm logic. "This is why you're my wife."

Eli took my hands and locked eyes with me. "I understand you're excited, but please chill. Before you ruin the evening for everyone else."

I smiled. Eli was right, as always.

My anxiety proved to be for nothing. I finished buying everyone popcorn and beverages before the doors to the auditorium even opened. Now all I had to do was sit through the next half hour of previews and ads.

"Take a deep breath," Eli ordered.

I complied.

"Take another one."

I complied again.

Eli pressed her hand to my cheek and brought her lips to mine for a warm kiss.

"Everyone's going to love it," Eli assured me. "It's a great film."

I took Elizabeth's soft hand and kissed her palm.

"You're right. I know you're right." Eli kissed me again. Her kiss had the power to make everything good for me.

"Full house," Shane interrupted.

Eli and I abruptly stopped kissing. Our eyes surveyed the auditorium. The lights were about to go down. The theater appeared sold out.

"Steve will be thrilled," Eli bubbled over. I was more low-key. I squeezed her hand and smiled my agreement.

If only the film does this well nationwide. My nerves wouldn't rest until I learned the box office take on Sunday.

"Danny, looks like your trust fund's safe for another year," Shane whispered, and he smirked to let me know he was joking.

"Shane! That's crass!" Eli scolded.

"Maybe, but with this box office, Danny can afford you for another year."

"Shane's right. Baby, you're an expensive habit."

I quickly kissed Eli as the previews began. "Have some popcorn," I whispered.

I was holding a large bag of popcorn that Eli had drenched with butter. She picked up a few kernels with her fingertips. Her smile was devilish as she pressed them into my mouth. I took her hand and slowly licked the butter from her fingers.

I smiled over her fingertips and Eli shuddered. There were at least ten more minutes of previews and commercials. I could afford the distraction that was Eli.

Finally, it was time. The studio logo appeared, then Dad's, before the film finally began. There was an opening sequence before the credits. I sat on edge, not knowing how my friends would react to seeing Dad's name.

As "A Film by Steven Newman," appeared on the screen, a loud wolf-whistle emanated from deep within the usually restrained, beautiful woman sitting beside me. This was followed by her loud applause. Everyone in the auditorium turned and stared. Whistling was completely out of character for Eli. I didn't even know that she could whistle.

I buried my face behind the popcorn bag. Shane smirked. Eli meant well, but her misplaced exuberance was embarrassing. I didn't want to be noticed tonight.

Over the bag, Rachel gave Eli a horrific stare. Reality check. Embarrassed, Eli sheepishly turned to me.

"I'm so sorry," Eli whispered. "I was excited."

I understood how badly she felt. "It's okay," I assured Eli.

After a while I placed the popcorn bag on the floor though it was still a third full, and I clutched Eli's hand for the duration of the film.

Occasionally I glanced at my friends and other nearby audience members. I was pleased to find them immersed in the story, apparently enjoying it.

When it ended, I turned to Eli. "Let's go," I said with urgency.

"Uh, no. I'm not leaving until I see <u>all</u> the credits."

I grimaced. When we'd returned from New York, my small, exclusive fan club informed anyone who would listen about my credit. Now Eli wanted our friends to see it. I hated the attention, but I was touched by her pride.

As my credit crawled down the screen, Eli let out another loud whistle. I shook my head, astounded. What else didn't I know about Eli?

"Since when can you whistle?" I asked.

Eli grinned. "There's a lot you don't know about me, Daniel."

I laughed at Eli's attempt at sounding mysterious. After all these years, we had no secrets.

By this time, the auditorium was nearly empty. My friends added their own applause. What the heck? I applauded my name too.

CHAPTER 79 - ELIZABETH

"Are you and Danny fighting?" Chloe asked while peeking her head into my bedroom. Her unexpected question jarred me from my studies.

"Why would you think that?" My note taking stopped. I was studying French and was having a difficult enough time as it was. I yawned. Why was I so tired?

"Elizabeth, you've been sleeping here the last few nights," she replied. "I'm not being nosy, but if you and Danny are having problems, I'm here if you want to talk."

"Thanks, Chloe," I responded with another yawn. "Danny and I are solid."

"Then why are you here?" Chloe knitted her brows, confused.

"Danny's with Rachel. Post-production."

Their short film was due soon, and they were working tirelessly to complete it. I understood the importance of this film. It was not only Danny's major; it was his life. Tonight Danny hoped to get off earlier and if he did he had promised to come by.

"I know," Chloe said. "I just thought you'd be sleeping downstairs so you could be together when Danny finally called it a night."

I yawned again then stretched my arms. My back and shoulders were achy.

"No. Danny will come here."

"You don't mind? Danny's always with Rachel lately."

"Chloe, you know they're only friends and work partners. Nothing else. I only mind, well I miss him of course. I hate not seeing Danny."

I let out another large yawn. My eyelids became slits. "I'm so tired," I complained.

"It's not even nine o'clock."

"I know. And I took a nap this afternoon."

"It's probably French. It's boring you."

"Probably, but I need to read at least five more pages."

Once Chloe left, I returned to my book. My eyes wouldn't stay open. One more page. One more page, I willed myself. I fought against my drooping eyes. Fail! Why fight a losing battle? I didn't care how early it was, if I couldn't keep my eyes open.

I changed into pajamas, crawled into bed, and instantly fell asleep.

I woke the next morning realizing three things. First, Danny was not in my bed and that meant he had worked late again. Second, at least I'd see him today in political science. And third, I was perspiring and could barely move.

Getting out of bed was difficult. Had my head gained weight? It was so heavy. Despite eleven solid hours of sleep, I was dragging my feet as I prepared for the day.

It was too late in the term to be sick. I couldn't afford to miss any classes plus I had too much studying to do. "Toughen up, Elizabeth," I urged myself. I needed to function today. I could sleep again later.

"Elizabeth," Professor Dennison said as class ended, "I'd like to speak with you."

Was I in trouble? I looked to Danny. He shrugged. My heart told me I'd done nothing wrong. My head told me, well it told me absolutely nothing. I had a pounding headache and absolutely no energy.

As the classroom emptied, I collected my books and with Danny by my side, I cautiously made my way to the professor waiting in the front by the lectern. My books seemed far heavier than usual.

"Danny, you can stay. It's nothing that you can't hear."

I placed my books on the first desk, glad to be eased of the burden. Danny stood by my side and reached for my hand.

"Elizabeth, are you all right?" Professor Dennison asked with concern.

"I may be coming down with a bug." I tried minimizing how poorly I felt.

"Eli, what's wrong?" Danny was alarmed.

"It's probably just a cold."

"Danny, Elizabeth looks awful." the professor asked. "Or are you not together anymore?"

"Of course we're together," Danny answered, surprised by the question. "I haven't been around much this week. My film is due in a few days."

Danny carefully studied me. I hated the scrutiny.

"Owen's right. Eli, you look awful. I'm taking you home and putting you to bed."

I shook my head no. "I have to study French."

"Elizabeth, French can wait."

"Thank you, professor. I'm sure..." my voice trailed off, the room was spinning.

CHAPTER 80 - DANIEL

"Eli!" Her feet gave out from under her body. I barely had time to react, but I caught Elizabeth before she fell.

"Elizabeth!" Owen exclaimed.

"She's fainted!" I'd never seen anyone faint before.

"I'll call emergency. Carry Elizabeth to my office."

I scooped Eli up in my arms and ran after Owen, sprinting to his office a short way down the hall. There I carefully placed Eli on the couch.

"Loosen her clothes," Owen ordered as he rummaged through his gym bag.

I elevated Elizabeth's head on a sofa pillow as I undid a couple of buttons on her silk blouse and unhooked her lacy bra.

Owen found a towel, and as he ran down the hall to the bathroom to wet it, I gently shook Eli. Her eyes slowly fluttered open. Only seconds had passed, but it seemed much longer.

Owen quickly returned with the wet towel. Kneeling beside the couch, I applied the cold compress to her neck while he called the health center. Eli looked around the office with glazed-over eyes before returning her vacant stare to me.

"You're in Owen's office. Honey, you fainted."

Then I touched Elizabeth's forehead. She was on fire!

"Danny, I'm scared." I patted Elizabeth's hand for comfort.

"The medics are on their way," said Owen.

"I've never fainted before." Elizabeth's voice was barely audible.

"That's okay. It happens," I said in the gentlest voice.

I massaged her fingers. Elizabeth couldn't see my fear. I had to be strong.

"I'm so embarrassed," she whispered and looked toward the professor.

"Don't sweat it, babe," I reassured her.

Owen was cool. He was probably glad this happened in his room so he could be of assistance.

Soon the medics arrived. After a cursory exam, I carried Elizabeth down to the van for the short trip to the infirmary.

When we arrived, I lifted Eli and carried her in. She was weak and helpless.

The nurse indicated an open examination room.

"Don't leave me," Elizabeth pleaded.

"I'm here, baby."

"I feel woozy."

"Here, let me." I effortlessly picked her up and Elizabeth cradled her head against my shoulder. Through my shirt, I felt her fever.

Soon after, the doctor entered. He glanced at me, hinting that I should leave the room. Eli clutched my arm. She stared at the doctor, but her eyes didn't focus.

"Danny stays." Eli's voice was weak.

The doctor sighed. He wasn't winning this battle.

Elizabeth had a fever of 103.8. Official diagnosis: flu.

"Elizabeth, you'll have to stay in the infirmary until your fever breaks and you regain your strength," the doctor said.

"How long will that be?" I asked.

"Probably three days. Possibly longer."

"My classes," Eli protested. "I have to study."

"Elizabeth, you're not going anywhere," I said firmly.

"You're contagious and you're weak," the doctor explained. "Elizabeth, you can't attend classes or return to the dorm."

Elizabeth's private room was like that of any hospital. It even included a television. The nurse gave Eli medication to bring down her fever and encouraged her to drink some apple juice. She carefully stuck Eli's left hand with a needle and attached an IV to keep her hydrated.

Lying in bed, her eyes glazed and barely open, Eli seemed so small. I sat down beside her and took her right hand.

"Eli, you need to sleep. I'll come back tonight."

"I'm tired," Elizabeth admitted.

I leaned over and kissed her hot forehead. "I love you, baby. I'll be back later." Elizabeth half-smiled and closed her eyes.

CHAPTER 81 - DANIEL

"Danny, where were you this afternoon? We had editorial reserved." Rachel barked.

The hairs on the back of my neck prickled. My intention was to have a quick bite in the cafeteria while going unnoticed. Instead, I had Rachel barking at me.

I didn't respond, afraid I would explode and say something I would later regret. Rachel knew how conscientious I was. Hell, I had more at stake than she did. Rachel should know if I blew her off there was a good reason. Yet there she was, addressing me as though I were a naughty child shirking my responsibilities.

Rachel sat down in a huff and only then noticed that I was alone.

"Where's your wife?" she snarled. Her voice was filled with rancor.

"In the infirmary with the flu," I snapped. Between Rachel's rudeness and worrying over Eli, I was in a sour mood.

"Infirmary! I had no idea…" she said contritely. "I thought…"

"Thought what?" I exploded. "That I was off getting wasted? Or maybe I was having sex with my girlfriend? I thought you knew me better than that! Screw you, Rach!" I slammed my plate down hard for emphasis.

"Danny! I didn't mean that." But of course she did.

"Then what did you mean?"

"I, I thought," she stammered." I was angry because you didn't call or text."

"Use your brains! Maybe I couldn't call because there are some things that are even more important than that damned film!"

"I'm sorry. I know how dedicated you are. How's Elizabeth?"

"Nice of you to ask. She'll be fine. Once she spends the week in bed. I've hardly seen her all week and now it will be another week," I grumbled.

"Poor you," Rachel said, her voice dripping in sarcasm.

"Yes, poor me. I don't like being without Elizabeth."

"This is not about you, Danny. Elizabeth's really sick."

"No shit, Rachel," I said curtly. "I WAS the one who caught her when she fainted. I simply prefer my girlfriend healthy and with me."

Rachel gasped. "You are so self-centered. You could have seen her all week but whenever I suggested quitting early you wouldn't hear of it. But now she's unavailable, so you're angry. I can't believe you."

"You are so wrong. Eli understood I wanted to work as much as possible. She knows I'm a perfectionists, and Eli understands this life. But damn it, I miss her."

"Where's Elizabeth?" Chloe cheerfully asked. She seemingly appeared from out of nowhere with her dinner plate in hand.

"Infirmary. Flu," I answered sharply.

"Oh. I half expected that," she said as she sat down.

"Why did you half expect it?" I grilled her.

"Don't you ever speak to your girlfriend anymore?"

"Of course I speak to my girlfriend," I snapped. "I've been working late and Eli's stubborn and doesn't want me to worry. So why did you half expect it?"

"Elizabeth looked awful last night. She even went to bed before nine."

"Why didn't you call me?" If Eli wasn't feeling well, Chloe should have called.

"Was I supposed to?"

"Yes!" I answered emphatically.

"You never told me that was my job," Chloe countered.

"Of course that's your job. Chloe, you're her roommate. If Elizabeth is sick, you call me. It's that simple. Eli can't be alone if she's sick."

Chloe and Rachel starred at me with wide eyes. Why didn't they understand? I had to take care of Elizabeth.

"What?" I asked angrily.

"This is too weird," Rachel muttered.

"Hey, guys." It was Shane and behind him was Cam.

"Where's Mrs. Newman?" Cam asked playfully. Rachel put her finger to her lips and gave them a warning glare.

"I wish you hadn't asked," Chloe groaned.

"Why?" Cam asked. Then he stopped in his tracks, alarm spread across his face. Cam looked at me, then at Rachel and back to me. "Danny, you haven't gotten divorced, have you? Is that why I haven't seen you with your wife all week?"

"I'm so out of here," Frustrated and angry, I bolted. "Eli is not my wife nor are we getting divorced. Oh, and Cam, she's in the infirmary." I bolted from the cafeteria.

I was sick of this! Just because I loved Eli, and we were living together, that did not make her my spouse. Until that day in the future when I proposed, Elizabeth understood I was not being serious when I called her Mrs. Newman. Why didn't our friends?

CHAPTER 82 - DANIEL

Before Rachel or Chloe returned from dinner, I entered their suite. I found Eli's overnight case atop her wardrobe. She needed clothes and toiletries. When Eli's health improved, she would want her books. I quickly packed and returned to my room.

My mood tempered as my thoughts turned to Eli. This afternoon was scary. I'd never seen a sober person pass out before. And Eli's head had been on fire. The nurses would take good care of her, but I wanted to make her smile.

Opening my closet, I pulled out two cotton shirts that were ready for the laundry. They weren't really dirty, but I'd worn them each a couple of times, and that made them perfect. I dabbed the collars with a drop of my cologne. Eli would love wearing these.

The infirmary was hospital quiet when I arrived and a security guard directed me to the elevator. The ten-room second floor looked like a miniature hospital. Room Seven was at the end of the hall. My heartbeat increased as I reached the door. I hoped to find Elizabeth awake and alert. I hoped her fever was down.

Eyes closed, Elizabeth was lying in bed. Her face was pale. Was she even awake? There was only one way to know. I set down the case, went to her side, and kissed her hot forehead. Green eyes fluttered open. Her usually bright emeralds were dull. She smiled demurely.

"Danny?" Elizabeth whispered. I sat down and clasped her small hand.

"I'm here, baby." My heart broke. It was unbearable seeing her so ill.

"I'm tired."

"Have you been sleeping?"

"Yes. I'm thirsty."

"Let me sit you up. I'll get you some water."

Carefully, as though she were made of crystal, I helped Elizabeth to sitting. I poured water from a carafe into a glass with a straw in it. Eli drained the glass.

"Better?"

"Much," she said in a stronger voice. "I feel awful."

"I can tell," I said, but I smiled affectionately.

"That bad, huh?"

I laughed, unable to mask the truth. "But you're always beautiful to me."

"Right answer," Eli chuckled. "Such a liar."

"So you'll keep me around?"

"For the time being." Sick as she was, Elizabeth still had her humor.

We smiled at each other as I played with her fingers. It wasn't necessary to speak. Eli's smile, filled with love and tenderness, spread warmth throughout me. I felt the best I had all day.

The nurse entered, interrupting. "Time to take your temperature," she announced.

I backed away and let the nurse place the thermometer in Eli's mouth. It was one of those digital models that didn't take long. The nurse frowned.

"What?" I asked.

"Elizabeth's fever is still over 103."

"I won't stay long," I assured the nurse.

"Yes, you will," Eli protested.

"E, I need you better."

The nurse handed Eli a glass of water and some pills. I assumed they were fever reducers.

"I'm tired of water. Can I please have some apple juice?"

"I'll be right back," the nurse said. And she was, bringing two small plastic bottles of juice.

"I'll check on you later." She smiled and left the room.

I opened a bottle of juice and handed it to Eli.

"Shouldn't you be with Rachel?" Elizabeth asked.

"Not tonight."

"Won't she be angry?"

"Elizabeth you're more important," I said trying to sidestep the issue. Eli's eyes opened wide. She figured it out anyway.

"You're fighting! Danny, you and Rachel had an argument, didn't you?"

"Yes," I confessed. "But I'd be here even if we hadn't."

"Of course you would." Eli smiled. "What happened?"

"Nothing, really. Rachel thought I blew her off this afternoon so I got pissed that she doubted my dedication and then she got pissed at me for missing you."

"Huh?" Eli crinkled her eyes in confusion.

"Then I got pissed at Chloe for not calling me last night when she knew you were sick."

"Was she supposed to?"

"Yes. How am I supposed to take care of you if no one tells me anything is wrong?"

"I'm an adult. I can take care of myself, Daniel."

"No you can't. Otherwise you would have been up here seeing a doctor instead of muddling your way through a Political Science class."

"I didn't want you to worry."

"Well guess what?"

"You're worried anyway."

"And I'm pissed at Shane and Cam for calling me on it."

"I think I'm the one you're really pissed at."

"How can you say that? You're lying in bed, sick in the infirmary."

"Exactly! So you're taking it out on everyone else. Daniel, I love you, but you're behaving like a petulant little boy."

"Eli!" I protested.

"All week you've been working late. On any evening you could have slept with me. It would have been nice, but I understood. If you were getting only three or four hours of sleep you wanted it to be solid. You have a very tight post schedule."

"I love that you understand. It takes the pressure off me. So why would I be angry?"

"Because you feel guilty. And second, you missed your chance to play and now my spoiled love, I can't play."

"I'm not angry, Eli. You're sick."

"That's why you're taking it out on everybody else. How would it look if you were angry with a sick woman?"

"Eli!" I flushed. My guilt showed through. But Eli was right. I was angry with her.

"You know I love you, Eli," I said contritely.

"Of course. Daniel, that's why you're embarrassed."

I moved in to kiss Elizabeth but she held up her hand to stop me.

"Danny, I don't want you to get sick. Then you'll be lying here when I'm ready to play again." Elizabeth spoke with such innocence I couldn't help but laugh.

"Eli, I'm not angry anymore," I said, and I smiled. Before Elizabeth could protest, I pressed my lips against her parched ones for a very chaste kiss.

"Danny! I'm contagious!"

"I swear to take full responsibility. If I catch the flu, I will not get angry with you. It will be completely my fault for not being able to resist you."

We both laughed.

"I hate this. I really do," I complained.

I took Eli in my arms wanting so badly to kiss her. She sensed it too.

"Daniel, you'd better go. I should rest and I need to protect you from yourself."

CHAPTER 83 - DANIEL

I should have gone to the gym. Instead, The Cellar beckoned.

Now that Eli had exonerated me, I was hyper. I needed to do something physical. Chances were Chloe or some other girls I was friends with would be at The Cellar. I could dance with them. Eli wouldn't mind. Eli was cool with me having friends who were girls.

I hadn't considered the early hour. The Cellar was nearly empty. On the assumption that a group would materialize, I took a seat at a round table meant for six. Then I ordered a shot of Jack Daniels, plus a pitcher of beer.

The pitcher came with four glasses, for the friends I anticipated, and to avoid looking like an alcoholic drinking alone. As soon as I was served, I threw back the J.D. Instant mellow. Then I slowly poured out a glass of beer; foamless, golden perfection. The beer's frosty smoothness was just what I needed. Heaven in a pilsner glass.

"Where's mine?" Phoebe exclaimed as she bounced onto the chair to my right.

"Me, too," Amelia purred as she slid onto the chair to my left. Shit!

"Ladies. Good to see you, too," I greeted them. Phoebe and Amelia were not exactly my first choice, but at least I was not alone anymore.

I poured from the pitcher and the girls happily took the beers.

"Talking to me again, Amelia?"

After she accepted that our fling had been just that, Amelia had turned toxic, and I avoided her. Rumor had it that she had been ready to call things off with her pompous boyfriend James over me.

"I can afford to give you a break. I'm out of here once finals are over. I'm transferring to Dartmouth."

"To be with James?" I asked with a raised eyebrow, though I knew the answer. "Sweet."

"So you see, you don't matter anymore."

"Amelia, you're breaking my heart." I laughed as I poured myself another beer.

"Where's Mary Poppins?" Phoebe asked cheerfully.

"Mary's so stiff." Amelia added. "I don't know how you stand it."

"If you're insulting my girlfriend, go drink someone else's beer."

"Touchy, touchy!" Phoebe chimed in playfully.

"You love making me uncomfortable," I laughed as did the girls.

"All I'm saying," Amelia explained, her chin lifted defiantly, "Your girlfriend's frigid and you're, well you're not, Dan."

"Does she float up into the clouds when the wind changes and gets under her designer mini-skirts?" Phoebe teased.

"Not funny, Phoebs. And my girlfriend is certainly not frigid." Then I chugged the rest of my beer and poured another. "Besides," I added, now feeling the buzz," I know what's under those designer mini-skirts."

"I'll bet," Amelia responded caustically.

"She's an ice princess, Dan," Phoebe added.

"Eli is no ice princess, Phoebs. Eli's hot."

"But she's a princess. She spends more on clothing than my father makes in a year."

"I doubt that. Your father's a CEO. He must earn at least seven figures."

"That's my point, Dan."

"Forget it. I am not discussing Elizabeth with you vultures."

"So where is Mary?" Phoebe asked. "Trouble on Cherry Tree Lane?"

"Not at all. Total bliss. Eli's in the infirmary with the flu."

Phoebe ran her fingers along my cheekbone and jaw. "Poor baby," she said sarcastically. "Sleeping alone tonight?"

"Have you ever?" Amelia's voice also oozed with sarcasm.

"Very funny ladies. I can go a few nights alone. I'm a big boy."

"Dan, you sure are." Amelia grinned and winked.

I groaned, regretting my choice of words.

After additional pitchers, and dances with the girls, it was time to go. Even I realized, if I spent any more time in The Cellar I would not be functional in the morning.

I needed to be more than functional. I had classes, studying, editing, and now the burden of visiting Elizabeth. It wasn't that I didn't want to see Eli, but this late in the semester time was my enemy.

Today had been a wasted day. I had accomplished nothing. Visiting Eli twice a day was a luxury I didn't have time for. There was nothing I could do for her, but staying away would break Eli's heart.

This was what Cam and Shane meant about me being married. I hated the obligations. If only Eli had found out about Reggie. She would have had no choice but to dump me. Then I could do what I really wanted; spend the night with Amelia who was being so flirty she was difficult to resist. Worse, Amelia knew it.

"Time to go," I announced.

"Drive us home?" Phoebe asked though it was more a statement.

Amelia perched her hands on my shoulder and smiled into my eyes.

"Pleeeeze?" she asked, and Amelia boldly kissed my lips. For a girl who had stopped talking to me for three months, Amelia was awfully playful tonight. Still, we were in public. If any of Eli's friends saw this, I would be in big trouble.

"Amelia!" I brushed her back. "I have a girlfriend, remember?"

"Oh pooh! Why does she have to spoil all the fun?"

"What about James?" I asked.

"He's in New Hampshire," Amelia answered matter-of-factly. "I told James the only way I would stop being naughty was if I spent every night with him. So we're spending the summer in Europe. Then it's off to Hanover. James and I will be like you and Mary."

I laughed caustically. Amelia would never be like Eli. I was unable to imagine Amelia being true to any man, but you never know. Maybe James was really a stud.

Buzzed as I was, I shouldn't have considered driving. But I wasn't leaving Donnelly. As the girls were clinging to me in an attempt to stay upright, I had no choice.

Halfway to The Village, Phoebe pulled out a joint and lit it. After inhaling she passed it forward to Amelia in the front passenger seat, as though in their states the girls needed any additional intoxicants.

If I crashed my car tonight, I would be in major trouble. Eli would be devastated upon learning the identities of my passengers. Dad would hang me for driving with however high my blood-alcohol level must be. And the Dean would probably suspend me.

I was not too drunk to understand the even hotter water I'd be in if illegal substances were found in my blood. This was upstate New York, not L.A. Steven Newman's name would probably be a detriment.

Phoebe and Amelia could barely walk. I helped them from my car and up the path to their house. Amelia was all over me as we stumbled through the door.

"Good-night," Phoebe slurred, and she winked as she staggered upstairs.

Amelia re-lit the joint and passed it to me.

"Amelia…" I protested. "It's late."

She brought it to my lips while pressing against me. "Dan," she ordered, "I want to party. With you."

Amelia starred at me until I took a hit. It had been a few weeks, and boy, had I missed it. I took the joint from Amelia's fingers and this time I inhaled deeply. Yeah, this was divine.

Loose from the effects of the joint, I smiled at Amelia and rested my arm on her shoulder. Her breasts pressed against me, soft and tempting. Mmm, Amelia.

After a few more deep hits, my brains were floating, completely detached from my body. Amelia kissed me, holding me tight. I kissed her back, responding to her lips and eager fingers stroking inside my now opened jeans.

I woke a few hours later stunned. Amelia's naked body was lying on the couch twined with mine. What the hell had I done?

Shit! Eli! Guilt consumed me. Elizabeth had trusted me. What had I done?

I dressed as quickly as I could, before covering Amelia with a nearby throw blanket. I had to get out of here.

As I drove back to Berkeley Hall, I concluded that I was the lowest form of humanity. If Eli ever found out, she would kill me. If I were the judge, I would let her go; justifiable homicide.

A steamy, shower made me no cleaner. I wished there was someone I could talk to, someone to tell me I would find the right path. I needed a priest, but I was Jewish. I needed a therapist, but I didn't have one. At three in the morning I couldn't exactly go out and find either.

How would I face Eli? I felt lower than low. What a fraud I was. She deserved much better than the real me I had successfully kept from her. Eli shouldn't visit Vancouver. She needed time away from me to find the better boyfriend she deserved.

CHAPTER 84 - DANIEL

Morning. My head was pounding. It had been ages since a night like last night. Dryness worse than the Mojave held my tongue hostage. I blindly reached to my desk for a fistful of Tylenol, which I downed with a half-liter of water.

I felt like shit, both mentally and physically. More mentally. From the moment my alarm clock rudely sounded, I launched into an endless set of mental gymnastics. I replayed the events of last night in great detail. I tried making sense of them.

There was no sense to be made. Unbearably, the only conclusion I reached was that I couldn't be trusted to behave responsibly. Living with Eli had taught me to see beyond myself, or so I thought. In one drunken evening I'd thrown it all away. I was twenty years old and needed a babysitter.

I grabbed a blueberry muffin and a cup of strong coffee at The Café before running over to visit Eli. I had an early class. I wouldn't stay long. The shorter visit would give Elizabeth less time to ask about last night.

I took a deep breath before entering Elizabeth's room. Would Eli notice my eyeglasses were covering dry, guilty eyes? I wore them often enough in the morning that they shouldn't raise Elizabeth's suspicions. I hoped.

I smiled as I approached her bedside. Elizabeth was ailing. I couldn't walk in and break her heart.

"Hey, you," I said cheerfully as I sat down on the edge of the bed.

Eli was awake and smiled, happy to see me. Of course Eli was happy to see me. She was oblivious to my morphing into a total bastard since I'd last seen her. Eli assumed I was a devoted, loving man who had slept alone.

"Danny," Eli whispered as she reached out her arms for a hug.

I gladly obliged. Eli felt so good. She always felt good. Why would I jeopardize this? What was wrong with me? Eli was the best, and she wanted me, only me.

I kissed her forehead. "Not as hot as yesterday."

"I'm down to 102."

"How are you, baby?" I asked as I smoothed matted auburn locks off her face.

"Much better now that you're here."

Another pang of guilt stabbed my heart like the sharpest Christian Louboutin stiletto. Elizabeth wasn't aware that she shouldn't love me anymore.

"Seriously Eli, how are you?"

"Tired. I need a nap even though I've barely been awake."

"I'm sorry, baby." I hated seeing her ill.

Elizabeth held my hand up to her lips and kissed my palm.

"I spoke to your dad last night." Mike was a safe topic. "Mike said he'd call you today. I told him not to worry. I'm here for you."

"Danny, you are, aren't you?" Elizabeth smiled.

I was such a fraud, but it was true. I was here for Elizabeth.

"I'm always here for you, baby."

My love for Eli had not diminished. An evening of sex with Amelia had not changed my feelings. It simply meant I was, as Eli described last night, a spoiled twenty year-old.

I should only get wasted when I'm with Elizabeth. Then I would be with the right girl when I lost control. Of course, Eli didn't like me getting wasted unless she joined me. The couple of times she had, Eli's lack of inhibitions frightened me, so I didn't let her get wasted anymore. This conundrum probably meant my committing to never getting wasted again. Another vice I was not ready to give up.

"Danny, you look worn. Didn't you sleep?"

"Not nearly enough. I couldn't stop thinking of you." At least that was the truth.

"It's only the flu."

"It's my job. I worry about you."

Elizabeth laughed, and I shrugged. Then I kissed her soft hands.

"Do you want to change your clothes?" I asked. Eli was wearing one of those flimsy hospital gowns. "I brought your case last night."

"Nobody told me." Eli frowned. "Can you unpack for me? Please, Danny?"

Eli was excited to see what I had brought. Unfortunately, there was nothing all that interesting: iPad, toiletries, underwear and nightshirts. And the framed photo Eli kept by her bed. Teddy had taken it of me embracing Eli on the mountain at Aspen.

"My photo!" Elizabeth cried joyously. "Now I won't be lonely."

Eli even hugged the photo. I wished it had been that easy for me.

I handed Eli one of the shirts as I untied the back closures holding the hospital gown together. Meanwhile, she held the shirt up to her nose and inhaled deeply. A smile lit up her face.

"It's my favorite scent. You," she gushed.

I couldn't help but smile back. Eli's glee was pure, almost childlike in its innocence. I was envious. How I wished my soul lived on her planet, one where desire was sated by the scent of cotton, faded sweat and cologne.

I removed the hospital gown leaving her bare-chested for a moment while I retrieved the shirt. Eli seemed quite comfortable sitting shirtless.

Elizabeth was so beautiful, even while sick. I had to touch her. So I eased her arms into the shirt but left the buttons open. My hand gently cupped Eli's breast as I kissed her cheek and then her neck.

"Danny, I'm sick," Elizabeth protested but did nothing to stop me.

Elizabeth was so soft and the faint scent of her perfume from yesterday lingered on her skin. Sick with flu, Eli was still lovely. My lips left her neck and met hers. With my hand massaging her breast, she was powerless to resist.

I didn't care that Eli was contagious. I needed her sweetness. Pure bliss.

Elizabeth abruptly pulled back. "Danny, no! You'll get sick."

"I don't care. Eli, I need you, baby," I said, and I kissed her again.

Elizabeth had no idea how badly I needed her. Could her kisses make me forget? And if I caught Elizabeth's flu, would that be my penitence for last night?

"I miss you so much," I told her.

"It's only a few days."

"I know. I can't stand being without you, Eli."

"That sounds so sad, Danny."

"I am sad. I'm sad that you have the flu. And I'm sad that we're forced to be apart. Eli, I didn't realize until this morning that I've become so dependent on you."

I realized too late what I had admitted. Would Eli take advantage of my vulnerability? I always feared letting anyone, even Eli learn of my weaknesses.

Elizabeth grasped my hands and locked her fever-glazed eyes on mine. The strength of her stare and the confidence from her heart gripped me with its pure intensity.

"I'm just as dependent on you, Danny. We need each other. That's what love is."

Eli was right. It was love. Relieved, I smiled. I should have known better. Eli always made it safe for me to confess my deepest fears.

"Would you please button my shirt now?" Elizabeth asked sweetly.

I complied, my fingers lingering on her skin. Elizabeth might have the flu, but she smiled in delight.

"I've got to go, baby. You need your rest and I have a class,"

Elizabeth squeezed my hand. "I'm really glad you came by, Danny."

"There is no place I would rather be. You know that, Elizabeth." Holding her chin in my hand I kissed her.

"I am a very happy girl. Except for the flu of course."

"Okay, happy girl," I laughed, and I kissed her very warm forehead, "Go to sleep and get better so I can make you an even happier girl."

Last night now seemed a lifetime ago. Chalk it up to behaving stupidly while inebriated. It hadn't meant anything to me. It hadn't meant anything to Amelia. Visiting Elizabeth had already cured me.

CHAPTER 85 - DANIEL

"Play that back again," I ordered.

Rachel groaned loudly, frustrated.

"What's wrong now?"

"Play it back, Rach. Last time, I promise."

Rachel raised a suspicious eyebrow. "Last time? Sure," she said sarcastically. "Why did I partner with you?" Rachel mumbled.

"Because you love me."

"I am not one of your adoring fans, Danny."

"I don't have adoring fans. Yet. But maybe I will after this film is completed."

"Danny, you're insufferable."

"And you love it because my perfectionist ways will get us an A."

"Why did my roommate have to be your BFF? Life would be so much simpler if I had partnered with a normal student."

"Rach," I paused, now serious. "I have to be this way. If I'm to be respected in this department, I need the professors and students to see that I'm working twice as hard as everyone else and turning out a film that's twice as good."

"But you don't have to worry. You're Steven Newman's son."

"But that's why. Otherwise everyone will assume that whatever I get is because I'm Steven Newman's son. This summer I'm going to be the best P.A. anyone's ever seen or Dad will never let me work for him again. The name opens doors, but it's also an albatross."

Rachel understood the added pressure I was under.

"People see your surface. They don't want to discover what lies beneath. It's easier to buy the stereotype. They have no idea how hard you work."

"Thanks, Rach. You're a true friend. One of the few."

"I'm glad my Dad's a dentist. It's easier." Rachel kissed my cheek. "There is one thing you've gotten because you're Steven Newman's son that I know you wouldn't trade," Rachel said playfully.

"What?" I asked, taking the bait.

"Your girlfriend. If you weren't…"

"Elizabeth!" I exclaimed. "Shit!" I jumped up in a panic.

"What?" Rachel asked.

"What time is it?" I exclaimed, so agitated I couldn't think straight nor could I find the clock affixed to the wall in front of me.

"It's almost eleven."

"Shit! I am so dead!" I slouched in my chair and snapped a pencil in two.

"Danny!"

"I told Eli I'd visit tonight. The infirmary doesn't let visitors in after ten. I'm screwed."

"Calm down. Elizabeth knows how busy we are. She'll understand."

"I promised, Rachel. I don't break promises. Ugh! I hate myself," I groaned.

Rachel put her hand on my shoulder. "Danny, you're way too hard on yourself. This isn't healthy."

Rachel might be right. Between the long hours working, concern for Eli, and guilt over Amelia, I was on edge. I needed to keep my wits about me.

I took a deep breath and slowly exhaled. I took a second breath and a third one. Then I smiled meekly.

"Thanks. I needed a reality check."

Rachel picked my phone up off the worktable and handed it to me.

"Here. Call her," she said.

This was the sensible solution that was eluding me in the near psychotic state that I seemed to exist in.

Elizabeth's phone rang five times before the outgoing message started. I didn't listen. I didn't want to leave a message.

"Eli's not answering," I said, panicked. "She sees it's me and won't pick up."

Rachel rolled her eyes. "Will you calm down and behave logically? Elizabeth is in the infirmary. She probably turned off her phone so she could get some sleep because she knows full well that her annoying boyfriend will call and wake her."

"What if Eli is avoiding me?"

"Because you're working and didn't visit her? Doubtful."

"It's possible."

"I've never seen you like this before. Elizabeth loves you."

"She did this morning."

A piercing brown-eyed stare chilled me to the bone.

"Daniel Newman, did you do something that would make Elizabeth not love you anymore?" Rachel asked sternly.

I couldn't answer. I was speechless. The truth of course was yes, but I couldn't tell Rachel. She would kill me. Eli was her best friend.

"Don't ask that, Rach." I implored.

"Danny!" Rachel gasped, her eyes opening wide in horror. "You did do something and you're afraid Elizabeth found out! You bastard! What did you do?"

My stomach wrenched. I groaned. How could I have let Rachel guess?

"Rachel, don't go there," I answered curtly.

"How could you do this to Elizabeth while she's in the infirmary!"

"Rach, stop," I begged. "I feel terrible enough."

"I can't believe you, Danny!" Rachel's voice rose angrily. I was thankful the room was soundproofed.

"I'm sorry. It's no excuse, but I was wasted. Please don't tell Eli," I pleaded.

"It's your job to tell her. Not mine."

"I'm not telling her. Eli will kill me. Worse she'll break up with me."

"If Elizabeth's smart, she should break up with you. I would."

"Rach, don't say that. You know how much I love Eli. It would break her heart."

"This is what you do to the woman you love? Unbelievable, Danny!"

"Rachel, it was one unfortunate indiscretion. It meant nothing to me."

"What a cliché," Rachel mumbled.

"Rachel, you have to believe me," I pleaded.

"I don't have to believe anything! I'm not the girl who lives with you."

"Rach, please."

"What do you want from me, Danny? Exoneration? Do you want me to say 'there, there cheat on your girlfriend. It will be alright'?"

"Promise me you won't say anything to Eli. Finals are coming."

"I hate you! I hate even more the position you've put me in! How am I supposed to be in a room with you and Elizabeth when I know your entire relationship is a lie?"

"It's not a lie. I love Elizabeth. It was one stupid mistake."

"Danny!"

My phone rang, and I jumped at the sound. The caller ID said it was Eli. "Hey, baby. How's the love of my life?" I tried sounding normal.

"Okay, I think." Eli's voice was strong.

"I assumed you were sleeping when you didn't answer."

"I was taking a shower."

"At eleven o'clock at night?" How odd.

"I fell asleep, some time around seven, I think, and I woke up drenched in sweat. I'll have to send your shirt to the laundry."

"That's okay," I laughed. Eli's voice put a smile on my face.

"I'm much better. I think my fever finally broke."

"Does that mean I can spring you?"

"I don't know."

"I miss you, hon. There's an empty space in my bed that's just your size, Eli."

"How I wish I was there with you," Eli sighed.

"I know, but there's a part of my heart that's been missing and I want it back."

"When did you become so poetic?"

"Don't tell anyone I'm a sentimental fool."

"It'll be our little secret."

Elizabeth and I shared a laugh. With Rachel in the room, none of this conversation was private, but Eli didn't know that.

"Danny, I have to see what the doctor says. He may keep me another day or two until I get my strength back."

"No. I need you Eli. I want you with me. Tomorrow you are coming home. I can give you Tylenol and tissues. And if you're not up to going out, I'll bring you sick trays from the cafeteria or chicken soup from the deli."

"What about your school work?"

"I'll neglect it less if you're home. And I won't feel bad for missing visiting hours like I did tonight because you'll be there whenever I get back."

"Were you upset about tonight? Don't be. I was sleeping."

"I didn't know. It was awful when I saw the time. I went off the deep end."

"Danny, you're the best! I can't imagine any girl being loved more than I am."

"I can't either 'cause I know how much I love you. It's getting late, hon. Eli, get some more sleep. I'll pick you up some clothes and be in my bed by midnight so I can be up bright and early to bring you home. How does that sound, baby?"

"The best news I've had all week."

"You have good dreams, Eli."

I ended the call and pressed the phone against my heart hoping her love would leave the device and enter me. A grin crossed my face. Eli's love had entered me.

"Unbelievable," Rachel declared. "Newman, you're mental. You're desperately in love with Elizabeth, yet you cheated on her last night. I give up trying to understand."

"Good," I snapped. "Don't understand me."

CHAPTER 86 - DANIEL

No sooner had I entered my room than I received a text message from Duncan. "Jam @ Kirks" it read. It was already eleven-thirty, but wired from my evening of hard work and confession, an hour of playing bass would do me good.

At the very least, I would return home tired enough to sleep. Besides, I wasn't picking up Eli until mid-morning. On the assumption that she was tired, we could take a cozy nap together. After lunch, when Rachel and I had the editing bay again, then I needed to function.

The guys were warming up when I arrived with a six-pack under my arm and some joints. I was glad it was only the four of us. Often I would arrive at Kirk's and find a party. Tonight I was not in the mood.

The guys surrounded me as I laid my wares down on the makeshift coffee table. Ron picked up a joint and sniffed its length. "This is good," he smiled.

Kirk lit one too.   He inhaled deeply. "Good shit, Newman," he proclaimed.

I smiled, pleased that they enjoyed my stash. For now, I popped open a beer.

I'd almost forgotten how much I enjoyed jamming. It had been a while. Eli enjoyed the music, but she didn't like me coming here.

This part of my life Eli and I mutually decided not to share. When I partied, invariably I would stumble home in the middle of the night smelling like pot and beer, wasted from one or both. Eli didn't have to say anything. Eli disapproved, but she was tolerant, never giving me an ultimatum. Eli knew by not stopping me that I probably partied less frequently than I would otherwise have done.

Shit! Phoebe and Amelia arrived with their posse. Who the hell let them in?

Through the corner of my eye, I saw Amelia perched on the edge of the coffee table trying to get my attention. It was a lose-lose. If I continued ignoring her, Amelia would win, knowing her presence was getting to me. If I looked her way, Amelia would win, thinking I was interested in spending another night with her.

I could safely ignore Amelia until we took a break. Unfortunately, that was soon.

Amelia lit a joint and greeted me with a peck on the cheek as I lay down my bass, acting as though she were my date. This was the last thing I wanted.

"Here," Amelia said, smiling coquettishly.

Amelia held the joint to my lips. I had no choice but to take it and inhale. A few hits would take the edge off. More than a few hits were what I feared.

"Thanks, Amelia," I said casually.

"Are you avoiding me tonight, Dan?" Amelia asked, her voice syrupy sweet.

"Why do you say that?" I asked.

"Eye contact. Since I arrived you've avoided making eye contact with me."

"Don't be ridiculous," But Amelia was right.

Amelia's stare bored into me. I could no longer avoid eye contact. I took a deep hit. Amelia smiled, and ran her finger along my jawbone, ending with gently touching my lip. My pulse sped up. I did not want the excitement generated by Amelia's touch.

Damn her! Amelia knew exactly what she was doing.

"Dan," she said deliberately, "You are afraid of me."

I laughed nervously.

"Mary Poppins isn't here and you're afraid we'll end up together again."

I inhaled another deep hit. Amelia was right. I didn't want her knowing that I knew.

"Don't flatter yourself, Amelia," I answered defensively.

"Mary still in the sick house?"

"I'm springing my girlfriend in the morning," I emphasized the word 'girlfriend.'

"Girlfriend? Yeah, right."

Amelia took back the joint and let her fingers rest on mine. She inhaled deeply and passed the joint back to me. Again her fingers lingered, touching mine. Amelia's fingers were warm and soft, and expert at getting what they wanted.

I was mellow, on my way to getting wasted. Amelia kept her hand on my face and reached up to kiss my lips.

"Amelia, cut it out. I'm taken." I couldn't help grinning, the grin of a wasted man.

"Dan," Amelia said in a flirty voice, "You know you want me."

I laughed nervously. Amelia was right. I didn't want Amelia to be right.

"Amelia, you're worse than poison."

"What's worse than poison?" she asked. Then Amelia opened a button on her shirt. She was bra-less.

I took another hit. My eyes fixated on her small but lovely breasts. Completely wasted, I had little control over what I said or did.

"Crystal meth," I laughed. "You're like crystal meth. Dangerous and unhealthy, but totally addicting." I desperately wanted to touch those breasts.

Amelia grabbed my hips and provocatively thrust hers against me.

"Then you're crack cocaine. A little has me wanting more."

Amelia and I giggled uncontrollably, two completely besotted souls.

"Let's get out of here, Dan," she whispered and sucked my ear lobe. Whoa!

I kissed Amelia's lips roughly. We shared hazy wasted smiles knowing what waited at her nearby house.

Sunlight, harsh and glaring woke me. Where the hell was I? Not in my bed, that was for sure. The hand wrapped around my hip was not small and the fingers were not delicate with perfectly manicured nails.

Shit! They belonged to Amelia! What little I was capable of remembering of last night came flooding back. Completely wasted, sex with Amelia had been unavoidable. But spending the night? Shit! I never spent the night with anyone but Elizabeth.

I grabbed my eyeglasses off the desk. I had to get out of here before Amelia woke.

A glance at the clock and I sat bolt upright. Shit! It was after eight already! I'd told Elizabeth I'd be by bright and early to spring her. It would no longer be so early.

"Good morning, Dan," a sleepy Amelia purred.

"I've got to get out of here," I said urgently as I slipped out of the bed.

Amelia reached for me. "What's the rush? It's Saturday."

I found my jeans. With my back to Amelia, I pulled them up and fastened the button. "Elizabeth is expecting me," I answered as I yanked the zipper closed.

"Come back to bed, Dan. She can wait."

I turned back to Amelia. "No, she can't. I promised Eli I'd be there. I'm so late."

My shirt sat dumped on the desk. I reached for it and shook it out. It's odor was unmistakable, yet I held the fabric before my nose for confirmation.

"Ugh! This reeks!" I couldn't wear this. Eli would kill me.

I did some quick thinking and remembered I had a week's worth of shirts in the trunk of my car, having stopped by the dry cleaner yesterday afternoon. Having forgotten to bring them up to my room, it was like having a closet on wheels.

What else smelled rank? I cupped my hands around my mouth and blew. Gross! Much as I assumed, my breath was disgusting.

"Ugh! Sour keg breath," I complained. I could not greet Eli in this condition.

"Amelia, hand me a towel. I need to shower." She stared as though she didn't understand my simple request.

"Do you have a spare toothbrush?" I added. "I can't smell like pot and stale beer. Elizabeth hates when I get wasted."

"Can't say I blame her," Amelia answered bitterly. "Ya think she suspects what happens next?"

I rolled my eyes. "Look, Amelia, I need that towel and toothbrush. I don't have time to get back to Berkeley," I said frantically.

"And I should help you cover-up your extra-curricular activities; why?"

I stopped short and considered it. I suppose I was asking a lot of Amelia by trying to enlist her aide in covering up my indiscretions.

"If you had to meet James, I'd give you a towel and a toothbrush without hesitation."

"Isn't that big of you." Amelia said sarcastically.

Amelia was proving to be a frustrating pain in the ass this morning. Maybe that's how she always was in the morning. I didn't know or want to know.

I took a deep breath. "Let's be adults, Amelia. The past two nights were fun. But we were wasted or they wouldn't have happened. You're James' lady. Eli is mine. I would never do anything to sabotage what you have with him. I expect the same from you. Otherwise, what were you doing spending the night with me? Towel?"

"You're so clueless, Dan. I'd have dropped James in a flash if you'd asked."

"I've never led you on, Amelia."

"Maybe not. But here you are. Again."

"I've got to shower, Amelia."

"You fucking bastard!" she cried. "I won't sabotage your relationship with Mary Poppins, but I certainly won't help you. Just get the hell out of here, Dan."

CHAPTER 87 - DANIEL

The sound of falling water greeted me as I entered Elizabeth's infirmary room. Then the volume of the shower decreased and finally stopped. Anticipating Eli's entrance me made me grin.

The metal against metal sound of the bathroom door brought me back to the moment. Elizabeth emerged dressed in navy plaid pajama pants and a magenta t-shirt. Her hair was in a towel and she was holding the shirt she had slept in.

"You're early," Elizabeth said smiling in delight.

Unbelievably, I was. After racing home from Amelia's, I had taken what was assuredly the shortest shower on record, brushed my teeth, and changed into clean clothes. My hair still damp, I smelled like me again.

"I couldn't stay away," I answered as I enveloped Elizabeth in my arms. I held her tightly, not wanting to let her go. Eli was my home.

I pulled the towel off Eli's head and let it drop to the floor, releasing a tumble of wet auburn waves. The light fragrance of Bumble & Bumble was intoxicating. I took her face in my hands. Elizabeth's eyes were clear, no longer glazed by fever.

"Baby, you look great. How are you today?"

"Not perfect, but much improved."

"Can I make you more perfect?"

Without waiting for an answer, I pressed my lips to hers. I wanted Eli to feel my love.

Eli's response was immediate; her lips parting for me. Three weeks. I could keep Amelia at bay for that long. I had no choice.

CHAPTER 88 - ELIZABETH

"It's so good to be home."

I playfully fell back onto the pillows. Danny followed, jumping onto the bed next to me. I laughed as my body bounced up in response to the force of his hard landing.

Then Danny propped himself on his elbow. Sapphire eyes glowed as he starred at me. I reached for him and eagerly pressed my lips to his, reigniting the kiss the nurse had interrupted. This time, Danny reached under my t-shirt and unhooked my bra. His touch sent shivers vibrating through me. How I'd missed him.

"Sure you're up to it?" he asked.

I wanted Danny so badly, but I remained weak. I hated disappointing him.

Danny read through my hesitation and removed his hand.

"It's okay. I'm perfectly happy cuddling. Baby, you need to recover."

"Thank you," I said, relieved that Danny had taken the decision from me.

Snuggled in each other's arms, we drifted off to sleep.

"I'm spending the afternoon with Rachel," Danny said as we returned from lunch. "I don't know when I'll be back. It could be late. I want you to rest, so I've instructed the roomies to take you to dinner. Those are orders, young lady."

Danny kissed my forehead for emphasis. I smiled shyly. Danny was making such a fuss. Still, his love touched me.

After Danny left me to join Rachel, I made myself comfortable among the pillows and settled in with a political science book. The pressure was on. I had fallen behind and time remaining in the semester was short.

But soon my eyelids weighed heavily. Danny's voice ordering me to rest echoed in my brain. I sighed, frustrated. As always, Danny was right. In half an hour, I'd read only one page. I was too tired.

Marking my place, I laid the book down on the desk, covered myself with the comforter, and closed my eyes. The scent of Danny, that wonderful, warm, masculine aroma, embraced me. Feeling loved and secure, I fell asleep within moments.

CHAPTER 89 - DANIEL

"That's it! I think." I checked the meticulous list of notes on my laptop that represented the work I wanted completed. Then I spun around in my swivel chair, a big grin on my face.

"Rach, we are out of here!" I exclaimed.

"It's only ten o'clock. Are you sure?" Rachel asked doubtfully.

"Yep. Don't you want to get out of here? I laughed. "It is Saturday night."

"Well, yeah. I'm just surprised. I didn't even make plans."

"So you'll go to The Cellar. I'm sure your friends will be there."

"Are you going?"

"Not tonight," I grinned, hyper with joy.

"Right. You have a hot date with someone who actually is your girlfriend. That is who you're spending tonight with or shouldn't I make that assumption?"

My smile dropped. "Rachel, don't start," I warned.

Why must she do this? Rachel hadn't spoken a word about Amelia all day. Couldn't she let sleeping dogs lie? I guess not.

"Just checking, because Elizabeth might notice if you don't come home."

"Eli will be very happy when I get home. But it's not going to be a hot date. Eli has the flu, remember?"

"Of course I do. I just didn't think that would hold you back."

"Then Rach, you don't know squat about me and Eli," I answered angrily.

"At this point, you're right. Elizabeth hasn't been available for girl talk in a while."

"It so happens I am perfectly happy simply being with my lady. I half expect to find Eli sleeping and if she is, I will gladly crawl in beside her because I am beat. If I'm fortunate and she's awake, then if she is up to it, we might watch a DVD. Hot night, huh Rach? It is for me."

Any night with Eli was a hot night as far as I was concerned.

"After this week, I didn't think you only wanted companionship."

"Then you insult both me and Elizabeth. Clearly you have never been in a serious relationship."

"You're right. I haven't. I do know when I am, I won't put up with any B.S."

"Good luck with that, Rach. He'll have some other flaw. We all do."

"Danny, you really have no shame, do you?"

I took a deep breath. I tired of Rachel's harping. It was threatening to end our friendship if she continued.

"Rachel, this is the last time I am going to discuss this. Either accept what I tell you or we can't continue as friends."

Rachel considered my words. "I'll try to understand," she relented.

"Good, because I value our friendship."

"So do I, but I value Elizabeth's more."

"I know you do. Rach, you alone understand how hard I fought my feelings for Elizabeth. But Eli understood my ambivalence toward being in a committed relationship. Hell, that was why I broke up with Juliette; she wanted me 24/7."

"I thought Juliette broke up with you because you were sleeping with Elizabeth."

"I was taking care of Eli, not sleeping with her. All right, so Juliette broke up with me. But I was about to because she wanted me 24/7."

"Aren't you with Elizabeth 24/7?"

"Yes. But it's different. I love Elizabeth."

"What about Amelia? Danny, you've made me this middle-man. I'm keeping secrets from my dearest friend knowing I'll be helping her through the heartbreak when it comes. And Danny, it will come. Donnelly is a small place."

"Rach, I'm not as bad as you make me out to be."

"What a relief," Rachel answered sarcastically. I ignored her.

"Fact is, I've only cheated a couple of times and that was when Eli wasn't with me and I've been wasted."

"So now she's home and finals are coming so you'll behave? What happens this summer when you're in Vancouver and she's not?"

"Nothing to worry about," I laughed. "Eli's coming up every weekend."

"And the other five nights?" Rachel asked caustically.

"Rach, you're such a cynic."

"I'm a realist who doesn't trust you, Danny."

"I will be the hardest working boy in Canada. Dad is depending on me. I can't afford to party. Dad's reputation is at stake."

"What about the girls? They have those in Vancouver."

"Are you kidding me? I'm working for Dad. If I did anything that could hurt Eli, Dad would send me packing in an instant."

CHAPTER 90 - DANIEL

The suite seemed eerily empty when I returned. A succinct note from Cam was affixed to the door. "She slept. We went to the deli. She ate. She went back to sleep. See you tomorrow." I was relieved that Elizabeth had eaten something. At lunch she had played with her food.

The bedroom door was ajar. Remaining silent, I pushed it open. My beautiful angel was in pajamas, cuddled up under the comforter, a sweet smile on her lips, fast asleep.

I closed the door and returned to the common room. I needed to unwind. Confession to a priest might soothe the soul, but confession to Rachel had the opposite effect. Unlike clergy, she was not shy with being judgmental. Now I felt even worse. Maybe that was good; a necessary kick in the butt to right me.

In the refrigerator I found a bottle of beer. I settled on the couch to watch an old sit-com while I downed it. The lack of sleep had caught up to me. An early night would do me good.

I tiptoed into the bedroom and removed my clothes. With utmost caution, I climbed over Eli and settled under the comforter next to her. I gently wrapped my arm around Eli and kissed her forehead. I was pleased by its coolness. My lady was on the mend.

Deep in sleep, Eli responded to my nearness. She grinned and mumbled incoherently. I almost laughed. Then Eli wiggled nearer, seeking comfort. Eli in my arms sleeping made me whole again. Life could not be better than this. Unless I did something stupid and blew it.

CHAPTER 91 - ELIZABETH

What a perfect day! I woke to sunlight filtering through the window shade, but my glee came from being clearheaded and well rested. I was finally better.

I turned my head and shifted my weight to glimpse the handsome man lying beside me. Danny's stubble-covered face brought me joy.

Danny and I hadn't spent a night together in nearly two weeks. Finding myself wrapped in Danny's embrace, I marveled that a man as strong as he was so soft; a man as arrogant as he was so tender.

My mind drifted to the upcoming summer break, now only three short weeks away. I was ambivalent. I looked forward to working for Dad and having my first year of college completed, but already I missed Danny.

Involuntarily, I pressed his hands tightly against me, and my stomach rumbled. Danny instantly nuzzled my neck and shoulder. The warm ticklish sensation made me squirm. Then Danny tightened his hold. I couldn't escape this tortuous pleasure.

"Stop!" I laughed. "Stop it!"

In a single, fluid motion Danny twisted me in his arms. I came face-to-face with his gleeful grin and glowing cobalt eyes.

"Good morning, beautiful," Danny laughed.

"I'm starving," I announced.

Danny pressed his lips against mine and ran his tongue across my lower lip, begging entrance to my mouth. I pulled back.

"That wasn't what I meant," I laughed. "I need food. When's breakfast?"

Danny twirled a lock of my hair around his finger, enjoying its smoothness.

"Baby, you're feeing better?" he asked hopefully.

"I think so," I answered hesitantly.

"You're not sure?"

"I won't declare victory until I make it through the day."

"Fair enough," Danny answered. Then he paused before adding, "I can help."

With a devilish twinkle in his eyes, Danny started tickling me again.

"Stop! Cut it out!" I protested to no avail as I squirmed against him.

Finally, Danny stopped and gathered me in his arms. He pulled me to his bare chest and declared, "I'm so glad you're back."

"Me too," I answered as my arms wrapped around Danny's neck.

No couple could be more content than we were.

CHAPTER 92 - ELIZABETH

"Is that really what you're wearing tonight?" Rachel shook her head, disapproving my dress, as I paused for her to zip me up. Tonight Danny and Rachel's short film was being screened and Danny and I were going formal, dressed in our outfits from Steve's premiere.

Rachel dressed in an untailored black blazer over jeans, more in line with what the other student-filmmakers were wearing, but not Danny.

"Tonight I'm Danny's arm-candy," I explained, "And he wants me as sugary as possible." Our clothing was over the top, but dressing-up was an easy way to please Danny.

"Arm-candy? That's so demeaning."

I eased my feet into my Jimmy Choo's. "I was joking, Rachel."

Then I picked up a lipstick tube, posed before the mirror and applied the soft pink color.

"Danny loves this dress. He's been looking for an excuse for me to wear it again, and tonight's the night."

"Tonight's the night! That better be with me, babe."

Danny brimmed with enthusiasm. He wrapped his arms around my waist, and mindful of my makeup, kissed my neck. I shuddered at his soft lips on my bare skin. Danny squeezed me tighter in acknowledgment of the pleasure only he could give me.

"I didn't hear you come in," I squealed in delight.

As I pivoted in his hands, my breath caught in my throat. Danny was so handsome!

I slipped my hands around Danny's neck and let him nibble at my lips and kiss my throat. My chin tilted upward. I gasped. I was all his.

"I'm going to brush my hair," an awkward Rachel announced, and she left us.

Danny released me and appraised my appearance.

"Eli, you look amazing, babe!"

I was glowing. Danny in his well-cut suit with his sparkling sapphire eyes set my heart a flutter. I'd be in trouble if he ever went corporate and dressed this way every day.

"You're pretty hot yourself."

I tried to regain my composure, but Danny pulled me back into his arms with a flourish and we laughed. Then he kissed my neck and shoulder again, sending bolts of electricity pulsating through me.

"Eli, we better get going," Danny whispered by my ear, unleashing more shivers. He thoroughly enjoyed my reaction to his breath against my ear.

"Damn!" I exclaimed, but I was laughing.

"We'll play later, young lady."

Touching Danny's face, I again kissed his lips, and he tightened his hold around my waist.

"We'd better get Rachel before we miss your screening," I whispered.

Danny took my face in his hands and turned on his full-wattage charm.

"I could always have Rachel represent me," he whispered.

"Then why did we get all dressed up?"

"Elizabeth, you have no idea what that dress does to me."

"Yes, I do. The same thing that suit does to me."

"Oh, babe. I love you so much."

Danny joined his lips to mine with searing intensity. I felt him hard against me as my arms around his neck pressed us closer. Danny cupped my face with one hand while we kissed, and his other hand reached for my zipper, pulling it halfway down. Exposed to his gentle touch, my pulse beat out of control. I did not want this moment to end.

A knock on the door interrupted us. Danny and I froze, locked in each other's arms. I flushed. Rachel!

"Are you coming? If not, I can go alone."

"We'll be right with you," Danny awkwardly replied.

"I'll be waiting." Rachel scowled before leaving the room.

"You have lipstick on your face. Let me."

I reached for a tissue and delicately dabbed Danny's cheek and chin while he grinned. Danny reached for my hand and delicately kissed my palm. I blushed and he smirked. Then I released my hand to adjust Danny's tie and smooth his lapels.

"Zipper me?" I asked.

As Danny fastened my dress, we grinned at each other, two mischievous children caught misbehaving by mother.

"Can we go now?" Rachel hissed as we emerged from my room.

"Yeah, Rach. What are you waiting for? We're going to be late."

I couldn't help laughing at Danny while Rachel rolled her eyes in disgust.

As I suspected, all eyes were on us as we entered the small screening room. So what if everyone else was wearing jeans? If the Newmans wanted to wear formal attire, who would dare question it?

"Mr. Newman, Miss Bergman. Nice of you to join us," the professor sneered. "Now we can begin."

If looks could kill, Danny and I would be dead from Rachel's fury. One of Donnelly's most conscientious student, and the professor had just called her out.

Danny settled in, holding my hand on his thigh. I filled with anticipation. Danny was so eager for me to finally see their film! He had wanted to surprise me. This was the first time he was even discussing the film with me.

The professor had compiled everyone's five to seven minutes long films into one DVD. The event would be over in less than an hour and a half.

Almost two-thirds through the program came Danny and Rachel's film. Pride filled me at the opening credit, "A film by Daniel M. Newman." I squeezed his hand and kissed his cheek. I imagined this was how Ellen felt at Steve's premieres. Did the exhilaration diminish over time? I hoped not.

Seven short minutes later it was over. Danny's film was great! I hadn't known what to expect. Short films were a genre I never paid any attention to. My parents always did features as did everyone else I knew unless they did television.

"I loved it!" I whispered to Danny.

We exchanged megawatt smiles and kisses. Then I leaned across to squeeze Rachel's hand and exchange quick cheek pecks. The next film was about to begin.

"We'll catch up to you at The Cellar," Danny told Rachel after the screenings ended. A group of student filmmakers was going. "We won't be long."

Danny took my hand. I had no idea where we were going as he spirited me away to his car. His energy level had plummeted compared to only minutes earlier. Inside the auditorium Danny had been gracious, chatting with everyone whether they were professors or other students. Now Danny was subdued.

We didn't go far. A few minutes later, Danny parked the BMW off the side of the road under a stand of trees and got out. This was the same beautiful hill overlooking the lake where we'd gone traying in the winter. Covered in grass, wildflowers were blooming and the deciduous trees were full with spring finery.

Danny opened my door, took my hand, and helped me out of the car. I obediently followed him off the path a short way and onto the grass. In my heels, walking was difficult. I held Danny's hand firmly to keep from stumbling.

Soon we stopped in a clearing. Danny pulled me into his arms and held me tight, his chin resting on my shoulder, while I wrapped my arms around him. We stood holding each other, silently contemplating. Not romantic, it was more therapeutic than anything.

"Thanks, Sweetheart," Danny finally said in a measured cadence.

"Is something the matter?" He should be thrilled from his triumph.

"No, baby. I need to decompress."

"Decompress?"

"Quiet time. Get my head together before heading back into the fray."

"The fray?"

"Tonight's been difficult for me."

"Why? I thought the screening went well."

"Maybe. I've been under a lot of pressure." Danny let go of me and rotated his shoulders and neck. "I'm so tight," he complained.

"Let me see," I offered. I reached up, placed my hands on Danny's shoulders, and began to slowly knead. Hardened knots in Danny's shoulders were tight as could be.

"Your knots have knots, dear." I empathized.

"If we were home I'd call Dad's masseuse, Johan. He's the best hands in L.A."

"I can try later," I smiled.

Danny reached behind, took my hands, and swung me around. He pretended to examine my hands and then gently kissed my palms.

"Johan's are bigger and stronger, but these will do," Danny said with a smile. Then he turned serious. "Tell me the truth, Eli. What did you think of my film? It's okay if you hated it."

I paused for a moment, searching for the right words. I had enjoyed the film, but unqualified approval was not what Danny wanted. He wouldn't believe me anyway.

"It's difficult," I slowly began. "I enjoyed your film. Very much, but Danny, I don't have the experience to judge. I've never seen short films before. I don't know what they're supposed to be like."

Danny took my head in his hands and kissed me. He smiled, relieved.

"Thank you, baby."

"I didn't really tell you anything," I protested.

"Yes, you did. You told me I can trust you because you won't bullshit."

"Feel better?"

"Yes. No, not really. I've been under so much pressure."

"You need to let it go."

"You're right. I bring it on myself, you know."

"I know. Only you expect perfection. Nobody else does."

"I have to be better than everyone, Eli. I have to."

I hugged one arm around Danny's waist and placed the other hand on his cheek.

"Danny, don't do this. You need to want to be the best for yourself. Forget Steven Newman."

"I can't. He's my Dad."

"I understand. It's why I won't study acting. I couldn't bear the comparisons with Mom. But you've jumped in with both feet. You can't avoid it. Summer is coming. Talk to Steve."

"Dad doesn't have time for me," Danny said sadly.

Then he gathered my hands and held me against his sculpted chest.

"I'm so lucky I have you Eli. You're the only one who understands me."

Danny pressed against me and we kissed, cautiously at first and then passionately. His hands were warm and secure against my bare back. Then Danny ran his fingertip up my spine causing me to squirm and giggle.

"Danny! Cut it out!"

"No," he laughed, "this is fun."

I pivoted to avoid being tickled. His arms were now around my waist; my back against his front. Danny swept my hair back and playfully kissed my shoulder and neck. Bliss! If only we had a blanket.

Soon Danny was leading me by the hand through the doors of the Student Center to join our friends in The Cellar. What a change! Danny's demeanor had transformed. He was happy again and full of energy.

"Come here," Danny ordered.

Smiling wickedly, Danny pulled me over to the corner just past the plate glass double-door entrance and gathered me in his arms, crushing his lips to mine. They were on fire. I eagerly responded, parting my lips, welcoming his exploring tongue. My arms around Danny's neck kept us glued together. Danny's strong but soft hands on my back, radiated electricity. Our hearts beat rapidly as one.

"You are so evil, Daniel," I whispered. Our foreheads touched. Danny again grinned mischievously.

"Isn't that great?" he whispered. My breath hitched. I was so aroused.

Before I could answer, Danny was kissing me again. We couldn't get enough of each other. There was something about Danny and that suit; he was so damned hot.

"E, we should probably get downstairs already," Danny whispered. His damned sapphire eyes melted me. Danny's kisses had left me intoxicated. I felt drunk.

"You're right. We should." I pressed against Danny. "Not yet."

"Oh, babe! You are so hot tonight," he whispered.

I nodded, grinning with lust. It was important that the most desirable girl Danny knew be me. If that meant participating in shameless public displays of affection, so be it. Being Danny's girl was all that mattered.

"Eli, have I told you how much I love you?"

"Not in at least an hour," I flirted.

"An hour? That's way too long. Baby, I love you so much it hurts."

"I feel the same about you, Danny. Can we go home?"

"We can't. I promised everyone we'd come to The Cellar."

"That's so unfair."

"Why is that unfair?" Danny smirked.

"I'm a spoiled rich girl. I want what I want when I want it," I said breathlessly into Danny's ear while I held his face in my hands.

"And what do you want, my spoiled rich girl?"

My lips against Danny's ear, I whispered, "You. I want to make love. Now."

I began kissing Danny again, enjoying his hands on my back and rear.

"E, we'd better stop. I can't resist you much longer."

"I can't resist you now."

Danny took my hands. "Come with me," he said with urgency.

"Where are we going?"

"Upstairs. Someplace private."

More than willingly, I let Danny lead us. If possible, the unknown was getting me even more excited. My pulse raced. Where were we going?

The third floor handicapped restroom? It was private. Danny locked the door behind us.

Giddy from our love fulfilled, Danny and I arrived at The Cellar. Several tables had been pushed together to accommodate the sizable group of film students. Arriving so late, there was only one chair left. Danny grabbed it and settled me onto his lap. I enjoyed Danny's strong arms wrapped around my waist, and the scent of his cologne playing on my nostrils.

This was Danny's crowd, not mine. He was the star and the ambitious student filmmakers showered him with the attention and respect worthy of "The Godfather."

I didn't know these students as Danny rarely socialized with them, but they all knew me or at least who I was. The students addressed me with cautious familiarity. I'd seen it before. I was the celebrities' daughter, and they made an effort to ignore it. They tried behaving casually, as though they didn't know who I was, but of course they did.

They were film students. They couldn't appear obvious, as though they wanted anything from me. Of course to a person, each one if they were being honest, wanted the world from me, and from Danny too. Becoming friends with either of us could provide the boost that might launch their hoped-for careers.

Too astute to be fooled, Rachel was uncomfortable with the attention she was receiving. She had friends in the department, but the interlopers were out in full force.

Surveying the scene, an amusing thought crossed my mind. Did anyone but me realize that Danny and I were the children they all hoped to eventually raise?

Boredom and lust were leading me to be unusually cynical this evening. I desperately wanted any excuse for Danny to take me upstairs and make love again. His knees rocking between my thighs didn't help. I flushed, about to combust.

"Will your parents be working together again soon?" A girl named Jess jarred me from my reverie.

"Dad's one of Steven's producers on the project Danny's working on this summer," I replied.

"I meant your mother," Jess brusquely clarified.

"Oh, her." I said, disappointed that Dad didn't count. "Nothing's on the calendar, but if the right project came along, they'd love it."

"Will you also be working in Vancouver?"

"God, no!" I exclaimed.

"Don't you want to be together?" Jess asked, surprised by my reaction.

"Of course, but not at work. I would never work with Danny. I'm perfectly content flying up every weekend to visit. Physical production doesn't interest me."

"Wouldn't it be fun hanging out on the set?" Jess asked.

"No, not really. Danny will be working. Besides, I have a summer job in L.A."

"Doing what?"

"Working for my Dad in development," I answered proudly.

Danny squeezed me tightly, and nuzzled my neck.

"And Daddy gives you off every Friday. Does Mike suspect the epic reunions we have planned?"

I circled Danny's neck with my hands and kissed him. "Probably," I answered with a flirty grin, though the thought of Dad embarrassed me.

Danny returned to holding court. Once more I was the bored, observing spouse.

Whoever had Rachel cornered, her fed up expression said that she'd had enough.

Rachel smiled, lips tight, ending the discussion. She stopped by Danny and I, en route to the restroom to escape.

"How's Barbie and Ken?" Rachel greeted us cheerfully. "What took you so long?"

"Ken needed to decompress," I answered.

"Decompress?"

"Danny needed an attitude adjustment, so we adjusted it."

Rachel snickered. "You went back to the dorm, didn't you?"

"No, we didn't," Danny responded.

"C'mon. I can tell. Elizabeth can't fool me." I flushed scarlet. "See. I'm so right!"

"You're wrong, Rach. If we'd gone back to the dorm, we'd still be there."

"We sure would be. Can we go soon?" I kissed Danny for emphasis.

"In a little, babe."

"I didn't ask before, but what's with Barbie and Ken?"

"We are not plastic dolls," I responded, and I frowned.

"I meant the clothes."

"I love that dress on Eli. I wanted her to wear it again."

"That is a great dress," a nearby girl chimed in. "Didn't I see that in "People"?"

"Thank you. Yes, you did," I answered pleasantly.

Danny grinned. "Why don't you wear dresses more often? I love your legs."

Danny had a point. I did prefer wearing skirts, but denim was the uniform at Donnelly.

The same girl stared, waiting for a chance to enter our conversation.

"Come with me to the restroom," Rachel said in an attempt to rescue me.

"I'll be right back." I kissed Danny's cheek and hopped off his lap.

"Hey," he said. Danny reached for my face and kissed me. "Don't be long, baby."

Danny's kiss left me nearly swooning, and I left with Rachel who rolled her eyes.

"You guys are disgusting tonight," she said.

"We can't help it if we're in love."

Rachel sighed. Did she know the fun I was having with her?

I followed Rachel into the restroom.

"I'm so sick of these people," Rachel ranted. "Either they're the biggest idiots or they think I am. They're so obvious. They think by being nice to me they'll become friends with you and Danny. I hate it!"

"Calm down, Rach. I'm sorry we put you through that. They are stupid if they think you don't read right through them. There's only one thing Danny and I can do."

"What's that?"

"Danny and I will stop being your friends."

"Perfect!" And Rachel and I burst into laughter.

"So you and Danny didn't go back to Berkeley? That's hard to believe."

"Well, believe it," I answered. "Danny was feeling down after the screening. He's been under a lot more pressure than you know. Danny fears everyone's waiting for him to fail. If he wasn't strong, he could have had a breakdown."

"He didn't say that, but Danny has been crazed lately," Rachel answered pensively. "It must be hell to follow your father when he's a legend."

"Exactly. That's why Danny needed to decompress."

"Decompress. That's a euphemism I haven't heard before."

"C'mon Rach. That wasn't what Danny meant."

"Maybe," she smirked, "But you can't keep secrets from me young lady."

Rachel raised an eyebrow, and I blushed.

"Let's just say that I'm a very nice girlfriend who is rightfully loved by her boyfriend and leave it at that."

CHAPTER 93 - DANIEL

There she was! I grabbed Eli's hand and pulled her back on to my lap.

"What took so long, babe?" My lips nearly touching her ear made Elizabeth shiver.

"There was a line."

"I'm tired of sitting. Let's dance."

Gleeful, Eli bounced off my thighs. I took her hand and led her to the dance floor. A slow song played. I found that very agreeable; any excuse to touch her.

I placed one hand on Eli's back and clasped her delicate hand. Soft and warm with a light floral scent wafting off her hair, she was magic.

Eli placed her other hand on my shoulder. Her feather light touch melted me. A lovely smile lit her face so brightly I basked in her glow. I removed my hand from her back and carefully spun her to the beat. Then she stumbled.

Eli smiled at her unexpected lack of grace executing a move that should have been perfunctory given her dance training. Another spin, another stumble. Eli shrugged, and then giggled. Oh, hell! I was responsible for her wearing those shoes. I certainly didn't want her re-injuring her ankle. One final spin and Eli was safe in my arms again.

I relished holding her, my hands circling her slender waist. Eli locked her hands behind my neck and leaned against me, scattering auburn waves to the beat of the music.

Eli was the picture of perfect contentment. I couldn't help smiling at my beautiful lady, so proud that it was me who made her this happy.

Sparkling emerald eyes enchanted me when she tilted her head up. Those full pink lips, slightly parted, bewitched me. Knowing how sweet they tasted, I had no choice but to kiss them.

"Can we go home?" Elizabeth whispered.

I smirked. I knew what she wanted. Anyone looking into her adoring eyes would know. It was unmistakable. I would play with Elizabeth a while longer. I enjoyed watching my usually controlled girl on the verge of losing it.

"Please, Daniel," Elizabeth begged. "I'm tired of being in public,"

I wanted her to ask for it. It was fun forcing Eli from her comfort zone. She spent too much time there.

"A few more minutes." If I could last that long.

Eli reached up to kiss me but I reacted first. I leaned down and trailed kisses from Eli's neck to her shoulder. She shivered and tightened her grip. Eli turned her head slightly to the side so I could kiss her neck and shoulder again. Her eyes were slits of ecstasy.

Eli abruptly reached her hands back around my neck.

"Kiss me like you're madly in love," she whispered.

"I am madly in love," I whispered back.

"Please, show it," Eli urged. "Those awful girls from The Village just arrived."

Shit! Amelia and Phoebe. Double shit!

"Why are they watching us? It's been over four months already!" Elizabeth complained. "Don't they get that we're not breaking up?"

"It still bothers you, doesn't it?" I asked uncomfortably, but at the same time relieved that Elizabeth only knew about January.

"No." My raised eyebrow signaled doubt. "Well, maybe sometimes. Only a little." Eli sighed. "Okay. A lot, when I'm forced to think about it."

"Elizabeth," I locked on her emerald eyes, "Lay it to rest, baby. It's not part of our lives. You're the only woman I've ever loved."

I took Eli's upturned face and crushed our lips together. My arms around her back, I held her as close as possible. My hand wandered down her back and squeezed her shapely bottom. I wanted Eli back in the mood.

"Danny, we're in public!" Elizabeth squealed. Too bad! That ass belonged to me.

"Not for long, Eli. Let's go."

We walked off the dance floor wrapped around each other and ran right into Amelia, Phoebe and Jasmine. I prayed we would safely leave The Cellar.

"Dan," Phoebe greeted me curtly.

"Ladies," I greeted them breezily. Eli said nothing.

"So, she's recovered from the flu, I see," Amelia sneered.

"How do you ...?" Eli began, a puzzled expression on her face.

"It's amazing what a few days in the infirmary can do," I answered, effectively cutting Eli off. Amelia and Phoebe scowled.

Elizabeth quickly recovered her composure. Remembering which team she was on, Eli smiled at me with adoring eyes.

"It was the exemplary home care that really made the difference," she said and squeezed my waist. Then Eli kissed my cheek.

"And that's exactly where we're going. Mrs. Newman needs more home care. Later, ladies," We left the three girls dumbfounded, with jaws dropped open.

CHAPTER 94 - DANIEL

Cartons surrounded me. Taking a break from studying, I was filing out Fedex waybills. Two more and I'd be done. Having spent the last two weeks writing papers and take-home exams, I was burned-out. I had earned a couple of hours off.

Elizabeth was taking her French final. She wouldn't be back for another hour. We were flying home in two days. I needed to call Mom and inform her of my important decision.

Mom was probably sleeping, but she wouldn't mind. Mom had always made it clear that I could call her anytime. Eli too.

"What's wrong?" Mom was awake and eating breakfast as she answered.

"Nothing," I assured her. "Eli is taking a final, so it's a good time to talk."

"What don't you want Elizabeth to know, Daniel?" Mom asked suspiciously.

"Mom!"

"You said Elizabeth wasn't there. Danny, you're hiding something."

I laughed at her analysis. Mom was right, of course. Then I explained my plans.

"Whatever you need, count me in," Mom enthusiastically replied.

"And Mom, I want to visit Grandma. I haven't seen her in so long. I miss her."

"Mother will love it! Did you call her?"

"Not yet. I will later. I'm going to bring Eli. Grandma knows Eli, right?"

"Mother last saw Elizabeth at your bar mitzvah."

"That's what I thought. Grandma will love Eli."

"Daniel, my mother's going to immediately ask me when the wedding is."

"C'mon, Mom. She won't do that."

"Danny, Dad didn't meet Mother until I had no choice because she learned I was sharing a studio apartment with someone named Steven, not Stephanie."

"You told Grandma Dad was named Stephanie!" I laughed, picturing a long-haired Dad wearing a dress.

"For about a month," Mom confessed. "Then guilt took hold, and I had no choice but to bring Dad home if I wanted Grandpa to continue paying my share of the rent."

"We all know Eli's name is really Elizabeth, so that shouldn't be a problem."

"Does this mean you're completely committed to Elizabeth now? I want honesty, Daniel."

"I love Eli."

"And she loves you. Tell me something I don't know, Danny."

Why was Mom doing this? Because she knew as well as I did that I could never lie to her.

"Danny, have you cheated on Elizabeth again?" Mom asked bluntly.

The question I was dreading. I couldn't skirt a direct question from Mom.

"It would break Eli's heart if she found out."

"Oh, Danny!" Mom was crestfallen. I hated doing this to her.

"You're disappointed," I said flatly.

"I am. I thought you'd finally grown up and understood what love meant. Every time I talk to you it's Elizabeth this and Elizabeth that. And when I talk to her, it's all about you."

"I love Eli. She's the most important person in my life."

"Daniel? This is how you treat the most important person in your life?"

"It's only happened a couple of times, Mom. Eli wasn't around and I was wasted." I doubted that made it any better.

"Being wasted is not an excuse," she scolded. "Danny, you're certain Elizabeth hasn't found out?"

"I'm certain, Mom. I'd be missing important body parts if she did."

"Florida?" she asked.

"Yeah, Florida," I answered sheepishly. That all I would admit.

"Danny, why are you cheating on the woman you say you love? Elizabeth will find out. Then she'll be devastated and you'll be alone."

"I fear that every day, but I've never made her promises."

"Daniel, you're living with her. I'm sure Elizabeth's made certain assumptions."

"Eli knows I don't want to be like Dad."

"What does that mean, Daniel?" Mom's measured voice was rising.

"I'm sorry, Mom. I don't want to hurt you," I said apologetically.

"I'm tougher than you think. I live with Steven Newman."

"Mom, I'm sure you love Dad. So do I. But he hasn't always been a good husband."

"Danny."

"Mom, I love you. Don't make me talk about Dad," I pleaded.

"Aren't you though? It still hurts. It hurts even more knowing that you know."

"And it's been years. I don't want to wake up in fifteen years when I have my own kids and wonder what dating other women would have been like. That would crush Eli. She knows when I tell her I'm ready to settle down it will be for real. Eli won't ever have cause to doubt."

"I love you Danny, but you're naïve."

"I don't think so. Mom, I know this sounds weird, but it's been good for me. I get completely disgusted with myself. By then of course I'm sober and I wonder what the hell I've done. I hate myself for betraying Eli."

"I'm glad you have a conscious. At least I haven't totally failed you."

"Mom, you haven't failed me."

I knew at some point Jewish guilt would enter the picture.

"There's nobody like Eli. No other girl comes close."

"Remember that Danny, because you're right. No one can compare to Elizabeth. I had no idea Dad had damaged you to this degree. I tried so hard to insulate you…"

"Yeah." I was quiet, contemplating.

"Remember Danny, you aren't Dad. When he was younger, this wouldn't have been a dilemma for him. Dad plows straight ahead, never considering the potential damage. He's cocky, arrogant and always willing to take the biggest risks. That's how Dad became Dad. He never doubts himself."

"You're such opposites."

"Imagine if we weren't," Mom laughed.

"It would be non-stop mania."

"Steven is the only man I've ever loved, but I'm glad you're not like him. You don't need to be like him, Danny. You're a much more sensitive man. That's why Elizabeth loves you and why you're emotionally torn."

A half-hour later we were still talking. I can discuss anything with Mom. If we spoke more often, perhaps I wouldn't get into the messes I found myself in. Maybe I didn't speak to her more often because I wanted to get into these messes.

I gave Mom a list of things I wanted at the beach house when Eli and I arrived.

"She'll love this!" Mom exclaimed. "How did I get such a romantic son?"

"Too many Miranda Jordan movies?" I laughed. "I want everything perfect for Elizabeth. It's important I make our time in Malibu special." I meant this wholeheartedly. I wanted it special for me too.

"Danny, when Graciela cleans the house tomorrow, I'll have her move my things and Dad's to another bedroom. You take the master."

"Mom, that's your bedroom and Dad's." Her generous offer was completely unexpected.

"We're rarely there. If you want the week to be special, then you'll want to wake up in the one bedroom with a full ocean view."

Mom's suggestion, so full of love, touched me. I smiled, picturing Eli waking and standing out on the balcony.

"Now who's the romantic?" I laughed. "Thank you. Eli will love it."

CHAPTER 95 - ELIZABETH

Wednesday morning, after an endless night of parties, Danny and I clasped tired hands as the 767 smoothly lifted off into the clear New York skies.

After the flight attendant took our drink order I rose to get my iPad from the overhead compartment. Before I could do so, Danny grabbed my wrist and gently pulled me back to my seat.

I glanced at him, puzzled. "What's up?" I asked.

Danny smiled uncomfortably. He slid his fingers down my wrist to my hand. His other hand touched my cheek, light and feathery and Danny kissed my lips.

"I've changed our itinerary," he said.

That explained his uneasy edge. Danny was afraid I wouldn't like the new plan.

"What change?" I asked warily. I would only be disappointed if Danny eliminated our stay in Malibu.

"We'll stop to get my car, and then go to the beach," Danny explained. "Saturday we'll leave for Rancho Mirage and visit Grandma until Monday. I haven't seen her in over a year."

"Grandma? We're visiting Naomi?" Yikes!

CHAPTER 96 - ELIZABETH

The limousine sat waiting in the guest parking space when we arrived in Malibu. After garaging the Porsche, we met the driver at the entrance and he brought our luggage in. Once he drove off, Danny opened the door. With a devilish grin, he scooped me into his arms and carried me inside

"Welcome home, Sweetheart."

"Danny!" I laughed. "What are you doing?"

"Carrying you over the threshold of our first home."

"Our what? Steve and Ellen gave you the house?" With the Newmans, it was plausible, and I was fuzzy-headed enough from lack of sleep to have missed something.

Danny finally set me down near the glass patio doors. In the distance the ocean was choppy with breaking whitecaps.

Danny's hands circled my waist. He kissed my neck. "Not yet, but they will."

"Danny, you asked them?" I was outraged.

"I won't have to. My parents are never here. They'll see how happy we are and they'll give it to us."

Out of the corner of my eyes I spotted a vase of stunningly beautiful red roses. There must have been at least two-dozen in all.

"Those are gorgeous," I gasped.

"Not as gorgeous as the girl I bought them for." Danny beamed with pride. "I want you to feel at home."

"Danny, you've succeeded," I squealed.

Danny gave me a warm welcome home kiss. "Let's go upstairs."

Then he took my hand, but let me lead us up to the second floor. At the top of the stairs, I headed to the left and Danny tugged me to the right.

"This way," he smiled.

I knew I was tired, but I was certain I hadn't forgotten the layout of the house. It couldn't have changed since January. I yawned. This was confusing.

Danny wrapped me in his protective arms. "Poor, sleepyhead. Our bedroom is this way." Danny's nose touched mine, and he gently kissed me.

Only one room was to the right of the stairs. "Isn't that the master?" I mumbled.

Danny smirked. "Not anymore."

"Are you kidding me?" I asked, momentarily awake again.

"Mom wanted us to feel at home. She thought we'd enjoy waking to the ocean view."

"Won't we be in the way?" I didn't want to live out of our suitcases.

Danny laughed at my interpretation. "Mom had Graciela move their stuff to a guest room. The master is ours, baby."

"This is what you meant when you said it was our house."

"Yes. So let's get to OUR room and take a nap."

Danny led me into the sizable master suite with its sidewall of glass leading to a private balcony and the ocean beyond.

The impressive king-sized bed faced a fireplace. The headboard was covered in tufted white silk and the linens were white Pratesi eyelet. Several light blue throw pillows contrasted.

The furniture, including a club chair with ottoman, and a settee, was either covered in white fabric or painted white. Even the floors were pickled hardwood partially covered by a white shag area rug. Open white wooden vertical blinds revealed the Pacific in the distance.

Despite being a vacation home, the bedroom had a large custom outfitted walk-in closet and a spa-sized bathroom. The over-sized bathroom was decorated with white wood cabinetry, white Carrera marble counters and tiles, and white plantation shutters covered the window beside the two-person spa-tub. The plush towels were naturally also white.

Both rooms were painted a cool light blue that matched the bed's accent pillows.

I almost didn't notice the small white table by the settee in front of the fireplace. On it's surface, a crystal vase contained two-dozen white roses with delicate long, green stems. They, like the red ones downstairs, were so fresh the buds were still tightly closed.

The rose in the center stood taller than the others. In contrast, it was in full bloom. I took a closer look. This rose wasn't in the water. It was made of silk!

I removed the silk rose from the vase and fingered its petals. How curious!

I looked at Danny who had come up beside me. He understood my confusion.

"Danny, they're beautiful," I said. "I can't believe how many roses you bought."

"Eli, this is it," he grinned.

Danny was pleased with himself, and why shouldn't he be? He saw how happy he'd made me.

I held up the silk flower. "What's with this one?"

"It's symbolic." Danny grinned again, and he clasped my hand. "Our love will last as long as that rose."

"It's silk," I said, "It will…"

"Never die," Danny completed my sentence.

Tears filled my eyes. I threw my arms around Danny's neck. I couldn't help crying. Danny held me tightly and let me. Then I smiled and gently touched his face.

"Danny, you're amazing! You're such a romantic."

"Don't tell anyone."

"I wouldn't dare. Everyone would hate me. It'll be our little secret."

It wasn't until Danny loosened his hold on me that I noticed a square blue box, unmistakably from Tiffany's, beside the vase.

"That's for you," Danny said and he handed me the box.

I smiled as I untied the white satin ribbon. The cube-shaped box was too large to contain jewelry. Opening the lid, I found …a box! A small, square crystal box cut to resemble a gift box with a crystal ribbon bow as the lid.

"It's lovely."

"I wanted you to have something of your own. You can put your earrings in it."

I was speechless. I understood the symbolism of this gift. Far from being merely an expensive box for trinkets, this was Danny's way of saying this was my home too.

CHAPTER 97 - ELIZABETH

A warm hand on my shoulder roused me. Hair tickled my face as Danny leaned over me to kiss my cheek. I stretched my arms in an exaggerated feline-like motion, reaching behind to capture him.

There was no better way to wake up. I hoped Danny agreed. Yeah, I knew he did. I smiled, satisfied with the turn of events since leaving Donnelly. I was now mistress of the Newman beach house. Unbelievable!

Well-rested and content, Danny rolled me onto my back. Propped on his elbow, his lips skimmed mine for a sweet kiss. Danny's heart beat against mine, strong and slow. His happiness pleased me immensely.

Before Danny left for Canada, he needed to believe that no other girl could fulfill his desires like I could. There was precious little time for me to work the magic to ensure his faithfulness. The calendar was not my friend.

Danny had repeatedly referred to this as our first night in our first home. The ultimate romantic, he had to have planned a celebration for later! But first, off to downtown Malibu for a light bite at Marmalade Café. Danny was starving. I wasn't. Still, he insisted I eat something. His plans must require me not to have an empty stomach.

Upon returning from dinner, Danny and I went upstairs to unpack. Six suitcases later, the walk-in closet had little room for future purchases.

"We'll need more closets when we live here permanently," Danny gripped as he appraised the situation.

"We can put non-essentials in the other bedrooms," I suggested.

"What about guests? There just isn't enough room to live here full-time, Eli."

I looked around the bedroom, taking in its sizeable dimensions. "This room is so large. Danny, we could build up that back wall and turn it into closet space."

Danny studied the wall. "That might help. It's an idea."

I rolled my eyes and sighed, frustrated. "Why don't we just level the house and start from scratch," I said sarcastically.

"Eli! That's a great idea! We'll hire an architect."

"Daniel!" I exclaimed, appalled. "I was being sarcastic. We love this house. I will not knock it down just to get closets."

"Baby, we'll remodel. An architect can rearrange the rooms. I'll call Mom for a name."

Danny was so enthusiastic I wanted to kill him. There was no way I was letting him near the phone.

"Stop!" I cried to get his attention. "Daniel, you will do no such thing!"

Danny stopped still, starring at me, stunned by my assertiveness.

"I thought you'd like that," Danny said quietly, hurt apparent in his voice.

"It's a little premature. Danny, we don't even own this house."

"Baby, we will." he answered with confidence. "My parents always give me what I want. I'll ask them. Mom and Dad can buy a new one."

I put down the sweater I was folding and approached him. Danny looked up from the underwear he was putting away and I hugged him tight.

"I love you very much," I said. "And I'm touched that you want to make everything perfect, but I have to draw the line. Danny, let's get a grip on reality. Steve and Ellen are very generous parents, and you're right, they do give you whatever you ask for. Danny, you will not ask for this house. If you do, I'm out of here. It's the end of us."

"Eli, you're serious?" Danny trembled, visibly shaken.

I had never threatened to leave him before. Danny knew I meant it.

"A house isn't a trinket or tickets to a concert. It's a big deal. Asking for this house would show me that you are more spoiled and immature than I ever imagined. That's not what I want. And they'll assume I was behind your request. That would humiliate me. I could never ask anyone to give me a house."

"Then where will we live?"

"Here, as planned. But we don't own this house unless it's offered. If it's not, we can buy another. There's no rush. We aren't even engaged."

I couldn't help thinking with some hostility, "Hell! You won't even promise to stop cheating. Who knows if we'll ever permanently live together in this or any other house."

I realized I remained bitter about Amelia and Reggie. I'd better get over it and fast. Danny had a special evening waiting, and I didn't want to spoil it. He needed to learn how amazing I would make life in this house be for him.

"There!" I declared as I closed the cabinet beneath the white marble sink. Finally. I had finished unpacking everything. So much stuff for only one week!

By the end of next week I'd have to pack it all up again. Not really have to, but I would. Danny, insisting that this was now our home, had made it clear that I could live here all summer. But I couldn't. This house didn't feel like home. It was Steve and Ellen's, not mine. Santa Monica was my home.

I turned to leave the bathroom and there was Danny, standing in the doorway.

"Will you ever be finished?" he asked. Danny's grin gave away his pleasure.

I held up my empty hands. "I'm done," I said, and I tried slipping passed him.

Blocking my way, Danny reached for my shoulder and pulled me into his arms.

"Playtime?" I grinned.

Then I reached my hands around his neck, and Danny lifted me up, his hands gripping beneath my skirt. While Danny held me securely, I wrapped my legs around his waist, purposely rubbing against him, lace silk to khaki. I pulled Danny's face to mine. His hands kneading my bottom left me gasping as our lips met. I reached for the hem of my polo shirt, and pulled it over my head, dropping it to the floor.

"Let's move this party to the hot tub," Danny whispered.

"Now?" I was disappointed by the interruption. Then I flashed back to him keeping me from the refrigerator before. Danny obviously had his reasons for moving downstairs.

Still. "In a little?" I asked hopefully.

Danny kissed my chest, then my shoulder, my lips and my neck. My back arched in response. I leaned deeply into his hands, pressing my breasts into them.

"Now," Danny ordered, "before we never get there." He was hard against me, probing.

"Too bad. Daniel, I'm not leaving this room until we make love."

Danny laughed at my boldness. Feathery soft, he ran his fingertips up my spine requiring me to unwrap my legs from around his hips or be dropped. Danny set me down, a soft landing. As he did so, he unhooked my bra and I pulled him down to me.

"Daniel, I want you now," I ordered.

"Eli, you're a demanding woman," Danny teased.

"I sure am. Now, let me make you a happy man."

"Skinny dip?" I asked after our playful quickie concluded.

Danny starred at my naked body with a triumphant smirk.

"No. Navy bikini."

"Nobody's here but us," I reminded him.

"Navy bikini. It drives me crazy."

"Danny, you're insatiable tonight."

"I hope so babe, 'cause you're an animal."

When I stepped out of the bathroom in my navy bikini, I zipped a gray hoodie halfway up before going down stairs.

Danny was already on the patio where he'd turned up the heated floor tiles and switched on the hot tub. He had also turned on a heating lamp by the nearby dining table, and had laid out large, fluffy turquoise beach towels, one for each of us.

"There's my Sweetheart," Danny said as I stepped out through the sliding glass door. "Kill the house lights, hon," he grinned.

There was a switch on the outside wall that controlled the lights in the great room. Once off, the only illumination on the patio was from the heating lamp and the stars.

I sauntered over to my smiling love and eased into his welcoming arms. A crystal clear evening, the moon sat low on the horizon. A bright orange orb glowing over the Pacific, craters so clearly delineated, the man in the moon was truly smiling down on us. In the distance, the lights of Santa Monica and further south, the Palos Verdes Peninsula, added a shimmer to the sky.

"It's so beautiful tonight," I whispered.

Danny's arms enveloped me. Our lips met, sealing our love. My heart pounded and Danny unzipped my hoodie. He slipped it off my shoulders and tossed it on a nearby chair. I stood shivering, even while Danny held me for another kiss.

Danny took my hand and led me to the in-ground hot tub. The warmth of the water and the power of the bubbles playfully encapsulated me. This was so much better than another round of love making in bed. We'd have time for that later.

Settled on the tiled seat with the jets on our backs, an errant bubble splashed my eye and tickled. I giggled and Danny gently wiped it away with his thumb. His hand lingered on my cheek as his eyes locked on mine.

"Do you realize, for once we are absolutely, completely alone?"

"Steve won't interrupt?" I giggled, alluding to our aborted hot tub romp in Aspen.

"Not tonight. I promise."

"Good. That was too weird."

"Now, what were we doing that evening?" Danny grinned.

"I think I remember," I flirted.

Danny's nose gently touched mine. I felt his sweet, warm breath on my face. My arms wrapped around his strong, wet back and our lips crushed together. The power of his kiss made me tremble.

Danny broke into the warmest, most pleased smile I'd ever seen. I slid on to his lap, straddling his hips to sit even closer than I already was. Danny's magnificent sapphire eyes bored into my soul as he took my face in his hands.

"E, I love you so much. Even more than in Aspen," Danny whispered.

Tears filled my eyes. I blinked hard to keep contained. Danny spoke with such sincerity. I felt so full.

"And I the same. Danny, I love you more than anything." I quivered.

Maybe I could trust Danny. At this moment I believed any and all things were possible. Danny's heart beat rapidly against mine that was beating equally fast. Our lips, our bodies, even our souls, joined together, pure powerful heat.

My head was spinning and I gripped his muscular back for support. I barely noticed when Danny removed my bikini top, but suddenly his hands, his lips; they were all over me. Like an expert musician, he played me perfectly while the crashing waves of the Pacific provided our own personal soundtrack.

My hands twined in Danny's hair. His wet skin against mine filled me with desire. Danny reached down to my bikini bottom, swiftly removed it and flung it on the deck, all the while grinning. I laughed, flashed him my own saucy grin, and removed his swim shorts that I tossed near the bikini.

"E, you're incredible," Danny murmured as I threw my arms around his neck.

"Danny, I love you," I whispered.

Never had I felt this free and uninhibited. I loved having our own home!

As our lips devoured each other amid the pulsating bubbles, I eagerly welcomed Danny entrance. Moving to the accelerating rhythm of music we could only feel in our souls, Danny and I exploded together, and then celebrated our love with more kisses, tender ones now.

Tenderly holding each other while our pulses returned to restful speed, I remained on Danny's lap while we silently celebrated our love on this magnificent evening.

"I need some water," Danny announced after a long while. The heat of the hot tub was getting to us.

Watching Danny climb out of the hot tub was a treat. My eyes were riveted to his perfection. "Behold Adonis," I thought. With his shaggy hair dripping rivulets down his muscular back, the Greek god would have been jealous.

Danny's back to me, I studied him toweling off. His broad shoulders perfectly tapered to his narrow hips and firm buttocks atop muscular athletic legs. I was completely infatuated. He was gorgeous. He was mine. Lucky me!

Danny abruptly turned back around. Caught! There was no getting around that I'd been starring! I shrugged my confession. Danny grinned, pleased with my enjoyment, and he tied the towel around his waist. Then he donned his hoodie and zippered it halfway up.

I swam to the side of the hot tub where Danny stood unfolding the other towel. He held it open for me and I climbed out. In the unlikely event that I had developed a case of modesty, Danny averted his gaze toward the ocean.

When I stood enveloped by plush terry, Danny rubbed me down. Then he wrapped the towel around me and tucked in the end creating a bandeau dress. Danny took me in his arms and I reached up, guiding his lips to mine. His tenderness sent sparks pulsating throughout me. How we enjoyed this close intimate moment.

"Oh, babe." Danny spoke softly, yet emotionally. "How will I make it through the summer without you?"

"Shhh." I placed my forefinger against his lips. "Don't think about that."

I reached my arms around Danny's neck and pressed against him. His strong arms lifted me off the hard tile floor. I tenderly kissed him and my movements loosened my towel dress.

"Baby, you'll be up every weekend, right?" Danny asked desperately.

"You know I will. Nothing can keep us apart."

"I need you, Eli."

"Danny, don't. I want to enjoy tonight." My towel came undone and fell to the ground. "Let's enjoy the moment."

Our lips crushed together, mine parting for his tongue to explore. Danny ran his hands down my back and held them on my bottom to support me. I gasped, feeling his hands on my bare skin. As we kissed, Danny became hard beneath his towel. In one fluid motion, I reached down and removed it.

"Eli?" Danny playfully admonished.

I took Danny's face in my hands, and while I devoured his lips he carried me to a lounge chair where we made love again.

After, Danny ran his fingertip up my side from my hip to my shoulder in feathery strokes causing a powerful, shiver to run through me. We were lying on the lounge facing each other. Danny's hand rested on my hip and I held his shoulder.

Danny moved to cover me as much as possible with the sweatshirt he was still wearing. My hands inside the hoodie laced behind his neck. I tilted my head up to his for a kiss.

"I can barely remember that we started today in New York. It's like a lifetime ago."

"And we'll go to sleep tonight under the stars of Malibu," Danny added.

"Inside, I hope."

"Chilly?"

"My own sweatshirt and towel would be nice," I pointed out.

Danny grinned. He scampered off the lounge to get both towels and my hoodie.

Danny wrapped his towel around his waist before sitting down again. Then he helped me into my hoodie. I lay the towel over me like a blanket and Danny took me in his arms.

"You're ice cold. Let me warm you up." Danny rubbed my arms, my back and my shoulders. "Is this helping?"

"Not really, but it sure feels good," I laughed.

Danny lifted me up to my feet. I tied the towel around my waist and zippered the hoodie half-way up to match his.

"Come sit by the heating lamp. It's snack time."

I obediently followed Danny to the warmth of the lamp-baked table.

While I sat on the curved two-person bench waiting, Danny brought cold water bottles from the nearby outdoor kitchen. I took a long pull, consuming nearly half of it at once.

"Stay right here, Eli. I'm going inside to get our snack." He stood and kissed my forehead. In my drunk-like state, I simply nodded.

I loved all of Danny's efforts to make our first night at home special. I considered all he had done. Whatever Danny was fetching from the kitchen, he had to have enlisted Ellen's assistance. Ellen was the best! I loved her nearly as much as my own mother.

"Close your eyes," Danny ordered as he backed out of the house through the sliding glass door. I had no choice and smiled at the mystery he was trying to create.

Eyes squeezed shut, I sensed Danny approach. I laughed at the absurdity of it.

"Keep them closed, Eli. I'm almost ready."

My lids must have fluttered. I placed my fingers over my eyes. I felt Danny's movements as the air current wavered. I heard him placing glass? No, maybe china? Could be both, upon the teak table. Had anticipation not been building inside me, I would have taken a deep breath to try sniffing my way out of this mystery. Giddiness prevented me.

A loud POP broke the spell. My eyes flew open and my body slammed against the bench back in startled response. Danny's laughter filled my ears.

I laughed too, for there Danny stood, wearing only a towel and a zip-up hoodie while pouring champagne into fine crystal flutes. How awesome was that!

Caviar and all its accoutrements were laid out on the table. The caviar was surrounded by ice in a beautiful crystal bowl, accompanied by a mother of pearl spoon. The chopped egg and crème fraiche were in matching bowls with small silver spoons.

Blini were stacked on the same fine china plates as those Danny had placed before us. Then Danny dramatically opened a napkin of apricot-colored linen monogrammed in brown thread with "J-N" and placed it on my lap, over my towel skirt.

Danny grinned, pleased with himself and rightfully so. He had pulled off this amazing evening from 3,000 miles away. I was speechless. My heart brimmed with more love than I knew possible. Danny had done all this for me!

I slid over to make room for Danny to sit beside me. He couldn't stop smiling and neither could I.

"How did you do all this?" I was completely in awe.

"I made a few strategic phone calls," Danny answered evasively.

"Ellen?" I asked, already knowing the answer.

"She helped," Danny laughed.

I picked up my champagne flute. "You sent your mother to Geary's?" I laughed.

Geary's is the elegant tabletop emporium in Beverly Hills where the fashionable brides of Los Angeles are listed for their china, crystal, silver and fine dining accessories.

Danny shrugged, embarrassed that I'd figured it out. He reached for his flute. Now serious, Danny's gaze met mine. He raised his flute, and I followed his lead.

My heart beat rapidly in anticipation, but anticipation of what? With Danny's departure looming on the horizon, did I dare hope that he would finally lay my doubts to rest? Was he about to speak the words I had been waiting for since our first date?

"I'm not good at this," Danny began. He took my hand. "E, I think you know how crazy in love I am with you."

I nodded and smiled nervously while trying to keep my emotions under control.

"I'm happier than I ever thought possible. It's going to be misery without you this summer, Eli." Danny stopped to kiss my fingers and smile at me. "We have a little over a week. Let's enjoy our home while we're together."

Danny lifted his flute a little higher. "Forever, Eli. To us and our life together."

Danny tapped his flute against mine. His toast was over. That was it? No promises?

I prayed that for once Danny couldn't read me. My disappointment because of what he had not said would spoil our perfect evening. One more week; we had one more week. Danny's words were getting closer.

CHAPTER 98 - DANIEL

Bright morning sun flooded the bedroom. Giddy from champagne, neither Elizabeth nor I had remembered to close the blinds last night. Through the open slider, the salty ocean tang filled the air, and crashing waves provided an enjoyable background symphony to our early waking.

Elizabeth's eyes fluttered opened. Smiling, she stretched like a kitten and playfully kissed my sleepy lips. Elizabeth had slept well.

Then Elizabeth rose up against the headboard, remaining covered by the sheet. "Can our forever start today?" she asked, downright perky.

It must have been earlier than I thought because I had no idea what she meant. I sat straight up. I had the feeling I needed to concentrate.

"I'm not following you, babe."

"Yesterday you said we could live here forever. Can forever start today?"

I was still confused, so I answered, "Technically, I think forever began yesterday but I'm still not following you."

"Ugh! Daniel!" she squealed with frustration. "Let's transfer to UCLA," she said with enthusiasm. "Then we could live here and commute."

"If I wanted to go to UCLA, I'd already be enrolled there."

UCLA was the last school on earth I wanted to attend except for maybe USC. That might be worse. There was a nationwide obsession with their film school. In that pressure cooker I wouldn't trust anyone.

"How about Pepperdine?" Eli asked just as brightly.

Eli had clearly thought this through. She did not wake up with an epiphany. I burst into full-fledged, gut-busting laughter.

"What's funny about Pepperdine? It's so close. We could even come home for lunch," she added in a flirty voice.

Eli kissed my cheek for emphasis in case I had missed her less than subtle innuendo.

"As lovely as that would be," I stammered, unable to stop laughing, "We would be expelled before mid-terms."

"Why?" she snapped. Elizabeth had reached her limits with my impertinent behavior. "We're both A-students at a much more academically rigorous institution."

I loved when my usually brainy girl would lapse into complete airhead naivety. Her innocence was adorable. I had no choice but to hug her. So I did.

"Eli, Grandma Margie would disown you. It's a Christian school.

Haven't you noticed the big cross on the front lawn?"

"They must have some Jewish students. It's in Malibu."

"There's probably a few," I admitted.

"It doesn't matter. It's not like we're religious." I began laughing again. "So glad I amuse you, Daniel." Eli was pissed.

I wrapped my arms around Elizabeth and swept her hair back so I could delicately kiss her shoulder.

"Baby, you always amuse me. It's part of your charm." It amazed me how the obvious had gone over her head. "Eli, Pepperdine's religious. We've probably violated at least several of their rules in the last twenty-four hours alone, one most enjoyably multiple times."

"I wasn't counting," she giggled. I hugged Elizabeth and kissed her neck again.

"Then there was the champagne, and we have at least one case of beer in the house. And I won't even mention the half-ounce of pot in my suitcase."

"There's a half-ounce of pot in your suitcase?" Eli was surprised.

"Leftovers, hon."

"Well it seemed like a good idea," Elizabeth said sadly.

"Donnelly may lack privacy, but at least nobody cares that my roommate's a girl. And we can do lunch there, too." I kissed the tip of her nose and winked. Eli giggled.

"There's a lot I want to do today," I said to change the subject. "Let's get up."

"It's only six-thirty," Eli laughed.

"Ugh! Jet-lag!"

"Let's go for a run on the beach?"

"Later for that, babe. Right now I know what I want."

Eli reached for my rough cheeks. Her nose rubbed against mine.

"I love breaking Pepperdine's rules," Eli said breathlessly before crushing her lips against mine and pulling me down on top of her.

In the kitchen after we dressed, Eli learned why I was anxious to start the day. Not only was there no food, the implements for cooking were either ancient or non-existent, a symptom of how seldom my parents had been here recently.

There was a good set of All-Clad cookware, but the toaster couldn't hold a bagel and the coffee maker required messy paper filters that we were out of. A trip to Williams-Sonoma would turn this house into a home.

Elizabeth was a breath of fresh air this morning. There was a bounce in her step and an electric smile that wouldn't quit. My mood matched hers and I smiled, knowing I was responsible for her glee.

Breakfast at Coogies was the perfect choice for omelets. Its location in the Malibu Colony Center was exactly where I wanted to be. There was one more errand in Malibu before Eli would truly feel at home.

Leaving Coogies hand-in-hand, Elizabeth was virtually skipping down the sidewalk. My smile expanded, as did the warmth I felt inside. Eli was as sunny as the cloudless Malibu sky. No June gloom today, either in the weather or in us.

"I need to fill a prescription," Eli announced. We were passing the CVS drug store, and I followed her in.

"Prescription?" Was something the matter?

Eli saw the concern in my face and giggled. "Birth control, Daniel." She stopped and quickly kissed me. "No babies for us this summer, young man."

I flashed to a magnificent vision of Eli cradling our auburn-haired baby in her arms, and I smiled. "You're sure?"

Eli's eyes opened wide in shock. "Danny! We have three more years of school and I intend on graduating with my stomach as flat as the day I entered."

"Baby, you would look beautiful with a bump."

Elizabeth flushed. "And you would be a great dad, Danny. But not until after we graduate, and not until there's a ring on this finger."

Elizabeth smiled as she shoved her left ring finger into my face.

"We don't have to be married."

"I do," Elizabeth declared as the pharmacist took her prescription slip.

"I need your address and phone number, please."

I leaned over Eli's shoulder. Much to my delight she wrote the beach address. Then she handed the slip and her health insurance card to the pharmacist.

"Thank you," I said to Eli.

I beamed with pride. Eli could easily have gone to Santa Monica for this. She was using our Malibu address!

The pharmacist handed Eli back her health insurance card.

"We'll be back this afternoon," I said. "Come on, Eli. Let's go to the bank."

Elizabeth followed me into the Bank of America branch and over to the bank officer's desk. The heavy-set, middle-aged woman wasn't busy and gave us her attention.

"May I help you?" she asked pleasantly.

Eli and I sat down. I took her hand and responded, "We'd like to open a joint checking account."

Eli gasped. If I hadn't been holding her hand she might have fallen backward off her chair. I grinned, enjoying her speechlessness. A joint account was news to her. This was my way of letting Elizabeth know we were truly making a home together.

CHAPTER 99 - ELIZABETH

A joint bank account! Men do not casually give a woman access to their money. As I didn't need Danny's money, that made this purely symbolic, and thus even more significant.

Danny might not have directly told me what I wanted to hear, but his words and actions since we'd left Donnelly were the functional equivalents. Weren't they? I wanted to think they were. Maybe, just maybe, I could finally relax.

"Why do we need a bank account?" I asked trying to sound nonchalant.

"Elizabeth, I want it. It's important for me to take care of everything while I'm away. You're my responsibility, baby."

Danny's responsibility? I grinned, turning to gushy-eyed mush.

The banker began inputting our personal information. I was giggly when I signed Elizabeth J. Jacobs in the line beneath where Daniel M. Newman had signed first. I couldn't find the words to describe how loved I felt.

"I have another checking account," Danny told the banker. "Can you please tell me the balance? I'm going to transfer funds from it."

The banker let Danny glance at her computer screen, careful not to let me see. I smirked. Danny and I had no secrets.

"I have over $257,000?" Danny said to himself in surprise. "Let's transfer $25,000 to the new account," he directed the banker.

"Why do you have over $250,000 in a checking account?" I asked disapprovingly.

A sum of that magnitude should be in an interest bearing account. I raised an eyebrow, bemused. Danny had an A in Economics and Ellen had once been a banker. This was so elementary; even I knew it was wrong!

"Pretty stupid," Danny admitted with a sheepish smile. "I didn't realize. It's trust income. The trust department automatically deposits it every month."

"I have to wait until I'm twenty-one," I complained.

"Sorry, babe. Guess your folks want to protect their innocent little girl from sweet-talking charmers who might take advantage."

I rolled my eyes. "I can take care of myself just fine," I scowled.

"Hey, I know you can. Baby, you're nobody's fool."

I smiled. "Thank you for the vote of confidence."

How ironic. My parents had been overly protective when they established my trust, and whom did I end up with? A man oblivious of the balance in his checking account who was generously sharing it with me.

I was over my pout. "It's nice not to have to worry and neither do you."

"Neither do I," Danny echoed. "You're right, Eli. I shouldn't keep this much in a checking account. When we get home I'll call my trust officer and tell her to reinvest any new income for at least the next six months."

"I'll need your driver's licenses," the banker curtly interrupted.

Danny took his wallet from his rear pants pocket and I opened my purse. We handed the woman our licenses. She glanced at them and then looked directly at Danny.

"You're very young. Do your parents approve?"

"It's my account. I can do whatever I want," Danny answered firmly.

"You are aware, with a joint account you both have equal access to the funds without the permission of the other."

The implication was clear. Had the banker inquired regarding my accounts, she would have changed her tune and fast.

I arrogantly raised my chin. Danny could tell by my narrowed eyes and scornful expression that I was moments from an ugly "do you know who I am" exchange with this woman. How dare she imply that I was some trashy gold-digger.

Danny met the banker's glance and held it. Firmly, without wavering, he answered her accusation.

"Yes, I'm fully aware. On second thought, I'll transfer $50,000."

The banker's jaw dropped, flustered by Danny's defiance. I knew she was thinking, "Spoiled rich boy. I hope she takes all your money."

Instead she gathered the account application and our licenses and said, "I'll be right back." She rose and took the materials to the teller's cage.

With the banker gone, I relaxed. "You told her," I laughed.

"I did, didn't I?" Danny chuckled.

"You don't have to do this."

Danny took my hands. He swiveled in the chair to directly face me. Danny's eyes were twinkling, but his face was filled with complex emotions.

"E, you don't need the money, but I like taking care of you. When I'm with you I never let you pay for anything."

"You're very old-fashioned that way. It's sweet."

"Think of this as a very long extension of me. If it's purchased north of Topanga, use this account. Hell, I don't care. Use it south of Topanga too. I love you."

"I want to take care of you too. How do I do that while you're away?"

"Baby, you take care of me every day. You don't even realize it. When we're apart, just knowing we're together, Eli, I'm a better man because of you. That's how you take care of me."

My heart melted. A tear pricked my eye.

The Williams-Sonoma on Beverly Drive contains everything you need for your kitchen and even things you don't yet know you need. Entering through the heavy glass doors is as exciting for adults as FAO Schwarz is for children.

While you salivate at the displays, and inhale deeply what the test kitchen has whipped up, an overwhelming feeling that everything in your own kitchen that hasn't been purchased in the last six months is antiquated overtakes you. Having a kitchen that actually was antiquated, and armed with Danny's Platinum Card, we needed massive self-control not to purchase everything.

I reminded myself that only the basics were necessary. Danny and I would barely be in this house until next summer. Williams-Sonoma would have new goodies by then!

Danny and I left the store with a stainless steel toaster designed for bagels, a coffee/espresso maker, mixing bowls, a waffle iron, two cookbooks, and a set of German knives. We'd also purchased a drawer's worth of small gadgets and implements, one or two of whose functions I was not certain of, but I loved their lime-colored plastic handles.

"Tell me again why we didn't valet the car?" I complained as we waited for the elevator in the parking structure.

My shopping bags were heavy. Danny couldn't help me either. He was carrying the larger items. I let the bags slide to the ground, ready to grab again when the elevator doors opened.

Danny laughed, "Mental lapse, I guess."

The elevator doors finally opened. I grabbed the bags by their handles.

"Elizabeth?" A man's voice forced my attention upward.

"Zac!" I exclaimed in delight. "Are you stalking me?" I laughed. "Every time I'm in Beverly Hills I run into you."

The elevator doors closed behind us. We'd catch another.

"Zac! Great to see you!" Danny released his packages, and the two friends embraced.

"Man, how have you been?"

"Great, Zac. How's Harvard?"

"Excellent. When did you get home?

"We got home ...when did we get home, Eli?"

I considered his question. "Yesterday," I responded, surprised by my answer.

"Only yesterday? We've been so busy. It feels like longer."

Zac noticed the Williams-Sonoma bags. "Are you going to some weddings?"

"No. We're stocking our house," Danny answered.

"Your house?" Danny's response surprised Zac.

"Eli and I are living at the beach house until I leave for Vancouver to work with Dad."

"Who's his star?'

"Vanessa Rogers," Danny answered, unimpressed.

"Vanessa Rogers! Whoa!" Zac exclaimed. "Can Steve hire me? She's hot."

"I hear she's a bitch. And Zac, she's married."

"Not anymore." Danny and Zac gaped at me as one. They had forgotten I was there.

"E, how do you know this?" Danny asked.

"It was all over the web. Vanessa's divorce was finalized in April. She said she was quote, 'excited to work with Steven Newman this summer' unquote. You boys really need to do a better job of keeping up."

Danny rolled his eyes.

"You better warn Ellen," Zac teased. "Vanessa's ex was married when they met."

"Zac! I'm sure Steve considers Vanessa nothing more than a highly-paid employee."

"Eli's right. Dad wouldn't cheat on Mom," Danny stated emphatically. "How's Gibby?" Danny asked Zac to change the subject.

"So far, so good. Dad's still clean. He's on tour most of the summer. I'm joining him."

"Babysitting?" Danny asked.

"Sort of. I'm turning it into an independent study on the psychological and sociological effects of touring."

"Gibby doesn't suspect?" I asked.

"Dad thinks it's cool. He's telling everyone to cooperate because it's for Harvard. To Dad, Harvard means it must be important."

"Maybe next summer you can conduct a study of people who go on location," I said with a smile that only Zac saw.

"Funny, Eli." Danny answered. "How about a study of the significant others who are left at home?"

Zac groaned. "I'd like to stay and mediate, but I have a dentist appointment."

"That sucks for you," Danny answered. "If you're not doing anything later, why don't you come to our house for dinner? Happy hour begins at five."

CHAPTER 100 - ELIZABETH

Dodgers! Friday evening was the opening game of the home stand and Danny desperately wanted to attend. The mere mention of his team reduced Danny to the stature of an excited ten-year old.

Nothing stood in the way of Danny and the Dodgers and we dressed accordingly to show our team spirit. Around my waist I tied a heavyweight blue Dodger sweatshirt and my ponytail poked through the back of my team cap. Danny wore a black t-shirt under his Dodger jersey and his own logo cap.

Friday evening rush hour traffic was heavier than anticipated. It was nearly six-thirty by the time we parked the car, purchased hot dogs and drinks, and found our seats. Our families jointly owned a block of eight season tickets three rows up from the field on the home plate side of the Dodger dugout.

I bit into my kosher dog slathered with yellow mustard. Its beefy juiciness coupled with the heat of the oozing mustard was perfection. I hadn't had one since last season. I giggled at the memory of bringing Grant Barnes. Attending his first baseball game, he had been clueless. The evening had evolved into a tutorial for the hapless star, all captured on the stadium big screen.

Danny glanced sideways at me, confused by my smirk.

"This is awesome," I stammered, and I raised my hotdog toward him.

Danny shook his head, perplexed. Better not to mention Grant. While grinning at Danny, I took another bite. He smiled at my deliberateness and then frowned.

"Eli, don't move," he said in a stern voice I knew I'd better listen to.

Danny leaned toward me. With a mischievous glint in his eyes, he licked mustard off the outside of my left hand up the side of my little finger. I gasped from the electricity. Did he realize how sensuous that was?

Danny smirked. "I didn't want the mustard to get all over you, babe."

I blushed deep crimson. "You really have no idea what that did to me."

Danny laughed, "I know exactly what that did to you. Now finish your hot dog. I want to show you off to the manager."

I devoured the rest and followed Danny down to the edge of the dugout. The manager was nowhere in sight.

"Hey," he called to the ballboy, "Give this to the big guy, and thanks."

Danny handed the ballboy a cream colored Crane card printed with his name and contact information in navy ink. I found it pretentious. Danny rarely used the cards, but he repeatedly told me I should get my own. I hadn't yet done so.

"Danny!" the Dodger manager greeted him warmly moments later. Then he shook Danny's hand and clapped him on the back. "Good to see you, son. I was wondering when you'd show up."

"I was in school in New York."

The lean, middle-aged manager looked me up and down, but in a fatherly way. Beneath his cap I noticed his receding hairline.

"Who's this lovely young lady, Danny?" His eyes crinkled as he smiled.

"This is my lady, Elizabeth," he said, wrapping his arm around my waist.

"Good to meet you, Elizabeth. Beautiful girl, Danny. I hope you like baseball."

Danny laughed. "Eli's a baseball geek."

"I am not a geek!"

"She's too pretty to be a geek."

"She is at that, but Eli's still a geek. This girl knows as much about baseball as I do, and she keeps a scorecard." Danny said proudly.

The manager appraised me with a studious eye. "I'm impressed."

After saying our good-byes and wishing a victory for the team, Danny led me back to our seats.

"How do you know the manager so well?"

"We met at a team charity event I attend with Dad every year. We missed last year. This year too," Danny brooded.

Soon, I bent down over the scorecard and began filing in the starting lineups as posted on the stadium scoreboard.

"Eli, you really are doing this?" Danny asked with wonder.

I met Danny's glance with steely resolve. "I wasn't going to until you bragged to the manager. Shame. I prefer giving my undivided attention to my date."

"Damn! I screwed myself, didn't I?" Danny laughed.

"Next time, keep things between us."

With Danny's help, I quickly finished filling in the line-ups.

"Do you want anything from the snack bar?" he asked.

"Maybe later. We just ate. You're hungry already?"

"I am for you, Elizabeth," he answered with a devilish grin. How trite! I giggled anyway, feeling the excitement rising to inappropriate levels. Then Danny took my face in his hands and kissed me as though we were alone and not in a crowded stadium.

"Looks like were interrupting."

A familiar voice caught our attention. Our eyes flew open and our lips broke apart. Danny and I exchanged horrified stares. We were so embarrassed.

"Dad!" I turned my head toward the row behind us.

"Mike, Randi." Danny stuttered, sounding as awkward as I felt.

"Teddy!" Even my brother was here.

The five of us stood and exchanged warm hugs and kisses. Danny was as pleased as I was for this impromptu reunion.

"We didn't know you were coming," I squealed.

"Looks like this is the only way I get to see my daughter," Dad said.

"We're seeing you on Thursday for dinner," I pointed out.

"Can I sit with you, Danny?" Teddy asked.

"Sure, squirt," he answered.

As the game progressed, Danny may have been keeping his hand around my shoulder, but he was engrossed in conversation with Teddy. My parents seated behind us were the ones on a date.

I struggled to keep my resentment at bay. Danny had spent all year with me. Teddy hadn't seen him since Aspen. I should be pleased that they got along like brothers. Alas, generosity was not forthcoming. I wanted Danny all to myself.

By the fourth inning I'd had enough of being ignored. Danny's awareness remained riveted to Teddy. How could my brother possibly be interesting enough to keep Danny's attention for this long?

As the third Astro was retired, and I recorded it on my scorecard, I stood to put my Dodger sweatshirt on.

"I'm going to the ladies' room," I announced. Then I handed Teddy the scorecard and stub of a pencil. "Here. In case I miss a batter."

Danny stood to remove his wallet from his back pocket and handed me a fifty.

"While you're up, can you please bring me a beer? And Cracker Jacks."

Danny quickly kissed my cheek, as though that made running his errands somehow more palatable. It didn't.

"Sure." I resigned myself to the task. "Want anything Teddy?"

"I'll have a beer too."

"Teddy…"

"Elizabeth's no fun," he said to Danny.

Danny winked at me. He found me lots of fun.

"I'll have a Coke," Teddy relented. "And some popcorn. Pleeeeeze."

I turned to Mom. "Want to come with?" I asked.

"You expect me to wait on line?" Mom answered curtly.

"It'll be good for your image," I retorted.

"Randi, while you're up, can you get me a beer and a Cracker Jack?" Dad asked.

"Can't you get it, Elizabeth?" Mom implored.

"No. I'm underage and they card everyone here."

"Oh, bother," Mom relented. "Let's go."

Miranda Jordan was not happy. It wasn't that she thought she was too important to stand in line, although that might have been part of it. Mom didn't want to be recognized. Had Dad not requested beer, Mom would not be accompanying me. She didn't care about Danny's request.

The line at the concession stand was shorter than expected.

When Mom ordered the two beers, the counter worker smiled and said, "I need to see your ID, Miss Jordan."

"But you know who I am," Mom replied indignantly.

"I really am sorry. I have to card everybody. It's stadium policy."

Mom removed her license from her purse and showed it to the young woman.

"This is why I didn't want to come," Mom grumbled.

After I pocketed the change, and we organized the snacks into two cardboard trays, Mom intentionally slowed her pace.

"I miss you, honey."

"It's only for a week." I tried to sound reassuring. What would she do when I graduated? I certainly wasn't moving back home.

"No, Elizabeth, it isn't. You're more like a visitor. You belong to Danny now."

"I am not his possession," I declared.

"That's not what I meant. He belongs to you too. You belong together. I've been watching tonight. Danny may be talking to Teddy, but he doesn't take his hand off you. It's like you're connected."

"I feel it too," I agreed.

"Dad and I were like that. My publicist hated it." Mom laughed at the memory. "She was baffled. What was Miranda Jordan doing with a law student?"

"And twenty-two years later, who's laughing now?" I giggled.

"Let's hope you have our track record."

"If only he didn't have to go to Vancouver. We're enjoying the beach too much."

"Elizabeth," Mom turned serious, "Danny's treating you well, I hope?"

"Of course he is." I frowned, taken aback by the question.

"Don't take offense, Elizabeth. I've always loved Danny like a son. I don't know how he is as a boyfriend."

"Absolutely wonderful. Mom, I'm so spoiled. Danny had dozens of roses, and champagne and caviar waiting when we got home."

Mom smiled, pleased. "Good. I was afraid Danny's interest might wane, or he'd miss his freedom. I never thought Danny would be interested in you until he was at least thirty."

"I've heard that before."

"Danny knows you love his real self, and he doesn't have to pretend."

"I think that's true for both of us."

We returned to our seats in the midst of a rally. Dad was leaning forward between Teddy and Danny who were also leaning forward. A quick glance at the field told me why. There were Dodgers on first and third, no outs, and the count to the batter was three balls and no strikes.

The one-one tie was about to be blown apart. I sat down carefully, balancing the lopsided tray on my lap. The batter swung and missed. Strike one.

As he stepped out of the batter's box I whispered to Danny, "Pass this to Teddy." He reached for Teddy's Coke and popcorn and passed them along.

Strike two. We needed a clean hit or a walk. A long fly would score one too. The tension mounted. Danny frowned. He looked at me as though something were very wrong. Then he took off my cap and turned it backwards. "Rally cap, babe."

The batter fouled off the next two pitches. My hands were glued to the cups in the tray, holding them steady. Danny tensely gripped my knee. The pitcher went into his wind-up and unloaded a curve ball that hung, a tantalizing offer to the batter.

Crrrraaaaaack! The sound of the sweet spot connecting with the ball reverberated throughout the stadium.

A thunderous 45,000 person roar erupted as the ball catapulted over the left field fence with the ferocity of a rocket. Dodgers 4, Astros 1!

Danny grabbed my face and brusquely kissed me. With the tray on my lap, I couldn't do anything but pray nothing spilled.

There were still no outs, and the Astros yanked their starting pitcher. This allowed a short respite. Danny took his beer and Cracker Jack from the tray. Finally, I could eat my ice cream. I loved the malted flavored ice cream cups that I never ate anywhere but at Dodger Stadium.

Danny took a couple gulps of beer. "Thanks, baby. I've missed you. I've been talking to Teddy too much."

"It's okay." I smiled, pleased with his acknowledgment. "You haven't seen Teddy since January."

"Thanks." Danny's lips brushed against mine. "I love you."

Then Danny kissed me again, longer and deeper. I was no longer pissed at all the time he had spent with my brother.

Final score: Dodgers 7, Astros 2; a happy ending for the Jacobs-Newman clan.

After lingering at our seats to let the crowds thin out, Danny glanced at the scoreboard clock. "E, we should go. Early start tomorrow."

"Danny told Grandma Slade we'd be there before lunch," I explained.

Danny hugged me around my shoulders, his arms wrapped like a human pashmina. My parent's lack of reaction pleased me. They were no longer uncomfortable with our affectionate displays.

"Elizabeth, you'll like Naomi," Dad said. "Danny's grandmother is a very sharp woman, and she appreciates other sharp women."

"That's why she'll love Eli," Danny answered, proudly kissing my head.

"I hope I live up to your expectations," I fretted.

"When do I get to spend time with my girl? You've been monopolizing her Danny," Dad said. He was smiling, so we knew he was teasing.

"I'm all yours a week from Monday," I replied.

Everyone quieted. Biting my lower lip and blinking hard did not prevent the tears I had hoped to contain.

"Eli, you're crying," Danny said in the gentlest voice.

"How do you know?" I sobbed.

"I feel your quiver, baby."

I buried my head against Danny to hide the crying I could no longer hold back. He stroked my head and held me tight.

"Hey, don't cry. Eli, I'll see you every weekend."

"I know," I whimpered.

"Baby, I'm going to miss you just as much."

"You are?" I doubted.

"Of course I am. Dad might work my ass off, but I'll never be too busy not to miss you. E, I love you too much, and I'll plan lots of fun things for us to do in BC."

"And I'll give you Fridays off," Dad added.

"You should get going. It's a long drive," Mom said.

"Can I come?" Teddy asked.

"No!" we answered emphatically and in perfect unison.

Danny looked at me for confirmation as he said to Teddy, "Maybe one night next week, squirt, if your sister approves." Teddy's face brightened. How he idolized Danny!

"Wednesday?" I finally answered.

CHAPTER 101 - ELIZABETH

Something was tickling my neck and shoulder as I lay on my side sleeping. I brushed it away. I felt the tickle again, only more so. This time I came to consciousness, unable to stop giggling and squirming.

The tickling stopped. My eyes fluttered open, and I found myself face-to-face with Danny's alert liquid cobalt ones.

Light, feathery fingertips traced an invisible line up my thigh, through my hip, and lighted on my face. I let my hand come to rest on Danny's taut waist while he closed the two-inch gap and touched his head to mine. Our lips met for a chaste kiss.

Danny, handsome in the early morning sunlight smiled, his dimple showing. It was impossible not to stare. His touch, his kiss, and his face were undeniably irresistible.

"Good morning, Sweetheart," Danny whispered.

His breath on my cheek excited me, giving me shivers, and Danny playfully twirled a lock of my hair around his finger. Then grasping through my hair he brought my head to his, and he kissed me hard. I smiled and moved my hand to his cheek. The roughness of his stubble was pure rugged masculinity.

I giggled at Danny's boyish grin. I loved when he was playful. I kissed him again.

"Yum!" Danny laughed.

"I can't be yum. I haven't brushed my teeth yet," I protested.

Danny tapped my nose with his forefinger. Sapphire eyes sparkled. "Maybe I like the taste of day-old hot dogs and malted milk ice cream."

"That sounds disgusting!" I squealed, and we laughed at the absurdity.

"Danny, you are so goofy this morning," I giggled.

Then I grabbed Danny's face and kissed him again. My leg slid over his and I felt his hardness rubbing against me.

"And you're so wicked. Have I told you how much I love you?"

"Don't tell me, Daniel." I looked him straight in the eyes. "Show me." And I climbed on top of him.

Danny was fully dressed when I finished showering. He was pulling the zipper on a small case lying on the settee. Clothing on hangers, including mine, lay on the bed.

I studied Danny, now freshly shaved, wearing chino shorts and a pale blue Lacoste polo shirt. Even with his shaggy hair needing a trim, he was preppy perfection. Juxtaposed with my appearance, a towel wrapped under my armpits and wet hair dripping down my back, I was far from perfection, preppy or otherwise.

Danny handed me a neatly folded pile of clothing topped with a pale yellow lace bikini and matching bra. I frowned. His presumption that he could choose my outfit down to my underwear disturbed me.

"Daniel," I smiled to cushion my words. "You're a control freak. You want me to look a certain way when I meet Naomi because you're anxious."

Danny smiled impishly. I had him.

"Do you mind?"

"No, not really," I sighed. "I wouldn't have bought these clothes if I didn't like them. But next time, ask. A simple 'Elizabeth, can I choose your outfit?' would have sufficed."

"Sorry, E," Danny answered with a wry grin. "Now give me your toothbrush and get dressed. I'm loading the car. Meet me in the kitchen."

Not wanting to keep him waiting, I quickly dressed and then I braided my hair. I probably would have selected the tiered cotton chambray skirt with its peek-a-boo triangular panel of white eyelet, topped by a pale yellow Lacoste polo shirt. With tan huaraches, I now looked perfectly preppy too, ready to take on the extreme desert heat.

Danny was seated at the kitchen table wolfing down a croissant and gulping a cup of coffee. A small glass of orange juice was sitting beside my empty plate.

"Croissant or muffin?" Danny asked rapid-fire.

"What about a bagel?" I asked as I joined him. That's what I really wanted.

"There isn't time. You'd have to toast it."

I looked at Danny as though he were nuts. I mean really, how long does it take to toast a bagel? Three minutes? Clearly he was more stressed than he admitted.

"Honey, you're scaring me," I said as I reached for a croissant and the jar of raspberry preserves. "I've never seen you so wound up."

"I'm excited about visiting Grandma, that's all. There could be traffic."

"There's always traffic, Danny. This is L.A."

Early Saturday morning is one of the few times traffic in Los Angeles is reliably light. Pacific Coast Highway, a cloudless blue sky, and virtually no other cars – this is what my convertible BMW was engineered for! Danny floored it.

Once we cleared the eastern suburb of Covina, it was clear sailing on the I-10. I glanced over and saw that Danny had calmed. His jaw was no longer clenched, and he'd loosened his grip on the steering wheel.

Catching my eye, Danny grinned. Behind dark glasses, his sapphires were twinkling. Danny reached for my hand, and caressed my fingers and palm.

"I'm okay now, babe. Back to normal." Danny had read my mind.

Just after eleven, we exited the freeway at Bob Hope Drive. Danny and I had arrived in Rancho Mirage. Now I was the apprehensive one. Soon, I would meet Naomi Slade.

I didn't know much about Naomi, but what little I did know was contradictory and it left me intimidated. By Danny's account, I was about to meet the warmest, most wonderful woman in the world. Kind, generous and loving were the words he had used.

In sharp contrast, Mom described her as formidable, comparing Naomi to matriarchs on prime time television dramas. Those characters, even the nicer ones, fiercely protected the family at all costs. These women were never cuddly, and they regarded newcomers with suspicion.

I crossed, re-crossed and then uncrossed my legs in rapid succession. My eyes could not focus on the passing landscape. I felt fluttery and I couldn't stop fidgeting.

"I'm scared," I told Danny as we continued down Bob Hope Drive.

"I can tell." Danny smiled supportively. "You can't sit still."

The car came to a stop at a red light, and Danny kissed my lips.

"Grandma is going to love you as much as I do."

Danny turned down a side street lined with country clubs. Far different from Los Angeles where members engaged in sport or dined, these country clubs were housing developments based around golf courses.

Privacy walls stretched as far as I could see with glimpses of majestic palm trees and endless red tiled roofs topping low stucco buildings. When Danny turned into the entranceway at the end of a particular wall, we had arrived.

Danny followed the "guests" roadway to the side of the gatehouse. A magnificent fountain of Spanish-styled tile spraying water at least ten feet up, greeted us as we approached. I expected no less from Ellen's mother.

"We're visiting Naomi Slade," Danny confidently told the security guard peering through the window of the heavily air-conditioned structure.

Then the guard phoned Naomi and found the guest pass pre-printed with Newman/Slade and the dates of our visit. Danny handed it to me so it wouldn't fly out of the car.

The dry heat was bothering me. Extremely arid, it was suffocating. I was thirsty, too. "Please hurry," I silently willed the guard who was giving Danny directions to 17 Bougainvillea Lane. I needed air conditioning and water, and I needed them now. There was no shade here.

Naomi had left the garage door open for us to park, shielding the car from the hundred plus degree heat. The BMW easily fit beside Naomi's large white Mercedes. In a third but smaller bay, a canopied golf cart was parked.

Danny opened my door and helped me out. He reached for my shaking hands, and smiled. "Baby, I love you and so will Grandma."

I knew that was true, and logically why wouldn't Naomi like me? Still I was apprehensive. I returned Danny's smile, and conjured my confidence.

"Come here, babe," Danny commanded in a gentle voice. He gathered me in his arms and kissed me. It was a warm, sweet kiss and its reassurance buoyed me.

"Eli, look at me." I raised my sunglasses, as did Danny. "Elizabeth Jordan Jacobs, you are the love of my life. If you weren't, we wouldn't be here."

Danny's eyes were twinkling, full of sincerity and love. Warmth radiated through our joined hands and my confidence returned.

"Thank you. I needed to hear that," I replied.

Holding my hand, Danny led me out of the garage toward the front door.

Naomi's house was an unattached ranch style. Like the others in the complex, it was covered in sand colored stucco and topped with a red tile roof. The path to her house was lined with lemon, orange and grapefruit trees bending under the weight of their fragrant, ripening fruit. Native plants grew on the side of the stone walkway.

Danny squeezed my hand and rang the doorbell. He was grinning, excited. I was nauseas.

CHAPTER 102 - ELIZABETH

"Grandma!" Danny exclaimed as the door opened.

"Danny!"

Naomi Slade, an attractive seventy-year old woman with a highlighted dark blonde bob, grabbed hold of Danny and warmly hugged and kissed him. Then she released him and examined his appearance, but Naomi wouldn't let him go.

It brought me great pleasure to witness my strapping boyfriend reduced to little boy glee as petite Naomi hugged Danny once more.

"I've missed you so much." Naomi's voice filled with pride. "Danny, you look wonderful."

"So do you, Grandma," Danny said joyously.

Watching this emotional reunion from the sidelines, I felt out of place. Why was I here? Danny appeared perfectly content alone with Naomi. Neither noticed my presence.

"When did you get so handsome, Daniel? I bet all the girls at Donnelly are chasing you."

My jaw dropped. There were women who afraid of losing their sons tried sabotaging their relationships. Was Naomi Slade one of those women?

Danny broke away from his grandmother. Embarrassed, he took my hand. "Grandma, I have no idea what girls you're talking about. There's only one girl I care about."

Naomi's eyes opened wide. Her hand flew to cover her mouth, mortified. "I'm so sorry," Naomi apologized. "I wasn't thinking."

"Grandma, I want to introduce you to Elizabeth."

"Of course you do, Daniel. That's why she's here. Let's go inside. It's too hot."

Danny and I followed Naomi into the substantially cooler living room.

"I'll get you iced tea. I made it this morning," she offered.

Naomi crossed to the open kitchen at the far end of the great room. There, she removed a glass pitcher from the refrigerator, poured two glasses of tea, added lemon slices, and carried them to us.

"Thanks, Grandma," Danny said as she handed us each a glass.

"Thank you," I stammered.

Danny took a large gulp; I sipped mine.

Danny smiled at me. "Grandma, Elizabeth is the most important person in my life. I love her very much."

Naomi regarded me coolly. "Elizabeth, you're as lovely as Danny described."

"Thank you. It's an honor to meet you, Mrs. Slade."

"Call me Naomi, dear."

"Thank you," I answered politely.

"Danny never told me he was dating anyone before he called last week. Neither had Ellen. She only said that you were beautiful. That didn't surprise me. Danny wouldn't date a girl who wasn't." Naomi paused to collect her thoughts. "This is a surprise. I thought it would be years before Danny brought a girl for me to meet."

"Grandma!"

"I'm being honest, Danny," Naomi said in a clipped voice. "I never thought you would be like your parents."

Naomi sighed. "You're so young. And Mom tells me you're living together."

Danny had never removed his hand from mine, and now he felt me trembling. It was painfully obvious that Naomi didn't approve.

Danny forced a smile at me. "I'm sorry, Eli," he said softly. "I thought Grandma would be happy for us."

"It's okay," I answered just as softly.

Danny's disappointment was evident. I felt so bad for him, his big day ruined.

"No, it's not okay," I corrected in my full voice. I didn't care what Naomi thought. Only Danny mattered. I gave him the supportive hug he needed.

"Thanks, Eli," Danny whispered.

"What kind of name is Eli?" Naomi interrupted with disdain.

Danny cracked a smile. He always enjoyed answering this question.

"I couldn't pronounce Elizabeth when I was a baby."

"A baby?"

Naomi was puzzled. Even I had to smile. "Ellen didn't tell you who I am?"

"Grandma, Eli's father is Mike Jacobs."

"Michael's daughter? Why didn't anyone tell me, Daniel?"

Naomi finally smiled. The mere mention of Dad had transformed her. "I've always been fond of Michael, and when I've met your mother, I've liked her too. I can relax now. You're not a gold-digger or an actress."

"Grandma, I'm not that naïve."

"Maybe, but beautiful girls know how to get what they want."

"That's for sure. Eli pulled all sorts of stunts before I finally asked her out."

"I did no such thing!" I protested. I never played games.

"Yes, you did." Danny twinkled his irresistible sapphire eyes at me, full strength. "Eli, you made me break your ankle."

"Danny, you broke Elizabeth's ankle?" Naomi asked.

"It was an accident, Grandma. Then I took care of Eli. All that time together made me realize that I loved my adorable little, gimpy best friend."

Danny looked into my eyes and quickly kissed my parched lips.

"Eli's such a manipulator." He grinned. "Good thing she's a spoiled rich girl, so we can trust her."

Monday after breakfast, Danny and I kissed Naomi good-bye and headed home.

"I'll see you soon, Elizabeth," Naomi said as she walked us to the car.

Naomi was spending part of the summer in Brentwood to escape the desert heat.

"I love you, Danny." Naomi said in as tender a voice as I had heard all weekend.

"I love you too, Grandma," Danny said as they warmly embraced.

As soon as we cleared the gate and turned onto Bob Hope Drive, Danny took my hand and kissed it. He was all smiles. I wasn't. I was simply relieved. The weekend was over and I had passed the test. I had survived Naomi's scrutiny.

"Grandma loves you," Danny gleefully exclaimed like a little boy who had found a bicycle parked beneath the Christmas tree. "I knew she would."

Naomi's approval was of utmost importance to Danny in a way I couldn't comprehend. I had a different relationship with my grandmother. I didn't try pleasing her. I was secure in Margie's love. If she approved of my boyfriend, good, that would be nice. If she didn't, oh well. She'd have to deal with it. We were adults. We could all peacefully sit around the Thanksgiving table. That's what mattered.

CHAPTER 103 - ELIZABETH

Grandma Margie had always lived nearby in Sherman Oaks. We had been close since my birth. Grandma had been a constant in my life, sharing not only big events, but also the mundane.

I didn't have much of a relationship with Dad's family. Bob and Frankie, Francine actually, were perfectly nice grandparents. We simply didn't see them very often. They maintained their home in Framingham, Massachusetts near Aunt Lisa, her husband Bruce, and their three children who lived in Newton.

Aunt Lisa was the Jacobs family princess who stayed near Boston and married a lawyer. Four years older than Dad, she had a PhD in nursing and was the director of her hospital's addiction rehab center. Uncle Bruce was a partner at a prestige downtown firm. He had the career Frankie and Bob had wanted for Dad.

Despite Dad's success, his parents weren't comfortable with either his career path or his movie star wife. Their expectations for me differed from theirs for my cousins too. Josh's acceptance to Penn was greeted matter-of-factly. The Ivy League was expected. My matriculation at Donnelly was an unanticipated surprise.

Was having a famous mother supposed to have robbed me of brains and academic ambition? I imagined Grandma Frankie's difficulty as she unexpectedly found herself with an additional grandchild to brag about at Hadassah meetings.

My cousins were very different from Teddy and I. Josh was older than me, Hannah and Justin were younger, and neither was Teddy's age either. Hannah, though only a year younger than me, might as well have been from another planet.

When Hannah had visited two summers ago, I found being her hostess difficult. Hannah didn't fit in. She didn't know how to react when she learned the identities of my friends' parents. Hannah was a tourist, starring, always on the lookout for celebrities. Of course there were celebrities. They were our friends. Welcome to my life, Hannah.

"Eli," Danny jarred me from my reverie. "You're so quiet."

"I was thinking about my grandparents."

"Grandma Margie's great, Eli."

"I meant Grandma Frankie and Grandpa Bob. I'd like them to meet you, but part of me doesn't think they care. They'd probably be perfectly content to wait until there's an engagement party and Dad sends for them.

Now if I was my cousin Hannah…"

"Baby, I'm sorry. It must hurt that they play favorites."

"Only when I think about it. Grandma Frankie and Grandpa Bob are proud of Dad, but our lives are foreign to them. It makes them uncomfortable."

I returned to starring out the window.

Soon, Danny interrupted my thoughts again.

"Why don't we visit Boston in the fall? We can stay in a hotel."

I was touched by Danny's thoughtfulness.

"Thanks. I'll think about it. Don't say anything to Dad," I cautioned.

Between the weekend with Naomi and now his talk about Boston, sadness overwhelmed me. Danny was leaving in six more days and he had not given me the guarantees I needed. The calendar hung over me like a thick, black thundercloud.

"We're living together," Danny told everyone. He took me to his grandmother's; he wanted to visit mine. Danny gave me $50,000 to spend on our home. Maybe actions speak louder than words. I wasn't convinced.

The ambiguity was killing me. I wanted the words. Without the words, I would be spending the summer in emotional limbo. I glanced at Danny. His peaceful smile told me he was oblivious to my turmoil.

Sure, I would visit Danny every weekend. That was our plan. But what about the rest of the week? Danny's assertions that he would have to behave or risk embarrassing Steve did not assuage my fears. I wanted him to behave because he loved me, not because he felt obligated.

I needed the words, but how to tell Danny without sounding like I was issuing an ultimatum. That wasn't what I wanted.

I continued staring at the passing landscape. Not much could be duller than endless strip malls flashing past at 80 miles per hour.

"E, why the frown?"

Danny startled me back to consciousness. Without noticing, we were now winding our way westbound past the glossy towers of downtown. Traffic had been light. If it kept up, we'd be early for lunch with the moms.

"Why the frown?" Danny repeated. His voice was kind and caring. Did I really look that sad? I hoped not.

"Nothing. Just spacing."

"I don't believe you. You haven't said one word in almost an hour."

"That long? Neither have you," I retorted.

"I've been concentrating on the road. What's your excuse?"

"There hasn't been any traffic to concentrate on. Try again."

"I was thinking how I woke up on top of the world this morning, but my lady is wearing a frown. If I quietly give her some space maybe she'll open up and tell me why. But you haven't, so what is it, baby?"

I took a deep breath. "I don't want to fight."

"Did I do something?" Danny asked with concern.

"No, you didn't do anything," I answered truthfully.

Fact is, it wasn't what Danny had done. It was what he hadn't done.

"Then what?" Danny asked.

"I don't want to have a fight," I repeated. "You're driving."

"Eli, you can't say that and not tell me,."

"Not now," I said firmly.

"Babe…"

"I want to stop at my house before we go to the club."

"Your house?"

"Santa Monica. I want to play tennis after lunch and hang out at the pool. I need to pick up clean whites and a dry bathing suit."

My efforts to change the conversation were transparent, but the longer Danny and I avoided Malibu, the longer I could avoid the conversation.

"Tennis?" Danny was surprised. "Can I borrow a shirt from Mike?"

"Sure," I said, relieved that Danny was buying into my plan.

"Why hang at the club? I was looking forward to taking you home, babe."

I was surprised to find tears spilling out of my eyes.

"Because we won't be able to all summer," I trembled.

"Is that what this is about? Sunday?" Danny's tender voice was full of love.

"Sort of," I admitted and more tears flowed.

Danny took my hand. "Baby, don't cry. I love you too much to see you so sad."

Mom was home when Flora opened the front door to let us in.

"Elizabeth! Danny!" Mom exclaimed as we nearly collided at the top of the stairs.

Mom was rushing out, already dressed for lunch.

"It's so good to see you!" Mom said and she hugged us. "Why are you here?"

"Eli had a sudden craving to be beaten at tennis," Danny answered and winked.

"I do not intend on being beaten," I answered and then added, "I need clean whites and a bathing suit."

"Can I borrow a polo from Mike?"

"Help yourself, Danny."

"Thanks. While I'm in your closet, can you find out why your daughter is so sad? All she'll tell me is she doesn't want to have a fight."

"Sure, Danny." Mom shook her head, perplexed. "Whatever."

"Thanks, Randi." Danny kissed my cheek and went toward my parents' room.

Mom followed me into my room and perched herself on my bed. Meanwhile, I rummaged through my walk-in closet, digging in the back for tennis clothes.

"Elizabeth, what's going on?" Mom asked when I emerged with a tennis dress and a floral Gottex one-piece with a matching pareo. "Danny says you're sad. Didn't you have a good time at Naomi's?"

"You know we did. I'm sure Ellen reported in," I giggled.

Mom laughed. I was right. "Then, why so sad? Danny's worried."

I bit my lower lip to keep my emotions under control. I didn't know how long I could hold out. Close as I was to my mother, I had never confided in her. Now I hurt because of it.

Mom intimidated me. Had I not feared her judgment, I could have relieved myself of the burden I was carrying. Mom didn't know the pain Danny had inflicted on me. Otherwise, she would tell me to drop him. Mom would be ashamed of my weakness. At times, I certainly was.

"Is this about Sunday?" Mom asked.

I nodded 'yes.' Speaking would bring unwelcomed tears. Now that it was Monday, the specter of Sunday had come crashing down like the proverbial ton of bricks in ways my mother could not imagine. Her husband was Dad, aka Mr. Perfect.

Mom's soft brown eyes met mine with a ferocity that wouldn't quit. She gave me the look that said she knew I was hiding something. Mom wouldn't rest until I spilled.

I turned away, my arms protectively across my chest. Tears flowed. I was shaking. Mom rose from the bed and gathered me in her warm embrace.

"Elizabeth," she said softly, "What is it, honey?"

Gut-wrenching pain paralyzed me. Mom had gone from opposing me being with Danny to whole-heartedly accepting us in large part because I was so happy. Would Mom consider me a liar when she learned the truth? Until today, I had been happy; Danny was wonderful. There was only one problem, and it killed me to voice it.

"Mommy, I don't trust Danny," I sobbed.

Immediately, I regretted my confession.

"Elizabeth, you live with Danny. What do you mean you don't trust him?" Mom asked, being kind for now, not judgmental. That would come later, I was certain.

"Mostly I trust him. I love Danny, but Mom, I'm afraid he's going to cheat," I sobbed.

The tears would not stop. I was trembling. The ugly truth was nearly out. Mom held me close and rubbed my back to provide comfort.

"You'll be seeing Danny every weekend," she pointed out.

"I know. But there's the rest of the week," I sniffled, tears subsiding.

"Why would you doubt him? Danny loves you."

"He's done it before," I whispered.

"Elizabeth! No!" Mom exclaimed softly. "Are you certain?"

"Yes," I whimpered so softly I was nearly inaudible.

Mom held me closer. She stroked my hair. Her voice took on a deflated edge. "My heart breaks for you, honey. How do you know?"

"Back in January. I overheard a girl at the library telling a friend. I confronted him then."

"What did Danny say?"

"It was a short fling. He saw her only once or twice."

"Elizabeth, you must have been devastated. Why didn't you call?"

"I was afraid to. You would have told me to break up with him."

"I would have," Mom agreed. "And you didn't want to hear that."

"No, I didn't. I called Ellen. She told me about Steve."

"I'm so sorry, honey," Mom said, sadly. "I know how much you love Steve."

I nodded.

"Elizabeth, I'm trying to process this. What did Ellen say?"

"Ellen told me Danny was sorry and to follow my heart."

"And your heart belongs to Danny."

I nodded as I answered tearfully. "I love Danny. I love him even more now."

"Has it happened again?"

"I don't think so," I lied. "But Danny's never promised not to do it again." I couldn't reveal my suspicions about Reggie. That would be too humiliating.

"Have you said anything to Danny?"

"Not in a while. I'm afraid. I might not like the answer."

"Elizabeth, I don't condone Danny's behavior. He took your heart and broke off a part of it. I can't look at him the same way anymore."

"Mom," I begged, "Danny can't know that I told you."

"Elizabeth, I would never betray your confidence," Mom promised. "Danny's behavior was reprehensible, but you say it hasn't happened again."

I nodded my confirmation.

"Danny's a sensitive young man. Hopefully seeing the hurt he inflicted made him realize the enormity of his actions."

"I hope so."

"Elizabeth, you were willing to forgive Danny because you loved him. What will make you forget?

"Words. Words will make me forget. I need Danny to promise he will never do anything to hurt me again."

"Let's think about this," Mom suggested. "You're living together?"

"Yes. We even opened a joint checking account."

"You did?" Mom was pleasantly surprised and smiled.

"Yes," I hesitated.

"You just returned from Naomi's, and I've seen you together enough to know how much Danny loves you."

"What's your point, Mom?"

"Actions speak louder than words, Elizabeth. Living together, joint bank accounts, visiting grandmothers; men don't frivolously do these things. Does Danny discuss your future?"

I finally smiled as I thought of how often Danny did.

"Danny talks about when we graduate and how beautiful he thinks I'll be when I'm pregnant. Danny wants lots of babies."

"Elizabeth, Danny certainly sounds committed. I wouldn't worry about it. He probably doesn't even think about you needing to hear the words at this point. Danny probably thinks telling you he loves you every day is enough."

"You think so?"

"Men do not discuss babies casually. It's the biggest commitment there is."

I hugged her tightly.

"Thanks, Mom. I better wash. I don't want Danny seeing my face tear-stained."

Mom left my room as I entered the bathroom. Through the running water I heard her and Danny.

"How's Eli?" he asked.

"She's good. Tell Elizabeth I'm leaving. I'll see you at lunch."

I splashed cold water on my cheeks and dabbed my eyes. Then I patted my face dry with a hand towel. Appraising my reflection, I was pleased to note my early season tan deflected attention from my puffy eyes.

I took a deep breath and exhaled slowly. Confiding in Mom made me feel better. She had not been judgmental nor had she told me to dump Danny.

Beyond the bathroom door, Danny was waiting. Poor boy! Today I was an emotional rollercoaster, and he had tolerated it. At least I was happy again.

I stepped into my bedroom and found Danny in Dad's white polo shirt. My sapphire-eyed sweetheart was staring at me.

My earlier sadness gone, I was able to appreciate how handsome Danny looked today. In contrast to his sandy hair, his tanned skin was striking. His eyes stood out more than usual. They were twinkling for me. Full, pink lips smiled my way.

"Feeling better?" he asked. Danny sounded hopeful.

"Yes," I answered, giving him my megawatt smile.

I took Danny's hands and pulled myself into his comforting embrace.

"Does this mean you're over whatever was going to cause us to fight later?"

"What fight" I asked innocently.

My hands reached up, and I brought Danny's lips to mine for a kiss.

"I have plans for tonight," I said breathlessly, "And a fight would be completely counterproductive."

"I know your plans, and you're right."

Danny's breath was on my face. He gripped my head through my thick waves and as my hands reached around his neck our lips met. Mine parted eagerly, sharing our love. All doubts vanished in the security of Danny's strong, loving arms.

Then Danny lifted my skirt and squeezed me. I gasped.

"Baby, I want you now," Danny whispered in my ear. "Do you know how tortuous it was sleeping next to you at Grandma's and not being able to love you?"

"Do you know how tortuous it was to feel you poking against me?"

Our lips joined again, our tongues exploring. Consumed by lust, Danny pushed my skirt and my thong down past my thighs where they fell to the floor.

Drunk from Danny's passionate sensuality, I couldn't react sanely. I was half undressed and his hardness rubbed against me. We had never made love in my parents' house. Yet here we were, powerless to stop.

"I love you, Eli."

"Flora will hear us," I protested while I unfastened his shorts and pushed them down far enough to fall to the floor.

"Too bad." Danny lifted me off the floor, our lips once more glued together.

On the way to the bed, Danny kicked the door closed. The highly charged moment left me feeling wasted, my mind turned to jelly. I was senseless. I wanted Danny as much as he wanted me, and I wanted him now.

Giddy from our furtive love making, we arrived at the Riviera Country Club. Freshly showered and wearing tennis whites, I hoped my mother wouldn't notice my damp, braided hair or more obvious, Danny's shaggy wet mane. Self-conscious, with grins that wouldn't quit, there was no getting around what we had been up to since Mom left the house.

In a lust-induced haze, I followed Danny to the dining room where we found our mothers already seated. Ellen rose and greeted us with hugs and kisses. Mom raised an eyebrow and shook her head. I blushed crimson. Danny sat by my side, confident and not caring.

Normally lunch at the club was relaxing. Today I couldn't get past Mom's glances and Danny's leg rubbing mine beneath the table.

I was relieved when Danny glanced at his Rolex and announced, "Time for tennis, Eli."

But my concentration was shot. Thoughts of our romantic interlude dominated. I spent the next hour going through the motions. My brain couldn't function. Neither could my body. I floated through the match.

Later that evening, we snuggled on the chaise beside the outdoor fireplace. "Will you ever tell me what we were going to fight over now that you say we won't?" Danny asked.

I thought before answering. "I'll tell you when we go to bed on September First." By then my insecurities would have been rendered moot, and we'd share a good laugh.

"Eli, I'll hold you to that," Danny chuckled

CHAPTER 104 - ELIZABETH

Wednesday Danny woke full of energy. Giving me a loud, playful smacker of a kiss, he bounced out of bed, near manic as he vaulted over me.

"E, go back to sleep. I'm picking up Teddy. It's going to be great hanging out with him."

I never heard Danny leave, so I knew I fell back to sleep. A check of the clock confirmed over an hour had passed. If I didn't want my brother catching me in my birthday suit, I needed to hit the shower and get dressed.

Danny and Teddy were in the kitchen when I came downstairs. The raucous scene reminded me of an exclusive fraternity. I was not used to this level of testosterone in my house.

Teddy was removing bagels from a brown paper bag and playfully tossing them to Danny. On the other side of the kitchen he caught the bagels and placed them in a large bowl. They were laughing, having a good time. My boys!

Danny spied me first. He smiled playfully and opened his arms to me.

"Here's your lazy sister!" Danny announced as he pulled me into his embrace. He was grinning. Teddy laughed.

"Danny, you told me to go back to sleep," I protested.

"So I did. Good morning, Sweetheart."

"Good morning," I answered. Then I pirouetted out of his embrace and over to Teddy.

"Hey, bro," I said, and I kissed his forehead after brushing a lock of wavy brown hair off his face. "Welcome to Casa de Jacobs-Newman."

"Elizabeth, this is so weird you living here with Danny."

"Whatever," I answered. I picked up a tomato from the counter and began to play one-handed catch.

"Come here, Eli," Danny said.

I caught the tomato one last time and in two strides I was at Danny's side. He embraced me again but this time he kissed me. It was awkward with Teddy watching.

"Teddy's here," I whispered through gritted teeth.

"I don't care." Danny kissed me again, not caring.

"Can you stop that?" Teddy asked. He flushed as red as the tomato. "That's my sister."

Danny stopped but kept his arms wrapped around my shoulders.

"Sorry," Danny apologized. "I love your sister. Eli's my lady." Then Danny noticed the tomato. "Can you please slice that, babe? I'm hungry." I groaned. Typical!

After clearing the breakfast dishes, Danny grabbed my hand and barked, "Teddy, fill the dishwasher. I want to show Eli the surprise."

What it could be? "It's in the garage," he added.

Teddy, already rinsing the dishes, smirked. He knew.

"My car!" I exclaimed as Danny pulled me into the garage. My Range Rover.

"It arrived last night," Danny explained.

"Thank you."

"I knew you'd want it, but today I need it."

The back seat was down and bicycles filled the space.

"Teddy and I are picking up the bike path in Santa Monica. Eli, you don't mind, do you?" Danny gave me sad puppy dog eyes. "I never spend time with Teddy."

"I know," I sighed. I was not happy with losing Danny for the day, but I was pleased to encourage their relationship.

Danny pulled me to his chest. "Eli, you're the best," he said and kissed me. "We'll be back by six." Danny kissed me again. "You can drive my car today. Have fun. Go shopping."

Danny pressed his keys into my palm. Then he pulled out his wallet and handed me a black American Express card and five one hundred dollar bills.

After my initial disappointment at not spending the day with Danny wore off, I realized he was right. It was time to get acquainted with my new hometown.

A trip to a nail salon was my first stop. I decided on a Shellac French manicure and a pink polish pedicure too. What the heck? I had all day, and I was wearing flip-flops anyway.

Next stop, the Malibu Country Mart and The Lumberyard.

I had never had much opportunity to shop in Malibu. When I was a kid, I stayed at the house and played on the beach. Later, we came for casual weekends and parties. The extent of my Malibu shopping experiences was trips to Ralph's for groceries or outings to movies.

Delighted with the variety, I discovered several boutiques that seemed to have been stocked just for me. Casual attire in soft cottons and linen were perfect for life in a town where it was acceptable to go out wearing a bathing suit with a towel wrapped around your waist.

Several shopping bags later, an iced tea break was in order. Walking up the row of shops to Coffee Bean and Tea Leaf, I passed a home décor shop. Well, Danny wanted me to make the house mine. Maybe later.

With surprising ease I was able to find a small table for enjoying my tea and chocolate chip cookie. Perched near the rim of the centrally located sand-filled playground, my table was an ideal place to kick back and relax. About a dozen children were playing on the slides, the swings and in the sand. Laughter and squeals were a pleasure to behold.

"Lucky children," I thought.

I smiled in their direction. As a child, I hadn't been allowed that freedom. My children would not be cloistered like I had been.

A cool breeze was blowing in from the Pacific. My loose auburn waves floated. I breathed deeply, satisfied. The salty air smelled so good. I could sit here all day!

Alone with my tea, I reflected on the past week. Hard to believe only a week had passed. Life with Danny had totally consumed me. I hadn't given Donnelly a moment's thought until now. I hadn't thought about Rachel or Chloe or even my local friends!

Leaning back in the chair, I sipped my iced tea. I inhaled deeply, absorbing the environment. Malibu had to be the most beautiful town in America. Everyone I'd met had been welcoming, too. I loved living in Malibu!

I enjoyed having a home that was mine, not my parents. I always thought having my own home would be cool. Sharing it with the man I had spent my entire life loving made it even more so. I was a real adult!

Most amazing was the growth in my relationship with Danny this past week. Danny might not have given me a ring, but I was as secure in his love as though he had. Now I regretted my tear-filled confession to Mom.

Mom was right. Actions do speak louder than words. How many girls with rings had the trust and love that Danny and I shared?

Sunday was coming, but I would make the most of the days we had left. I would be cheerful. Danny deserved to see me happy. He deserved to be showered with attention and treated like a king. Nothing would make me happier than to make the remainder of the week the best Danny had ever experienced.

With a bounce in my step and renewed purpose, I set out on the second half of my day determined to make this portion as Danny-centric as possible.

After stashing my bags in the car, I strode into the décor store. Something had to be right for our home. Even if it were only a vase, it would please Danny if I added my imprimatur.

Just inside the small store, I found it. Only it couldn't be brought home today or anytime soon. Across the back wall was a magnificent seascape mural. Our living room was bland; it cried out for a mural. The wall behind the sofa was the ideal place. I would not say a word. I only hoped it could be complete by his return in August. I loved surprising Danny!

For today, I purchased two fringed throw pillows in an ombre-dip mélange of sea foam and sky blue. They would liven up the room and look great with the mural that in my mind was as good as painted.

As expected, my boys were not home when I returned. First, I put away the food I had picked up for dinner. Teddy would be surprised that I could cook!

Next, I snipped the tags off the pillows, plumped them, and placed them on the sofa. There! They looked as inviting to the eye as they were cozy to lean against.

Upstairs I hung my new purchases in the closet, carefully placing Danny's on his side. I hoped he liked what I bought. I had walked over to Kitson's after I crammed the pillows in the car. It was an exciting experience, clothing shopping for a man! I bought Danny several graphic t-shirts and colorful casual shirts. Then I crossed to the James Perce store and purchased the softest sold colored t-shirts ever. They would be perfect for Vancouver.

It was three o'clock, and I was wiped. I changed into one of Danny's old shirts, opened the slider to enjoy the sea breeze, and crawled into bed.

Two hours later I awoke, well rested. I stretched my arms and yawned. Surrounded by the scent of my favorite person, I didn't want to leave the bed. It was too cozy!

This is what I needed while Danny was in Vancouver. Would Graciela think I was gross if I ordered her not to change our sheets until Danny returned? I could satisfy my desires by hiding his pillow each week before she arrived.

I willed myself to sitting. Danny and Teddy would be home shortly and I wanted to prep dinner. After a day spent bicycling, they would be starving.

Rising slowly, I spied the silk rose on my pillow. I picked it up and held it to my heart, then sighed, satisfied.

With my heart full of love, I ran to the balcony. Danny and Teddy had to be on the beach. The house was too quiet for them to be inside.

There! I spotted them easily enough. Danny and Teddy had just completed a ride in on a wave using bogie boards. Playfully running in the surf, kicking water at each other and high-fiving, my eyes could have been following two very tall ten year olds.

For the first time, I noticed how much Teddy had grown since January. He couldn't be more than two or three inches shorter than Danny. Teddy must have been hitting the gym, too. His shoulders were broader, and he had the beginning of a muscular physique. With his curly brown hair and warm brown eyes, Teddy must be driving the girls at Bromley crazy. From this distance, I found myself watching two very attractive men.

What an awkward thought! Teddy was barely fifteen. He was my baby brother, not a man. For the first time I understood how Teddy had felt when he found me keeping house like a newlywed this morning. No wonder he seemed uncomfortable.

I thought Danny glanced my way, so I waved the rose. It didn't catch his blind eyes' attention.

I ran back in to change into the bathing suit I had purchased earlier. Turquoise with a floral print, the tank with narrow lingerie straps was cut low in front, but not too low, and similarly cut low in back, but not too low. In contrast, the legs were cut high, almost to my hips, but the matching pareo covered that feature.

I was acutely aware of Teddy's presence and the need to be the proper big sister. That was why I'd bought this suit. The others in the closet were revealing bikinis meant only for Danny. I wouldn't wear those in front of my brother.

Before heading out, I stopped in the kitchen to prepare a marinade for the grilled shrimp appetizer. I squeezed juice from a few limes, chopped some cilantro, added a little olive oil and mixed in a few dashes of cayenne powder. After adding the shrimp, I covered the bowl with plastic wrap and placed it in the refrigerator. In half an hour it would be ready.

One more finger fluff to my hair and I was good to go.

CHAPTER 105 - DANIEL

Before I spotted her, I sensed Elizabeth approach. I looked up. Her new bathing suit emphasized every luscious curve and turquoise was a great color on her. The pareo tied around her swaying hips emphasized the narrow waist I couldn't wait to get my hands around.

Eli's attempt at modesty failed. It amazed me how much sexier she was in this one-piece confection than the two girls flirting shamelessly with Teddy and me were in their show-all bikinis.

Through sunglasses, our eyes made contact. I instantly filled with warmth that lit my face and made my eyes sparkle. I loved Eli's newfound confidence. There I stood, chatting with two attractive and practically naked girls, yet she didn't so much as flinch. Eli knew as well as I did that she was my lady, forever.

Sometime during the last two weeks at Donnelly I had made that decision. After the embarrassment of Rachel learning of my pointless fling with Amelia, I knew I had to stop denying the inevitable. Elizabeth was my great love. I couldn't live without her. It was time to grow-up and stop sabotaging our relationship.

Moving in, taking her to meet Grandma, opening a bank account, those were my ways of telling Eli I would take care of her now. I hadn't said the words or given her a ring, but in my mind she had crossed the threshold and had become a Newman.

The words would come later. That was the other decision I had made. Elizabeth and I came from homes where one parent or another had spent time away on location. Intellectually we knew what it meant to be separated. This summer we were the ones forced apart. Eli and I would be together most weekends, but could our love sustain us through a separation that was nearly half as long as our entire relationship?

Elizabeth shouldn't feel pressured. She needed the freedom to decide if she wanted this life. Eli might decide it wasn't for her. She should make that determination with a clear mind and an honest assessment. If this were for Eli, once settled back at Donnelly, I would tell her the words she so desperately wanted to hear.

"There 's my lady," I said cheerfully as Elizabeth neared.

Eli's smile was as bright as the sun. The boogie board I was holding under my arm fell to the sand, leaving my hands free to circle her waist. Eli went up on toe to kiss my cheek. I surprised her by clasping her against my damp chest.

"I missed you, babe," I whispered.

"I missed you too."

Eli lost her balance. I caught her around her waist. She shrugged, giggling at her clumsiness. The high-pitched delight in her laughter was music.

Eli felt so good. I kept her in my hold as I eyed her ensemble. "Nice," I said. "You've been shopping." Elizabeth blushed.

I let one hand leave Eli's waist to hold her face, and I quickly kissed her. Eli melted in my arms. Then I moved my hand to her shoulder, holding Eli close, and I clasped her hand. Elizabeth's fingers were so soft. Freshly manicured too.

"I bought you some things too." Elizabeth smiled, pleased with herself.

"Thanks, babe."

Elizabeth need not have bought me anything, but the pleasure she derived from making me happy showed in her sparkling emerald eyes.

I ignored Teddy and the girls as I kissed Elizabeth to show how much I loved her.

"Do you mind?" Teddy interrupted.

"Sorry, Teddy. I missed your sister."

"She's your sister?" the dark haired girl asked.

"Yes," Teddy answered.

"You didn't say you had a girlfriend," the sun-bleached white blonde sneered. Her coloring reminded me of Juliette. I didn't want that memory.

"You didn't ask," I answered flippantly. It was really none of her business.

The blonde was dumbfounded, but Eli smiled.

"Teddy might be auditioning for a girlfriend," I added as an afterthought.

Teddy's grin told me he liked that idea. Eli's glare told me she didn't.

"Time to start the grill," Eli announced, purposely changing the subject. "Teddy, you need to shower before dinner," Eli said crossly.

Point made. No girls for Teddy. Big sis defending his virtue, though that contradicted the summer goal he had earlier confided.

Teddy sighed, disappointed.

Eli reached for my hand. "Let's go, Daniel," she ordered.

I reached for my boogie board and let her lead the way.

"Eli, I thought Teddy could have some fun. He's fifteen already."

"He's just a kid!" she growled.

"I was younger," I said in a gentle voice hoping to quiet her.

Eli stood before me defensively; her hands on her hips, her chin tilted defiantly, fire in her green eyes.

"Teddy is not you," she said and frowned.

I tried pulling Eli into my arms but she wouldn't budge.

"Eli, honey c'mon," I said, and I held out my arms for her.

Elizabeth folded her arms across her chest and glared.

"I'm angry, Daniel." Eli scowled.

Despite her crossed-arms stance, I wrapped my arms around her. Elizabeth pressed her head against my chest and sobbed. She was shaking and clung to me.

Eli was not usually this emotional or irrational. I could only come to one conclusion; Eli must be hormonal. I would say whatever needed saying to placate her.

"Honey, I'm sorry. I didn't consider your feelings. All I thought was how Teddy's fifteen. It's time already. I wasn't thinking how you feel responsible for him."

Thankfully Eli's crying stopped. I lifted her chin and looked into sad, red eyes.

"I love you, honey. Now let's kiss and make up."

CHAPTER 106 - DANIEL

"Where's Teddy?" Eli asked as soon as we entered the empty great room from the garage.

Hormonal or not, Eli and I needed time alone, so after dinner we drove into town for gelato. All was quiet when we returned home. The place seemed deserted.

"Teddy's probably in his room. I'll check." I knew what I'd find.

Teddy's downstairs bedroom was a mess. The bed linens were disheveled of course, and Teddy's swim trunks and clothes were dumped on the floor along with two used condoms and their wrappers. I grinned at his success.

Teddy was singing in the shower. I loudly rapped on the bathroom door.

"Yeah?" Teddy called out. His voice was muffled by the sound of the water.

"We're upstairs. And clean up this mess," I ordered. Then I left for the great room.

Eli was waiting; her arms crossed across her chest.

"Teddy's in the shower. He'll be up soon."

Eli dropped her defensive position. I took her hands and drew her to my chest.

"Baby, I missed you today," I said softly.

"Danny, I missed you too. It's almost Thursday," Eli said sadly.

"Is that what this is about? Babe, you've really been emotional today."

"Maybe," Eli sniffled.

"Hey," I said and Elizabeth raised her eyes to mine. "You'll be in Vancouver on Friday. We'll be apart for only five days."

I brought Elizabeth's hands up to my lips and kissed the tops of them. How could I convey to Eli the extent of my love? I told her, 'I love you' so often I needed another way to make Elizabeth understand the depth of my feelings.

"Baby, I can't stand the thought of not waking up next to you every morning. If I were working in L.A., you'd send me off after breakfast. I would have to have a great day.

And Eli, how will I get through the night? Coming home to you is what I look forward to everyday. Hanging out with you is the best. Making love to you, well nothing compares to that."

There were tears in Elizabeth's eyes. A couple trickled out, and I wiped them away with my thumb.

"That was so eloquent. Danny, you've never... That was so beautiful, it hurts."

"Hurts? I don't want you to hurt."

"In a good way. I mean... I don't know what I mean. All I know is I love you so much and your words really touched me."

Elizabeth's sweetness shone through. I reached for her face and held it to mine. Our lips joined. Eli's eagerly parted, welcoming me, allowing my exploration. Her tongue found mine and caressed my mouth. Eli's love was transporting me. Never had I experienced a kiss as emotional as this one.

When it ended, I held Elizabeth's delicate frame against mine and stroked her silky hair. I leaned my chin into Elizabeth's shoulder and with my eyes closed I inhaled her intoxicating floral scent. There could never be anything better than this moment.

Teddy bounced into the room. "Where's my gelato?" he asked. His exuberant entrance startled us.

Eli didn't move, but I opened my eyes and stopped stroking her hair.

"Teddy, your timing sucks, man."

"Sorry," he laughed. How typical! "So where's my gelato?"

Teddy was like an overgrown child. In his Bromley logo pajama pants and t-shirt, he certainly looked like one.

"There's ice cream in the freezer," Elizabeth responded.

"Get me a bowl?"

Eli rolled her eyes and resigned herself to playing mom. She left my arms for the kitchen, leaving me empty in more ways than one.

With Eli's back turned, a sly grin crossed Teddy's face.

"Thanks, Danny," he smirked and high-fived me.

I embraced Teddy and clapped him on the back.

"Who did the honors?" I whispered, hoping Eli wouldn't hear.

No such luck. The ice cream scoop loudly clanged against the stainless steel sink; a deliberate attention-getter that Teddy and I ignored, though he snickered. Teddy could afford to irritate Eli. He wasn't sharing her bed.

"Ashley," he answered. The blonde.

Teddy was completely sober, but he was flying. His smile was infectious. I had experienced this same joy my first time too.

"Was she good to you?" I hoped so.

"Real good," Teddy laughed.

Eli slammed the freezer door shut. Teddy and I exchanged nervous glances and laughed. We were two naughty boys pissing off mom.

"Then Tiffany joined us," Teddy added.

Eli exited the kitchen carrying a bowl of ice cream and a spoon. The steam spouting from her ears threatened to melt the snack.

"No, shit!" I exclaimed, and I stared wide-eyed at Teddy. "You're legend bro! That's never even happened to me."

With angry, narrow eyes Eli shoved the bowl at Teddy and growled. "Daniel Martin Newman! Have you forgotten that I'm in the room?"

"Uh-oh!" Teddy laughed. "Your wife is really pissed, bro."

Eli's face turned scarlet. I was in big trouble.

"Theodore Sean Jacobs! I don't want to hear this!" she barked. "This is not a fraternity. This is my home!" Eli screamed.

"Elizabeth, calm down," I urged her.

Eli glared straight at me. "Daniel!" she snarled, "You were behind this. That's why you insisted on gelato."

Furious, Eli turned toward me, hands on hips. I took advantage and wrapped my arms around her body to still her.

"Shush, Eli. Calm down," I murmured.

Elizabeth relented and began crying. "This is our home," she whimpered.

I stroked her back. Elizabeth clung to me. She sobbed against my chest. I let her hysteria subside and gradually her grip softened.

"Is Elizabeth having a nervous breakdown?" Teddy chuckled. I glared, fed up with him.

"She'll be fine," I snapped. "Teddy, excuse us. Elizabeth and I need our privacy."

Without waiting for either to respond, I scooped Eli up in my arms and threw her over my shoulder.

"Daniel!" she protested, arms and legs flailing against me. But I didn't care, and I grabbed the chenille throw to wrap around her.

Once outside, I slid the door closed against Teddy's prying. I gently placed Eli on a chaise and tucked the throw around her.

Eli reached for my hand, her ire gone. A tear rolled down her check, and I leaned forward to brush it away.

"You were acting like the old Danny," she complained.

"Can't I be immature? Sometimes?" I tried to make Eli smile.

Instead Elizabeth dropped my hand, drew up her knees and tucked in to hide her face. Eli was crying again, but softly.

"Babe?"

"Danny, if I say I'm scared, would you be angry?"

"Angry? Never. What are you scared about, honey?"

"Vancouver. This summer. Us."

I pursed my lips in contemplation. This was not unexpected.

Eli sat up straighter. "Maybe I should move out," she said sadly.

"Of course not! That's the last thing I want."

I slid down. Eli moved over, allowing me to lie on my side facing her. I took back the hand she'd dropped and laced my fingers through hers. Eli's face, Eli's body, her entire being froze, fearful.

"E…"

"I can't live like this, Daniel. This limbo is killing me."

"I can't live like this either."

Panoply of emotions crossed Elizabeth's lovely face. One moment there was disappointment, the next there was hope, and lastly, there was plain confusion. I put my finger up to her lips to signal quiet.

I continued holding Eli's hand, letting our twined fingers rest upon her thigh. I closed the gap between us and quickly kissed her. Eli didn't react. I felt her inner debate. Would remaining true to herself equate to leaving me?

"E, you've been waiting a long time for me to settle down." I smiled warmly and Eli rewarded me with an upturn of her lips. "I'm almost there, baby."

"What does that mean?"

"It means if I weren't leaving, I would give you what you want. Without hesitation."

"I don't understand. Are you setting me up so if you cheat this summer you'll say 'don't be mad, I never made you promises?'"

"God no, Eli. I love you." I twinkled my eyes at her. "Three months is a long time to be apart. You might get tired of the flying. You'll find other things to do on the weekend. I don't want you feeling obligated."

"Do you really think that?"

I shrugged and smiled impishly. "It could happen."

Eli reached for my cheek. Her hand was cold from the night air.

"I could never tire of visiting you."

"Eli, you're being naïve," I whispered, my forehead touching hers.

"I don't think so."

"Lots of guys work at the studio. One of them might ask you out."

Elizabeth burst into a fit of giggles.

"It could happen, Eli. You are gorgeous."

Elizabeth smiled as she rubbed her nose against mine.

"I would turn them down. I have a boyfriend, remember?"

"That's exactly what I mean. Elizabeth, you might want to say yes."

"Daniel, anyone who would ask a girl out who lives with her boyfriend is a cad. Besides, they'll know who my dad is and be intimidated. What about you? Lots of girls work on a set."

"Any girl who would want a guy who lives with his girlfriend is a slut." I mischievously raised an eyebrow. "Hmm. Now that I put it that way…"

"Daniel!" Elizabeth feigned annoyance. She knew I was teasing.

"I will be too busy working to notice any girls. Besides, when they see how amazing my lady is, they'll know they have no chance."

And I flashed Elizabeth my flirtiest grin. She blushed.

"Daniel?"

"Elizabeth?"

Eli reached her hands around my neck and kissed me.

"Some ambitious young suit might try taking advantage because of your parents. Dating Elizabeth Jacobs could be very attractive for their careers."

"I'm taken, Daniel."

Elizabeth's breath tickled my cheek as she spoke.

"It could happen, Eli."

Elizabeth pressed her lips to mine while her hands held my face to hers as though we were glued together. I delicately ran my hand down Elizabeth's pareo-covered thigh. A shiver ran through her.

"I'm taken, Daniel," Eli repeated in a whisper.

"I hope so," I whispered back.

My breath on Eli's face made her shudder.

"Why are you being insecure?" Eli asked. "I've never seen you like this."

I gave Eli a quick lip nibble.

"I don't want to lose you. Any of these scenarios could happen."

"Daniel?" Eli knew I was hiding something.

I inhaled deeply. "I'm acutely aware that I'm the only boyfriend you've ever had. Being apart, you'll have time to think about it. Maybe you'll decide you're too young for this." I gestured toward the house. " Maybe you'll decide you want to experiment with other men."

Eli laughed. "That would be disappointing."

"I'm serious, Eli."

"So am I." Then Elizabeth smiled. "Daniel, you're right. I am too young to settle down, but I couldn't be happier."

Eli pressed her lips to mine for another heart-felt kiss. "I love you Daniel. That's not going to change."

I touched her lower lip with my finger. "I love you too. That's why I want you to have options."

Eli took my hand and pressed it to her cheek. Then she kissed my palm. Eli's laughing emerald eyes never left me.

"You didn't move me in here to give me options. So cut the crap, Newman. This is the most bogus conversation I've ever had."

My mouth opened wide, then closed. Elizabeth's directness took me completely by surprise. I loved it! She was so hot!.

"You're right. This is bogus. I don't want to give you options. I felt obligated because I'm leaving." I kissed the top of Eli's head.

Elizabeth pulled back a few inches to make eye contact. "Daniel, you are a very complicated man. That's part of why I love you. In this case, there's something in your head, something intangible that even I can't comprehend. I don't know if you even understand it. But if that infinitesimal fraction of one percent is telling you to hold off until you return in August, I can live with that."

"You can?" Elizabeth understood!

"Yes, I can," Elizabeth smiled. Her delicate fingers cupped my face. "Because I'm getting what I want, so what's three more months when I've been waiting nineteen years." Eli laughed.

"You're so confident."

"Completely." Eli wrapped her hands around my neck. Through my hair she pulled me to her. My arms clutched Eli's body against mine, my hands resting on her upper thigh.

Elizabeth's full lips parted. Our tongues met, caressing. She had never tasted sweeter. Her leg curled around mine, gripping me in a vise. The pareo slipped open exposing Eli's thigh. My hand stroked her thigh, enjoying its smooth softness. Eli responded by moving as close to me as possible, sliding her leg up to my hip. My desires rose hard against her, probing, wanting entrance.

Eli abruptly uncurled her leg and stopped kissing me. What the...?

"Teddy," she whispered. "He can see us."

We both laughed having forgotten our houseguest.

"One more kiss," she said, not wanting us to end.

I grabbed Eli and attacked her lips again. My hand caressed her thigh. Teddy be damned! He could avert his eyes. Elizabeth was right. I was spoiled.

CHAPTER 107 - ELIZABETH

Call me selfish, but I was looking forward to my brother's departure. With so little time left before Sunday, I didn't want to share Danny a moment longer than necessary.

Hearing Teddy in the living room, Danny and I decided we'd better get out of bed. While he took a quick shower, I threw on yoga pants and last night's hoodie. Grubby, with my hair a tangled mess, grooming could wait. I wanted Teddy gone.

But first Teddy had to be fed. I raced to the kitchen to get breakfast started. Being boys, Danny and Teddy virtually inhaled the scrambled eggs I cooked. They gobbled up bagels too.

Normally a raised eyebrow from me got Danny to slow his pace, but not today, no raised eyebrow. I wanted Teddy out of here so badly I didn't care if I finished eating my meal alone.

Danny was a study in motion. Whether he was taking the quickest shower and literally throwing on shorts, or wolfing down breakfast, Danny was operating in warped speed hyper mode this morning. He wanted Teddy gone too.

Danny fairly ran in from Teddy's room, my brother's backpack slung over his shoulder. I was starting on the second half of my bagel but Danny grabbed my shoulders and smacked a loud kiss on my cheek.

"Gotta go, babe. I'll be back soon."

"Don't get a speeding ticket," I warned.

The way Danny was moving, I was afraid to see the speedometer.

"What will you be doing?" Danny managed to stop long enough to ask.

"I'm feeling lazy. I'll just lie on a lounge chair and bake in the sun."

"Sounds good. I'll join you late, but we won't have long. We're going to the stadium later. The Braves are in town."

"Can I come too?" Teddy piped in, having quietly arrived from his bedroom.

No! I wanted to be alone with Danny, even if we were with 50,000 strangers.

"Eli?" Danny asked, his eyes pleading Teddy's case.

I sighed loudly. Danny gave me no choice.

"Teddy can come but we're dropping him at his house after the game."

Danny hugged my shoulders and kissed the side of my forehead.

"Thank you, Sweetheart," he said and rushed off to the garage.

"Thanks, sis," Teddy called while running after Danny.

I didn't like it, but I understood. I would see Danny every weekend. He wouldn't see Teddy again until August if not later.

"Mind if I come too?" Dad asked, as we were getting Teddy. "I wouldn't normally ask, but as you're already taking Teddy...."

"Sure, Dad." I frowned. How could I answer otherwise? "What about Mom?" Or all of Santa Monica for that matter?

Danny opened the front passenger door. I hesitated. Did Dad expect to sit there?

"Go ahead Elizabeth. We're intruding on your date."

I climbed into the car while Dad and Teddy settled into the back.

"Where's Mom?" I asked again as we headed east on San Vicente.

"She's meeting friends for an early dinner before going to a screening," Dad replied.

"What's she seeing, Mike?" Danny asked.

"Some weepie chick flick. Don't ask. I didn't pay attention."

"E, why didn't you go with her?" Danny asked.

"You know me better than that," I snapped. "I resent 'weepie chick flicks.' It's so sexist to think all women like movies that make them cry. I don't."

"Sorry I asked," Danny relented.

"Mom didn't invite me," I awkwardly admitted.

"Kids, thanks for letting me and Teddy tag along," Dad interjected.

"Yeah, Dad. It's not like Danny and I ever get to spend time alone anymore."

"Tomorrow we will," Danny announced. Seeing my disappointment, he picked up my hand. "Tomorrow will be Eli's day. Nobody else is invited, okay?"

"I have witnesses, Daniel."

"I promise. Tomorrow is about you. We'll do whatever you want and then we'll have a nice, quiet dinner at Geoffrey's. How's that?"

I immediately cheered up. A day alone with Danny, followed by a romantic dinner – works for me!

If only the Dodgers would score a couple of runs early and then settle into a low-scoring pitchers' duel. Then the game would end quickly and we could shed my father and brother.

At least Dad understood. When we reached our seats, he insisted that Teddy sit with him in the row in front of Danny and me.

"Enjoy," Dad said, and he kissed my cheek before sitting down next to Teddy.

In the top of the second inning, just as the Dodgers completed a double play, a familiar voice interrupted us.

"Can I join you?"

Danny and I stopped our celebration kiss mid-stream.

"Steve!" I exclaimed, thrilled to see him.

"Dad! This is unexpected."

I jumped up and enthusiastically hugged Steve. He was forced to balance his tray carrying two loaded hot dogs and a beer, on the seat so he wouldn't drop them.

Steve and Danny warmly embraced. By this time Dad was standing too.

"Steven, glad you made it," Dad said while clapping his hand against Steve's shoulder in a brotherly greeting.

"Thanks for the text, Michael. My driver dropped me off. Is there room in your car for me?"

"Should be. We came in Elizabeth's Range Rover."

"Dad, I thought you weren't coming home until tomorrow," Danny said.

"I thought so too, but I'm meeting with the studio in the morning."

Steve sat down beside Dad and turned to him. "Personnel issue," he said quietly as though it were a code.

"Talent?" Dad responded just as softly.

I had a feeling Dad and Steve didn't want anyone listening. So I tried as hard as possible to block out all the other stadium noises to hear them.

"You'll be there, right?" Steve asked Dad.

"Yeah. It's my film too. I want a happy director."

"But it's their money. And they want her."

"You may be stuck, bro."

"If I can give them another name by tomorrow."

"I hear you," Dad said empathetically. "But there are three problems."

"Curiosity because of my insistence..."

"Main one. Plus she's perfect for the part and it's been publicized."

"A beautiful, young bitch. Nobody can play bitch better," Steve groused.

Were they discussing Vanessa Rogers? She was Steve's announced star, and Vanessa was young, beautiful and an infamous bitch.

Dad snapped his head around and caught me. He must have felt my ears boring into their backs. I tried to look innocent but I'm sure I failed.

If I was correct, why was Vanessa so disliked by Steve?

Dad turned back to Steve. "Come by early for breakfast. We'll talk then when we'll have privacy." He emphasized the word privacy.

It wasn't until we had dropped Steve, Dad and Teddy off that I could reflect on the overheard conversation. Dad must have thought I knew whom he and Steve were referring to. In reality, I was far from certain and was guessing.

Nearly my entire family was involved in this project. Prior to now I hadn't paid much if any attention to it. Would Steve's 'personnel issue' impact Danny? I hoped not.

And poor Dad! If Steve couldn't get an actor replaced, Dad would be under a lot of stress. We could all be in for a long, hot summer.

CHAPTER 108 - DANIEL

Eli's Day was here! I had the morning planned, and I knew Elizabeth would love it.

A sleepy smile played upon Elizabeth's full pink lips. Thick auburn waves flared in all directions. I smiled in memory of the mess I'd made of them last night. Then I slid over, closing the inches-wide gap. The comforter covered most of her, though a lightly tanned shoulder attached to a slender arm faced me.

Careful not to wake Elizabeth, I smoothed the waves off her neck and shoulder. I reached my arm around her, pressing my body against hers. Elizabeth's narrow frame was soft and fragile.

Ever so gently, I kissed her neck and shoulder. Eli's squeezed-tight closed eyes didn't fool me. The silent, laughing smile and delightful squirm told me all I needed to know. She was awake. I leaned over her shoulder and kissed her cheek.

"Good morning, beautiful," I whispered.

"Good morning," Elizabeth whispered back.

Her voice was musical; the sound of Eli's smile. I held her securely, pleased that Elizabeth enjoyed my touch on her bare skin as much as I did.

"It's Eli's Day. How do you want to spend it?" I asked while stroking her thigh.

"Daniel Martin Newman," Elizabeth said in a devilishly seductive trill.

"Am I in trouble?" My question was light and teasing.

Eli rotated in my arms to face me. Her hands went around my neck. An infectious grin lit her face.

"You sure are," Eli pronounced, and she joyously pressed her lips against mine.

Yep, I was in trouble. And I planned on enjoying every minute of it.

"What's next?" Eli eagerly asked while we lay in each other's arms relishing the warm afterglow of making love.

I smiled at her childlike curiosity, a complete contradiction of her very womanly behavior.

"It's your day, babe." Then I kissed her parted lips before she could reply. Elizabeth's hand on my cheek held us together and she smiled.

"You haven't shaved in a few days." Eli stroked my two-day growth.

"Am I hurting you?" I hadn't thought about my rough stubble against her soft skin when I decided not to shave yesterday. Sometimes I got so sick of it. Ironic, as only a few years ago I had wanted so badly to be a man I had shaved peach fuzz.

Elizabeth gently caressed my cheek.

"I like it. It's very masculine." Then she kissed me. "Let's run on the beach?"

"Run on the beach?" Ugh, no! Eli had already sapped my energy.

"It'll be fun. It's such a beautiful morning."

"Haven't we had enough exercise already?"

Elizabeth considered this. "How about a walk?"

"Okay," I sighed, "But not too long. I did plan one part of the day."

"You did?" Eli asked, curious.

"I did, baby. I have coming to our home," I said slowly and deliberately to build suspense, "Not one, but two masseuses so we can have massages, together, outside on the patio."

"Seriously?" Elizabeth asked. She was so excited.

"Seriously," I laughed.

Elizabeth reached for me and kissed me again. I ran my finger up her spine causing her to squirm. "Daniel, you're the best."

"No, you are." I pulled Eli to me and devoured her luscious lips.

We never made it to the beach. We barely made it to a quick shower before the massage team arrived.

An hour and a half later, we were like two extra limp noodles.

"First shower," I ordered Eli.

I knew full well that she'd be in the bathroom for at least half an hour. I could take a much-deserved nap.

San Vicente Boulevard, Brentwood's main shopping district, was unusually busy today, but this was where Elizabeth wanted to be. The wide boulevard is lined with upscale shopping, restaurants, and a Whole Foods market. The passing runners reminded me of what we hadn't done earlier and I grinned at the memory of our more enjoyable work-out. Keeping fit the Newman way. I sighed, content.

Some things about Elizabeth I would never understand. Maybe all girls were like this. I didn't know. I lacked experience. But on a day when we could have done anything, or gone anywhere, Elizabeth insisted that what she wanted to do the most was shop at the Free People boutique.

"Didn't you buy new clothes two days ago?" I had asked, half hoping my question would make Elizabeth rethink her retail plans.

Instead I was the recipient of a glare that made me feel completely inept.

"Those are for the beach. I can't wear them to the studio. And forget about couture." In case I'd been ready to suggest Beverly Hills.

I understood, but I had to laugh. Unless you're working in Hollywood, which she was, Free People's edgy feminine styles did not qualify as work clothes anywhere else. Elizabeth would be in for a rude awakening if she ever worked on Wall Street or at a law firm.

Eli in a business suit! I caught myself laughing out loud as we neared the store entrance. My arm was around Eli's shoulder and she cocked her head in my direction.

"What?"

She was adorable, no doubt about that.

"Nothing," I smiled. "A thought struck me as funny."

Elizabeth shrugged and narrowed her eyes. She was confused, but not enough to further inquire.

"Elizabeth!" A very attractive blonde salesgirl warmly greeted Eli as we entered the store. She was probably my age or a little older and, I assumed, an aspiring actress. If I were she, I would remember Elizabeth Jacobs too.

The level of attention she would lavish on Eli would be in direct proportion to her ambition. I was twenty years old and already a jaded cynic. Not so Elizabeth.

"Monica, I need some new clothes. I start my summer job on Monday."

"Oh, of course," Monica concurred with the appropriate level of understanding.

I laughed again. Only in Brentwood!

Eli frowned, looking at me crossly. I shrugged. It didn't work. She was pissed.

"Don't mind him, Monica," Elizabeth said sourly.

Of course that's exactly what Monica now did. She minded me. Monica regarded me, all of me, and looked me straight in the eyes while turning on her best business smile. Had I not been accompanying a favored customer, say we'd met at a bar, I would have been the recipient of the flirtatious version of that smile.

"Who's this?" an intrigued Monica asked Elizabeth.

"My roommate. He's sharing a private joke with himself," Eli answered coolly.

"I'm sorry, babe. I'll explain later," I kissed Elizabeth's forehead. Roommate, huh? "Go find lots of nice things, honey," I instructed.

With Monica's assistance, Eli did indeed find lots of nice things. Guaranteed, she would be the most fashionable summer intern in Culver City.

Once Elizabeth entered the dressing room, I removed my American Express card from my wallet and handed it to Monica.

"Whatever Elizabeth wants, put it on this," I instructed.

"You didn't have to do that," Eli protested afterwards.

Her pleased smile told me otherwise. Eli would have to get used to my spoiling now that she lived in my house.

After driving down to the heart of San Vicente, we stopped in M.Fredric for a few more things. Later, strolling down the boulevard, we picked up a light snack at Whole Foods that would tide us over until dinner.

Again my arm was around Eli's back, my hand resting on her shoulder, while I carried her shopping bags. She was enjoying the chivalry. I was too. On Eli's Day, Eli did not carry shopping bags.

I stopped in the middle of the sidewalk and kissed her. Eli's face lit with joy.

"I love you, babe," I murmured.

Then Eli did the unthinkable for Eli. She grabbed my cheeks and kissed me in the middle of the busiest street in Brentwood!

Click! Click, click, click.

"Eli, someone took our picture."

"What!" She exclaimed, horrified.

"That wasn't a tourist."

"Why?" She frowned.

"Don't sweat it, baby. At least you were kissing me," I grinned.

Elizabeth smiled. "I was, wasn't I. But why would anyone care?"

"People Magazine."

"The premiere?"

"We're gossip worthy. It's almost two months and we're still together."

"Does that mean they'll be speculating about our wedding and kids?"

"Probably. Better keep a flat stomach or they'll say you're pregnant."

When we returned home, what little was left of the afternoon Elizabeth wanted to spend relaxing on the sun-drenched patio.

"I'll be down in a few," I told her after she had changed into a bikini.

I didn't want Elizabeth watching me go through my side of the closet to prepare for packing. I planned to leave as much as possible here and take more from Brentwood. Elizabeth should not feel as though I'd moved out.

Tomorrow I would bring my filled suitcases to my parents' house. I was leaving Sunday in the early afternoon from Santa Monica Airport. Dad wanted to settle me in at the hotel in Vancouver and share dinner before he left for an early evening meeting. I hated being alone in a hotel room. My iPad would be my savior this summer.

After arranging my clothes for easy packing, I changed to swim shorts and hurried out to join Elizabeth.

CHAPTER 109 - DANIEL

Waiting for Eli. Waiting for Eli. Waiting for Eli!

I sat in the great room waiting for Eli. In keeping with the drama of the day, she insisted on making a grand entrance.

CNN did not hold my attention this evening. I was antsy, though we had plenty of time to get to Geoffrey's, one of the most romantic restaurants in Los Angeles. With its cliff side location and to die from ocean views, it was a Malibu institution. Though Geoffrey's was perhaps five minutes from our house, I still found myself constantly checking my watch.

If this is what Elizabeth meant by making it feel like a date, then I was glad we were beyond the dating phase. Now that I thought about it, I couldn't remember ever formally picking Elizabeth up for a date. In the dorm, I simply knocked on her door and waited while sitting on her bed. Even for our first date I did that.

Before I saw her, I sensed Elizabeth's presence on the staircase. Always beautiful, my eyes were riveted to the gorgeous woman who stopped mid-step when she saw my jaw drop open in awe. Elizabeth was absolutely stunning.

I walked over and took her hand. She smiled demurely. I kissed Elizabeth's hand French-style, while my eyes locked on her shimmering emerald ones. Eli blushed. She was amazing, no exaggeration.

Elizabeth wore an ankle-length skirt of lightweight sea foam green cotton. A slit reached up her right leg to mid-thigh allowing movement despite the skirt's straight style. Eli's off-shoulder peasant blouse of gauzy white cotton fell to her hips. A narrow double-wrapped bronze leather belt accented Eli's waist. It matched the flat sandals on her feet.

Similarly casual, I wore chino shorts and Italian leather flip-flops. My white t-shirt with its rough-edged v-neck made it appear as though the man wearing it had cut it open himself. Not this man. Over it I donned a light blue linen shirt, which I wore open. I chose these shirts because Elizabeth had bought them. Let her see that I genuinely appreciated her gift.

Elizabeth's waves tumbled past her shoulders, thick and glossy. She didn't wear any make-up. With Eli's natural beauty, it was unnecessary.

"Wait right here," I ordered. "Don't move."

In a few long strides I picked up my phone from the coffee table. For a phone, it had a pretty good camera. My model impatiently fidgeted while I opened the camera app and focused.

"Don't move. Smile."

I pressed the shutter icon. Perfect!

"Now you'll never be further away than my pocket."

I smiled as I saw her fight a frown. Eli blinked hard. Damn! I had made her think about Sunday. I gathered Elizabeth into my arms.

"We are going to have the best time this evening, right?"

"Right." Eli's smile returned. "I'm sorry. I didn't mean to get emotional."

"I'm trying too," I admitted. "Tonight should be as memorable as our first date. We have Rach to thank for that one, you know. She forced my hand."

"What did Rachel have to do with it?"

"She never told you? Rachel was sick of me living in denial. That afternoon she and I returned to Berkeley Hall only moments before you arrived with Jackson. I yanked Rachel into the stairwell so you wouldn't see us."

"Danny, you spied on me? That's creepy."

"I wasn't spying! Seeing you with Jackson was the kick in the butt that I needed."

"You were jealous!" Eli gasped.

"No I wasn't!" I protested, embarrassed by the memory. "Maybe... No, not jealous. Fearful. I thought Jackson might ask you out, and you'd say yes. You were so animated."

"I like Jackson. He's a good guy."

"Yeah, well Rach saw my reaction. She made me realize if I didn't make my move, somebody else might and I would lose you."

"Thank you, Rachel," Eli said and smiled. "She's such a good friend."

Soon I ushered Eli into Geoffrey's. Checking in with the hostess again reminded me that tonight was our last night out in Malibu for a long time. I wanted a keepsake.

"Would you please take our picture?" I asked the hostess, and I handed her my phone. Eli beamed.

Then the hostess led us to an intimate table on the ocean view terrace. What a beautiful, clear evening. The moon sat low over the Pacific. A light breeze blew in. Heating lamps kept us comfortable.

I reached for Elizabeth's hand. I didn't know if I could let go of it. Not ever.

If a magical power could be harnessed to slow down time, this would have been the night I'd have chosen to utilize it. I wanted to cherish every moment, as did Eli.

While we dined, we couldn't take our eyes off of each other. At every opportunity we shared quick kisses. Electricity pulsated between us.

"It really does feel like our first date," I observed.

Dinner was winding down. Eli and I shared crème brulee made richer by a bottom layer of chocolate mousse. I slowly sipped a cup of coffee.

"No, it doesn't," Elizabeth contradicted.

"It doesn't?" I grimaced. Hadn't I succeeded in making this evening just as special?

"Tonight is so much better," Eli answered enthusiastically. Her warm smile lit her face and erased my frown. "That was a great evening," she continued. "I'd love to go back to the Beach House, but tonight is better. I was such a wreck."

I laughed and squeezed her hand.

"Me, too. I spent half the night wondering what the hell I was doing."

"Well I spent half the night wondering what the hell you were doing too!" Eli laughed. "It took you forever just to admit it was a date even though it was so obvious. I mean really, who drives two hours to a romantic lakeside restaurant with a buddy?"

I laughed at the memory. "It was that obvious?" I asked.

"Yes. But that's you. So until you were ready to admit it was a date, I felt that element of doubt. What if I had misread your signals? And then you had all these warnings."

"Was I that bad?" I knew the answer.

"Yes, but you were so cute. I didn't care because then you kissed me, and I nearly died. I wanted more. I had to have more."

"Like this?"

I reached for Eli's beautiful face, cupped it in my hands and slowly kissed her. She gasped in delight.

"Not quite." Eli smiled her brightest smile. "It was more like this," she teased.

Elizabeth pressed her lips to mine while my hands in her hair held us together. Her hands went around my back. Eli's soft pink lips parted, and she expertly teased my tongue with hers. She tasted sweeter than she ever had. When I had to inhale, Eli's eyes opened wide in amazement.

"Am I still alive?" she asked.

"I think so." I smiled at her pleasure. "Want to do it again?"

"Yes, please."

With urgency our lips met, and I held her in my arms for the longest kiss. Eli's face glowed with love. Our faces touched against each other and she tenderly kissed me.

"I only imagined we could be this happy back then," Elizabeth whispered.

"And we are," I added.

"We are," Eli breathlessly agreed, and we shared a quick kiss.

"Are you ready to go home?" I asked.

Eli's eyes lit up. "Let's go dancing," she announced.

"Dancing?"

We usually didn't dance except when we were at The Cellar or at a party. The only place I knew for dancing was a dive bar a few miles down Pacific Coast Highway.

We were the only Porsche in the parking lot when we arrived. That and the preponderance of pick-ups should have been clues as to what to expect inside, but Eli and I were too into each other for it to register.

Country night! There was a live cowboy band. Even sawdust was spread on the worn wooden planked floor. The other patrons wore jeans and cowboy boots. Many even had Stetson hats.

I felt many sets of eyes starring at us. A beach prep and his fashion model date were out of place in this crowd.

Elizabeth wanted to dance. We would dance.

The band was playing a Texas two-tep. "C'mon," I said, and I pulled Elizabeth to the dance floor. Eli gave me a look that said, "You've got to be kidding."

"Baby, you wanted to dance," I reminded Eli as I began to lead her around the floor.

"I can't believe we're doing this," Elizabeth laughed.

I grinned at Eli and we chuckled, as I positioned her hands. For a trained dancer, Elizabeth was so clumsy. She was definitely out of her element and unhappy happy about it. Dance was one skill I was not supposed to be superior at.

"How do you know the two-step?" Elizabeth blurted in frustration.

"Three years ago I spent half the summer in Oklahoma."

"You never told me that," she said sourly.

"I didn't? Well, three years ago I spent half the summer in Oklahoma," I laughed.

"So you said," Eli answered coolly.

"C'mon, don't be sore. Just follow my lead. You'll get it, Eli. It's fun."

Determination rapidly replaced Elizabeth's confusion as she doubled her efforts to learn.

"What were you doing in Oklahoma?"

"Working on a failed political campaign." I smiled wryly.

Eli laughed. "Of course it failed. They never elect Democrats in Oklahoma."

Elizabeth was correct, and I laughed at the memory of the most futile campaign my family had ever supported.

Having gotten the hang of the two-step, Elizabeth now enjoyed herself, even smiling at her stumbles. She relaxed, and had a good time, going with the flow. And when she did trip because her new sandals slipped on the sawdust, Eli happily let me catch her and shrugged it off.

We didn't leave the bar until nearly two o'clock! Giddy with laughter, I held Eli against the side of the Porsche and kissed her.

"This was fun!" she admitted.

Elizabeth's hands reached around my neck and as I held her we kissed as passionately as we had at Geoffrey's.

"E, let's go home."

"I hope so, Daniel. It's two a.m."

I pulled my lady into the house. Before the door from the garage had even fully closed I was on her. My body pressed Elizabeth against the wall. Our fingers twined.

My other hand cupped her face, forcing Eli onto her toes for our lips to meet. She held tightly to my back while I hungrily devoured her. Time stood still.

Then Eli's leg found the opening in the skirt created by its slit. She rubbed her foot against my calf, adding to the excitement. Our hearts pounded.

It didn't seem possible, but I leaned in even closer. I unbuckled Eli's belt and let it drop to the floor. Not a word was spoken. Our kisses did all the talking.

When Eli wrapped her leg around my hip, I couldn't resist any longer. I lifted her off the floor. She wrapped both her legs around my hips and I carried her to the sofa. Her hands held tightly around my neck. A lustrous smile lighting her beautiful face signaled Elizabeth wanted me as much as I wanted her.

We collapsed onto the cushions. The slit made it easy to remove Eli's silk lace thong and lift her skirt out of the way. Eli's fingers expertly opened my shorts and pulled them off. Our bodies joined for the most insane pleasure.

I held Eli in my arms, luxuriating in her musky-floral scent. I willed my nose to remember it forever, the fragrance of my dearest girl. How I would miss her!

Eli's delicate fingers entered my t-shirt, tracing tickling patterns on my chest. I didn't want to squirm. I took Eli's hand, kissed it, and kept it. Elizabeth purred like a kitten, a very contented kitten. Our lips met for a quick kiss.

"I love you, Daniel," Elizabeth whispered.

Elizabeth's heart and her warm, glowing eyes meant every word.

This time I kissed her longer and then I held her face in my hand.

"Elizabeth Jacobs, you have no idea how much I love you."

Elizabeth giggled in response. "I think I do," she said and smiled.

"Yeah, you do," I agreed.

Then we lay quietly, Eli snuggled in my arms. Despite the hour, we never slept. I know I didn't. We simply enjoyed the quiet solitude of being together.

Elizabeth tipped her head upward. Deep emerald eyes, glassy from the hour, gazed at me. She smiled, oh so tired.

"Let's go down to the beach. I want to watch the sun rise," Eli suggested.

It was black out now, but this time of year the sun rose early. That was in only a couple of hours. I kissed Eli's nose.

"Great idea," I said enthusiastically.

I scooted off the sofa. Kissing Eli's forehead I said, "I'll be right back."

I returned a few minutes later. Elizabeth was sitting, knees pulled in, holding the chenille throw tucked around her. She smiled at my entrance.

"I was cold," Elizabeth explained.

"Here, Sweetheart," I said, and I handed her a grey Donnelly sweatshirt.

Eli rose and slipped her arms into the hoodie. The extra long sleeves swallowed her arms so I zippered it and cuffed the sleeves.

"This is yours," Eli laughed.

"It's the warmest one we have."

"I like big sweatshirts," she assured me. "You changed."

I was wearing sweatpants and a pullover sweatshirt. "I wasn't wearing any pants anyway," I added.

Eli laughed. "I noticed. And you took out your lenses too."

I had my glasses on. "It's late. My eyes are dried out."

The crescent moon over the ocean appeared close enough to touch. Its low-wattage glow reflecting off the gently breaking white caps cast an ethereal air to the blue-black sky. It kept the otherwise dark pre-dawn hour from complete blackness.

Just up from the water's edge, far enough back not to get wet from the tide, I shook out the chenille throw. When it settled on the chilly sand I again reached for Eli's hand and helped her down to sitting between my legs. I wrapped both arms around her shoulders and we sat watching the surf ebb and flow. With my love in my arms, the moon lighting the scene, and the sound of the pounding surf, it was magic.

Time passed. The moon had set. The sun was rising. Darkness slowly receded. Pink tinged the horizon; an indication that another beautiful day lay ahead with no coastal fog to mar it.

In advance of the approaching high tide, the waves were breaking more often and more powerfully than before. I had sited our blanket perfectly. We sat close enough to enjoy nature's wake-up call, but far enough away that we stayed dry.

Elizabeth sat cross-legged, leaning against my chest like a ragdoll while my arms held her snugly. Exhaustion soon claimed us. Eli's eyes were tired, swollen slits. I was afraid to know what I looked like.

Elizabeth and I were making a memory we were certain to cherish forever. I yawned again. I couldn't wait for the sun to rise a little higher so we could crawl into bed.

Eli smiled and caressed my stubble-covered cheek. Even in this condition, she was exquisite. I gathered all the energy that remained to kiss her. Then Eli yawned and stretched her arms like a kitten.

"Oops!" she said awkwardly, smiling sheepishly.

I laughed softly at her indiscretion. With the level of comfort we shared, it didn't matter. At dawn, it was even appropriate.

"Too bad we didn't stay up 'til dawn on our first date," I remarked.

"I'm glad we didn't."

"Tonight wouldn't be as special if we had."

"Yeah," Eli answered. "Tonight was the best."

"I would have thought a different night topped your list."

Eli giggled. "That one's down a few notches. Any night where you vomit cannot be number one on your list."

I laughed at the memory. "That still bothers you?"

"I was so embarrassed."

"So what made tonight the best?" I asked.

"I like our freedom here."

"And that we made love?"

"Yeah, that's always nice."

Eli kissed my cheek. We were both so mellow.

"You know, Danny, that first night I would have if you'd wanted to. It's not as though we'd just met. I wanted to. Badly. But that month you made me wait, it seemed like forever."

"It did? Poor baby," I teased.

"Oh come on Danny! You have to know that every time you kiss me it's like I'm going to die. It was torturous."

"Do you still feel like you're going to die when I kiss you?"

"Yes," she admitted, but Eli blushed.

"I think we've more than made up for the wait."

"You were so afraid," Eli giggled. "It was as though you were the virgin."

"I wasn't afraid. I wanted everything perfect because you were a virgin."

Eli giggled again. "Danny, you were afraid you'd end up in a monogamous relationship where you'd spend every night and day with me. You were afraid I'd move in with you."

"Uh, Eli?"

"Yes, Daniel?"

"Isn't that exactly what happened?"

"Yes." Even this tired, Eli grinned, victorious. Somewhere along the way I'd released myself from my fears. "Do you regret it, Danny?"

"Not for even one minute, babe."

In my sleepy haze my lips found Eli's, and I kissed her, proof of my undying love.

CHAPTER 110 - ELIZABETH

The official beginning to the day I was dreading began rudely with the alarm clock going off. Danny had set it for noon. We'd be alert enough to get through the day and yet be sleepy at a reasonable hour to get our bodies back on a normal schedule.

How ironic – yesterday had been the best day of my life while today was one of the worst. A large part of me wanted to go back to sleep and not wake until Monday. I sighed. Avoidance was not to be.

Perhaps it was the strong coffee Danny was continually gulping, but he was handling the lack of sleep much better than I was. My yawning was incessant. If only I could stay awake until we arrived at the Newman's later.

"There's my long-lost son and his girl next door!" Ellen greeted us with hugs. Her attempt at humor fell flat. Danny and I were too brain-dead.

"Actually, Elizabeth's not from next door, Mom."

"I know where Elizabeth lives, Daniel."

"We've been busy, Mom."

"I'm sure you have been. If I'd lived at the beach with Dad when we were your age, I'm sure we wouldn't have shown our faces in public much either."

"Mom!"

I laughed at Danny's uncharacteristic discomfort, and then I yawned.

"Has Danny been keeping you up, Elizabeth?"

"We stayed up to watch the sun rise at the beach," I answered.

"Nice. As I said, Daniel."

Danny kissed Ellen's cheek.

"We'll be upstairs packing, Mom."

"Don't forget, we're all having dinner together tonight."

"Where?" I asked.

"Here," Danny answered.

"I thought Danny and Steven would enjoy a home-cooked meal before going off for three months of restaurants and caterers."

"Thank you, Mommy," Danny responded with a playful wink.

"Good. Then we don't have to get dressed-up."

Ellen gave me a hard stare. Suddenly I was conscious of my gym shorts and tank top. Danny wasn't dressed any better.

"Yes, you do," Ellen stated bluntly. "This isn't Malibu, Elizabeth."

"Randi can bring you something. I'll call her," Danny said.

"Maybe I need to keep clothing here too."

Upstairs, Danny deposited two of the three suitcases he had brought from Malibu on the floor. Tomorrow they would all be loaded into the limo that was coming for Steve.

Then Danny left me alone while he went to fetch a collapsible luggage stand from another room. Like the largest black wave, the enormity of tomorrow swept over me.

When he returned, I was seated cross-legged on the end of the bed, my hands supporting my moping face. I felt as sullen as I looked. Upon seeing me, Danny propped the stand against the wall and sat by my side.

"Eli," Danny said softly, and he took my hands.

I tried not to, I really did, but I couldn't. Like an open spigot the tears I'd kept hidden poured out. Danny's strong arms enveloped me and held me close, secure. The comfort they usually brought did not come, however.

Danny continued letting me cry. He understood that I needed the release. Better today, than tomorrow.

"Let it out, baby. You're hurting," Danny said in a kind voice while he held me.

"I'm sorry," I sputtered. "I don't want to ruin the day."

"You could never do that, honey."

My crying slowed, and then it stopped. There was a wet stain on Danny's shirt. He gently wiped my face with his thumb.

"I love you, Eli. It won't be that bad. I'll see you on Friday."

"I know."

Danny lifted my chin and kissed me. The sweetness of his lips made me smile.

"I'll make it the best reunion," I said cheerfully.

"I'm sure you will. Every week."

CHAPTER 111 - ELIZABETH

Today I was determined to keep a smile on my face. I wanted our last day to be happy.

Oddly, I felt light-hearted having released all my emotions in the last few days. I had achieved clarity. Now, I almost looked forward to putting Danny on the plane so I could begin my real summer.

My job started tomorrow. I couldn't concentrate on work while living in girlfriend mode with Danny the focus of my attention. Putting Danny on the plane was such a definitive act it would automatically propel me forward.

The early morning sun filtering through the blinds filled me with joy. I loved living here, and not only because I shared the house with Danny. At dinner last night I felt out of place, stifled. Returning to Brentwood, even for one evening, was like retreating to childhood.

"How are you enjoying playing house?" Mom had asked as if it were a game.

Danny and I were not "playing" anything. This was our life. I resented Mom acting as though it was nothing deeper than a thinly veiled excuse for us to fool around.

Danny and I were adults. We had spent the past year being adults. I could not return to my parents' home and be treated like a child. I could not return and be forced to act as though Danny and I had never happened.

I rose from the bed, threw open the blinds, and inhaled the salty ocean air coming through the partially opened glass slider. I wanted to be ready when Danny returned from the Jacobs-Newman golf outing.

CHAPTER 112 - ELIZABETH

The tarmac at Santa Monica Airport was quiet this afternoon. As Danny drove through the gates, the roar of the turbo-charged Porsche matched that of the lone plane taxiing down the runway for take off.

Steve was stepping out of his limo when Danny pulled up beside the plane. The driver unloaded Danny's three suitcases and one belonging to Steve and carried them to the Gulfstream to be loaded in.

Steve approached and opened my door. At the same time, Danny opened the small trunk of the Porsche. While he removed his backpack and laptop, Steve reached for my hand and helped me out.

"Elizabeth, we'll see you Friday, right?" Steve asked.

"Yes. Friday." I bit my lower lip that had begun quivering.

Danny placed his bags on the ground. Steve held me but turned to Danny.

"I'll know by Wednesday if the plane is available."

Danny nodded.

"Otherwise you'll go commercial. Sorry, honey."

"That's fine," I answered quietly.

All that mattered was seeing Danny. I'd be in First Class so I didn't really care. One more year with Danny and I might begin to care.

Steve wrapped his arms around me. His warmth always brought me comfort.

"You be good, Elizabeth."

I smiled at his addressing me like a little girl.

"Keep an eye on my man for me," I said.

"I certainly will. Anything for my favorite girl."

Steve hugged me tightly, and I hugged him back.

"I never imagined you'd be the girl putting Danny on the plane today. I'm glad it is. He's in good hands."

"Thanks, Steve. I love you too."

"Elizabeth, while Danny's in Vancouver, the beach house is still yours to live in. It's your home now, yours and Danny's."

"Thank you, Steve."

I hugged him tightly. I loved Steve so much. How fortunate I was to have two loving fathers. Steve kissed my forehead and handed me over to Danny.

"Don't be long. I have a meeting," Steve told his son before taking his leave.

As we watched Steve climb the stairs to the plane, Danny took my hands. Our eyes locked on each other's. My insides trembled. I didn't want them to. Danny should remember me as happy.

There was no time for further thoughts as Danny cradled me in his arm and kissed me. His tongue teased my lower lip that parted, giving him entrance. I moaned as he pressed against me. Danny's fingers ran down my side to my thigh, and then squeezed my rear through my skirt. My tongue danced with his and Danny hardened against me. My head was spinning. Then Danny pulled back, ending our kiss.

"I'm going to miss you, babe," Danny whispered.

"I'll miss you too. Terribly."

"What are you doing today?"

"Steff and Emma are coming for dinner. They had no idea that I was in town."

"I bet they don't know where you're living either."

"I've been occupied, Mr. Newman."

"You certainly have been." Danny tenderly kissed my lips.

"They'll be surprised that I can cook," I laughed.

"Secret facts about Elizabeth Jacobs," he laughed. "I'm glad you'll be with friends. When are you moving back home?"

"I am home, Daniel. Our home. I've made up my mind. I'm staying in Malibu," I answered with a confident smile.

"That's great," Danny said, but I wasn't sure he meant it as he hesitated. "I didn't think you'd want to be alone."

"I won't be alone. You'll be there with me."

"How am I there?" Danny asked, puzzled.

"You're everywhere. Danny, your presence is in every room. And at night, I'll put on one of your shirts and curl up with your pillow. It'll smell like you're with me."

"What made you decide?"

"Are you happy that I did?"

"I'm the one who's leaving. All I need to be happy is knowing you're happy."

I touched my hand to Danny's smooth cheek. He reached for my hand and we kissed again.

"Our home is my home even when you're away. To move out would nullify the past seven months. It would be as though the past ten days had never happened."

Danny's sapphire eyes twinkled at me like the finest gems as he smiled at our shared memories.

"If anyone had told me a year ago that I'd be living with a girl, I'd have told them they were nuts. There was no way I wanted to come home to the same girl every night."

"I guess you don't know yourself very well," I laughed.

Danny shrugged, and he smiled impishly.

"Yeah, I guess not. And if anyone had told me that girl would be Elizabeth Jacobs, I'd have said they must be smoking some very strong weed."

"Thanks a lot, Daniel. Was the idea of me that repulsive?"

"Honey, you know you were never repulsive. But to me Elizabeth Jacobs was a scrawny kid with thick eyeglasses. And then there was that brother-sister thing."

"That never hung me up."

"So it took me a little longer than you to get past that. But once you re-entered my life, it only took me a couple of months to get past the incest thing and take you to bed."

"Danny," I purred.

"Eli, you know you drive me crazy."

"Yes I do, Daniel. And I will continue to do so for the rest of your life."

"You'd better, Sweetheart. I'm counting on it."

Danny laced his hands into my hair and pulled our lips together. Mine parted to receive his love. My arms reached around his back to hold us firmly together. Our hearts beat rapidly as my head was spinning from the power of Danny's kiss. Every emotion we were feeling about his departure we now shared.

"Daniel, you'll see Elizabeth on Friday. We have to go," Steve called from the door of the Gulfstream.

Danny stopped kissing me and called back. "I'll be up in a minute, Dad."

For the first time, I sadness overtook me. Steve calling Danny was a chilling reminder of where we were and why. Up until now it had been easy to block out reality.

"Baby, don't be sad. Friday will be here soon."

"I know. I'm trying. You'll have a great time in Vancouver," I said enthusiastically.

My hands remained around Danny's neck keeping us close.

"I'll be working really hard."

"It's going to be an amazing experience. Everyone will be impressed that Steve's son takes his job so seriously."

"I do take it seriously. I may have this job because of Dad, but I'm going to prove to everyone that I deserve it."

"Of course you deserve it. You're smart, conscientious, and hardworking."

"And I already have a fan club," Danny smiled. I rolled my eyes.

"Steve and I are so proud of you. Danny, I respect you so much."

"Baby, I love you. You're going to be great at your job too."

"I hope so. I want Dad to be proud."

"Of course Mike will be proud. He's lucky to have you. You're an amazing woman, Elizabeth."

My insides wanted to explode from joy. I squeezed his hand. I was glowing.

"Daniel, I love you so much," I squealed.

"Daniel, c'mon! I can't be late to my own meeting," Steve yelled down again.

"Be right there, Dad!"

"You'd better go." I said tentatively.

"Yeah. I don't want Dad getting angry." Danny smiled at me. "I'll call you tonight, baby. Let's Skype. You'll think I'm there."

"Not quite."

"Use your imagination. I will."

Danny pulled me to his chest. His arms wrapped around me and my hands clasped tightly around his neck. This would be our last kiss and we made it count.

"I'll see you Friday," Danny said when we finally parted.

"I love you, Danny."

"I love you too."

"Steve's waiting."

I smiled at Danny, wanting to make a good memory. He quickly kissed me again and smiled a warm, encouraging smile.

"I'll call tonight. Have fun with the girls."

I nodded as we slowly parted and Danny walked toward the stairs to the plane. One solitary tear slipped out of my eye and down my cheek as I watched him.

Three steps later, Danny bounded back to me.

"I forgot these," Danny said while picking up his backpack and laptop. "One more kiss," he ordered, and I happily obliged.

Danny grinned as we parted. "Gotta go," and he ran for the stairs.

I watched the flight attendant pull the heavy door closed. Only then did I return to the Porsche. I sighed and leaned against the side of the car, my arms folded across my chest shielding me from the chill I felt inside. I smiled and waved to the plane, certain that Danny could see me from the window. He had to see me smiling.

The plane soon taxied down the runway. As it lifted off into the clear, sun-drenched sky, tears fell from my eyes. "Friday will be here soon enough," I told myself.

Then I smiled, pleased that for the second time this year I had successfully started a new life. I climbed into the Porsche, started the engine and began my drive back home to Malibu. I had dinner guests to prepare for.

To Be Continued...

ABOUT THE AUTHOR

Born and raised in New York City, I was always a California girl at heart, obsessed with sports cars in a town with no parking. I couldn't wait to leave. So I did.

After graduating from Vassar College where I studied Psychology and Economics, I headed to Los Angeles. Then, after a brief stint in Washington, D.C., to earn my MBA, I headed back to the beach, and became a film production accountant, working on films you've probably never heard of.

I wrote my first novel at the age of six, and didn't write another until Hollywood Princess. I'm a news junkie and a baseball addict who loves a good love story. There are too many tragedies in the world. Why not provide an escape?

Now living in Connecticut, I'm married to a New York-based film producer. We have three children; two are not yet old enough to read this book, though one keeps trying to peek.

www.danayannlevin.com
www.facebook.com/DanaAynnLevin
twitter.com/OfficialDLevin

www.ingramcontent.com/pod-product-compliance
Lightning Source LLC
Chambersburg PA
CBHW060345260626
47160CB00006B/2212